C.A. WITTMAN

THE VISITORS

Publisher: Expert Subjects, LLC
4775 Collins Avenue, suite 3206
Miami Beach, FL 33140

Disclaimer: This book is a work of fiction. Names, characters, places and incidents are either the product of the author's imagination or are used fictitiously. Any resemblance to actual events or locales or persons, living or dead, is entirely coincidental.

The Visitors
An Expert Subjects' book, published by
agreement with the author

Copyright © 2014 by Celena Wittman

All rights reserved.
No part of this book may be reproduced, scanned or distributed in any printed or electronic form whatsoever, without permission.

ISBN: 978-0-9886765-7-2

Printed in the United States of America

Cover design by Marija Vilotijevic

Expert Subjects, LLC

For my children

Chapter One

The children arrived in early September, just five days after the letter. It was a thin, wispy, white envelope. Sara almost missed it lying there at the bottom of the mailbox under a stack of more voluminous pieces of mail. Being too thin to grasp, she slid it out, staring at the neat, formal writing addressed to Mrs. Annette Deureaux, her Maman. There was no return address.

It was unusual for her family to receive personal mail. Sara's parents had no friends or relatives that she knew of. Other than weekly afternoon tea with a small group of churchwomen in their rural neighborhood, the Deureauxs kept to themselves. Depositing the mail in her backpack, she began the two-mile walk home. It had not rained for three weeks and a heavy, humid stillness enveloped most of Maui in the absence of the usual trade winds.

As she passed the small Catholic Church that her family attended, a faint trickle of sweat began between her shoulder blades. She did not gain relief from the fierce heat until her walk lead her through the shelter of a grove of Norfolk pine trees and thickly gnarled hau bush. Yellow guavas littered the damp ground. Sheltered from the sun, some of the fruit was squashed and oozing pink, pulpy flesh.

A sweet, earthy smell wafted through the air and swarms of gnats rose up from the abundant rotted fruit, giving way to mosquitoes as Sara drew closer to the stream that was almost dry. She traversed a one-lane bridge and began her upward climb, the last strenuous bit.

Once home, the girl removed the mail from her bag, setting it on the kitchen counter, a neat stack on an equally clean and neat surface. The pots and pans hung uniformly over the counter space. On the kitchen table sat a small basket of fresh herbs that Maman must have just picked. Sara ran her slim brown fingers through the mint, cilantro and basil, breaking off a mint leaf and crushing it to release the pungent aroma.

Maman came in the house just a minute later, pink and sweaty from her gardening, a large straw hat hiding half her face. She removed it carefully, revealing thick hair tied loosely back, more grey in color than brown. She hung the hat by the front door.

"Do you have homework?" her mother asked in her broken country French: a Louisiana creole dialect. She and Papa spoke no English at home; as a result, Sara also spoke the rare dialect.

"*Oui*, I was going to check if there was laundry to hang first."

Maman nodded curtly.

"The baskets are by the line. Don't drop the damp clothes."

Maman routinely warned her not to break or drop things, although she was fifteen and could not remember when she had last ruined something—but praise, Sara never heard.

"Hello?" came a voice from outside.

Maman frowned, her large hands smoothing back stray hairs as she peered out of the window to see who the unexpected visitor was. Sara stood on tiptoe to look over her mother's shoulder. It was Keoni, a neighbor from down in the valley, holding a styrofoam cooler. Papa came out from his workshop and met Keoni on the porch. In greeting, he slapped her father heartily on the back.

The Visitors

"I brought you folks some fish and tago. We get plenty. There's some big ones in here, ahi."

He held up the cooler with a smile. His teeth were widely spaced apart in his brown face, the two front ones missing. This gave him mostly a gummy look. Papa took the small cooler and set it down on the porch. He opened the lid to look in and smiled appreciatively.

"Thank you. Have a smoke?"

Reaching a weathered hand into his white linen shirt pocket, he produced a hand rolled cigarette and matches, handing these items over to Keoni before stepping off the porch and leading the man away from the house. Sara watched the two men walk toward the driveway, Papa's tawny build slight next to Keoni's broad, powerful shoulders and legs, both thick with well-defined muscle. Only the men's feet were similar: hard, rough and cracked, like most islanders. Their conversation carried clearly in the stillness.

"How was the fishing?"

"It was some hot. Whew. I think there be a storm comin dis way, you know?"

Maman turned away from the window, her grey eyes flicking over Sara.

"Sara, mind you hang the laundry."

Maman picked up the mail her daughter had deposited earlier and took it to the living room to place it on the coffee table for Papa to look over later. As she came back into the kitchen, Sara spotted the thin white envelope.

"There is one more." She pointed to the last piece of mail left behind.

Maman bent over, her hands on her hips, to examine it closer, and stayed there, as if frozen in that position, her thick body growing rigid with visible tension. Sara felt an odd, lurching feeling in her belly as she watched her mother bent over the strange letter. Rising slowly to her full height, her hands still on her hips,

Maman's eyes did not leave the envelope and its black formal lettering. She did not look up, but said in a quiet voice, "Go get your father."

Sara stepped from the house, willing herself to stay calm and composed, although her heart had sped up at her mother's reaction to the letter. Maman would not appreciate Keoni following her father back to the house with neighborly concern. Slowing her movements to a stroll, she approached the men who were smoking casually as they leaned against Keoni's Toyota pickup, filled with coolers of fish and several six-packs of Budweiser.

Sara caught Papa's green eyes with her own dark gaze and he straightened up immediately, focusing on her with his full attention.

"Maman wants you to come," Sara said in French, hoping her voice sounded light.

"Get trouble?" Keoni asked.

Her father smiled easily. "Ah no, the oven is acting up. Annette has a cake in it. I better go see what the problem is."

"OK, my man, next time."

The two men clasped hands and Keoni jumped into his truck, pulling out of their driveway. Papa stood and waited as if he hadn't a care in the world, sucking on his cigarette and holding his calloused hand up in a friendly farewell. When Keoni's truck was well out of sight, only then did Papa begin walking toward the house.

Maman was sitting in her rocking chair where she did most of her smaller mending projects in the evening hours. A ripped sleeve along the seam, a hem that needed to be let out; she usually fixed these with swift, deft fingers. She still held the letter, two slim sheets of paper filled with small delicate writing that shook with feathery lightness in her trembling hand. Her grey eyes were large and full of fear. Maman was a strong woman who did not upset easily. Sara could not ever remember her being afraid.

"I thought we were done," was all she said.

The Visitors

Papa hurried over to her with Sara close behind. He took the papers from her hand and she let go of them willingly. The writing was in English.

My Dearest Annette, it began. *There has been a sudden turn of events...*
Papa pulled the letter away from Sara's view.
"Sara, you have things to do?"
"*Oui.*"
Sara turned to go, leaving her father to read whatever news had upset her mother so much.
"Let's try to look at this reasonably," he said.
"Reasonably!"
"Annette."
There was a warning tone in his voice.
"We do not have a choice, and you know this. It is only for a month that we will have them. Only for the beginning," he added.
His words were followed by an odd, stifled cry that came from Maman. Curiosity getting the better of Sara, she walked quietly back to the living room and stood in the doorway. Maman leaned forward in her chair, her hand doubled in a fist and pushed forcefully against her own mouth to block the sounds of crying. Her body shook convulsively as Papa kneeled in front of her, gently pulling her up into his arms. Sara could see her mother's face damp with tears. She had never known Maman to cry before, had never seen her parents embrace for any reason, but now her father cradled her mother against his chest, whispering into her ear. She turned away from this intimate scene, a sick feeling settling in her stomach.

Outside, the damp clothes that Maman left wrung and draped neatly in baskets, sat on the grass under the clothesline, and Sara found some solace in the mundane hanging of the clothes to dry. When this task was done, she returned to the house, finding it empty and quiet. Usually at this hour Maman would be prepping food for dinner. But the kitchen was as neat and spotless as when she'd arrived home. Unsure of what to think, she decided to start on her homework, but not before stepping out to the back porch to retrieve her dog's food dish and fill it with the dried food kept in a bucket in the broom closet. She whistled for Blackie, unsure if he would come while she stood there. He had been strangely skittish around her ever since her illness.

Last year, Sara suffered a fever that lasted for weeks. Her parents did not take her to the doctor; they were too private even for that. Instead, Sara had lain in bed, her body wracked with pain, her lips cracked and bleeding from a searing heat that coursed through her: a heat so intense that even her eyeballs felt like glowing coals in her skull. It was only the brown, powdery medicine mixed with water that Maman fed her with a spoon that had broken the fevers. The sweating would come then, soaking through to her mattress, and Maman was forced to move her aching body to remove the wet bedding and replace it with fresh, dry towels.

At one time, Sara had felt very light and realized that she was looking down at herself from the ceiling of her room. There Maman sat holding rosary beads, her face grim, lips moving soundlessly in prayer as she gazed down at her daughter. Sara saw herself stretched stiffly on the bed, her eyes open and unseeing, the pain and heat absent from her senses. All that remained was relief and a calm resignation. But it had only been momentary before a sucking, rushing pressure began to pull at her. She'd tried to fight it. Whatever it was, it wasn't a part of her. It pulled with the strength of an unnatural force, bringing her back to her body.

When Sara recovered, she found some things about herself changed. She now healed much faster from minor scratches and scrapes, and her constitution was stronger. But most importantly, her dog and only companion no longer seemed to trust her. While her pet remained playful and friendly with Papa and non-interactive with Maman, only with Sara was he different. Over many months,

The Visitors

she worked at getting him not to show his teeth when she approached. At best, he would stand a short distance away with his tail between his legs, a wary look in his eye, even when she spoke softly and encouragingly. Finally resigned that Blackie was no longer her friend, Sara asked Papa for another puppy.

"No Sara, Blackie is the only pet you will have," was Papa's reply.

Now Sara stood for a moment on the porch, hoping Blackie would approach even to the bottom step, but he never came. The girl stepped back inside, knowing he would eat his food when she was not around.

"Hide in here! Don't look, don't look!"

Someone covered Sara's eyes, but she could still hear children shrieking, the sound of flesh tearing and the anguished cry of a woman.

Now it was dark; a feminine voice spoke in soothing murmurs. Fingers pushed open her lips and something was shoved into her mouth. She began to scream.

Light flooded her vision. Papa stood in her room. Sara sat up in bed, an acrid taste on her tongue.

"Did you have the nightmare again?"

He came to sit on the side of her bed. Sara nodded, pushing her thick, heavy curls back over her shoulders. A thin sheen of sweat covered her body from the terror of the dream.

"Papa, don't leave," she whispered.

"No, I'll stay here awhile," he promised, patting her dark hand with his own fairer one before gently caressing her damp brow.

"Lay back now, Sara, and try not to think of it."

Sara collapsed back on her pillow, her eyes falling on Mother Mary's picture. Papa's gaze followed hers.

"Mary watches over us, child," he said in a hushed voice that rang out clear and soothing in the still night. "You must pray for yourself, Sara. Wash away the darkness that clouds your mind." Sara shut her eyes, reassured with Papa's continued presence.

"Oh most merciful Jesus, lover of souls," she began. "I beseech thee, by the agony of thy most sacred heart, and by the sorrows of thine Immaculate Mother, wash clean in thy blood the sinners of the whole world who are to die this day."

She continued the prayer, feeling her heart return to a regular rhythm and her breathing become even.

Papa patted her hand and stood up. Leaving the propane light on, he closed the door quietly behind him. The prayer having calmed her, she waited with her eyes shut for sleep.

The usual Saturday morning sausage omelette and biscuits were already on the table when Sara walked into the kitchen. Maman was just bringing the silver pot filled with coffee. Sara grabbed the sugar bowl and creamer from the counter, taking them to the table for her mother. After their meal, she would help Papa load crates of vegetables from their large garden into his old, rusty pickup, to be sold at the swap meet, an outing that she looked forward to every week. When the morning rush of the swap was over and Papa no longer needed a second set of hands, it was her turn to browse the eclectic group of vendors and look for items of interest that she may or may not buy.

"Sara, you're to stay home today," Maman said as she sat in her usual seat.

"Doesn't Papa need help?"

A wave of disappointment so strong washed over her that she experienced an immediate loss of appetite.

The Visitors

"Your mother will need even more help," her father said, emerging from the hallway looking crisp and washed in a fresh, white linen shirt. His wet hair was combed neatly back and parted at the side. He sat easily at the table, waiting for Maman, who took her seat a moment later. All three bowed their heads for grace.

"Bless us, oh Lord, and these, thy gifts, which we are about to receive from thy bounty, through Christ our Lord. Amen."

The prayer finished, Papa poured himself a cup of coffee, spooning in several teaspoons of sugar and a splash of cream. Maman cut into the omelette with sure, efficient strokes, and reaching for Papa's plate, she deposited a heap of steaming egg.

"We are going to have some visitors," Papa said as he waited for Sara to be served before reaching for an already buttered biscuit. "Your cousins are coming to stay a little while."

"I have cousins?"

Sara felt mildly alarmed at this new bit of family information, as well as a thrill of excitement. She herself was *hanai*, although the details of her adoption were a closed subject with her parents. Sara knew that if she were White like Maman and Papa, they would have preferred to keep this a secret from her. However, she was a mulatta, the term Maman used to describe her ethnicity, and it was so obvious that Maman could not ignore it.

"Maman will need some help getting the guest rooms ready," her father said between bites of omelette.

"There is a lot to do in the next few days," Maman continued. "The rooms need to be cleaned, there is the washing…"

She went on naming various chores that she and Sara would need to attend to, but Sara had stopped listening, thinking only of the cousins that were coming to stay with them. She had never heard her parents talk of other family members. Maman's reaction to the letter yesterday flashed through her mind and she could hear Papa's voice saying again, *"It is only for a month that we will have them."* She wondered why her mother had reacted so strongly to the news.

How were the cousins related? Did they come from Maman or Papa's side of the family? Her throat constricted with familiar frustration when she thought of how much information her parents kept from her. Papa's hand lightly touched Sara's fingers.

"What is it?"

He always knew when something was troubling her.

"I don't understand…"

Maman looked up from her plate, her hard grey eyes fixed on Sara. The rest of the sentence died on her lips. She grew emboldened again when her mother made a stab at her eggs and resumed eating.

"I don't understand why I am not trusted. Neither of you ever really tell me much of anything."

"We tell you as much as you need to know," Maman spoke sharply, deflating the mild rebellion that had risen up in the girl. The rest of the meal was eaten in silence. When Papa was finished, he wiped his mouth in broad strokes with a cloth napkin and stood up from the table. Pulling a cigarette from his shirt pocket, he walked outside.

"May I be excused?" Sara asked. Maman gave a curt nod and Sara jumped up, running out the front door after her father. Smoke from his cigarette curled in the still air as he walked down the hill to a small building where the crates of vegetables were stored for the swap meet.

"Papa," Sara called out. Her father stopped and waited for her. Streaks of early morning light sliced through the dark sky—an orange river of color spilling out from the eastern horizon. Sara ran up to her father, the grass cool and dewy wet under her bare feet.

"Who are my cousins?"

It was hard to tell in that dark morning, but Sara thought she detected sadness on her father's face. Wordlessly, he reached out his

The Visitors

hand to stroke her cheek. Taking a breath, he opened his mouth as if to say something, changed his mind and walked away.

"Papa, tell me, *sil vous plait.*"

"Sara," his voice cracked, "I need you more than ever to be a good girl for your Maman and me. Will you do that for us?"

"Are we in some kind of danger?"

The sky grew paler as they stood in the yard. Sara could now see the strain on her father's elderly face.

"You must know, Sara," he paused, running his tongue over his dry lips. Again he tried to speak but seemed at a loss for words.

"*Oui,* Papa?" Sara urged.

"You must know that Maman and I love you, whatever happens."

Sara was struck with his use of the word "love". It was not like him, and she found no comfort in the endearment, only alarm. She started to ask what might happen, but her father took a step back.

"Go and help Maman now. There is much to be done before your cousins arrive."

Chapter Two

The trill of the bell signalling the end of school elicited a rustling of books and scraping of chairs against the wood floor, as students moved with an alacrity that had been absent for most of the day.

Mrs. Knowles, a slim red-headed woman, the only Caucasian in a sea of Japanese faculty, was new to the island, having recently moved with her family from Santa Monica, California. She fanned herself with a sheath of papers, watching the exodus of students. All day the heat in the room had been whipped into a hot wind by the overhead fan. Her students, red faced and droopy eyed, endured her lecture on The Great Depression and FDR's New Deal, but once the bell rang, kids again became animated with laughter and smiles. They joked with one another, jostling for position to get outside. Only one stayed behind at her desk, quietly writing in her notebook, her hand scribbling furiously over the pages. For a moment the girl looked up, and Mrs. Knowles smiled at her but received no acknowledgement. Her dark, almond-shaped eyes were set in a face of exotic beauty, which the teacher could not quite ethnically pinpoint. They stared straight through her. Sara was lost in her own world, and not for the first time.

The Visitors

Academically, Sara Deureaux by far outshone her classmates, Mrs. Knowles thought, and her grasp of history was astounding, yet mentally she was often absent. Sara was a curious combination of the best and worst student. There were many students who did not pay attention in class, turned in mediocre work, if at all, and when called on, did not have a clue as to what was being discussed.

Sara, a chronic daydreamer and avid reader who habitually read other history books in class, was among the worst when it came to not paying attention. When called upon, she would stare blankly, her eyes hazy as is if returning from another world. Yet once focused, she usually had a thorough grasp of the subject, often adding fascinating tidbits of information or asking thought-provoking questions that had ignited many a class discussion.

"Sara."

Mrs. Knowles spoke the girl's name gently. Her head was bent over her notebook again as she resumed writing. Mrs. Knowles stood up from her desk and walked over to the girl, placing a hand on her squared shoulder. Sara set her pen down, revealing a middle finger stained with ink, and quickly looked up. Mrs. Knowles could see that she was startled.

"Sara, school's over. You don't want to miss your bus."

"Oh, pardon."

The girl, forgetting to use English, began to speak in rapid French, her inflection and body language apologetic, although Mrs. Knowles could not understand a word. Gathering her things, she rushed out of the classroom, brushing past Mrs. Sakamoto, the tenth grade Home Economics teacher. Mrs. Sakamoto shook her head, smiling. She was a short woman of barely five feet, wide hipped, with thick soft, doughy arms and a round, good-natured face. She wore her coarse, thick black hair to her shoulders with a fringe of girlish bangs.

"School's out. Time for party," she joked, lapsing into pidgin as she sometimes did. Mrs. Knowles laughed. She had grown to appreciate Mrs. Sakamoto's clownish and humorous demeanor. A favorite with the students, she was a refreshing break from the stern and austere attitude of the rest of the faculty.

"Well here's the info for the book fair," Mrs. Sakamoto set some papers on Mrs. Knowles' desk and turned to leave.

"Theresa, do have a minute?" Mrs. Knowles called out.

"I don't know, Angela. I have my own party to go to. Wash the dog, grade papers."

Mrs. Knowles smiled and gestured to one of the seats. "I wanted to ask you about Sara Deureaux. I was told that you used to teach at North Shore Elementary. Sara went there, didn't she?"

All traces of humor left Mrs. Sakamoto's expression at the mention of the girl.

"I was Sara's primary teacher for third grade." Mrs. Sakamoto pulled out a chair from one of the desks and sat down. "Some sweet, Sara." She shook her head. "And smart."

Mrs. Sakamoto gave Mrs. Knowles a sharp look. "She could easily start university tomorrow and do just fine."

Mrs. Knowles nodded her head in agreement. "Yes, I can see that scholastically she's way ahead, but she tends to keep to herself. No one bothers her, yet she doesn't seem to have any friends. Whenever I see her outside of class, she's either reading, studying or eating lunch by herself. It's strange. Even the most outcast kids have developed relationships with at least one other person."

Mrs. Sakamoto sighed as if she had had this conversation before.

"Her family's very private, you know. They're like the homeschooler families, into their own way of doing things. Sara's family sends her to school, but school life ends when she leaves the campus. I saw her develop relationships when she was a little girl but she was never allowed to take it any farther than within the bounds of school

The Visitors

life. You know how it is with kids. They visit at each other's houses, spend the night. For a while in my class she had a little group that she went around with, but she fell away from them because she was not a part of the sleepovers, movie outings or beach time."

"But why would her parents keep her alienated like that?" Mrs. Knowles asked.

Mrs. Sakamoto shrugged and pulled a handkerchief from her dress pocket, wiping the sweat from her nose and forehead. There were other things about the girl that she had noticed, but could never make sense of. Odd occurrences happened when Sara was around; objects sometimes moved on their own, and a few times the girl had had strange fits in her class when she was small. She had yelled out in French, her eyes glazed over, a great gush of words flowing from her mouth. It was as if she were proclaiming something. Both times, it had been frightening to see. This she had reported to the principle, but in the end nothing changed much for Sara, only a growing isolation from her peers.

"What is it?" Mrs. Knowles asked, not missing the discomfort on Theresa's face.

The woman shrugged. "You know some of these families these days who move here to Hawaii from the mainland, don't want to learn about the culture. Don't want to have anything to do with anyone, just hole up in their own little world."

Mrs. Knowles frowned, thinking of how lonely Sara's life must be. Every girl should have at least one close friend her age to confide in and share life's ups and downs with, the woman thought. She imagined a younger Sara giggling with the other girls, playing tag and make-believe games.

The door to the classroom flew open and Jenny Knowles, Mrs. Knowles' daughter, came bursting into the room, red hair flying behind her, hazel eyes wide with alarm. The girl's face was flushed with excitement.

"Mom, Mrs. Sakamoto, come quick, there's going to be a fight! Some girls are ganging up on that girl Sara."

The two women leapt to their feet and ran outside after Jenny, who pointed across a dry, brown field. Three local girls in jean shorts and t-shirts stood with arms crossed before the girl, who looked almost ethereal next to them in her light homemade linen dress. Although it was 1984, Sara often wore clothes that were reminiscent of the 1930s. The ringleader leaned toward the girl, pointing her finger accusatively. Mrs. Knowles recognized the shorter, wiry girl who was full of attitude. Her name was Sunami, and she was a notorious troublemaker. Well, she wasn't going to make trouble this time. Mrs. Knowles began to walk toward the girls but was stopped by Mrs. Sakamoto, who grabbed her arm.

"Wait, try see." Mrs. Sakamoto said, gesturing to the tense little group. Sunami's hand had dropped to her hip and Sara was speaking. A moment later the girl's posture relaxed and there was the distant sound of laughter. Sunami reached out and gave Sara a playful shove before jutting out her chin and giving a masculine flick of her head. She turned to leave, followed by her two much larger sidekicks, who could have crushed Sara's lithe frame if they had wanted to. Mrs. Sakamoto nodded her head admiringly.

"Now that's the way to handle things."

She grinned a lopsided comical smile that was almost always contagious. Sara had not moved, however, the route 32 bus pulling away from the curb prompted her to run in its direction. Mrs. Knowles watched her jog half way across the field before giving up in a state of despondency when she saw the bus chug off.

"Jenny, go and get Sara. We'll give her a ride home," she said. But Jenny was already running off in Sara's direction, her pale, coltish legs taking long, exuberant strides.

It would be a pleasure to get to know the girl a little, since she had often been the topic of conversation within their home. Many times, Mrs. Knowles brought up the subject of her student with her husband or discussed the girl with Jenny, who was equally curious. Jenny made a few friendly overtures toward Sara, but each time, her efforts were met with polite indifference.

Since school began, Jenny had a slow start making friends herself. Instead she'd suffered countless racist attacks, shockingly vicious. Mrs. Knowles was not prepared for the fact that being White in Hawaii, especially for an adolescent, could sometimes be a liability.

Within seconds, Jenny caught up to Sara. Smiling and gesticulating as she talked, she pointed in Mrs. Knowles direction. Moments later, the girls fell into step alongside one another as they walked back to the classroom.

Chapter Three

Sara chewed at her nail, glancing outside the passenger window of the tan Volvo. Riding in someone else's vehicle was a new experience: one she knew her parents wouldn't approve of. Never having missed the bus, it was the worst day that she could think of for things to go wrong. Her cousins were arriving that afternoon and Maman had been sterner than ever, reminding her not to dawdle on the way home.

Saturday, after Papa had left for the swap meet, Sara's mother did not speak to her for most of the day, though she bristled with agitation. Working side by side from morning till night, they washed and scrubbed everything. Monday morning, Papa left and came back in the late afternoon with a truck full of wide, flat boards. When Maman saw the lumber, her lips grew thin and pinched.

"We don't need that!" she'd snapped.

Papa, unmoved, replied evenly, "You don't know what we'll need."

Sara had helped her father carry the boards down the hill to the old stable that never housed a horse, only two Holstein dairy cows that she often milked before her illness. The cows were Maman's business now. Both animals had grown dangerously wild around

Sara, rolling their eyes and kicking their hooves whenever she came near.

Last night, Maman pulled down the wide, glass jar that held the greyish, foul smelling medicine. A flour sack full of the same stuff lay open on the floor and Maman filled the jar to the top with the powder, using a plastic scooper.

"What's all that medicine for?" Sara asked.

"Go and get your storybooks and take them upstairs for the younger ones," was all Maman said. Late into the night and in the morning when Sara awakened for school, she had heard her father down the hill hammering and sawing. He had taken a break to drive her to the top of the road, where she waited with some of the other kids in the valley for the school bus.

"Sara," her father said, touching her hand gently before she hopped out of the pickup truck. "Your cousins will be here today. I want you kids to stay away from the stable building. You're not to play around there."

"*Oui*, Papa."

She'd dared not ask him why, knowing there would not be an answer anyway.

"What did those girls say to you?" Jenny asked, interrupting Sara's thoughts. She swung around in the front seat to face Sara, her hazel eyes a soft golden color from the flecks of amber in them. It was amazing how similar she looked to Mrs. Knowles. Jenny waited, her face an open book of expectancy. Sara felt the warmth of embarrassment creep up her neck and into her cheeks. She didn't want to talk about Sunami

"I saw those girls bullying you, Sara. Did they threaten to hit you?" Mrs. Knowles asked, glancing at her through the rear view mirror. She squinted at the odd play of light on the girl's reflection. It gave her an almost transparent look.

"No, no," Sara stammered, talking down at her hands folded tightly in her lap. "It was just a misunderstanding."

"Why? What happened?" Jenny asked.

Neither one of them was going to let up until Sara told them the whole story, which was really only a minor confrontation, but wouldn't be if Sunami thought she'd been snitched on. Sunami was not a girl to make an enemy of. Jenny must have understood this. More than once, Sara had witnessed Jenny pinned against the lockers by Sunami and other brutish *tita* types.

In elementary school, White children and locals played, for the most part, peacefully amongst each other. But by high school earlier friendships forged in kindergarten and nurtured through the primary years dissipated into groups of racial solidarity. Hawaiians and Portuguese hung together, all of the anger, resentment and pride of the culture channeled through the youth. Samoans stuck with Samoans, Tongans with Tongans, and the Filipinos, although small, could be fierce, their strength lying in the fact that they traveled in packs. Japanese were the elite. They were the brightest students, the prettiest girls in the yearbook, and along with the White children, the students that the teachers favored and focused on. But while the Japanese were accepted as part of the island melting pot, Whites were not. There were some White mainlanders that did fit in seamlessly with the locals but they were like the Portuguese, speaking heavy pidgin, having adopted the values, body language and attitude of the local youth, completely divorced from mainland culture. Jenny was the epitome of the type of *haole* that local kids loved to hate. Pale with red hair, meek-mannered under pressure, and a recent transplant: she was the perfect target.

Both Jenny and Mrs. Knowles were waiting for Sara to explain what had happened. She could feel their eyes boring into her.

"Does Sunami bother you often?" Mrs. Knowles asked gently.

"No." Sara said no more. The subject was dropped and an uncomfortable silence settled between them as they rode through the town of Kahului. Eventually markets and businesses gave way to

The Visitors

abundant fields of leafy sugar cane in various stages of growth. A massive pickup truck filled with laborers, mostly older Filipino women clothed head to toe with their faces and heads covered in t-shirts and scarves, ploughed through a fallow field of burnt soil.

"They must be so hot," Jenny remarked.

Several miles later they came to a single traffic light that marked the center of a dusty beach town. Once the hub of Maui in the 1950s, it was now quiet and desolate. Tourists hardly ever came as far as the northeast side of the island, and when they did, they drove straight through the town.

Mrs. Knowles drove through the town as well, the highway winding over a cliff that plunged down to the ocean, its blue depths a mirror of the sky.

"What a gorgeous sight," she remarked. "I never get tired of the beach."

A few surfers paddled languidly in the placid water twenty yards out, waiting for waves. Gradually, the highway grew windier and Jenny rolled down her window, pushing her pale face out into the warm air.

"I feel sick," she said after a bit.

Mrs. Knowles looked over at her daughter, who suddenly belched, throwing her hand over her mouth.

"Wait, wait, let me pull over!" Mrs. Knowles yelled, as if Jenny had suddenly become hard of hearing. There was no shoulder. Groaning, she frantically looked for a place to stop.

"There's no one behind us," Sara offered.

There hadn't been since they left Kahului. Glancing briefly in her rear view mirror and seeing that Sara was right, she came to a screeching stop. The passenger door was flung open and Jenny, with no time to unbuckle, leaned out of the car, violently spewing the sour liquid contents of her stomach on to the hot, black asphalt, where it evaporated almost immediately. A fetid steam was all that was left from her upset. They waited there for a minute as Jenny hung limply out the door.

"Honey, are you okay to sit back up?" Mrs. Knowles asked her daughter.

There was no reply but a moment later the girl slowly eased back into the car, closing the door.

"I need to leave the windows down," she mumbled.

"Yes, of course," Mrs. Knowles agreed, as they continued the drive, traveling at half the speed so that now they only crept along. Sara began to worry about getting home later than her parents expected, especially with all the added tension of the strange cousins' arrival.

A few times, they stopped where there was a shoulder so Jenny could get out and stand in the humid, salty air for five minutes at a time. Her lively face was now ashen and tired.

"How much farther out is your house?" Mrs. Knowles asked.

She sounded tired herself, a trace of uncertainty in her tone.

"It's just here." Sara said, as they rounded a curve and a string of mailboxes resting domestically on a long woodened frame came into view.

"If you pull over here, I can walk the rest of the way."

Mrs. Knowles pulled up along the mailboxes, peering down the dirt road that Sara traversed every day.

"I think Jenny might need a cup of water and to rest a bit before we turn around. I'll just take you out to your house."

Alarmed, Sara fell back against her seat. This was terrible, of all the days for her teacher to pay a visit. Yet she knew that it would be rude to say no and deny them water and rest after they had been kind enough to bring her all the way home.

Potholes in the road only allowed for them to travel at ten miles per hour, and at that pace, Jenny seemed to finally revive a bit, looking about curiously.

"Wow! You live out in the boonies," she exclaimed, craning her neck to get a better look at everything. Mrs. Knowles exhaled sharply

The Visitors

as they drove over a tiny bridge with no guardrails. Moments later they were pulling up to Sara's driveway in a thick cloud of dust.

"Is it okay to park here?" she asked, looking around the large dirt entryway.

"Yes."

Sara grabbed her backpack and scrambled from the car before Mrs. Knowles had turned it off, but her heart sank as she looked toward the house and saw Maman standing on the porch.

"I hope she's not in trouble," Jenny remarked, as she and her mother got out of the car. A sturdy looking older woman, bulky and round in the middle and wearing a plain, high-necked, navy blue dress falling to her ankles walked toward them. Her face was flat and unwelcoming. She looked nothing like Sara, although Mrs. Knowles heard the girl call her Maman. The four of them met midway between a humble looking brown house and the driveway. Sara began speaking rapidly in French. The woman stood with her arms crossed, listening with barely concealed rage. A few times, her hard grey eyes swept over Mrs. Knowles and Jenny, the frown on her face deepening as Sara spoke.

Mrs. Knowles felt her own temper flare at the woman's blatant hostility. How dare she be so rude after they had just driven out of their way to bring her daughter home? Well, she would just have to demonstrate to the old battle-axe what etiquette was. Thrusting her hand out to the older woman with a determined smile on her face, she introduced herself and Jenny.

"Yes, I know who you are already," the woman said in heavily accented English, the words choppy and blunt. "Come with me."

She did not take Mrs. Knowles hand. Instead, Sara's mother turned on her heel and walked briskly back to the house, leaving the three of them to trail behind her.

It was the astounding beauty of their surroundings that captured their attention though, taking the sting out of Mrs. Deureaux's appallingly rude behavior. Great fields of verdant, green tropical foliage stretched out in every direction, the grass tinged brown from the dry spell. Coconut trees, palm trees, avocados, star fruit, citrus and guava bushes grew profusely. At the bottom of the sloping land were a thicket of banana trees and then the ocean, so close that it looked only a ten-minute walk away.

"My God," Mrs. Knowles whispered.

"This place is awesome," Jenny said in a hushed tone.

On the porch stood a shoe rack where Jenny, Mrs. Knowles and Sara deposited their slippers. Mrs. Deureaux, barefoot, went into the house ahead of them without a word.

"Please, come in," Sara said. She opened the front door with unsure movements. Mrs. Knowles, noticing that her daughter was looking increasingly uncomfortable, wondered a little late if it had been wise to accept such an unwilling invitation.

Stepping into the home, they entered a tidy kitchen with fresh flowers decorating the dining table and dried herbs hanging from a low beam. Mrs. Deureaux was filling a glass with water from a faucet that looked as if it lacked sufficient pressure. An agonizingly slow stream of water fell from the tap. Jenny stood briefly near her mother but, curiosity getting the better of her, she took a few steps more into the kitchen and poked her head around an entranceway that must have led to their living room. Mrs. Knowles was about to grab her daughter's arm when Jenny suddenly smiled and waved her hand.

"Hey," she called out.

There was no response from whomever it was she was greeting, and the smile faded from her lips. Moments later a tall, willowy girl in a homespun dress similar to Sara's emerged from the other room. Her steps were awkward and slightly wobbly, as if she were carefully negotiating herself around an ice rink. Striking pale-green eyes set in an even paler face assessed their little group. The girl's eyes were

The Visitors

all the more striking next to a shock of dark hair that fell thick and heavy over thin, wide shoulders. Every part of her seemed to contrast with another part, giving her an unnerving beauty. There was no color in her complexion. Her skin was as smooth and flawless as a white orchid. The girl stared wordlessly at them.

"This is Sara's cousin, and she's not speaking English," Mrs. Deureaux said brusquely, handing Jenny the water and then hovering near her while she drank it. When she was finished, Mrs. Deureaux all but snatched the glass from her fingers, silently dismissing them as she turned her back to the sink to wash the glass. Sara's cousin hadn't moved, only stood staring uncannily. Mrs. Knowles noticed that Sara stared back at the girl as if she had never seen her before.

Looking at her watch, she inclined her head toward the door.

"Jenny, it's time to go. Thank you for the water." She spoke to Mrs. Deureaux's back.

"Yes, goodbye," Mrs. Deureaux said without turning around

The strange girl did not move after Jenny and her mother left. She continued to stare at Sara, who introduced herself.

"*Bonjour. Je m'appelle Sara. Je suis enchantée,*" but the girl did not respond. Instead she slowly tilted her head to the side as Sara spoke, her eyes unblinking.

Maman's large hand came to rest flat against Sara's back, pushing her toward her odd cousin and the living room.

"Go and meet the other ones," she said.

The girl stepped aside so Sara could pass, almost losing what little balance she had, but Maman caught her roughly by the sleeve of her dress to steady her.

In the living room sat two young children that couldn't have been more than six or seven. Both fit easily in Papa's favorite chair. The fourth cousin, a tall boy that looked to be Sara's age, stood near his younger siblings, his white hand resting lightly on the armrest. The two little ones sat staring in the same manner as the older girl. They reminded Sara of two little birds, their dark eyes sharp and observant but without comprehension.

Only the older boy seemed to hold a flicker of a thinking mind in his expression. He smiled as Sara looked at him: a strange smile. His lips moved but the rest of his features seemed divorced from his expression, lending an eerie, unnatural look to his face. He reminded Sara of a ventriloquist puppet that had been brought into her class when she was a small girl in elementary school.

She smiled back, unsure.

The boy walked toward her on slender legs that looked as if they might give out on him any moment. He managed to keep himself much steadier than his sister. Extending his long white arm, he offered his hand to Sara.

She took it in hers but was jolted when she felt nothing but air, although she saw there was physical contact between them. A second later, she felt his skin, cool and dry, and she grasped his hand firmly with her own, disoriented by the odd effect.

"Hello," he said in English, the word sliding from his lips as if being tested when he spoke. "I am Samuel." Each word was said separately in a ponderous, slow fashion.

"*Parle vous Francais?*" Sara asked him. There was a long pause, and a strained silence filled the room.

"*Oui,*" he finally responded, again in that strange, slow way of letting the word slip as if unsure from his mouth.

"*Je m'appelle* Sara," she replied. The older boy nodded but the other three only stared. There was no comprehension, only a keen interest in the sharp pairs of eyes. All of them were slender to the point of frailty, and their bones protruded from their milky white skin; skin that emitted an odd pallor of health and newness although they were absent of any color.

All the while Maman had not said a word. Sara looked to her mother for some sort of guidance but Maman's strong ruddy

The Visitors

features were set into a deep frown. A fierce hatred glinted in her grey eyes, which were fixed solely on the older girl, who seemed oblivious of any ill will. The sound of the front door opening and Papa coming into the house broke the spell of tension that had been building. The smell of tobacco preceded him as he strode into the living room shirtless and musky with sweat from his work down the hill.

"Well now," he said in a loud, jovial voice that Sara had never heard him use before. "Have all of you met Sara?" Samuel nodded his head.

"Sara," he said, as if to reaffirm to himself that it was indeed her name. The other children remained silent.

"It's time to go upstairs and see your rooms," Papa said.

He continued to talk in a loud, pleasant voice as if they were all in a play.

"What are the other children's names?" Sara asked.

"Names," Samuel said. He reminded Sara of a toddler learning to talk.

"Never mind their names," Maman snapped. "Help Papa get the children up the stairs."

She left the living room then and the house altogether, slamming the front door after her. Sara watched her father bend over to pick up the little girl. Her thin arms snaked around his neck, and a disconcerted expression clouded her father's gaunt face as he lifted the girl from the wicker chair. The little boy raised his arms up too, and so did the eldest girl. Samuel just cocked his head to the side as if he were trying to understand something.

"Sara, pick up the other little one," Papa instructed. "Samuel, help your sister." Papa waited for his words to register. "Samuel, help her." Papa pointed to the older girl. Samuel's blue eyes suddenly brightened with understanding and he walked with unsteady legs to the girl, taking her hand. Sara wasn't sure about the two of them together, as he seemed not much better off than his sister.

Her father led the way to the stairs. Sara turned her attention to picking up her young male cousin and was startled again when she grasped nothing but air, all the while seeing her hands under the boy's arms. Seconds later, she felt his body as she lifted him up. He seemed to weigh almost nothing. The boy gazed shrewdly at her as she walked with him up the stairs.

Papa went to the room with the twin beds. "The boys will sleep here," he said.

Sara set her young cousin down and watched in dismay as his legs buckled under him and he fell in a twisted heap on his side. This did not seem to bother him. He did not look startled or hurt, only intent on looking at everything around him.

"It's okay, Sara," Papa said. Carefully, he set the girl on one of the beds before picking up the boy. Samuel and the older girl stood watching, still holding onto one another.

"These two little ones cannot walk yet," he explained. "In a few days, they will have the strength."

"What happened to them? How come they cannot walk?"

"I can handle it from here. Best to get started on your homework," was the only answer Papa gave.

It was late for them to be eating: already seven o'clock. Their family usually sat down an hour earlier for dinner. When Sara entered the kitchen, she saw that Maman had set the table for three as usual. Papa was already seated.

"Won't Samuel and the others be eating?" Sara asked.

"They're not to be eating. Just leave them be," Maman said as she set the ladle in a little dish on the stove next to the pot of stew. Sara sat down, slow and unsure. "But they look like they could eat. Aren't they hungry?"

The Visitors

Maman came to sit at the table, her expression stern. "You're not to be feeding them…"

In a flash, Papa's hand came to rest over Maman's as if warning her of something. Maman's mouth closed shut, cutting off her words, clearly tinged with the distaste that she'd shown earlier toward the children. A look of despair washed over her features.

"You're not to feed those children," she began again. "Are you understanding me, Sara?"

Sara nodded, her skin prickling and warm all over as she finally gave into what she already knew on a subconscious level. They were in some kind of trouble. This she knew, even if she had no other knowledge of why or how. Papa said the blessing. It was then Sara's turn to serve the stew. As usual they ate quietly. The only sounds were their spoons clinking against their dishes and the slurping and chewing of their food. It was silent upstairs.

Chapter Four

"Angela, we've been over this several times," Tim Knowles said to his wife, who reclined on the flowery brocade sofa, an uncomfortable antique piece of furniture that had once belonged to her great-grandmother. A martini rested in her slim hand as she massaged her temple with the other, eyes closed and brow wrinkled. Tim sat down next to his wife, pushing her red hair back over her shoulder and massaging the little worry lines between her brows with his thumb. She sighed, taking a sip of her drink.

"What should I do?" she asked.

"Nothing. There is nothing you can do for this girl. Her family isn't breaking the law because they like to be private. She's a good student, like you said, and doesn't get into trouble." Tim ran his hand through his hair. He was out of answers, not knowing what else he could say that would convince his wife that this girl's home life was not her business.

"The parents are unnaturally private, Tim. You should have seen—"

"Yeah, yeah you told me already, how rude her mother was. Look, are we done talking about this weird family? Because I have some news myself."

The Visitors

Angela sat up, setting her drink on a coaster that rested on the coffee table.

"What is it?" she asked.

"Well something strange happened today."

"Oh yeah?" Angela leaned forward, lifting a slim eyebrow as she studied her husband, who looked slightly uncomfortable.

"You remember my Uncle Arnold, right?"

Angela nodded. The image of an older, dowdy man with a slight British accent came to mind. She had only met him and his wife Sue a handful of times during her eighteen years with Tim. At their wedding reception, his uncle had given a nail biting toast, his stuttering such a hindrance to his speech that it had taken him a full two minutes to get out three sentences. Red-faced, he'd raised his glass before he was finished and sat back down, his wife patting his hand gently. As a wedding gift, he had given them a Ford station wagon in anticipation of a growing family. After that there'd been a few short visits over the years, and the funeral of Tim's parents, before they had fallen out of contact altogether.

"I just got news today that he's passed away," Tim said.

"Oh?" Angela reached for her husband's hand. "I'm sorry, Tim. Here I am going on about my student and I had no idea about your uncle. I know when you were a kid you used to spend a lot of time with him. Here on Maui, right?"

"Yes," Tim said.

He looked distracted and Angela tightened her grip on his hand. "What is it?"

"Well along with the news of his passing, apparently he also left me a house on the island." Angela sat up straighter. "The executor of the will spoke with me today. My Aunt Sue has been sick with Alzheimer's for some years now, and my Uncle Arnold had her put in a nursing home. It's odd how he never let me know about Aunt Sue or his will. I'm his only family, really."

Tim shook his head thinking about this. Angela waited.

"Anyway, he bought a two acre parcel with a house on the northeast side of the island back in the late seventies. From what the executor Eric told me, it was just an investment. He never stayed in it. There is some money as well that is being used to pay for the nursing home where my aunt lives. Whatever is left after she passes I will also inherit."

"Oh."

Angela let go of her husband's hand. They had been saving money to purchase a home and now they suddenly had one with two acres of land?

"I know it's shocking," Tim said. "I get this call at work. There were some problems locating me after our move here. Uncle Arnold has been gone since July."

"Will you be visiting your Aunt Sue?" Angela asked.

"I was able to get the name and number of the nursing home. She's in northern California, in Petaluma." Tim went to the bar and fixed himself another martini, taking a deep swallow.

"Tomorrow, we can go take a look at the place. There's a family living there. Eric wanted to know if we wanted to move in or leave things the way they are. Of course I wanted to discuss it with you first, but it sounds like just what we were looking for Angie, a house in the country. It has four bedrooms and two baths."

Angela couldn't help but smile, and Tim smiled back, coming to sit next to her again.

"What do you say we take a ride out there when I get off work?"

"I say yes," Angela whispered. Tim leaned over and kissed his wife, stroking her face.

"I think we're going to be just fine here, Mrs. Knowles."

Angela nuzzled up to her husband and closed her eyes. Maybe it would be all right. She had been homesick, missing her friends and the variety of things to do in Santa Monica. Jenny was on the phone

The Visitors

every weekend talking to her two best friends. Living in their own home would really give them a fresh start. Before long, Jenny would make connections at school. It would work out. It had to.

"Hey, this is the way to Sara's house," Jenny exclaimed, perking up a little from her bout of carsickness.

What had begun earlier that evening as a joyous occasion to see the new house had gradually fizzled into a sombre mood. Angela wondered if Jenny would be able to handle the daily trek to school on a curvy road that upset the poor girl's stomach to the point that they were forced to pull over numerous times.

Tim's smile faded, and he glanced at his daughter every few minutes through the rear-view mirror. Angela squeezed her husband's arm in an attempt to dispel his worry, but Jenny's comment added a new tension. Tim's jaw hardened.

To Angela's dismay, a row of mailboxes loomed up ahead of them and Tim put on his blinker, making the left turn onto the same dirt road she and Jenny had traversed the day before. Fortunately, Jenny didn't remark on this being Sara's road. Angela turned to look back at her daughter, who reclined against the door directly behind her father. Her eyes were closed, the lids pale and threaded lightly with veins. Her hand rested on her stomach and her legs were sprawled across the seat in an attempt to get comfortable. The dirt road, uneven and full of potholes, yawned out before them and they bumped along, quietly raising clouds of dust.

"Driving out here will be hard on the car's alignment," Tim remarked.

The road forked and Angela held her breath, wondering, but they did not make a right hand turn in the direction of Sara's house, instead they turned left.

Old style plantation homes with wide porches and low pitched gabled roofs sat picturesquely in spacious lots. All were overtaken by fuchsia, bougainvillea and bright yellow hibiscus growing with robust profusion along fences up against the exterior of the homes and out in the fields. As Tim took in the scenery he was unprepared for the two shirtless boys on bicycles that came careening from around the bend of the road, almost riding into the car. Tim swore as he turned the steering wheel hard, pressing the breaks. But the boys' reflexes were faster and they were already dodging past them, laughing.

"Whoa brah, you see the look on dat haole's face?" one of the boys called out to the other. The sound of their laughter faded as they sped by. Dirt and pebbles shot out from under their tires, spraying the back of the car. Tim shook his head angrily, his mouth tight and grim. He righted the car and continued on. Just around the bend that the boys came from was a driveway off to the left, shaded by an old mango tree, its branches spread out wide, a cluster of white balloons strung from one of the branches.

"This must be it," Tim said.

He turned left into a driveway shaded by several tall Norfolk pines. The ground was littered with brown and orange leaves from the mango tree. The trees gave way to the pervasive bougainvillea. At the end of the driveway and off to the right sat a modest sized white clapboard house with a wide veranda and a low-pitched roof. A silver Mercedes was parked in front of the home.

"This shreds!" Jenny exclaimed opening her door before her father had cut the engine. Tim's features softened as he stepped out of the car following his daughter's buoyant gait. The front door opened and a man with a greying ponytail in brown slacks and an Aloha dress shirt emerged from the house. He carried a thin folder under his arm.

"I like it already," Tim called out once he had climbed the porch steps. He clasped his hand with the older man's, whose smile was a bit lopsided due to a slight droop on the left side of his face. His left eye was also a bit smaller than the right but his handshake was strong, the skin calloused and rough, like that of a laborer.

"Aloha, I'm Eric."

He had an easy way of talking and Tim felt himself beginning to relax.

"This must be quite a surprise," Eric said.

"You bet," Tim replied, assessing his surroundings appreciatively.

"Dad, can we look around now?" Jenny was bouncing on her toes, her hands in a begging position.

"Honey, Eric is going to show us around right now," Angela said.

"Let her run and take a look. I'll take you two around and she can join us when she's gotten some of that juju out of her system," Eric said with a laugh.

Jenny squealed, darting off. Eric opened the screen door and stepped aside to let Angela and Tim walk through.

"This home is more than fifty years old. It was built in 1929 and renovated a few years before your uncle acquired it in '79. It's what they call a craftsman bungalow, a popular style back at the turn of the century."

He waved his arm around for emphasis and Angela gasped, taking hold of Tim's arm as they looked around them. A large living room with a beamed ceiling, tiled fireplace and inglenook adorned with picture windows that featured a view of a lush, green pasture took Angela's breath away. Tim felt stunned. "There's quite a bit of built in cabinet space." Eric continued opening one of the low-lying cabinets revealing a deep, wide space lined with shelves.

"Is this a redwood floor?" Tim asked.

"Yeah, a lot of homes here in Hawaii were built with redwood up until the sixties."

Angela placed her hand on a yellow rocking chair that sat before the fireplace, drawing Eric's attention.

"The caretakers have agreed to have the place ready in two weeks, as was part of the agreement."

Angela thought she detected something in his expression... uncertainty?

"If they need more time, that's perfectly alright. We have to give a month's notice anyway, right honey?" She looked to Tim.

"Absolutely," Tim agreed.

"Just the same, they've already started packing and this home will be free and clear in two weeks." He cleared his throat. "Let me show you the kitchen."

Leading them through an arched doorway, he revealed a good-sized kitchen and dining area sequestered by more picture windows.

"Now I've been told that some of the electrical wiring is faulty," Eric remarked, continuing with the tour. Angela and Tim followed him to the first of two bedrooms that were accessed by walking through the living room and down a short hallway. Each room held a twin bed. Toys and children's books were neatly kept on dark brown shelves. Tall, wide windows just a foot above the floor lit up the little rooms with grey evening light. As they walked back to the living room and around to a second hallway to view the other two rooms, they met Jenny who had just skipped back from the kitchen.

"I love this house!" she yelled. "Mom, Dad, did you see the master bedroom? It's awesome! There are French doors that open out to the yard and you can see the neighbor's horses. There's even a little garden right outside the room."

"Yes, we're going to take a look right now," Angela laughed.

This was a dream. How they had gotten so lucky, she could not understand.

"Honey this is wonderful," she spoke into Tim's ear, who pulled her closer as they followed Eric.

The master bedroom had its own bathroom with a deep, old-fashioned claw foot tub and a tiny sink with spigot handles labeled for

The Visitors

hot and cold. Angela wandered out of the French doors, stepping onto a circular patch of cobbled stones with two wooden folding chairs set out for relaxing. Pink, white and purple impatiens grew all around, lending a cheerful atmosphere to the small garden.

A gardenia bush still bloomed, the perfumed scent of the white flowers wafting in the still air. Jenny joined them and ran outside to smell the gardenias. Angela watched her daughter run ahead in the yard as Eric pointed out the special features of their bedroom. This led to a conversation between Eric and Tim about the electrical wiring in the house, electricians to contact and the use of candles and kerosene lanterns once upon a time.

"In fact, the folks on the ridge are still off grid, just one family, actually. Nice people but they like to keep to themselves. They have a daughter just about your daughter's age."

"Sara," Angela said.

"That's her name. Quiet girl."

"I'm her history teacher."

"That so."

Tim placed his hands in his pockets, growing silent.

"I think I'll go see if I can catch up with Jenny," Angela said stepping out to the little garden and picking a gardenia. The sweet, musky aroma of the flower flooded her senses for a moment as she went out into the yard and toward a knoll that rose up gradually. Walking up to the top of the small hill, she scanned her surroundings. It seemed like more than two acres, she thought. Her eyes alighted on the figure of someone standing in the distance. As she drew closer, she could make out the shape of a woman. A long dark braid hung down the center of her back and she appeared to be staring down at something. It wasn't until Angela was yards away that she noticed for the first time a cluster of headstones. The sound of her feet swishing in the dry grass disturbed what was clearly a moment of reflection, and the woman turned around.

"Oh, I'm sorry." Angela said. "I didn't realize…"

The woman's broad features were without expression, only her brown eyes, wet with tears, portrayed emotion. A tense silence stretched between them, broken by the sudden trill of an 'apapane. The small red bird alighted on an Ohi'a Lehua bush, its head dipping rapidly into the spiky red flowers before taking flight again. A light breeze blew tendrils of the woman's hair across her high cheekbones. Without a word, she walked toward a cluster of bamboo that knocked together in the wind. Parting the spindly stalks, she stepped through them, leaving Angela alone at the smattering of graves, her heart knocking in her chest.

"Mom," Angela turned around to see her daughter running up to her.

"Isn't this great? Oh my God!" Jenny's hand flew to her mouth. "A cemetery," she whispered. "That's kind of creepy."

Angela wanted to say something but her throat was so dry that she found herself just croaking, "Yes."

"Are you okay? You look like you just saw a…" the word died on Jenny's lips.

"Did you see a ghost?"

Forcing herself to smile, she put an arm around her daughter.

"No, no. My stomach was just a little upset. I'm feeling better now."

Angela's eyes rested on the headstone that the woman had been standing in front of. "*Beloved Tutu*," it read. "*Margaret Kahiamoi 1879 to 1979, May she rest in peace.*"

"She was old." Jenny remarked, her brows drawing together as she read the inscription. Fresh flowers placed by the headstone were tied with string in a little bundle, purple and pink impatiens, gardenias and ginger.

"Those are the same flowers in the garden outside your bedroom," Jenny said, stooping to finger the ginger bulbs.

The Visitors

"Jenny, don't touch those. It's disrespectful."

Jenny stood back up, her face pinched with thought. "I think Margaret Kahimamoi was a relative of the people living in the house that Dad inherited." A sudden gust of wind, the first real trade wind in a month, flattened the grass and ballooned out their shirts.

"We should head back," was all Angela could think to say. All of the joy had left her daughter's face as she remained next to the small gravesite looking around, her expression pensive.

"This is someone's home," she said. "I don't understand how it belonged to my uncle. Didn't Dad say he never lived here?"

"Sometimes people buy a property as an investment," Angela explained.

"But why would a family sell their home to my uncle and then stay living here?"

"Honey, I'm not sure about the particulars. But we do need to get going. I'm sure your father's wondering where we are."

Jenny rolled her eyes. "It's not like it would be hard to find us," she said, as she began to walk toward the house.

Angela followed her daughter, the wind pushing back at them. She thought of California, and a wave of homesickness washed over her. For the first time, she wondered if it had been a bad idea to move to Hawaii.

Chapter Five

Sara did not go to school the next morning. It was dark as usual when she awoke. She dressed in the dim, flickering light of a single candle on her dresser, not bothering with her propane lamp. After brushing her hair, she pulled the front back neatly, without the aid of a mirror. Maman considered them to be the height of vanity. There were no mirrors at her house or in the bathrooms at school, and Sara could not remember when she had properly seen her full reflection. Other than the odd warped image of her face in the lid of a shiny pot or the transparent, shadowy reflection of herself in a windowpane, she had very little idea of what she looked like.

The sounds of her parents moving about alerted her that they were up, but it remained quiet in the upstairs rooms where her cousins had retired the night before. There was a sharp rap at the door and Sara opened it to see Maman standing, already dressed, her features hollowed and shadowed from the light of a tapered candle that she held in the dark hallway. She sniffed approvingly when she saw Sara ready for the day.

"Come and help me with the children," she said.

The Visitors

Sara followed her mother upstairs where she was directed to go to the girls' bedroom. Knocking softly on the door, she waited. Hearing nothing, she slowly opened it. A smudge of morning light relieved some of the darkness in the room and Sara lit the lamp mounted in a metal sconce on the wall, using the flame of her candle. A golden hue flooded the room and revealed the two girls lying in bed on their backs beneath the floral quilt. Their eyes were already open.

"It's time to get up," Sara said.

They both stared at her inquisitively but did not speak or move. Sara pulled back the quilt and gently helped the eldest girl to sit up first. Again there was the odd feeling of touching nothing before the girl's body became corporal in her hands. She held her sitting position. Sara noticed that she wore the same dress that she had worn yesterday. Unsure what to make of this or if she should help her change into a different dress, Sara decided to sit the smaller girl up and go get Maman. She could hear her mother barking orders in the other room and then the heavy footsteps of the older woman making her way to the girls' room. Maman stood in the doorway, taking in the scene.

"The boys are ready. Take them downstairs and sit them in the living room." Sara left the room and found Samuel and the smaller boy holding hands as they waited by the stairs. She was surprised to see the younger boy standing.

"Bonjour," she greeted Samuel, who cocked his head, deciphering her greeting.

His lips suddenly stretched back in that odd frozen expression of a smile when he seemed to understand, then greeted Sara haltingly.

"Bon jour."

Sara took the small boy's hand from Samuel, not trusting them to walk down the steps together. Samuel went ahead, seeming much sturdier on his feet than before. The younger boy walked carefully and Sara held his hand tightly as he negotiated each step. Guiding the children to the living room, she found Papa sitting at his desk, his head bent as he wrote on letter paper. He looked up as they filed into the room and greeted them with a friendly nod. Maman brought the girls down shortly and then bustled about in the kitchen filling four glasses with water. Sara watched as she pulled out the jar of medicine and began to heap teaspoons of the powder into each glass, which gave the liquid a greyish, clumpy look.

"Carefully observe, it is four teaspoons to a cup of water," Maman said. "They take it twice a day; once in the morning, once in the evening. Is that clear?"

Sara nodded and helped her mother carry the glasses of medicine to the children. Each drank the rapidly congealing drink without incident. There was not even a wrinkle of the nose or a grimace at the repugnant smell and taste. This was all they were given. Maman did not offer them the breakfast of oatmeal she had made. Again Sara sat down to eat with her parents, leaving the cousins to wait quietly amongst themselves, the soft light of dawn finally creeping through the windows.

"Sara, I want you to water the garden this morning. Take Samuel down the hill with you and show him what to do," Maman said between bites of food.

"*Oui.*"

Maman grunted her satisfaction over her cereal and did not look up when Papa excused himself. Sara knew he was headed for the old stable building where he would probably spend most of the day again.

After breakfast, Maman went to the bathroom, coming back with the jar of cream that she insisted Sara wear every day.

"I already put that on," she said when she saw the jar in her mother's large hands.

"It's for the children. They must wear this one everyday like you, Sara. Have Samuel put on this cream before you two go outside."

The Visitors

Sara followed her mother into the living room where the children waited. Only Samuel stood by the window looking out, but he turned around when he heard them come into the room, his face without expression. Maman opened the jar, offering it to Sara, who dipped her slim finger into the silky, goopy stuff and cupped a few tablespoons worth into the palm of her hand while her mother briskly set about applying the cream to the little boy first. Her eyebrows rose up and down in a disconcerted, startled expression while she touched him. It was the same expression Papa had worn when he had lifted the girl to take her upstairs. Sara offered the cream to Samuel, making the motions with her hands to show him what to do. The eldest girl stood up and came to watch, her expression keen.

He dabbed a long, skinny finger into the goop that she held out and rubbed some slowly onto his pale face. He was so white that Sara could see the faint blue of his veins snaking under his skin. She nodded, smiling for encouragement to show him he was doing it right. He smiled back, nodding in imitation, flashing white, oddly shaped teeth that over lapped in a crooked, jagged fashion. The older girl followed suit, her face impassive and her eyes unblinking as she rubbed the cream on herself.

Next, Maman pulled from the coat rack a large straw hat, placing it on Samuel's head. She then handed him a long- sleeved raincoat. When he put it on, it hung to his knees. In this gear, she allowed him to leave the house. Sara grabbed an apple from the kitchen and shoved it in her dress pocket as they made their way outside into the pale morning. Although Samuel was steadier on his feet, he still walked slowly. *They must all be recovering from a serious illness,* Sara thought. She frowned to herself, wondering again where they had come from and why they'd come to stay.

"The main water tank is by the driveway," Sara told Samuel in French. She was not sure he completely understood her when she spoke but thought he would soon learn—all of the children would.

French was a better language to speak then English, she decided. French was mostly spoken at home and there seemed to be no indication that her cousins would be going to school. *"It is just for a month,"* she heard Papa's voice in her mind.

They walked to her father's workshop where the buckets were kept. A low whine from the small dark shed alerted Sara that Blackie was there.

"It's okay," she called out to the dog, hoping her voice sounded soothing. Samuel tilted his head to the side, his light brows pulling together. There was a sharp bark and another mournful whine. Samuel slowly tilted his head to the other side.

"Dog," he said in English.

"Oui c'est mon chien," Sara said. "Blackie. He's afraid of me now," she explained.

"Dog," Samuel said again as they entered the shed. Sara could make out Blackie's shape in the corner of the building. He was crouched up against the buckets, his ears back and his tail between his legs. She sighed as she knelt down, holding her hand out toward the animal. Samuel did the same, imitating her calls. Blackie only moved farther into the corner, his pitiful whines giving way to his bladder as a small puddle spread out between his legs.

"Blackie," Sara called out softly, moving closer to her pet. Samuel followed her, his low voice calling the dog. "We just need the buckets," she whispered, edging closer. Blackie's whines gave way to a low growl, as his pointy ears flattened back farther and his mouth pulled away from his sharp canines. Sara felt her throat tighten as hot tears prickled her eyes. Why was he so afraid of her?

It was Samuel's grunt of surprise that she heard first before she took in the dark shape hurtling at her throat. Quicker than she had time to think, she caught Blackie's lunging form, the force of him knocking her back on the floor. His teeth sank into her hand and a second later she was sending him hurtling across the workshop, his fangs ripping through her flesh as he disengaged. There was a thud as her dog hit the opposite wall, sending the buckets rolling in different directions. Yelping, he scurried past them, his hind legs sliding behind him in his haste to be away from her.

"Ow! Ow!" she cried, pulling herself up. Samuel's eyes were as wide as a baby's. Sara examined her hand. The webbing was torn between her thumb and index finger. Her flesh was shredded from the lacerations of the dog's teeth, gaping open in ragged pink folds. Blood immediately began to well up and drip onto her dress and the floor. Sara grabbed a clean rag from one of the shelves, pressing it hard against her hand to suppress the bleeding as Samuel watched. Red soaked through the white rag. Sara folded it in half and pressed it again against her hand. Samuel reached for another rag without being asked and handed it to her. His small helpful action surprised her, considering that he and his siblings appeared nearly helpless, with little comprehension of anything.

"*Merci*," she said while interchanging the rags. She knew the bleeding would slow soon. She never stayed hurt for long when she cut herself. Holding her hand to her chest with the rag in place, she grabbed one of the buckets that had toppled over and a watering can. Looping the handle of the can over the index finger of her good hand while curling her remaining fingers over the handle of the bucket, she lifted them up and pointed to the other bucket and a metal scooper with her toe.

"Get those, Samuel."

She watched him digest her words and stare down at her pointed foot. She nudged the bucket for emphasis. Finally understanding, he bent down to pick it up, his thin body swallowed up momentarily in the yellow plastic of the raincoat as he retrieved the bucket and scooper. Sufficiently supplied, Sara led Samuel to the water tank, a large dome of metal capable of holding twenty thousand gallons of water. A couple of faucets protruded off the side of the tank and

Sara turned one of these on to fill their buckets. Once both buckets were filled, Sara picked up one and gave Samuel the watering can and scooper to hold. He was not strong enough to lug five gallons of water down the hill to the garden. She would have to come back for the second one herself. It was usually an hour to an hour and half process but Sara didn't mind. It was a lot better than hand washing clothes or churning butter.

Sara's hand throbbed as they slowly made their way to the garden. Some of the water was sloshing against her dress in her effort to only use her good hand to carry the heavy bucket. It was a tedious walk and her arm began to ache from the weight of the water. Samuel stumbled a few times but managed to keep his footing.

The two reached a tall fence that ran the perimeter of the garden: an obstacle to cattle that sometimes escaped neighboring pastures. Sara set the water bucket down and flexed her hand a few times to wake up cramped muscles before opening the gate. Picking up the bucket again, she plopped it down inside the enclosed area and waited for Samuel to step in before closing the gate after them. Rows of seedlings, lettuce, chard, Chinese cabbage and collard greens stood wilted from the spell of hot, dry weather and now the returning trade winds whipped at the fatigued plants, further drying the earth. The mature vegetables were faring better, although the string beans were browning early. It would rain soon. Sara knew that when the trade winds became strong, they pushed rain-laden clouds over the land.

Quickly she showed Samuel how to pour water a little at a time around each plant. With Samuel busy, Sara hurried back up the hill for the second bucket. She took a moment to peel the rag back from her hand and inspect it. The bleeding had stopped. It still throbbed though, and she ran her hand under the faucet, letting the cool water wash away the dried blood and relieve some of the pain. By evening she knew her wound would be almost closed up. In a few days, her hand would be back to normal. There would be no scar.

The Visitors

Samuel was using the last of the water when Sara returned. While setting the second bucket down, her apple fell from her pocket and rolled over the newly moistened earth, flattening a struggling lettuce seedling. Picking it up, she rinsed the dirt off and took a bite. It was crunchy, sweet and juicy. Samuel watched. He stood stark and thin, his long arms dangling at his sides.

"Do you want a bite?" she offered. He wasn't going to do very well on that medicine Maman was feeding him, she decided. He took the apple in his long white fingers and bit into it, chewing loudly not bothering to close his mouth, as he should. His strange teeth fascinated Sara, how they folded over each other. While he ate, he stared at the apple as if not knowing what to make of it. After swallowing, he looked up at Sara with unfathomable blue eyes. Sara motioned for him to eat more. He took another bite, crunching loudly, again examining the apple. He ate it quickly, turning it around in his hands; some of the juices dribbling down his chin. He even ate the core. He's starving, she thought.

"Feel better?" she asked when he was finished. He didn't answer, just stood running his tongue all around his mouth, staring at her. She pointed to the water bucket and told him to continue watering before grabbing the newly empty bucket to refill.

On her third trip, Sara had to stop and rest several times. With her left hand out of commission, her right arm ached from the continuous weight pulling on her muscles. Dragging the bucket into the garden, she saw that Samuel had abandoned the watering. He was nowhere in sight.

"Samuel!" she called. All was quiet in the garden. Sara left the enclosed space and wandered around the fenced area. "Samuel!" she called again.

There was a gurgling sound in the bushes, followed by loud retching. Sara ran toward the sound, peeling back the branches of hau bush. She found her cousin bent over, spewing up chunks of apple.

Flecks of the fruit dappled the leaves and ground around him. Brown liquid gushed from his mouth as he emitted agonized heaving sounds. Sara placed her palm on Samuel's contracting shoulders, as liquid shot out of his mouth and dribbled out his nose. Oh God, the apple had made him sick, but why?

"Samuel," she spoke his name soothingly but the vomiting continued. Samuel gave another loud groan and a giant heave. He fell to the ground and his body convulsed then stiffened, his face turning blue. Sara ran to the stable where her father was working.

"Papa!" she screamed. It seemed her father just appeared as soon his name left her lips. "It's Samuel." She pointed to the bushes. "He's sick, something's wrong!"

"Go get Maman!" Papa yelled back before running in Samuel's direction.

Sara sprinted up the hill, winded by the time she arrived on the front porch. Flinging open the front door, she burst into the living room. Maman was ironing clothes and the eldest girl folded crisp, starched items while the two younger children looked at picture books. All of them looked up at the sudden intrusion, only Maman's face registering that something was wrong.

"It' Samuel…he's sick," Sara said between gasps for air. Maman set the iron aside. Her eyes flashed with anger that superseded any anger that Sara had ever seen before.

"He is only sick if you fed him. Have you been feedin him, girl?"

Sara nodded, her head feeling wooden. Maman moved toward her and slapped her cheek so hard, her ear rang. Sara's skin stung with the sensation of a thousand prickles, as a red welt rose rapidly on her dark face. The cousins looked on, their expressions unchanged except for the older girl, whose eyes met Sara's with pupils so enlarged that her eyes appeared black with a rim of green. A shadow of a smile played on her pale mouth. Her expression did not escape Maman's sharp eyes.

The Visitors

"Do not watch us, girl!" Maman yelled.

But she did not avert her eyes. It was Maman who turned away to go into the kitchen, where she grabbed the jar of the medicine and began to make the drink. The older girl pulled herself up. She was still unsteady but appeared to have better balance than the day before. She walked carefully to the kitchen and planted herself before Maman, holding out her slim arm.

Her voice was husky. "Me. *Donnez moi ca,* Annette," she said, which in English meant, *Give me that.* Her words were slow and strange sounding. She spoke unaccented French, but the flow of her words had a halting quality. Maman ignored her, stirring the powder into the glass of water. Sara watched her mother's hands begin to shake under the steady gaze of the girl. "*Donne!*" she demanded, still holding out her arm as she began to open and close her hand. Maman's nostrils flared, but when she spoke it was in a quiet, steady voice.

"Sara, walk to me slowly and carefully take this medicine to Samuel." Sara walked toward her mother. Her cousin's hand dropped, but her head whipped around, her dilated eyes resting on Sara.

"Walk slower, Sara, and do not look at your cousin. Keep your eyes on me." Sara felt her heart speed up as she took small steps toward Maman; all the while the intense gaze of the eldest girl was scrutinizing her.

"That's right," Maman coaxed.

A sheen of sweat spread across the woman's forehead as beads of moisture gathered above her lip. She began to hold the glass out to Sara. Sara kept her eyes on her mother as she raised her own arm inch by inch until her fingers touched the glass. She still felt the girl's eyes boring into her.

"Sara," it was the sound of Maman's voice but her mother's lips hadn't moved.

"Sara," the voice came from beside her and Sara swallowed, looking at the girl who spoke her name with a perfect imitation of her mother's intonation. Her pale eyes blazed dark in her gaunt, white face.

"Look to me," Maman said while pushing the glass fully into Sara's grasp. "Walk past me now to the back door," Maman continued to speak in a quiet, calm voice. "When you get outside, hurry."

Sara followed her mother's directions, moving at sloth speed down the hall and out the back door that their family never used.

Once outside, she picked up her gait and noticed for the first time that she was damp with sweat. Her dress clung to her skin. Papa was already heading up the hill. He held Samuel in his arms. The boy's long legs were draped over his arm.

"Oh Papa!" Sara called out, rushing to her father with the drink. Papa laid the boy down in the grass and grabbed the glass from Sara, dipping his creased, rough fingers into the sludgy liquid. He rubbed the sludge on the boy's blue lips. Pulling his lips open a bit, he dripped some of the medicine into his mouth, while attempting to hold his head up. Sara sank to her knees and cradled her cousin's head while her father dribbled more liquid. This time Samuel's Adam's apple bobbed, signaling the motion of swallowing. Papa dribbled more liquid and again Samuel's throat muscles constricted. While Papa kept up a consistent drip, Samuel's normally white complexion gradually returned as the blue receded.

The boy's eyelids began to flutter open, followed by a long, ragged gasp for air. Papa set the glass down and Sara remained on her knees, letting Samuel's head rest against her chest. All was quiet except for the calls of the myna birds and the distant sound of a lawn mower. After a while Samuel's breathing became even, his eyes opened and closed again, and his limp body rested against Sara. He appeared to have fallen asleep. Papa set the glass down.

"You mustn't feed the children," he said. "Help me carry him to the house. He will have to sleep it off. This is a setback for him."

The Visitors

Sara slipped her arms under Samuel's shoulders while Papa grabbed his legs. Both stood up, lifting the boy and carrying him up the hill to the house. Maman was waiting for them at the back door.

"He can't come in," she said flatly. Papa nodded as if he understood perfectly.

"We'll put him in the truck," he said.

Maman followed them out to the driveway, where she watched with her hands on her hips as they climbed clumsily into the bed of the truck with Samuel and laid him down.

"Sara, go and get that old blanket in the workshop," Papa commanded.

Sara jumped from the truck and ran to grab the wool blanket that lay folded on the shelf with the hand towels. She hurried back and handed it to Papa, who folded it lengthwise before rolling Samuel to his side and slipping the blanket under him. Sara peered over the side of the truck bed. Samuel seemed stabilized; his breathing was even, though the skin on his face was slightly reddened in what looked like the beginning of a sunburn.

"Go and finish your watering. I will watch him."

"Papa, I'm sorry," Sara whispered. Her father's eyebrows drew together, but he did not reply. Sara turned away, tucking her head down as she headed for the garden.

Chapter Six

It had grown exceptionally quiet since the children's arrival. On the fifth day, Sara noticed the absence of birds. There were no animals of any kind. She had not seen Blackie since he had bitten her that day she poisoned Samuel with the apple. The cows in the pasture would have fled if they could, she realized.

As she supervised the needlepoint project of the youngest girl, whose name, she learned, was Carmilla, she pondered what it meant. Her young charge sat primly, following the pattern expertly on the small canvas that she held in her lap, her fingers nimble and efficient. Everything her cousins learned, they mastered with peculiar alacrity.

On the first day the cousins had gone outside, it had quickly been discovered that their white complexions could not take much of the sun, even when slathered in Maman's special cream. All of them suffered burns that were gruesome to look at, their skin cooked to the point of bubbling, oozing sores. But they healed quickly, much quicker than Sara, even. Sara had seen the fleshy part of the youngest boy's leg split open from a particularly severe burn. Within only two hours of staying inside, Michael's wound had healed, the skin

The Visitors

returning to normal. These strange, disturbing occurrences were amongst many Sara could only contemplate. Her parents had made it abundantly clear that they would not discuss or explain anything in regard to her strange cousins.

While the two boys and the younger girl were put to work doing various projects in the house or amusing themselves with a book, the eldest girl was kept locked in her room. Her door was fitted with a knob that locked from the outside. She was only permitted to join her siblings for nightly excursions around the property.

Carmilla set her needlepoint down and stood, stretching her body. She walked to the bookshelf, examining the spines of the books by running her fingers lightly over them. There was something different about her, Sara thought, studying the girl. Carmilla, feeling her gaze, looked up, her dark eyes penetrating and sharp as ever. She seemed taller than before. The light cotton frock she wore was an old dress of Sara's, and two days ago it had fit the girl's slim, small figure perfectly. Now the length of it was shorter on her, markedly so.

"Carmilla, come here," Sara beckoned.

Leading the girl to her room, she motioned for her to stand up against the wall. Grabbing a ruler from her desk, she placed it on the top of her dark head, creating an even, horizontal line that she marked faintly with her pencil on the bare wall. Carmilla watched all of this with the keenest of interest but said nothing. She and Michael never spoke.

"It looks like you grew recently," Sara explained. "Just a few days ago you were not so tall. I am making this mark so I can chart your progress."

Carmilla slowly cocked her head as Sara spoke. It seemed she was interested in Sara's remark, which was unusual for her. Projects, she made a visible effort to understand and learn, but conversation had never attracted her attention much. Sara put the ruler away.

"Grow."

The sound of a strange, husky voice made the hairs on the back of Sara's neck stand on end. Carmilla stood very still, her dark eyes blazing in their intensity.

"Grow," she said again in the same slow way that Samuel and her older sister spoke.

"*Oui*," Sara nodded.

Carmilla raised her arm and pointed to the mark on the wall. Her hand continued to inch up above the mark. She turned to look at Sara, her narrow face full of consternation, as if she wanted Sara to understand something.

"You are growing," Sara said.

Carmilla's hand dropped to her side while she continued to stare at Sara. Through her girlish, narrow features the wisdom of someone much older emanated from her eyes and the stillness of her frame.

Since the children's arrival, Sara had never seen either of the little ones run about playfully, laugh or take interest in things that most small children found pleasure in. The picture books had been pored over the first day of the cousins' arrival and had not been touched since. Dolls had been examined methodically and tossed away with indifference. Colorful beads and Play Dough that Papa had picked up from the toy store, much to Maman's disapproval, had been left untouched. Instead, the children had been more interested in various chores given them and learning skills that Sara had initially thought were beyond their comprehension. Yet they had learned quickly and easily.

In one night, the eldest girl went from banging keys on their old Steinway piano, kept in the small library adjacent to the house, to playing haunting adagios. It had been only three hours ago that Sara had showed Carmilla how to needlepoint, yet in the last hour, she had become so precise and quick with her stitching it was as if she had always known what to do. None of it made any sense.

The Visitors

The sound of the front door opening and Maman's heavy footsteps pulled Sara from her thoughts. Taking Carmilla's hand, she walked with the girl from her room into the kitchen. She could already hear her mother interrogating the boys as to where she and Carmilla had gone.

"We are here," Sara called out.

Her mother stepped into the kitchen, staring for a moment at the two of them.

"And where have you been?"

"I was noticing something," Sara began, swallowing back the fear of her mother's anger. "Carmilla seems as if she has grown since she came here. The dress she is wearing is shorter on her than it was a few days ago."

Maman's eyes assessed Carmilla briefly before she reached for the girl and roughly grabbed her hand, yanking her forward and pushing her toward the living room. She stumbled over her feet and caught herself before turning to stand and glare at Maman.

"Go and finish your needlepoint, Carmilla."

Carmilla did not move, only stood very still, her expression pensive, as if she were trying to understand something.

"I said go and finish your work, girl."

Carmilla's arm rose up and she pointed at Maman.

"You," she spoke, her voice ponderous and husky. "You are a slave."

Each word was pronounced clearly and singularly as if she were laying down blocks. Maman's face grew slack. The color drained from her cheeks. Carmilla continued to stare, her body held erect, her chin up as if she were in command. When Maman said nothing, the small girl went back into the living room with eyes full of contempt. Sara followed her and watched as Carmilla took her seat and resumed her needlepoint. The boys continued reading. Whatever they may have overheard held little interest for them. They did not even look up.

It was six-thirty and the sun was already dipping into the western horizon. For the rest of the afternoon, Maman spent her time in the small sewing room. She did not come out until it was time to make dinner. Sara joined her and assisted in making a meat pie. There were no words exchanged as Maman dipped cubes of beef in seasoned flour for browning. Sara chopped vegetables. When the pie was complete, Maman grabbed a small knife and made a few quick slashes in the center of it before rubbing her hands on her apron and glancing at the clock over the stove.

"It's time for the children to go out," she announced.

With relief, Sara left her mother's side and went first upstairs to unlock the door for the eldest girl. As she reached the top of the steps, the sound of humming came from the room. Sara paused on the step and listened. The girl was singing to herself, her voice rising and falling in a lilting manner that was beautiful to hear. Sara crept forward but the humming stopped. After a minute she went to the door and unlocked it. There the eldest girl stood in front of the window with solemn features. The window appeared to be undulating. Sara blinked, not sure what she was looking at. Something flew at her face, a buzzing, whirring brown insect. It was a cockroach! The sticky claws caught in her hair and she frantically grabbed at her curls, trying to disengage the awful creature. When she looked up, the window bubbled into a moving mass of skittering creatures that suddenly took flight. An angry cloud of roaches swarmed toward Sara. The girl was untouched by the hurricane of insects dive-bombing Sara's face and hair. A great noise overpowered the room, whirring and humming. Screaming, Sara beat at the air around her, frantically trying to dislodge the horrid things that were now crawling through her hair and down her dress. She did not hear Papa's voice calling her name. She slapped at his hands pulling her up from a crouching position.

The Visitors

"Sara what is it? Why are you screaming?"

Her father's voice cut through the buzzing sound. It was quiet. The sensation of dozens of little claws skittering over her skin was gone. Sara opened her eyes. The insects were gone. Papa stood watching her. His bushy eyes brows were pulled together, thin lips tight and brown eyes full of worry. "What is it?" he asked softly. Sara glanced at the eldest girl, who remained standing by the window, her face without expression. Too stunned to speak, Sara burst into tears.

"What happened?" Papa directed his question to the girl. "What have you done?"

The girl tilted her head, her pale eyes wandering toward the doorway. Sara followed the girl's gaze to see Maman standing partially in the room. Shadows fell over her larger frame as she stood silently watching.

"Go and rest in your room," Papa said. "The children can walk on their own tonight." Sara left the room, brushing past her mother. Samuel, Carmilla and Michael stood at the bottom of the steps, looking up. Only Samuel's face had anything that approached a normal expression of concern. Sara hurried down the steps, not wanting to be alone with any of them, but what she saw before her arrested her movement. Carmilla was standing next to Michael. Just five days ago when they arrived, both children had been the same height. Now Carmilla was clearly several inches taller than her brother. Even since the afternoon, she was visibly taller.

"Sara?" Samuel called out. Sara pushed past them, her head spinning. Rushing to her room, she closed the door firmly behind her.

"They must go!"

The children had left the house for their nocturnal walk, allowing Maman to give in to her anger and fear.

"We have nowhere to send them, Annette."

Papa's voice became muffled as he moved to the living room. Sara quietly opened her door a crack to listen.

"You see where they are in their development, Louis. We cannot keep them. We have no help, no one who understands what to do. How could they send us the children in this state?"

Her father laughed softly, the sound tinged with bitterness. "How, indeed," he replied. "I have already sent off a second letter explaining our predicament and the state of the children. We can only wait for an answer." There was a long pause.

And then Maman asked, "How long do we have?"

"I'm not sure. A few weeks, maybe."

"She said we were free," Maman's voice was full of anguish. "If something happens to Sara…I don't think it is safe for her to be here."

"Let's not be rash, Annette. A mistake was made. We did get the children too late. I'm sure once the contact gets my letter, someone will be sent to retrieve them."

The distant sound of piano music coming from the library cut into the conversation and they were both momentarily silent, listening to the eldest girl play.

"I saw Michael drawing earlier today," Papa finally said. "He must be the artist."

There was no reply from Maman. Sara carefully shut her door and went to sit on her bed, trying to digest what she had just heard and what was happening in her home. But no logical explanation came to mind, only a feeling of loneliness and alienation. Who were the children? Why did they have them?

Chapter Seven

Jenny retied both of her shoelaces for a third time before depositing her empty lunch containers in the rubbish and finally deciding to poke her face outside the cafeteria. Sunami was nowhere in sight. She could see her math class just a short walk across a field of dry brown grass. Groups of kids milled about talking, laughing and pushing each other playfully. Jenny stepped out of the cafeteria and, taking a deep breath, strode across the field, keeping door number seven within her vision. The math classroom should be open. It was almost time for fifth period. Once inside, she would be safe with Mr. Hanzawa—a balding, sleepy-eyed older man. His benign look belied the fact that he could be unmercifully strict. She did not hear Sunami approach her from behind. The painful tug on her ponytail snapping her neck back brought her to a quick halt.

"What boddah you?" Sunami let go of her hair and swaggered in front of Jenny, flashing silver front teeth as she smirked. Jenny felt her face grow warm. She looked past Sunami at the classroom just a few yards away. Sunami's smirk grew into a wide grin and she took a step back from Jenny, lifting her chin.

"Try go for it, *haole*."

"I just want to go to class," Jenny stuttered.

"So, go fo it bitch. Go to class." Sunami didn't budge. Jenny took a tentative step toward the classroom and another. When Sunami remained standing where she was, Jenny continued forward, mildly relieved. Her relief was short-lived. Sunami rushed toward her, pushing her forcefully to the ground, giving her a sharp kick to the shin. Jenny covered her legs with her hands, only to receive another kick to her left hand.

"Ow! Please stop," Jenny cried.

The chant of "fight, fight" filled her ears as a group of kids encircled her, laughing. Someone hit her hard, catching the tip of her ear, setting off a stinging, buzzing sensation. When Jenny looked up, a boy spit in her face. The sound of the bell calling a return to class and the voice of a teacher yelling "Break it up" dispersed the menacing crowd. Hot tears flowed from Jenny's eyes as she tried to wipe away the slime of saliva smeared across her nose and forehead.

"Jenny?" Jenny looked up to see Mrs. Sakamoto standing over her. Bending down, the squat woman helped her to her feet. She could barely stand, her leg already swelling from the blow of Sunami's foot.

"Here, lean on me," Mrs. Sakamoto offered. "We go to the nurse's office, poor ting." Leaning on the soft shoulder of the teacher, she limped along to the health room.

Nurse Ikeda, a small wizened, old woman, with lines etched deeply into her forehead, took in the two of them with a shrewd gaze.

"Why don't you go and wash your face," Mrs. Sakamoto said, pushing Jenny gently toward a small sink in the back of the room. "I've got Jenny Knowles here, Jean. She was beat on." Nurse Ikeda's small brown eyes rested on Jenny, who stooped over the sink, splashing water on her face.

"She's going to need ice on that leg," she said, standing to her full height of four eleven. She shuffled over toward Jenny, lightly running her fingers over the girl's swollen red leg. "Dry your face, dear."

The Visitors

Jenny took some paper towels and pressed them to her face as the nurse tutted over her.

"Hand is swollen too. Had a fight?"

"More like ganged up on," Mrs. Sakamoto cut in.

Nurse Ikeda pulled two ice packs from the freezer and wrapped each one in a light cotton cloth before handing the packs to Jenny and leading her over to one of the plastic chairs. A second chair was brought for her to prop up her injured leg. Gingerly, Jenny placed one of the packs against her leg and held the second in her swollen hand.

"Jenny, was Sunami involved?" Mrs. Sakamoto asked. "I saw her there with some of them that was bothering you."

Jenny remained quiet.

"We can't help you unless you tell us." Mrs. Sakamoto stood over the girl, who did not look up or utter a sound.

"Theresa, she needs to rest," Nurse Ikeda gently interjected.

"OK, when you're ready, I can help."

Jenny lifted her eyes far enough to see the thick, round calves of her teacher under the swish of a skirt leaving the room.

Telling on Sunami is as sensible as slitting one's own wrists, she thought, remembering and now understanding Sara's reticence. No wonder she hadn't wanted to talk. Mrs. Sakamoto would not be there when she was cornered alone and had to face Sunami's fury. It wasn't only Sunami; it was also the kids in her neighborhood, mainly the boys that lived in the red house on the corner. They were Sunami's cousins, nephews of the Kahiamoi family whose house Jenny had just moved into. Since the move, the Kahiamoi's had moved into a smaller *ohana* on the property where the red house was. Whenever Jenny thought of it, her stomach felt sick.

Over the past weeks, she had begun to despise the house and the valley they lived in. Catching the bus and walking home after school when her mother stayed behind with extra work was unbearable.

She was continually taunted, harassed and threatened, arriving home in tears or full of fear. Jenny had hoped to see Sara since her move but Sara had only been to school a handful of times in the last few weeks.

Jenny shifted the ice pack on her fingers and chewed at the inside of her cheek, a nervous habit that her friends back home liked to tease her about. Her mother would want to know what happened when she saw her. If she admitted to being ganged up on, there was no doubt that her mom would want names. Peeling the ice pack off her lower leg, she stared down at the swelling. There was no way to hide it. She was wearing shorts. And then suddenly remembering her gym sweats in her locker, she mentally gave a sigh of relief. If Mrs. Sakamoto didn't talk to her mother about the incident, she might be able to avoid the interrogation. There were lots of fights at school and usually teachers or security just broke them up without further incident.

Mrs. Ikeda had gone into the back office. Pulling the ice pack off, she inspected the swelling and was relieved to see it had diminished somewhat. Jenny stood up, wincing as weight was put on her leg. It was still very sore. Quietly, she replaced the ice packs, leaving the cloths in a small laundry basket. Having waited until ten minutes before the next bell, she would have just enough time to get to her locker, pull the bulky sweat pants over her shorts and walk to her mother's classroom for her last period. There she could wait in relative safety.

Limping out of the health room, Jenny glanced about the empty campus before crossing the quad to the freshman building and walking through the shaded corridor. It smelled faintly of warm cement and cigarettes. There was an open space between the freshman and sophomore structures that was unofficially allotted as the student smoking section. It was usually packed during breaks and lunch with kids who carried well-established nicotine addictions, some of them having picked up the habit as early as third grade. The smell of

The Visitors

cigarette smoke grew stronger as Jenny stepped out into the scruffy little courtyard, the ground more dirt than grass. A boy sat on a large irregular shaped stone, a popular seating area. He was listening to a walk-man with a cigarette dangling from his lips, reading what looked to be a science fiction novel. He glanced up, smiled and removed his earphones.

"Hey," he called out.

Jenny smiled back, uncertain. She knew who he was, everyone did. He was probably the most well liked kid at school. His name was Charlie, an old fashioned name for the 1980s, and an odd name for a kid that was born in Hawaii. Charlie was *haupa hauole*. One of his parents was White and the other of local ethnicity. Jenny knew that he surfed and hung with locals and Whites alike. His father, Tom Baldwin, she had overheard her parents once say, was a wealthy business tycoon from the mainland. He had a passion for Hawaiian history and had authored two books on the subject. Charlie's mother was completely Hawaiian, a rarity. The family was well traveled and Charlie seemed to have cousins and friends everywhere. He did not speak pidgin, although he spoke fluent Hawaiian, also unusual.

"Jenny, right?" he asked.

"Um, yeah. And you're Charlie." He nodded, taking a final puff off his cigarette before grinding it out.

"Cutting class?" He grinned.

"No, not really."

Jenny looked down, not wanting to go into the woes of her unfortunate status. He seemed to catch on quickly, switching the subject to himself.

"I only have four subjects. It's my last year. Waiting for my brother to pick me up. He borrowed my truck."

Jenny nodded, not sure of what else to say, but wanting the conversation to continue. The hiss of music crackled from the headphones that hung around his brown neck.

"What are you listening to?" She asked.

He looked a bit sheepish and she waved her hand apologetically.

"Sorry, you don't have to tell me."

He smiled again and Jenny felt a little lightheaded. She had never seen a boy more good looking than Charlie. His eyes were the color of emerald water set in dark, well-defined features. Only kindness shone through.

"It's OK," he shrugged. "Here, have a listen." He unwound the headphones from his neck and held them out to her. Jenny stepped up to him and placed the speakers on her ears. The energetic sounds of percussive drums intermingled with seductive flutes and the chanting, wailing voices of a foreign tongue, immediately transported her imagination to exotic landscapes. She had never heard anything like it.

"What kind of music is this?"

Charlie laughed, although his response was drowned out from the cacophony of stereo sound pouring into Jenny's ears. He pulled the speakers away.

"You're yelling." Jenny reddened. "It's Persian. Pretty cool, huh?"

"I've never heard Persian music before."

"No, especially not around here, you wouldn't."

The sudden trill of the bell signaling the end of fifth period jolted Jenny back to reality. She needed to get to her locker, put her gym pants on and go to her mother's classroom before she ran into Sunami or one of her gang. Charlie, catching the look of worry and fear on Jenny's face and assessing the swelling of her leg, stood up and dog-eared his book before closing it.

"I'll walk with you. I'm headed that way myself."

His keen perception of Jenny's need for a chaperone was welcomed, so was the pretence of having to walk through the hallway of the sophomore building. It was a relief to have him with her. His presence almost erased the memory of her violent experience

The Visitors

earlier that afternoon. He waited with Jenny at her locker while she retrieved her pants and slipped them on over her shorts.

"So you're new here, right?"

"Yeah, we moved here from California over the summer."

She glanced quickly up at him, feeling her face growing warm. He smiled. Embarrassed at what she knew was an obvious blush, she turned quickly away to pick up her backpack but Charlie grabbed it for her.

"Let me help you with that."

"Oh, I can manage."

His eyes flicked over her swollen fingers and he tossed the strap of her bag over his shoulder. As they walked through the growing mass of students, Charlie must have greeted at least twenty people between the short distance of the lockers and her mother's classroom. Mrs. Knowles was standing outside the door when they arrived, her face flushed from the heat of the room. A look of pleasant surprise lit up her features when she saw Jenny with Charlie. Charlie handed Jenny her backpack and held up his thumb and pinky, the three middle fingers folded down for a *shaka* as he turned to leave. She returned Charlie's *shaka* with unsure motions. Never having made the sign in her life, she felt a little silly and nerdy looking.

"I didn't know you knew Charlie Baldwin." Jenny ducked her head, not wanting to get the third degree from her mother about him.

"I don't really."

"How funny. I was going to stop by the Baldwin's on Saturday to talk with his father about coming in as a guest speaker in the spring." Jenny felt her stomach do a complete flip, but she shrugged and entered the classroom, sitting at her usual desk. The remaining fifty minutes of school were spent replaying meeting Charlie, their brief conversation and their walk to her classroom over and over in her mind.

Angela looked up from the stack of essays on her desk and studied her daughter's face as she sat reading. Lately she had begun to look pale and pinched. Although Jenny never talked about it, Angela knew she was being bullied at school and she knew it was the reason she had remained behind in the classroom with her that afternoon under the pretext of an upset stomach and being worried about motion sickness.

When Angela expressed her concern to Mrs. Sakamoto, the only colleague that she felt she could talk to, she was tsked away.

"We can't hover over them. They have to learn to stand up for themselves," Mrs. Sakamoto reasoned. But Angela wondered. She wondered when she saw bruises and scratches on Jenny that she wouldn't talk about, or the way her daughter had begun to hunch her thin shoulders as if trying to appear less conspicuous. Even Tim said that she was overreacting.

"Jenny needs to find her own way in relating to her peers and standing up for herself better," had been his advice. The move to the new home had put a strain on their marriage. It did not take Angela long to learn about the previous owners. A friendly overture for tea and cookies at her neighbor Ann's house left her feeling tense and unsure.

"Of course it's not your fault," Ann murmured, pouring the steaming liquid from the white and gold-rimmed china teapot into a matching teacup.

"Keoni's brother warned him about borrowing too much when he renovated the house. It was just unfortunate that their grandmother fell ill a year later. The hospital bills and the cost of having an in-home nurse were enormous. It's a shame, really, the Kahiamoi's used to own this whole valley. All of the local families here, what's left of them, were related to Margaret in one way or another. The

The Visitors

minister of the little church up the hill, Clair, is Margaret's daughter and Keoni's auntie. Now the family across the way from you, that's Ben and Linda and their three boys. Ben is Keoni's brother. There is a third brother, Fess. He's gay," Ann said with a grimace. "He lives with his partner Manuel at the end of the road."

Ann lowered her voice.

"Fess could have paid for everything. He's got the money, but from what I hear, he's somewhat ostracized from the rest of the family."

Later that evening, Angela passed on the gossip of their neighbor to Tim, whose jaw hardened.

"Maybe we should give the house back," she said quietly. "It doesn't feel right to me."

"And lose my uncle's money, money that he intended me to inherit just because someone else was irresponsible with their finances? He bought property as an investment, Angela. How could he have known the troubles this family was going through?"

"He must have known something, Tim. He let them stay on as caretakers."

"We are living here now!"

Her husband's fist came slamming down on the coffee table, making her jump.

"My uncle bought this house fairly. He was kind enough to let the previous owners stay on for as long as they did."

Angela shuddered, thinking of the conversation as she watched her daughter. Jenny looked up and attempted a smile that flickered uncertainly on her lips before fading away. Her hazel eyes returned to her book.

One year, Angela said to herself, *and that is it*. She was not going to stand by and watch her daughter's self-esteem torn down by these children and the community that they lived in. If they didn't belong here, well they would just go back to California. She did not voice to herself *with or without Tim*. It was too painful to think about.

Their daughter was floundering. She could not abandon Jenny to be abused, a scapegoat for every wrong that her race had committed. *It is not our fault*, she told herself, while the memory of Keoni's wife standing in the small family cemetery loomed ominously in her mind. How could her family live in a home that had displaced another family? A family whose relatives were buried in the back yard? Angela stood up to dispel the thought and was startled by a sudden gust of wind that shook the building, followed by fat drops of rain that began to splatter against the westward windows. It was finally raining.

Chapter Eight

Once the rain began, it fell in torrential sheets, violently uprooting the dry earth, sending boulders, trees and mud toppling down cliffs and embankments.

Water gathered on the dirt roads and highways in bubbling rivulets, becoming surging streams of run-off, flooding the larger roads in the sudden deluge. Roofs in need of repair lost shingles and pieces of corrugation. Flash floods shot through dry streambeds, sweeping everything in their path out to sea. It did not let up for two days. By late Friday night the rain had turned to a fine mist.

Jenny lay in bed listening to the raging howl of the wind tides that snaked through the valley and seemed to grab the house with invisible hands, shaking it in a fury of shrieks. Thunder exploded from the dark night sky and lightening illuminated everything like an x-ray of the day.

The large picture windows rattled as if haunted by ghosts. She squeezed her eyes shut, willing herself to fall asleep. Taking deep breaths that came from her belly, an exercise she once learned in sixth grade as part of an acting workshop, she gradually began to relax. *Breath in, slowly breath out*, she silently crooned to herself.

Ignoring the creaks of the house and the rumbling of thunder, she focused deeper on her breath…and then it seemed to happen seamlessly; she found herself walking outside toward the graveyard, but it wasn't scary.

There was the gravestone: *Beloved Tutu, Margaret Kahiamoi, 1879-1979*. A glow from the sliver of moon overhead bathed the stone in pale, soft light. Jenny touched it and felt a wave of comfort as she looked up at the moon. Its light pulled her away to the road and over the bridge that led to Sara's. She was moving faster now. She found herself in Sara's driveway, staring at the dark, plain house. The wind picked up, grabbing at her. A soft laugh hissed in her ear. Struggling to leave, the harder she tried to pull away, the closer she got, until she could see a pale face in the window looking out, the eyes boring into her.

Jenny woke up with a start, her body slick with sweat. Her t-shirt clung to her body and her sheets were soaked from perspiration. It was still night, but the wind had died out and a stagnant silence seemed to envelope her room. A flicker of something caught Jenny's eye from outside the window. When she looked, there was nothing. The dream had cast a numb fear over her body and she ached to stretch and go to the bathroom but was too afraid to move. After a few minutes elapsed, she slowly reached up to push her bangs off her forehead and slid farther down in her covers. She tried to put the awful nightmare out of her mind, surprised that she had fallen asleep in the first place during such a loud storm. She did not sleep again until the first streaks of early dawn light dispelled the stifling darkness. Reassured by the approaching day, she finally let her tired eyes close.

It was noon when Jenny did wake up. Her throat felt dry and her face was warm from the heat of the sun that flooded her room with

The Visitors

light. She needed to remind her mom about buying curtains. She sat up and stretched. The sounds of birds chirping and dogs barking dispelled the memory of the fear she had felt during the storm and the nightmare. With the sun shining brightly, she felt hopeful. It was quiet in the rest of the house.

"Mom, Dad?"

There was no answer, only the lingering smell of coffee. Jenny padded into the bathroom and blinked at her reflection. She looked tired. Her eyes were a bit puckered, her face wan. She removed her sleep shirt and wrapped a towel around herself. Tying her hair up, she grabbed her toothbrush, smearing it with peppermint toothpaste.

Someone was bustling around in the living room.

"Mom?"

Jenny walked down the short hallway that led to the living room and glanced around. There was no one there. Some papers were stacked on the coffee table, probably essays her mother was correcting. Jenny observed for the first time how out of place their new modern furniture looked in contrast to the country-like interior of the house. A sudden crash in the kitchen brought the girl to her toes with fright.

"Mom?"

Jenny closed her eyes a moment, sick with fear, before tiptoeing to the kitchen and peering into the warm, yellow glow of the room. The broom closet door was open and the broom and mop had fallen to the floor. Relieved at the normalcy of what she saw, she picked up the cleaning items and put them back into the closet. As she pulled her hand back, something dry and brittle brushed up against her skin. Poking her head into the closet she saw a bundle of leaves hanging against the back wall. Pulling the bundle out, she stared at the cluster of old, brown *ti* leaves, tied neatly with faded yellow yarn. *Someone must have hung them a while ago and forgotten about them,* Jenny thought. She tossed them on the counter when she heard the front door open and her mother clearing her throat.

Mrs. Knowles stood by the shoe rack removing her slippers, a stack of mail in one hand. She looked up with surprise when she saw Jenny.

"Honey, what are you doing standing there in a towel?"

"The broom and mop fell out of the closet in the kitchen," she started to explain, but her mother cut her off.

"Oh, well why don't you get dressed? Did you want to walk with me to the Baldwin's?"

Jenny shrugged. Her heart sped up as soon as her mom mentioned the name and she instantly thought of Charlie. However, a memory of seeing him holding hands with a girl just yesterday dampened the enthusiasm. There was no point getting all worked up over a boy that was already taken. She imagined that the visit at the Baldwin's might be tedious and boring. It might be hours of sitting and listening to old stories that mostly didn't interest her, sometimes poring over ancient looking documents. But staying home by herself was even more unappealing. She thought of the sounds she had heard in the living room earlier, as if someone were moving about, and then finding no one there.

"Where's Dad?" Her mother stiffened visibly, her face flushing.

"He thought he might try his hand at golf. He left early this morning."

Jenny frowned at this remark. Several times she had heard her father say that he couldn't stand the game.

"Sweetie, go get dressed. Are you coming with me or not? I need to leave here in twenty minutes."

"I'm coming," Jenny said, making up her mind. "I just need to take a quick shower."

"By the way, Becky sent you a letter."

"Really?"

Her mother handed her an oversized envelope, well padded. All of Jenny's uncertainties flew from her mind as she took the letter, overjoyed to receive a tangible object from her best friend. The bubbly, cheerful handwriting made Jenny smile. Here was something that she could look at when she went with her mom: that and a book.

All about them, the vegetation glistened from the residual dampness of the storm. Jenny followed her mother to the Baldwin's, side-stepping some water that ran down the center of the road. Large potholes cratered the road, the dirt worn away by the hard rain. Unearthed stones lay everywhere. They were so clean it looked as if someone had taken the time to purposely scour each and every one. Within five minutes, they reached the bottom of a graveled driveway that lead up to a tall, white fence and bushy eucalyptus trees. Angela walked ahead and opened the gate. There stood a modest, brown house in the middle of a recently mowed lawn. A small vegetable garden off to the side was made up of several large, raised wooden beds in full view of the sun. Jenny followed her mother up the wide porch steps, where they waited after Angela rang the doorbell. Looking around, Jenny felt surprised at the simplicity of the place. She had imagined Charlie's home to be more like one of the estates in Beverly Hills. Everyone knew his family was wealthy and his parents were known for their philanthropy in the community. The door opened and Jenny's mouth went dry when she saw Charlie standing there bare-chested in surf trunks. He looked surprised but smiled immediately, stepping aside to let them in.

"Hi, come on in."

He extended his hand out to Jenny's mom, who took it with a pleased expression on her face.

"I'm Charlie."

"I'm Angela. It's nice to meet you properly, Charlie." Jenny groaned inwardly at her mother's remark.

"Likewise. Hey Jenny, how's it going?"

"Good," her voice came out a whisper and she felt her face grow warm with embarrassment.

"Have a sore throat?" he inquired cheerfully. Jenny shook her head, not trusting herself to speak. "Can I get you anything? Coke, sprite, water?" Jenny's mom smiled looking around. "My dad should be home any minute. He went out riding this morning."

"Well in that case, a coke sounds great," Angela replied.

Charlie grinned. "You got it." He glanced at Jenny.

"Yeah, sure, a coke is fine." Her voice sounded way too high. She looked away quickly, taking pretend interest in a black and white photo of three Hawaiian cowboys atop horses, wrangling several cattle out of the ocean. Charlie's gaze followed hers.

"My uncles. Well, actually my mom's uncles. They're my great uncles."

"How wonderful to have captured so much of your genealogy," Angela remarked, her eyes sweeping the walls with rapt interest. Jenny could see it was going to be a long visit. She recognized that fanatical look in her mother's eyes when she was in the midst of old and ancient things, and Charlie's home was like a museum. There were black and white pictures everywhere, as well as old wooden masks, canoe paddles, lauhala skirts, ukuleles and baskets.

"Be right back," he said, leaving them alone to explore his living room. Jenny walked to one of the bookshelves, reading the titles of the various books but they didn't interest her. Mostly they were thick volumes of historical matter interspersed with economics, business and politics. She clutched her own novel, VC Andrews' Flowers in the Attic. She was halfway through the book and it would give her hours of reading pleasure, along with the letter from Becky.

The Visitors

It seemed only moments before Charlie returned with a wooden tray and several glasses of ice-cold soda, fizzing invitingly. He set the tray down and politely handed Jenny's mom the first glass, then Jenny, his eyes meeting hers briefly.

"My dad says you're really interested in Hawaiian history," Charlie said conversationally, settling into an easy chair while Jenny and her mom took up residence on a brown plush sofa.

"Yes, I find it fascinating, really. Next spring in my class, I'll be going over the events and politics surrounding Hawaii becoming the fiftieth state. It's great to have someone like your father with all his knowledge of Hawaiian history as a reference. There is a lot to go over."

Charlie nodded, taking a sip of his drink.

He's like a grown up, Jenny found herself thinking as she watched him from under her eyelashes, barely raising her eyes.

The door opened and an older man with thick, white hair, t-shirt, blue jeans and cowboy boots stood in the entry way. He smiled broadly when he saw them.

"Aloha," he called out, removing his boots and striding over to them. Jenny's mom made motions to stand but Charlie's father reached her before she did.

"Oh, no, no, no, don't get up, my dear." He bent his tall frame and thrust out his hand. She took it, smiling. He carried the same kindness in his light eyes as his son. Turning to Jenny, he shook her hand as well.

"Beautiful girl. See where she gets it from though," he said in a booming voice, giving Jenny a quick wink from under a bushy eyebrow.

"So Charlie has set you up with some refreshments." He turned then to Angela. "How have you been enjoying Maui so far?"

"It is a beautiful island." She paused. "It has just been a bit of an adjustment."

He laughed.

"Yes, I'm sure. Always is, isn't it Charlie?" His son nodded. Tom Baldwin's features settled into benign contentment. "In my study I have a copy of the official ballot for the proposition of statehood that you might find interesting."

Charlie stood up. "Dad, I'm going to take off soon, go surfing."

"Hum? Oh fine." Mr. Baldwin smiled, his face craggy and tan from years of sun.

Charlie looked at Jenny. "Want to come meet our dog Ikeala?"

She stood up, relieved by his invitation. As they slipped out the front door, she could hear her mother saying, "I've read that although it was a landslide vote in favor of statehood, there was still some controversy around the decision."

"Yes, most of it undercover," Mr. Baldwin said. Their voices faded as Charlie shut the door.

"Get my dad talking about Hawaiian history and the sun will be going down before your mom gets out of there."

"Oh she loves it," Jenny said. The two grinned at each other and she followed him down the wide steps and out to his sunny yard, where he took her around to the back of the house. Putting two fingers in his mouth, he whistled, and a golden retriever came stiffly out from under the house. The dog stretched and walked sedately over to them.

"She's a bit old, aren't you, grandma?"

Charlie scratched the dog roughly around her neck. Clouds of fur came off in his hand, floating down to the ground. There was a sound in the bushes at the back part of the fence line. Charlie's dog grew rigid and her tail went up as she focused her attention in that direction. The muzzle of another dog poked through an opening where a portion of the fence had collapsed. Ikeala gave a short, gruff bark and briskly sauntered over to the emerging figure of an all-black dog. With its tail between its legs and its head lowered, the dog came into full view and stood still as Ikeala smelled its back end and its mouth.

The Visitors

When the intruder proved not to be much of a threat, she lost interest and walked away toward her food and water dish. Charlie laughed.

"She's not much of a watch dog," he said as Ikeala began to lap up water. The black dog, feeling safer, slowly wagged its tail.

"Come here, boy."

The dog dropped to its belly and began to inch toward them. Jenny and Charlie burst out laughing.

"He's been coming around the last few days. I don't know who he belongs to. When he first showed up, he was wicked skinny, looked like he hadn't eaten in days. I gave him some food and he's been coming around ever since."

The dog paused near a cluster of ti leaves, which reminded Jenny of the bundle that she had found.

"This morning in our house I found some old ti leaves tied together, hanging in the broom closet."

"People hang them to ward off spirits."

Jenny felt a chill go down her spine at his words.

"Do people around here really believe in spirits?"

"Sure they do." He glanced up briefly noticing the disbelief on her face.

"All over the world there's a strong belief in spirits, not just here."

"Yeah. I suppose," Jenny said grudgingly. Feeling creeped out, she changed the subject.

"I heard that your family is related to the Kahiamoi's."

"Most of the local families here in this valley are all part of the same family. The house your family moved into once belonged to my great Aunt Margaret Kahiamoi. My mom says that all of us here in one way or another are descended from her. You saw the old cemetery in the back of the property?" Jenny nodded. "Aunt Margret is buried there."

"I know. I saw."

Charlie pointed eastward. "Up on the ridge when King Kamehameha invaded this island, it's been said that some of the warriors that fought against his army were forced to jump from the cliff like the warriors at the Pali lookout on Oahu. Our family is descended from many of those warriors. Sometimes their spirits still come through this valley as night marchers."

Jenny felt her throat tighten. "What are night marchers?"

"They're warrior ghosts. They come out on certain nights, usually around sunrise or sunset." He paused, thinking. "It's bad luck for someone not of the bloodline to see them." He gazed at Jenny thoughtfully. "My dad said there was a *heiau* up there until about 1960 or so."

"What's a *heiau*?"

"It's like a temple, except the structure is much simpler. The ridge was considered a sacred place, and my great Aunt Margaret, who was a Kahuna, used to go and pay her respects there. Somehow, I don't really remember the details, but the banks got a hold of that property. It was considered sacred ground, but the *heiau* was torn down and now a family lives up there." He shrugged. "It's the family with that girl, Sara. Did you ever meet her?"

Jenny nodded.

"My mom goes up there sometimes with some of the other women after church on Sundays to visit. She says she feels like the place is haunted."

Jenny stared down at her feet and flicked her big toe in the grass.

"We didn't know about your family when we moved into the house. My dad inherited it from his uncle. We found out later."

Charlie touched her arm, and she felt a small shiver run up her skin.

"Hey listen, that's not your fault. You're just a kid, and Uncle Keoni should have told the rest of the family that he was having trouble. We would have helped. But he never said anything and the next thing we knew, the house was already sold."

"So if the Kahiamoi's had ti leaves hanging in the broom closet, was there a spirit haunting the house?"

The Visitors

Charlie looked uncomfortable for a moment.

"The ti leaves are to protect against any spirits in general," he said vaguely. Jenny was about to ask what spirits might be around her place, when the sound of voices interrupted their conversation. Charlie walked toward the front of the yard with Jenny following behind. Two women were coming through the gate. One was middle-aged, tall and big boned with a wide kind looking face. The other was short and older.

"Hi Mom, hi Auntie," he called out. The two women waved back, walking slowly in their direction.

"This is Jenny Knowles," Charlie said, once they were all standing a few feet from each other. "This is my mom, Kanani, and my Aunt Clair." The older woman took Jenny's hand in both of hers and smiled, looking into her eyes.

"Aloha, Jenny. Welcome." Jenny was taken aback at her warmth.

"Thank you."

Clair released her hand and began walking toward the house. Charlie's mom reached out and gave her a firm hug. She smelled of sweet ginger and sunshine.

"Uh oh, here comes trouble," Charlie said. "What up, *tita?*"

Jenny was released from Kanani's embrace as she turned to see whom her son was talking to. A familiar girl's voice called out.

"Hey Auntie." And "Wus up, *haupa?*" addressed to Charlie.

Jenny's heart quickened as Charlie's mom stepped aside and she came face to face with Sunami.

She was wearing surf trunks and a rash-guard, her hair slicked back, still damp from the ocean. She froze when she saw Jenny. A much younger girl emerged from behind her, also in miniature surf trunks worn over a pink one-piece bathing suit.

"Sunami, have you met Jenny yet? She's new here," Charlie's mom said. Sunami gave Jenny a once over with her dark eyes, her expression unreadable.

"Yeah, we met. Wus up?" She gave a flick of her chin and began walking toward the house.

The small girl tugged on Kanani's dress.

"Auntie, Sunami says we get ice cream." The woman smiled, taking the little girl's hand.

"Let's see what we have. Jenny, would you like some ice cream?"

Jenny felt sick with fear. The thought of going back to her house, haunted or not, was much more enticing than eating ice cream with Sunami, but she didn't want to appear rude. She would have a small scoop and head back home. There was still Becky's letter to read and probably her dad would be home in the next hour or so.

"Sure," she replied with false cheerfulness.

Sunami had already gone inside.

"I'm going to take off," Charlie said.

He jogged across the lawn back toward the house and called out from the bottom of the steps. "Hey Sue!" Sunami poked her head out of the door. "How were the waves? Did you go to Insiders?"

She shook her head. "No cuz, I was at Hookipa. Get four footers, mostly."

Charlie grinned and jogged back toward the gate.

"See you, Jen," he said. Jenny watched him disappear behind the gate.

"Did Sunami and Mele go to your house?" a woman with a deep voice asked.

"Yes Auntie, they went inside."

The gate opened and a large, buxom woman with a head of coarse black curls falling like a cape over her broad back strode into the yard. Her thick neck all but disappeared within her breasts and wide shoulders. Jenny stood alone, as everyone had gone up into the house. The woman paused, her dark round eyes slowly traveling from Jenny's face down to her feet and back again.

The Visitors

"Who are you?" she asked bluntly. There was no warmth or kindness in her face like the other women. Instead she crossed her arms, waiting.

"I'm Jenny Knowles. My mom…"

"Oh, you part a da new family went move into Keoni and Leilani's house."

Jenny felt her face grow hot. "Yes, we moved here a few weeks ago."

The woman's dark eyes hardened. She dropped her arms without further comment or introduction to continue on her way to Charlie's.

"Sunami," she called as she marched up the steps like a war general, her back as straight and flat as an ironing board. Jenny swallowed and for the second time thought of walking back to her own home. *I'll just stay a few more minutes,* she told herself. She could always lie and say she had homework. That would be the polite way to handle leaving instead of silently slinking off and adding to her already unsavory reputation as the girl whose parents had moved into a house that didn't belong to them.

"Oh there she is," Clair said as Jenny entered the kitchen. The older woman held out a bowl of ice cream. "Have a seat, dear."

"Thank you." She sat in one of the high backed wooden chairs, ducking her head over her bowl to avoid Sunami's glowering stare.

"How long has your mom been a history teacher?" Kanani asked. She had a melodic, soft voice and a graceful way of moving that made Jenny feel at ease.

"Um, I'm not sure, a long time. Since before I was born. She can talk about historical events for hours."

Kanani laughed. "Then she probably won't mind if she's here way into the night. Tom is the same way." Jenny took a quick bite of ice cream, noticing that Charlie got his smile from his mom.

"Will you and your parents be coming to church tomorrow?" Clair asked.

"Auntie, they're not part of the congregation," the larger woman spoke up.

"Since when has that stopped anyone from coming to God's house?"

The large woman pursed her lips but said nothing more. Clair smiled at Jenny.

"You and your family are always welcome to attend the services, which, by the way, Linda," she interrupted herself, looking at the scowling woman, "whatever happened to the Deureaux's? They haven't been to service for some weeks now and I was noticing that it's Annette's turn to host tea at her house tomorrow."

Linda shrugged, looking uncertain.

"Maybe we should send someone out there to check and see if everyone's alright and if she is hosting," Clair suggested.

"I'll ride up there later and see," Linda said.

"No need, we can send the girls. Sara doesn't get out much and she will probably be happy to see them." Clair winked at Jenny. "Do you know the way to Sara's?" she asked.

"Me?" Jenny's hand rose to her chest and stayed there when Clair mentioned that Sunami knew where to go.

"Sunami, come," the older woman motioned with her hand. Jenny's eyes darted over toward the window where Sunami had been standing. Her face was unreadable as she walked to the table.

"When you girls get finished with your ice cream, please walk to Sara's and ask Annette if she is coming to service tomorrow and if so, if she is hosting tea time at her place."

"Yes, Auntie," Sunami mumbled, a flicker of uncertainty drawing her brows together. Clair smiled again and slowly took a bite of her ice cream. The smaller girl tugged at Sunami's shorts.

"I go, Sunami," she whined, "Can?" Sunami pushed the girl's hand away.

"No, Mele, stay here." Sunami turned away from the girl.

"Let the Keiki go wid you," Linda said.

The Visitors

Mele immediately smiled, catching Sunami's hand and jumping up and down, her curls bouncing on her dark head.

"What, Bo da dem?" Sunami exclaimed, her irritation radiating from her curled lip. "Mele walk slow."

"Did I ask you?" Linda's voice was hard and Sunami fell silent.

Ten minutes later, Jenny found herself joining the two girls on the front porch, wishing fervently that she had gone home instead of going into the house for ice cream. Without a word Sunami abruptly began walking away, Mele skipping alongside her and Jenny lagging behind. Once out of the gate, the girls turned left and Sunami looked briefly over her shoulder, rolling her eyes. She stopped, exasperated and shook her wrist in a way that made her fingers snap together. Jenny had seen other locals do that. It meant hurry up.

"Come on. We ain't got all day," Sunami growled.

Jenny picked up her pace until she was walking alongside Sunami, with Mele between them. The younger girl began to sing to herself and Sunami glanced down at her with the same look of uncertainty she had when Clair suggested that they walk to Sara's. Other than Mele's singsong voice, the only sound was the flap and scrape of their slippers on the dirt road.

It would be Jenny's second time going to Sara's. Was it only three weeks ago? So much had happened. While she hoped that she and Sara might become friends after she moved to the small valley, it was not to be. Sara had become more reclusive. A few times when she'd tried to speak with her, the girl had been distant to the point of indifference. She wondered if it was such a good idea to bother Sara's family. The image of her mother's hard gray eyes and frowning face loomed large in Jenny's mind.

As they passed through a groove of Norfolk pine Mele called out, "Guavas. I want one."

Her voice was deep like Linda's and she stared up at Sunami, waiting.

Sunami sighed and walked to a bush laden with the yellow fruit. It was close to a stream that was full and rushing from the previous night's storm.

When Mele followed, Sunami said, "Try wait, please."

Jenny watched, fascinated with this other side of Sunami. Her lithe, agile figure stretched for the largest guavas that hung over the turbulent water. Snatching two of the yellow fruits with slim, long fingers she walked slowly back to where Mele and Jenny waited. Mele's pudgy hand reached out but Sunami broke the fruit in half first and then grimaced. Jenny, curious, stretched her neck to see and wrinkled her nose at the white maggots that wiggled in the pulpy, pink flesh.

"No good?" Mele asked. Sunami shook her head and tossed it.

"It's *pilau*."

Opening another one, she inspected it first by poking around with her finger. Satisfied, she handed the fruit to Mele and then looked up at Jenny. The two girls stared at each other and Jenny felt her heart quicken.

"You Sara's friend?" Sunami asked.

Mele was slurping the fruit and its sweet scent wafted through the air, intermingling with the smell of wet earth.

"Not really. My mom and me gave her a ride home once," Jenny said, intrigued with the fact that Sunami was conversing with her. Sunami's eyebrows arched at Jenny's reply.

"She rode in your car?"

Jenny nodded. Sunami looked back down at Mele, that odd expression on her face again and then Jenny knew what it was; Sunami was worried. The girls began walking again but Sunami was walking slower and her face had scrunched up in a thoughtful scowl.

"Why didn't we just call Sara's mom? Wouldn't that have been faster?"

The Visitors

"They no get phones up dat way." Her expression turned pensive. "Did you see those *haoles* when you went drop Sara dat day you give her one ride home?"

"Her cousins?" Jenny asked.

Sunami shrugged.

"They don't look like no cousins of hers. The white, white ones, those are the ones I saw. They're whiter than you." Sunami turned to look at Jenny, assessing her. "There's something spooky over there."

Sunami's words triggered Jenny's memory of her nightmare and she shivered, although the air was humid and warm.

"What's spooky?" Mele asked. Sunami waved the question away.

"How fast can you run?" she asked Mele.

"Fast," Mele replied smugly.

"Cannot," Sunami challenged.

"Try look, I can run!" Mele shot off running as quick as her short legs could carry her. Sunami turned to Jenny.

"Animals are spooked by them," she said quickly.

"What?" Jenny asked startled at Sunami's confession.

"Animals, stupid!" Mele was still running.

"My horse almost went throw me when I went riding by there. Sara was with one of those bleached, white *haoles*. When I try ride past them, my horse got spooked and that *haole* chick, she was with…" Sunami's words trailed off, as she didn't seem sure how to explain.

"Junior said their dog has been hanging out in the bushes round his place. At first when he try bring him back, he started whining when he get near Sara's place. Another time I try bring the dog. Sara was outside. When I went walk Blackie to her, he quick bit my arm and run away." Sunami held out her arm to Jenny and showed her the recent scar of the bite above her wrist, it had darkened and puckered a little.

"I think I just saw that same dog at Charlie's. He was wondering where it came from."

"Did you see how fast I ran, Sunami?" Mele called from a short distance.

"That's not fast," Sunami called back.

"Yes," Mele argued. Sunami didn't reply.

"OK, try look," Mele called taking off again.

"There's four of them," Sunami said, her eyes on Mele running ahead. "I went by there yesterday with Junior to swim in the pools and I saw that same girl that spooked my horse, but she was bigger." Sunami glanced at Jenny, perplexed. "You don't know em?" she asked.

"Not really. I only saw them that one time and Sara doesn't really talk to me about anything."

Mele ran back and she stood in front of them, panting. "Did you see how fast that was?"

Sunami nodded, grinning, flashing her silver smile. It was the first time Jenny had seen her really smile without menace behind it. The three continued walking, but with Mele close, Sunami was quiet the rest of the way.

There was the same graveled driveway to the little brown house. Mele ran ahead singing again.

"Mele, wait," Sunami called as the little girl ran to the porch.

The front door opened and a pale, willowy boy stepped out, staring at Mele. The little girl stopped singing and stared back at the boy. *It must be the older boy*, Jenny thought, the one she had seen standing next to the window in Sara's living room. The older boy had smiled but the other three just sat staring at her. He looked different, though. *Didn't he have blonde hair?* She wondered. This one had brown hair. Someone else stepped up behind the boy; a young, broad-shouldered man with blonde hair that fell to his shoulders.

He was just as white, and when he saw Mele, he said, "Hello," and then asked her something in French. Mele was speechless. Jenny and Sunami came to stand next to her. Jenny frowned; something

The Visitors

didn't seem right. Were there other people like them that she hadn't seen on her brief visit? The young man smiled at them. It was a strange smile because the rest of his face appeared frozen. Only his lips moved, revealing odd shaped, overly crowded teeth. His eyes, a pale blue, appeared fathomless. It was hard to know if he was looking right at you or somewhere beyond. Someone from inside the house spoke in French, it sounded like Sara's voice, and then Sara appeared looking as confused as Jenny, Sunami and Mele were feeling.

"Yes?" she said questioningly.

Her hair was not tied back the way she usually wore it. Instead it fell in rich, thick waves and curls down her back, enhancing her beauty in a way that was striking. Someone else came up behind her, a tall woman, and then the woman pushed past her and came to stand by the young man, followed by a teenaged girl. Jenny felt her heart speed up and the hair rise on her arms as the woman glanced at them. Was she the same girl that Sara's mother had introduced as her cousin who didn't speak English? But how could that be? She was taller and more filled out, older somehow. Jenny glanced again at the young man and realized that he was the older boy, but then, the other two… The thought trailed off in Jenny's mind. There had been a small boy and girl sharing a chair in Sara's living room.

"We weren't sure…" Jenny began, but was at a loss for words.

It only took Sara a few moments to realize what Jenny was seeing. She spoke in soft French to her cousins to go inside. Wordlessly, all obeyed, except the woman.

"You're white," Mele said to the woman, whose gaze was fixated on the girl. The woman's laughter was as unnerving as her stare: a sound like brittle, discordant bells. Mele stepped back. The woman stepped forward and held out her hand to the girl.

"Do you want to touch my skin?" she asked.

Her voice rose deep and resonant from her chest; it had an odd metallic sound. Mele shook her head no and Sunami walked quickly to the little girl and picked her up protectively, sizing up the strange lady. The woman's green eyes slowly focused on Sunami and her smile evaporated. With no expression, she looked like an intricately carved statue. Sara spoke to the woman in French and gestured to the inside of the house. Her body language was that of someone negotiating with a particularly dangerous animal. She made no sudden movements and she spoke slowly and softly, smiling a little to encourage her.

"I have to go now," the woman said. "Annette doesn't like visitors, but I do." She said all of this while looking at Mele, who turned and buried her face in Sunami's chest. The woman went inside and Jenny exhaled. She had no idea she had been holding her breath.

"Why are you here?" Sara hissed.

Sunami's eyes narrowed.

"What kine *haoles* are those?"

"They are my cousins. I told you. You have to go before Maman comes up from the garden."

"Auntie Clair sent us," Sunami said lifting her chin. "She wants to know why your family not come to church, and if your mom is hosting for tea and *kau kau* tomorrow."

Sara licked her lips and craned her neck to look at something in the house. She looked terribly worried, and Jenny felt sorry for her.

"While my cousins are here, we won't be going to church," Sara said, "Now please go before I get into trouble."

Sunami and Jenny stepped away, walking out of the yard but stopped when they heard Sara gasp. When they turned around, she waved them away and then ran off her porch around the backside of the house. Sunami and Jenny picked up speed, walking quickly back to the road, keeping a brisk pace until they had traveled down off of the ridge and were back at the bridge.

The Visitors

Sunami still held Mele tight in her arms and the little girl lifted her head.

"Sunami, who was that *haole* lady?"

Sunami was quiet and then she smiled at Mele. "Can you keep a secret? Cannot, right?"

"Can," Mele was indignant.

"Don't tell about the *haoles*, OK?" Mele looked uncertain.

"I got candy and so does Jenny. If you don't tell, get candy, but if you tell…" Sunami's face hardened. Jenny felt herself cringe at Sunami's threatening look. Mele's eyes grew large.

"I won't tell," she whispered.

Sunami smiled and set the girl down.

"I have a Snickers bar when we get home."

Delighted with this news, recent events were immediately forgotten as Mele ran up the steep road. Sunami turned to Jenny and put a finger over her lips.

"Don't tell no one, *haole*." Sunami's eyes were fierce.

Jenny swallowed, her throat suddenly dry. Whatever burgeoning friendship she had imagined with Sunami seemed as far away as the two thousand miles that separated Maui from California. Sunami quickened her step, moving ahead of Jenny. Once they crested the top of the road that brought them back to the valley, an old Toyota pickup slowed as the driver edged past them and waved. Sunami waved at the man who smiled, his front teeth missing. Junior, Kawika and several other boys sat in the back with their surf and boogie boards. As the truck pulled away from them, Kawika raised his middle finger at Jenny and the truckload of boys threw their heads back, laughing. Jenny hunched her shoulders and hurried to catch up with Sunami and Mele, her mind buzzing with a whirlwind of emotions from the afternoon's events.

Chapter Nine

"Sara, did the girl get started on her dress?" Maman asked as she came in the door. Hanging from her thick arm was a large wicker basket of vegetables, fresh from their garden.

"*Oui*, Maman," Sara replied.

Maman never talked directly to the eldest girl but used Sara, Papa and sometimes one of the other children as an intermediary. For the past week, the eldest girl had been once again trusted to join the rest of her siblings during the day to attend to minor chores.

Maman set the basket on the kitchen counter and surveyed the surroundings briefly before sniffing and pulling two heads of bok choy from the basket. They were handed to Sara to wash. She took the greens, her heart still crashing against her chest. Maman had not seen Sunami, Jenny and Mele. Samuel had warned her just in time. Still the idea of her mother's wrath if she were to know that the girls stopped by made Sara's hands shake as she searched in the cabinet for a colander to put the lettuce in.

"How far has she gotten with it?" Mama asked.

Sara willed her voice to be steady before she spoke. "She has already cut the pattern."

The Visitors

"I have done more than cut the pattern, Annette. I have begun sewing the pieces," the eldest girl said. She had come to stand in the doorway between the kitchen and living room, staring at Maman, her pale lips twisted in a smirk, although the rest of her face remained unnaturally still. "There are three main sections Annette, three," the girl reiterated. "It is so simple," she said quietly.

Maman's ruddy complexion reddened. She stared back at the girl but appeared speechless for a moment. Sara watched her mother's shoulders slump, and a fierce grief washed all authority and anger from her features. Maman's hand flew to her hat and she seemed disoriented.

"Maman?" Sara stepped toward her mother, unsure. Fear of her mother's anger was now replaced with worry. She reached out her hand but Maman roughly pushed it aside.

"I must go out," she announced, shaking her head as if to dispel something. Sara could see that she was trembling as she shook her head harder before flinging the door open and almost running outside. Sara started after her mother but Maman waved her away. She was headed back down the hill toward the garden. Sara did not follow her but she did see Maman cross herself several times slowly. Her shoulders shook with grief and for the second time, Sara saw her mother cry.

It was quiet when she re-entered the house. The only sound came from the thin stream of water that flowed from the faucet. Sara scanned the empty kitchen before turning the water off. In the living room, the cousins were busy with their hobbies and projects. The eldest girl had resumed her seat, her head bent over her work. She was smiling as she hand sewed precise, even stitches. Her long fingers flew over the material.

With each passing day, Sara felt increasingly frightened of her cousins, Samuel being the exception. He lacked a certain menace that the others radiated from their being. There was no one to talk to about how worried they made her feel. Stranger things had begun to happen, terrifying hallucinations that usually occurred when she felt intense fear toward one or the other of the children. Once, on a nightly walk, when Sara was alone with Samuel, she had asked him if he knew where they had come from, hoping to gain some insight.

"No," he'd replied, "I thought you knew."

His answer had only added to her confusion. But in the last few days, there seemed to be an increasing awareness amongst her cousins, as if they were finally waking from their amnesia. It seemed there was a growing understanding about something, even if they never spoke of it.

Sara continued to study the older girl. She was not a girl anymore, really, but a young woman. She seemed to harbor information. It was in her eyes and body movements.

"I don't know your name," Sara said. As soon as the words left her lips she clamped her mouth shut, surprised at her own boldness and unsure of what the girl might do.

"Don't you?" the girl replied. She did not look up but continued sewing at a rapid pace. "Such a simple garment," she said. "Only three main sections, really. I will have the dress done in no time."

Her voice was resonate and grating at the same time. It reminded Sara of a vague memory that she couldn't quite grasp. She longed to snatch the material and needle out of the girl's hands and slap that awful smile off of her bloodless lips. Papa had told her that she must be careful with her body language around her cousins, to remain neutral in temperament even if Maman could not. Most of all, he had warned, she was never to yell out in anger or to strike one of them. Sara was surprised that Papa would tell her to not hit her cousins. She had never struck anyone in her life, nor ever wanted to until this afternoon.

Samuel cleared his throat and stood up to stretch his long legs, interrupting Sara's thoughts. He and Carmilla had been reading all

The Visitors

morning and Michael was drawing as usual. Samuel walked across the living room and stood looking out the window. Usually when he did that, it meant that he was restless but this time he was also frowning.

"What's wrong, Samuel?" Sara asked. He turned to look at her but said nothing. Instead he left the room and Sara could hear him climbing the stairs to the bedroom that he shared with his brother.

Michael tore his completed drawing out of his art book and tossed it aside, starting on another piece. It was a picture of a woman in a dense forest setting. Sara bent to examine it. She was a dark-skinned woman with a strong, lean body. She wore some kind of animal skins and carried on her shoulder a bow with a quiver of arrows. A sheathed knife was strapped to her leg and she stood tensely at the edge of a clearing, looking straight across the open space that was bordered by more forest on the other side. It appeared to be dusk, and low-hanging fog shrouded the trees on the other side. Through the heavy mist Sara, thought she could barely make out the figure of another woman, the object of the first woman's attention. It was such a masterful piece of work that Sara was stunned at its detail, depth and realism. Sara pointed to the woman with the arrows.

"Who is this woman supposed to be, Michael?"

The boy shrugged, his hand rapidly producing shapes and ridges on a fresh sheet of paper.

"She comes from the tribe of the Night Hunters," the older girl answered for him. "Their tribe descends from the ancient Amazon warrior women, but you will never find a word written of that particular band."

Sara was stunned to hear the older girl talk so casually and to actually explain something. The children rarely spoke, even Samuel, whom Sara felt closest to, remained as reticent as his siblings.

"You should have it," Michael said, as he looked up at her, pushing his dark hair away from his white forehead. "It is where you come from."

His words jolted her. "Where I come from?"

Michael did not answer, his focus turned back to his new drawing. The older girl had stopped working on the dress, her gaze fixated on Sara. Her face was as immobile and expressionless as a stone, her green eyes opaque in the afternoon lighting.

Chapter Ten

Jenny sat on her bed trying to block out the sounds of her parents arguing. It had started that evening when her father came home.

"We are not a religious family," she had heard him yell. "If you want to go, go."

"I am just asking you to come for one day. It's a way to get to know our neighbors."

"You see that's how it starts. It won't just be one day. They'll want to know if we'll be there next week."

There was the sound of her parent's bedroom door slamming and then it was quiet. Jenny picked up the Polaroid pictures that her friend Becky sent and looked at them again. She tried not to think about the fact that her parents seemed to argue every day lately. Her friends' faces stared cheerfully back at her and a wave of homesickness washed over her, bringing tears to her eyes.

"You're so lucky to be on Maui," Becky gushed in her letter. "We're all making plans to come and visit you next summer. Did you ever sign up for hula lessons?" Jenny smiled when she read that, remembering her excitement at wanting to learn the dance. She realized that since the move, she hadn't given it a single thought.

A sharp knock at her window startled her. She stood up, terrified to see the silhouette of someone standing outside looking in on her. Whoever it was knocked again and she heard her name called. She peered out and was relieved to see Sunami scowling at her. Jenny unlatched the window, swinging it open. Sunami stepped over the sill into her room. She was back in jeans and a t-shirt, her wiry body looking bigger in the large clothes.

Looking around, she stared for a moment at Jenny's poster of Rob Lowe and the other of Madonna in a flood of stage lights, arms covered in bracelets.

"Do you like Madonna?" Jenny asked.

Sunami snorted. "Who? That *haole* chick? I listen to reggae, Bob Marley."

She glanced around some more. "This use to be Mele's room."

"Oh, she's Leilani's daughter?" Jenny asked.

Sunami rolled her eyes. "Duh, you didn't get that yet?"

"I just thought she was your sister," Jenny said quietly, not wishing to offend Sunami more. Sunami kicked off her slippers and sat on Jenny's bed.

"Mele's my cousin. That man in the truck who waved to me when you was wid me is Uncle Keoni. He's Mele and Ikaika's dad."

Jenny wasn't sure which one was Ikaika, but she didn't tell Sunami that. There were so many kids in the red house that it was hard to keep track of who was who. She did know that the Kahiamoi's and the family in the red house were related, but she wasn't sure how.

"So, is Leilani related to you by blood, or is Keoni?"

"Leilani and my mom are sisters."

"Linda is your mom then?"

"Nope," Sunami replied, and didn't explain further. Suddenly she stood up again, her scowl deeper. She walked back to the window looking out into the night.

The Visitors

"What do you think is going on at Sara's?" she asked.

"I'm not sure," Jenny said.

Sunami turned to study her. "Why did your family come and take my auntie's home? This is her house. Grandpa Kahiamoi built it. Tutu wanted Mele to have this room. Before she died, she said Mele would be safe here. Tutu was a Kahuna Pule."

Jenny felt her face grow warm.

"You know what a Kahuna is?" Sunami asked.

Jenny shook her head no. She remembered hearing Charlie use that same word to describe Sunami's grandmother. Sunami clenched her hand into a fist and punched it into the other one. "Kahuna is like *da kine,* those black robe men in the church."

"A priest?" Jenny whispered.

"Yes, but stronger. Your family is going to pay. You took a home that don't belong to you. If something happens to Mele, something will happen to you."

Jenny hugged herself, her chest heavy with mounting frustration. "I don't want to be here!" she yelled.

Sunami's eyes widened.

"Our family didn't know. If it were up to me, I would leave this house and I would be on the next plane back to California."

The local girl's features softened some. "Meybe you can talk to your dad den," she suggested.

Jenny nodded. "I will."

Sunami shrugged, looking uncomfortable. "I'm going to talk to my uncle," she remarked.

"About the house?" Jenny asked.

"No, about those white cousins. Once when I was at my uncle's, I saw he had one book with drawings that looked like *da kine.* I started to look at it but his partner, Uncle Manuel, saw me wid it and he snatched it outta my hand. He grabbed some papers too was on his desk and took everything to his room."

Sunami frowned as she thought back to that day. "Uncle Fess asked me what I'd seen in da, you know, *da kine*, and I told him, I no see nothing. I thought meybe there might be some dirty pictures in there they didn't want me to see. Uncle Fess was some kine worried about dat book. I never told him about da drawing of the white *wahinies* I saw swimming in the pond at night and the dead men around em. Uncle Fess just told me then not to be gettin into Uncle Manuel's tings."

"Are you saying the women in the book looked like Sara's cousins?" Jenny asked.

Sunami nodded.

"What do you mean there were dead men around them?" The thought made Jenny feel sick.

"Dead, you know, croaked. The way the men was dressed it looked like, you know, from a long time ago. I thought it was kinna spooky that drawing, because the women were swimming in the pond and no care no how that there's dead men laying on the ground."

Jenny thought about the afternoon she and her mother had dropped Sara off and she had caught a brief look at her cousins. There had been small children in the living room that day but today all of the children were grown. Jenny shook her head at her own thought. It was impossible. There must have been more cousins that she hadn't seen. But the woman who talked to Mele had looked so much like the girl that Sara's mother had said didn't speak English.

"What?" Sunami asked, studying Jenny's expression.

Jenny shook her head again. "It's just that none of it really makes any sense."

"You saw it too, yeah? Those *haoles* grew as if overnight. Sara's family is hiding dem. They're not natural, dats why. I never met no *haoles* dat white. They never go to school."

"So if you talked to your Uncle Fess, do you think he might know or tell you more about that book? It seems he doesn't want you to know."

The Visitors

Sunami stood up, struck by Jenny's words. "I might be able to get dat book. Me and Junior can get in there when they're not home."

Jenny grimaced. "You could get in a lot of trouble for that."

Sunami grinned. "They won't find out. Next time they both go out we'll get in there. You with me?"

Jenny shook her head. "I don't want to break into someone's house. It's illegal."

Sunami's lip curled and her eyes hardened. "Look bitch, your family went took my auntie's house. You owe me."

Jenny took a step back, her lip trembling.

"K'den, I'm pau," Sunami said, accepting Jenny's silence for acquiescence. She swaggered to the window and pulled the latch, pushing it up to step out. "I'll tell you what I find out," she said, before letting the window close gently behind her.

Jenny latched it and watched Sunami walk away with her loping stride until she was finally swallowed up by the darkness.

Chapter Eleven

Sara's heart pounded in her chest and her hands began to sweat as she looked over her shoulder one last time. *I want you kids to stay away from the stable building. You're not to play around there*, she could hear Papa's voice saying in her mind. Her father was in his workshop. She had no idea when he might return to the stable and the project that had kept him so busy the last several weeks. Swallowing, she tried the knob before she could give it any more thought.

The door opened easily. There was an earthy, musty smell to the room. It was not a real room in the sense that the floor was dirt. Only pieces of construction equipment littered the place. Sara left the door open a crack. She stepped into the space and looked around. So far there was nothing unusual. The room stretched out before her, long and dark, illuminated faintly from some light that came through a small window. She could see some of the flat boards piled in one corner that Papa had purchased before the children's arrival. Farther back were some indistinct, large objects. As Sara's eyes adjusted to the light, she realized that they were crates of some sort. There were two of them, roughly put together from the wood, looking like crude coffins, and another much larger wooden container.

The Visitors

Lifting the lid of one of the makeshift crates, she found it empty. Relief washed over her. She made her way to the container, reading the huge block lettering on the lid: MATSON.

Frowning, she pulled the much heavier lid back and examined the contents of a wide deep space divided equally into four compartments. Hay filled each space. Sara lifted some of it, letting it fall from her fingers. Closing the lid, she looked about, her mind churning with mounting frustration. Nothing made any sense, yet every fiber of her being was taut with an intuitive sense of danger.

At lunch Maman looked tired, the skin over her high cheekbones peaked and pale. When the eldest girl went up the stairs at one point during their meal, Maman's face reddened and her grey eyes followed her movements. Papa placed his hand over hers to quell the terror that was so plain on her face. After their meal, Maman didn't stay behind to attend to the regular household chores. Instead, she announced that she would be in the garden.

Once her parents left, Sara gathered up the dishes and brought them to the sink. The cabinet door under the counter was partially open, revealing the brown burlap bag of medicine. She closed the door with her knee, wondering what the acrid smelling powder was made of and where Maman had obtained it. She kept so much of it, always had, as if she already knew that one day the strange children would come to live with them.

Turning on the water to wash the dishes, she did not feel his hand at first but saw from the corner of her eye Samuel's arm extend out to her and then the weight of his touch exert a pressure on her shoulder. Sara jumped, the dish she was soaping sliding from her hand. She caught it again with her heart in her throat.

"Samuel, you scared me."

She turned to see the young man watching her intently, his brows pulled together.

"Who are you?" he asked, his hand still holding her shoulder.

Sara pulled her body away from him and set the plate down, turning the water off.

"What do you mean? You know who I am."

She stepped back but he stepped toward her. His brows pulled tighter together and he looked about him, as if trying to understand something. Sara could not stand to watch his face for very long. Any expression he exhibited remained completely divorced from the rest of his features. A smile could appear on his lips that never reached his eyes or crinkled his skin. Before knowing the children, Sara, realized she had never noticed how expressive a normal face was. Samuel's face at that moment was more extreme than usual and it was terrifying to look at him.

"Sara, yes," he said, "I know that is your name. But why are we here with you and the gypsies?"

"What gypsies?" she asked, a searing heat of alarm sweeping through her body. Samuel's large, white hands moved to his face and he began to rub at his temples with long white fingers. "How is it that you and the gypsies took over the infantry? Why is it just the three of you raising us? Where is everyone? Why are we the only ones?"

"What?" Sara felt her tongue go dry.

Samuel took another step toward her until his face was inches from hers and he was peering intently into her eyes. She leaned away, the edge of the sink pressing into the small of her back.

"Fear," his voice was soft, his breath, rotten. "It emanates from you and the gypsies. How is it that we are left to be brought up under the care of a high servant that is full of fear? How can you not know the most basic lesson that fear is dangerous?"

Sara brought her hand to her face, covering her nose. She felt like she might pass out. His breath was so rank, she could almost taste it. But his words were enlightening. The most awful hallucinations that she had experienced around the children were when she had been afraid or even uncertain.

The Visitors

"Tell me this, Sara. How long have I been asleep? You must know that."

Sara shook her head. "Asleep?"

"She doesn't know." It was the oldest girl who spoke.

The younger children followed her but she waved them away before coming to stand next to Samuel. The two of them towered over Sara, their white faces immobile with flat, hard eyes.

"She knows even less than you," the oldest girl continued. "She doesn't even know her true name and she is under the impression that those two ridiculous people are her parents. Such is the way of foolish plans, Samuel." The girl snorted, her lips twisting in a smile as she stared at Samuel, clearly enjoying his confusion.

"So you have finally woken up, have you?" she continued. "Look around. We are all here under your careful vision, whatever that was supposed to be. This girl has been rendered useless as a servant. She's had no proper training. It's a pity, seeing as she comes from the first line."

The oldest girl reached toward Sara, who flinched, and picked up a lock of her curls, letting the hair cascade over her white fingers. "I have been aware for quite some time, Samuel. But I will leave you and your memories to get acquainted."

She laughed, pulling Sara's hair tighter, yanking her neck back with surprising strength.

"She is a beautiful specimen," the girl said, her pupils so enlarged that every bit of green was eclipsed in her excitement and her eyes became like black, glowing coals in a white stone face. "Imagine such a fine specimen as this high servant taking orders from slaves."

Samuel frowned and left the kitchen. The older girl, seeing his sudden loss of interest, released her grip on Sara and followed him into the living room.

"What was your plan for us, Samuel? Why are the pure ones being raised with us in this house secluded from society? We don't even know where we are. And you, you are a fatalist. How did you get a hold of me? You need to remember," the older girl said quietly. "I can already feel that I am not well. Who will take care of us after the transformation? Certainly not an ignorant servant and those inept slaves?"

    Samuel was silent. Sara struggled to regain her breath as she listened. With her last bit of energy, she bolted from the house and out to the road. She ran, not thinking of where she was going but only that she wanted to be far away from the awful cousins and her parents.

Chapter Twelve

Mrs. Sakamoto closed her attendance book and tapped the top of it with her pencil. Earlier that morning, she had noticed that Sara Deureaux was absent from her class again. This was her fifth absence, which was unusual for the girl. There had been the time last year when she was sick for weeks, but her father had taken the time to stop by the office and explain the situation. What could be keeping her away?

School was over for the day. A long day it was too, with two fights in the yard and the humid heat. After the storm of a few days ago, it had grown increasingly muggy, but just in the last moments, a breeze was beginning to pick up and billow through the open window. *A relief*, Mrs. Sakamoto thought to herself, as she stood up and made her way to Angela's classroom.

She found the younger woman sitting behind her desk, her head bent over a stack of papers. She looked tired.

"Knock, knock," Mrs. Sakamoto called out.

Angela looked up and smiled faintly.

"What? That's all I get outta you," Mrs. Sakamoto said with a laugh.

Angela's smile widened but it did not dispel the sadness in her eyes. Her skin was puffy from lack of sleep.

"Come on in," Angela said, her cheerful words belying her fatigue. "I've just been loaded down with these papers. But it's nice to take a break for a moment."

"Where's Jenny?" Mrs. Sakamoto asked.

"Oh, I sent her home on the bus. It's easier for me to get this work done here. I get too distracted when I'm at home."

"I know that," Mrs. Sakamoto agreed heartily. "You know, I was wondering if I could get you to stop by Sara's, since you live near her, and see why she's not coming to school. I'm a little worried about her. It's not like her to miss school. Today she missed a quiz in my class."

Angela nodded, waving a slim wrist over the stack of papers on her desk.

"She's missed a three page paper that I assigned last week. It's worth twenty points on her grade." She sighed.

Mrs. Sakamoto watched the younger woman shrewdly. Something was bothering her.

"You know, that time I gave her a ride home, her mother was extremely rude to me. I mean Jenny was really car sick from the ride out there. When I asked Sara's mother for a cup of water, she acted as if my request was completely unreasonable. It just really put me off."

Mrs. Sakamoto nodded.

"There were some other children there," Angela continued, "Her mother said that Sara's cousins were visiting. I met one of them briefly. She was really kind of..." Angela pursed her lips. "She looked ill. Sara's mother said that the girl didn't speak English. I know that Sara and her family speak French. Maybe her cousins are visiting from France and the visit might be keeping her home."

"Well, Annette can be willful, so I've heard," Mrs. Sakamoto said. "But I think for Sara's sake and her grades, we need to know why she's not in school."

The Visitors

"I think it would be best if I phoned over there, rather than stopping by."

"They don't have a phone, you know."

Angela sat back, struck by this new information. "I'll stop by later this evening," she said and sighed again, glancing back down at the papers in front of her.

"That's it," Mrs. Sakamoto said, "Show them what you got."

In jest, she curled her arm up to make a muscle and frowned down at the doughy skin. "Is that all I got?" She shook her head. "Sad, so sad."

Angela threw her head back and laughed. Mrs. Sakamoto winked before leaving the classroom. *It's good to see Angela laugh like her old self*, she thought, as she made her way back to her classroom to close up for the afternoon.

"Sunami, where do you think you're going?"

Sunami paused on her walk to the bus, turning around to see her sister heading in the same direction. She carried her oldest child Mitchell on her hip and Joseph, just one year younger, was asleep in the stroller that she pushed. Her protruding midsection advertised baby number-three. Sunami rolled her eyes.

"I'm going by Uncle Keoni's."

"No you're not. I told you this morning, you're babysitting for me."

"Did you hear me say yes?" Sunami snarled.

"I told you I got plans."

"Yeah, plans to party."

"Mom told you before she get sent away that you need to help me."

"You know what, Kayle? I watch your boys so much they think you're their auntie. Mom's in prison for burglary, trying to steal shit to pay for babies you keep poppin out every year."

Sunami watched her sister's face redden and her nostrils flair. Just a few years ago, Kayle had been a beautiful talented hula dancer. But having babies in her teen years and heavy drinking had bloated her features. Her once curvy body was now heavy and thick.

"Mom's in prison because she's a drug addict but you're too much a mama's girl to admit it."

"What eva," Sunami scoffed while turning away.

Kayle's words stung and Sunami didn't want to give her sister the satisfaction of seeing the hurt on her face.

"I'm going to tell Uncle Keoni and Auntie Linda you're not helping like you should."

Sunami boarded the bus, ignoring her sister. She hated going home to a house without their mother. Kayle was always bossing her around and bringing her stupid-ass drunken friends home. There were no adults to put anyone in their place. Tomorrow she would go home though, Sunami thought. It wasn't good for the boys to be alone with their mother too much. But today she needed to find out when Uncle Fess and Uncle Manuel were going to be out of the house. Some days ago, before she and Jenny walked to Sara's house, Mele complained that there was a spooky white lady watching her sometimes when she slept. Mele complained of it again the morning after their visit to Sara's, except that time Mele called her the White Lady from Sara's. Sunami sat down next to her friend Cammy.

"Hey stupid," she greeted.

"Shut up," Cammy grinned. "You think you're so smart, what grade you get on Mr. Ikeda's science test?"

"I aced it," Sunami said.

"Yeah right," Cammy hooted.

Sunami laughed along with her friend, letting her believe she had failed. No one saw the word written in capitols at the top of her paper: EXCELLENT! She received 100%. It had been easy. She'd

The Visitors

always liked science, especially the study of movement and energy. Sunami tried to fold up her test before anyone could see it but Cammy saw her shoving the paper in her bag.

"What, no good?" Cammy had asked, as they left the classroom.

Sunami shrugged and Cammy flashed her own paper, D+ written in bold red across the top.

Cammy stopped laughing and lifted her chin to alert Sunami to Jenny who was boarding the bus, her head down and shoulders hunched forward. Some of the kids jeered as she tried to sit in the front. Giving up, she made her way to an empty seat next to Junior and directly in front of Sunami and Cammy. Hesitating, she looked up, briefly catching Sunami's eye, then attempted to sit down.

"*Haole!*" Junior called out, making a braying noise like a donkey.

The busload of kids exploded in laughter, and before Sunami could think of what she was doing, she wacked her cousin across the head with the palm of her hand.

"Ow, watch it!" Junior growled.

"Shut up, dummy!" The other kids quieted, watching this interchange. "Scoot ova!' Junior moved closer to the window, smirking. But he said no more and Jenny sat down, looking straight ahead. The rest of the ride was uneventful and when the bus pulled over at their stop, Jenny, Sunami, Junior, Ikaika, Kawika and a few others were the remaining passengers.

As they filed from the vehicle, the trade winds wailed up from the valley. Jenny tried to situate her backpack on her shoulder as her hair whipped about her face. A strong gust pushed the children back in their effort to walk and billowed up Kawika's t-shirt, giving him the appearance of an inflated kite. The boys howled at this trick of nature and each pulled at his shirt trying to create the same effect.

"Hey, come try this one!" Ikaika yelled, waving at his cousins to come join him on a small bluff, his shirt ballooning out around him. The boys ran to join him and it became a game to follow the wind.

Jenny let them run ahead and hoped they would keep going until they arrived home and stayed there. It was hard to see straight with the wind pressing against her eyelids and her bangs flying in her face. She didn't notice Sunami waiting for her until she felt, rather than saw, the presence of someone walk up next to her.

"What? Go home now?"

Jenny shrugged. Where else would she be going? The girls walked in silence, the wind assaulting them from every direction. Leaves fluttered in the air and small sticks and branches lay scattered along the dirt road. Jenny tucked her head down, the only way to move forward and see without dust or debris getting caught in her eyes.

Sunami's startled gasp alerted her to look up just in time to see limbs, hair and fabric all askew in a great flapping, chaotic mess of motion. Then she was being knocked to the ground. She fell hard, scraping the back of her bare legs, feeling someone falling on top of her. The blow knocked the breath out of her and she was so startled that it took her a moment to realize that the person who had run her down was Sara. Sunami stood over them both. A shaking Sara stood up, dark eyes wild with emotion.

"Pardon! Pardon!" she said several times and held out a hand to Jenny, but then all at once burst into tears, her body trembling violently. Sunami remained still, rigid with visible discomfort at this intense display of emotion. Jenny pulled herself up and put a hand gently on Sara's quivering shoulders and then grimaced when she felt she was touching nothing for a moment. Her attempt at comfort prompted Sara to grab her hand and squeeze it tightly. Again that odd feeling, but it was so fleeting that Jenny wasn't sure if she wasn't just overly disoriented from being suddenly ploughed over. Feeling maternal, Jenny pulled Sara closer to her side. In this way the three girls continued their walk. As they passed the red house, a great whimpering and howling broke forth from the pit bulls tied up in the yard.

The Visitors

"Ey, quiet!" Sunami called out to the dogs but her reprimand only elicited an even higher pitched howling. Jack, the dog closest to the road, began to lunge at his leash, his body straining to break free, his teeth bared.

"Jack!" Sunami called out, but the dog appeared to be beyond reason. His powerful body reared up and his face bulged at the constraint of the collar tightening against his neck. Sara removed her hand from her face and stared wide-eyed at the dog.

"We need to hurry past," she said, picking up her pace, and the other two girls followed suit.

Although it wasn't spoken, all knew that they were headed for Jenny's. The horses acted as wild as the dogs when they passed near them. Sunami watched in astonishment as the animals reared up, their eyes rolling back and their ears flattened, as they came thundering down before turning and fleeing to the other side of the pasture. All the while, the wind grew stronger, and the girls pushed onward. When they arrived at Jenny's, she ran up the steps and threw open the unlocked door. Breathing a sigh of relief, she stepped into the calm and warmth of her home. The other two girls came in, shutting the door on the rushing, howling wind. It was quiet, except for the low moans and occasional shrieking outside. Once inside, the girls stood silently staring at one another. Each was flushed from the wind, exertion and personal emotions.

"What happened?" Sunami finally asked. Sara bit her lip and looked down.

Jenny, seeing the girl's discomfort at the forward question, diverted the attention away from Sara. "Does anyone want anything to eat or drink?"

Sara shook her head no, but Sunami looked over toward the kitchen with interest.

"Like what?" she asked.

Jenny headed toward the kitchen, her guests following her. She felt a surge of excitement to have company, friends over, even if it was under odd circumstances. Opening the cabinet where her mother stored the snacks, she pulled down a box of Ritz crackers and a half-eaten bag of Oreos. Sunami's eyes lit up when she saw the food. Jenny opened her fridge and examined the contents.

"We have cream cheese that you can put on the crackers."

"Shoots," Sunami said.

"There's milk to go with the cookies, or Coke."

Jenny looked over her shoulder at Sunami, who was grinning with pleasure, and Sara, who stood silently. Jenny grabbed the cream cheese and both drinks. She directed Sunami to get some cups and a butter knife. Sunami gathered these items and Jenny picked up the crackers and cookies. The girls walked to Jenny's room, spreading out the food on her large, colorful rag rug. Sara did not touch any of it and moments later she stood up and walked toward the window, looking out. She pulled her thin arms across her body and shivered. Sunami munched on a cookie and took a large swallow of milk as she examined Sara.

"Why are animals spooked by you?" she asked. Sara turned slowly back around to face the girls. Her eyes were moist with gathering tears and her lips trembled.

"I don't know," she said barely above a whisper. "It started happening last year after I recovered from my illness."

Jenny frowned, trying to make sense of this answer. Sunami held another cookie in her slim fingers and turned it around thoughtfully.

"How would getting sick make animals spooked of you?"

"I'm not sure," Sara shrugged.

"What were you sick with?" Jenny asked. Again, Sara shrugged.

"Well what did the doctor say?"

"I never saw a doctor. My parents don't like them."

The Visitors

The girls fell into silence. The only sound was Sunami munching contentedly on an Oreo.

"I should probably go home," Sara said, but as soon as the words left her mouth she shuddered. Jenny stood up to stand near her for comfort.

"You can stay longer if you want and when my mom gets home, she can give you a ride home. Do you want to do that?"

Sara stood quietly thinking, then nodded. Jenny turned around to grab some pillows from her bed, but what she saw next made her freeze in mid-movement. An icy terror enveloped her body as she stared in shock at her large vanity mirror. There she stood plainly in the reflection of the glass but Sara was nothing more than a wisp of herself. In the mirror Jenny could see right through Sara and she appeared not like a normal person but a ghostly apparition. Sunami, catching Jenny's expression, quickly stood up to see what she was staring at. Jenny and Sunami were reflected back boldly but Sara was like a projected image. You could see the wall and window right through her.

"Jesus!" Sunami exclaimed staring at the mirror. Sara looked at one girl then the other, confused but growing more afraid at their sudden alarm as they stared at the mirror.

"What is it? What's happened?"

"Try look!" Sunami yelled. "It's like you're almost no there."

"Where?" She looked at her reflection in the mirror alongside the other girls, but she saw nothing unusual.

"Don't you see it?" Jenny whispered. She waved her hand in front of Sara, all the while looking at the mirror. As she reached to touch her, there was the strange feeling again, so fleeting it was almost like she didn't experience it. Jenny felt the palm of her hand make contact with Sara's chest but in the mirror the image of her hand went right through her. Sunami jumped back and whipped around to gaze at Sara incredulously. Sara blinked, and tears spilled from her eyes as she reached to wipe them away.

"What's going on?" she cried. "What's in the mirror?"

Jenny pulled her hand back. "It's like you're only partially there," she tried to explain as she studied Sara's transparent image. Sunami was scowling, and Jenny recognized that when she made that face she was thinking.

"How long you was sick last year?" Sunami asked.

"A long time, maybe weeks. I don't know."

Sunami nodded taking in this information. "Where did those cousins come from?"

Sara's dark face grew ashen but her jaw set stubbornly and she didn't respond. The sound of the front door opening and closing made the girls jump.

"Jenny!"

"Yes, Mom," Jenny called back. The girls listened as Jenny's mother made her way to the bedroom and opened the door.

"Oh!" Angela was so startled that her eyebrows rose high on her forehead and she stood speechless for a moment.

"Hi," Jenny said, waving her hand slightly. Angela took in the looks of uncertainty on the girls' faces and the snacks spread out on the floor. Everything appeared normal, except each girl looked uncomfortable, as if they had experienced some kind of shock.

"Is everything okay here?"

Sunami and Sara were silent.

"We're just hanging out," Jenny responded quickly. "But I was wondering, can Sara get a ride home? It's so windy out."

"Yes, of course," Angela said feeling more uncertain at the unlikely trio in her daughter's bedroom. "In fact, I was going to go to your house this evening, Sara, and inquire as to why you are missing so much school."

Sara looked down at her hands but she didn't respond.

"Um, right," Angela said. "Will your mother be home?"

The girl nodded and then turned to Jenny.

The Visitors

"Thank you for having me over."

"Sure."

Sunami bent down and grabbed a few more cookies.

"Kay den," she gave a brief *shaka* to the girls and a curt nod to Angela. "Bye, Mrs. Knowles, I can walk home." Sunami sauntered from the room and Sara followed her.

"Well," Angela said, scrutinizing Jenny, who began to pick up the snacks from the floor. "I won't be too long."

Jenny didn't reply. Angela walked back to the living room where Sara stood waiting. Sunami had already left the house. *If I'm not mistaken*, Angela thought to herself, *it looks like she's been crying*. All three girls looked like they had experienced some sort of fright. It was unusual to see the three of them all together in her daughter's bedroom. Angela couldn't shake the fact that it seemed like something had happened to them.

The wind rocked the car as they drove slowly to Sara's. The pale light of evening was gradually darkening into night. Angela couldn't help but feel a certain apprehension. She already had one bad experience with Sara's mother and now Sara appeared uncomfortable about going to her own house.

As they approached the front door an older man came walking up the gentle slope of a hill that led down to an orchard of banana trees. Sara hurried toward him and the man quickened his stride. As he drew nearer, Angela noticed that his weathered face was creased with worry but there was a kindness in his eyes that Sara's mother did not have.

"Papa!" Sara called out.

Her father waved. His linen shirt flapped around his body from the wind, his hair dancing crazily around his slim, pointy face. When he finally reached what was the front yard, he gave a brief smile.

"Hello," he said. Angela held out her hand and he took it, his grasp firm and calloused.

"I'm Angela Knowles, Sara's history teacher."

"Yes," he said in a neutral tone. He did not invite her in but stood waiting.

"Mr. Deureaux, I am sorry about showing up unexpectedly but I was told that your family doesn't have a phone?" He smiled wryly.

"My dear, there are no poles out on this ridge. We couldn't have a phone if we wanted to. Our property is completely cut off from county amenities."

Angela cleared her throat. "I see. Sara has been missing a lot of school the past few weeks. She is a great student. However, if she continues to miss school, it will affect her grades. Actually, her absences have already had a negative effect on her grades. It's possible that she might be able to make up some of her missed work, but she needs to come back to school. Is there a reason why she has so many absences?"

Sara's father smiled again. "She will be in school tomorrow. Thank you, Mrs. Knowles."

Sara stood by his side, her body leaning somewhat toward his wiry frame. He made no further comment on Sara's absences or otherwise, and it was clear that the conversation was over. Angela nodded.

"Yes, well, we will all be happy to see Sara again. She is really very bright."

"Thank you."

"I should get going," Angela found herself saying lamely. "I need to get dinner started."

Sara's father put up his hand in a gesture of goodbye. He turned away from Angela, beckoning Sara to follow him back down the hill. She stood for a moment, watching them. Again, she had been thoroughly dismissed.

Chapter Thirteen

"I want to know what is happening?" Sara demanded. She waited with her parents in Papa's workshop for the children to take their nocturnal walk. Maman had grown more fearful listening to Sara explain the turn of events earlier in the day.

"It's not possible," Papa replied in a quiet voice. "You must trust us, Sara, that there is a reason. Soon your cousins will be gone and we can return back to our normal lives."

"No! I'm tired of this. I'm tired of not knowing or understanding what is happening, pretending that it's not unusual that there are four people living with us that are unnaturally pale, never eat and have grown inches in just weeks. How can you say we will return back to normal? We will never be normal. You need to tell me why. I need to know, Papa."

Maman stood up from the small bench she had been sitting on for the past hour. Her mouth was hard and turned down, her lips just a slash on her round face, her cheeks splotched with red.

"You!" she screamed, pointing a finger at Sara. Flecks of spittle sprayed the girl's face. "This is because of you! She made us take you." Sara shrank back from her mother's fury.

"Annette," Papa said in a warning voice.

"We'll never be free of them," her voice broke, and Papa took her in his arms. Sara watched as her father's hand stroked her mother in an effort to calm her and felt, not for the first time, like an intruder that had disrupted their neat, orderly lives. *You do not belong*, a small voice whispered in her head. Hugging herself, she closed her eyes as she began to sway on her feet. She did not hear or see the tools on the countertop begin to jump about, clanging loudly as if imbued with life, or the shutters on the window fold closed on their own and rapidly open up again. She did not even know that she was speaking, shouting.

Grabbing her shoulders, Papa began to shake her.

"Sara!"

Her eyes fluttered, facial muscles twitching.

"She is having the spell," Maman said quietly, pinching Sara's chin and tipping her head back. This usually broke her trance.

"Back into the light! Back into the light!"

The strange, deep voice cried from the girl's vocal chords. All at once, it ended. The dancing tools fell with a resounding clang, lying still, and the shutters ceased their movement midway across the window. Sara's eyes flew open. Maman and Papa were both standing over her, each holding an arm. Frowning, she pulled away from her parents whose faces registered a worry that she could make no sense of.

"You must not let yourself go like that," Papa finally said. She had no idea what he was talking about.

Their remaining wait in the workshop was in silence, the wind raging outside, whistling through crevices in the small room. There was a definite empty feeling when Sara and her parents returned to the house, an absence of the cousin's presence. Their home was beginning to feel foreign as if it didn't belong to them anymore.

The Visitors

Maman immediately retired to her room. Sara watched her father as he poked around inside the fridge for something to eat. Although her stomach growled, her eyes burned with fatigue. Not bothering to say goodnight, she went to her room and sat on her bed, listening to the wind beat against the house. She stared at the picture of Mother Mary that sat on her dresser, remembering Papa's suggestion that she pray to her. Sara closed her eyes, trying to think. What could she do? If she only knew or understood what was happening around her, then she could make a plan.

She did not hear her closet door open over the fierce noise of the storm. It was only when she opened her eyes and saw Samuel standing in the small space that a searing fright raced through her body. He stood watching her, his expression flat. Putting one long finger to his lips he stepped from the closet. Sara shrank farther back on her bed, her eyes darting to the door.

"Sara, I need to talk to you," he whispered.

She did not trust herself to speak as he walked to her small desk and sat in the chair. He did not say anything for quite a while. It was only when she felt she might come apart with tension that he spoke.

"I have been thinking all this afternoon and evening since you left, and some memories are coming to me, but they are fleeting. She is right, though. It was partly my plan for us to be here, and I remember a little. I remember that I knew that you would be here. For what purpose, I cannot tell you."

Now that Samuel was speaking, Sara noticed that his sentence structures were elegant and old-fashioned. He leaned back in his chair, silent again. The house shuddered and there was a loud bang, the sound of thunder. Sara jumped, but Samuel was unmoved. A low rumble rippled overhead, followed by more furious shrieks of nature.

"What I cannot understand," he began again, "is why you are in fear almost constantly. The gypsies, yes, it is expected." His brows pulled together and he rubbed his forehead. "Even Louis, whom you call Papa, has a more centered demeanor."

Sara bit at her lip, not sure what to say.

"It is obvious that you are a high servant but you don't seem to know it. You have had no training."

"Do you know where you come from?" Sara ventured. "Or why all of you are so different from other people?" Samuel crossed his legs and held out one of his hands before himself, spreading the fingers.

"There is something called the true physical. Have you heard of it?"

Sara shook her head. She could feel herself beginning to relax once she realized that Samuel was not there to harm her.

"Let me see how best to explain this."

He looked around and his eyes lit on an eraser lying on her desk. He picked up the rectangular, pink object and held it up for Sara to see.

"What is this?" he asked.

"An eraser," Sara whispered. She watched his hand close around it and become a fist.

"Is this an eraser?"

Sara frowned. "No, it's your hand."

"Why? Why is it my hand and not the eraser?"

"Just because your hand has closed around it doesn't make it an eraser."

He smiled that odd smile that only stretched the lips. "Yes. We can apply that same concept to you. Your name is Sara Deureaux, and you live here in this house with two people that you call Maman and Papa. But are you really Sara?"

Sara felt her heart quicken. What was he saying?

"Again, the fear," Samuel said softly. "I am asking, is this what makes you Sara? Or put another way, are you Sara?"

"I don't understand. I don't get it. Are you saying I am someone else?"

The Visitors

"Are you?" His eyes blazed and he rested his chin in his hand. Sara gritted her teeth. She felt as if her head would explode. She was frightened, disoriented and tired. "You are confusing me, Samuel. I don't know what you're trying to say."

"You are confusing yourself. It is simple."

Sara sat up as the shadow of a thought began to take shape in her mind. "When I touch you, or any one of you, I don't feel you at first," she said softly, thinking. Samuel waited, watching her. Sara looked up at the ceiling. What was he trying to tell her? She needed to know. It was the first time someone was making an effort to speak with her about the strange circumstances surrounding her life, yet he spoke in riddles. Suddenly there was a spark of comprehension. The hallucinations usually happened around the older girl or when she was feeling afraid or worried. She thought again of Samuel holding the eraser out and his hand closing around it. Sara stood up and walked toward Samuel, holding out her hand.

"May I have that?" He placed the eraser in her palm and she closed her fingers around the rubbery object. *The eraser still exists,* she thought, *but if the eraser could think...what if it thought it were now my hand?*

"Is the true physical like this eraser?"

"What do you mean?"

Sara felt an excitement building in her. She paused, not sure how to explain.

"This eraser is truly an eraser. But what if it can think, and when my hand surrounds it, it thinks it is now also my hand?" she asked.

"In a way it is part of your hand," Samuel said. "The problem is that it has forgotten itself and thinks it is only your hand. We are like this." He pointed to his hand. "Outer circumstances, our bodies, emotions, they are a part of us for a while, however, it is not the true physical." He was quiet for a moment, letting that sink in. "So are you Sara?" He waved his hand from side to side. "Yes and no." He sighed. "This would have been one of your first lessons."

Sara went back to sit on her bed. "It still doesn't really explain why it is so strange when I touch you."

"What I am, I am, but I am not," was Samuel's only explanation.

"I don't get it."

"That is enough. We have more pressing matters to attend to. Since it is clear that you know very little of who you are and Annette and Louis will not be volunteering any information, we will have to glean what we can from the little that we do know until my memories fully return."

"Why not just wait until you remember? That would be easier."

"Because, Sara, we are all in danger and my full memories might return too late."

"What are we in danger of?" Sara asked softly.

Samuel held up his hand.

"It is not wise to go down that route. It will serve no purpose in helping us out of our predicament and it will surely increase your fear, which you must learn to control if we are to have any success." Sara swallowed and took a breath. He made some sense and somehow she felt she could trust him.

"First, I need to know where we are and what year it is."

"We are in Hawaii, on the island of Maui, and it is 1984."

Samuel's nostrils flared, and he nodded slightly.

"I see. And what are your first memories of being here?"

"We moved here when I was really young. It just seems I was always here."

"Please think hard. Do you have any wisp of a memory of where you came from?" Sara thought, but nothing came to mind, only the nightmare.

"What is it?"

"I don't remember where we moved from. The only thing I can think of that would be my earliest memory is of this dream." Sara paused, thinking. "I am in a house that seems very large and ornate." Samuel leaned forward. "There is a woman and she is saying, "don't look, don't look." Sara felt her heart speed up at the thought of it and for the first time made an effort to separate herself from the fear that she felt rising in her chest.

"Good," Samuel said, noticing her effort.

"'Hide in here,' she says. I'm pushed into this big, deep closet, and I can hear children screaming. Something is killing them. I can hear a woman crying." Pinching her eyebrows to stop the tears from flowing, Sarah remembered the woman's anguish and forced herself to continue.

"There is a second woman who is trying to soothe me but she scares me. Her voice is like the eldest girl's. Then someone is trying to put something in my mouth. It tastes so bad."

She looked at Samuel and was taken aback at the intensity that emanated from his blue eyes.

"That is not a dream," he finally said. "It is a memory of your first right. You have passed through the sickness, I assume."

"I was really sick last year," Sara confirmed.

Samuel nodded and stood up. "You have been made complete then, but without your education. It is important," he paused, seeming to pick his words carefully, "that we try and piece together our situation. There were plans made and they have obviously gone most grievously awry. There are contacts that need to be found. I am going to need you to collect as much information as you can. I cannot go amongst people. My appearance would cause suspicion. There is really not much time. Already, I have seen the signs that *she* is growing ill."

Sara understood She to mean the eldest girl.

"Soon I will be next, and then Carmilla and Michael." Samuel's eyes bore into her. Willing herself to remain calm, Sara dropped her own gaze to the floor.

"Those people who you call Maman and Papa are slaves. The fact that they have kept so much information from you has done you a great disservice. I am not certain whom you belong to but someone has been trying to hide you here on this island and I'm not sure why. The gypsies know and She knows. I think She knows everything already. Normally, there is something called an infantry. That is where we grow into ourselves. In the infantry, we are guided and educated until our memories return. Here, there is no one to guide us. I only have partial memories." Samuel broke off, as if trying to recollect something and Sara waited for him to continue.

"Tomorrow when Annette and Louis are out of the house, I want you to look in their room and see what information you are able to find."

"I have to go to school tomorrow."

"We don't have much time, Sara. In the end, we are all working together. However, the final transformation is the most treacherous. Everyone here, your neighbors, they are not safe."

"What transformation?" Sara whispered. The question was left hanging.

"In the late afternoon the gypsies are usually both away from the house for quite a while. When you come home from school, we can take advantage of that time. I can keep watch for you."

Sara dared herself to look up at Samuel. He stared back at her, his face composed into the usual expressionless mask. Without another word, he quietly let himself out of her room, closing the door gently behind him.

Later that night, Sara lay in bed in the darkness listening, not daring to close her eyes and sleep. At one point, she awoke with a start, realizing that she had dozed off. It was very quiet, even the wind had

The Visitors

died down. Rising from her bed, she walked to the window, looking out into the night. From the light of the stars she could barely make out the outline of the coconut and banana trees. Something moved amongst the foliage. Sara strained her eyes following the shadow of a figure that disappeared behind a cluster of large, fat leaves and then re-emerged again. In full view, Sara recognized her. The oldest girl was walking toward the stable, her movements fluid and sure.

The rest of the night was spent waiting. It was early morning when Sara finally heard the front door slowly creak open and the soft footsteps of the girl returning up to the children's rooms.

Chapter Fourteen

The last of the plants were watered. River gazed admiringly at this latest crop. The marijuana had grown exceptionally tall and bushy, the leaves broader than normal. Ripening buds, thick and greyish green clung to the stems between the leaves. He rubbed his palms together and grinned at Don and Leonard. If all went well, this harvest would bring in a cool 200K. With the money he had already saved from previous crops, River looked forward to purchasing his first piece of property.

"Yeah man," Leonard said, rubbing his palms together, and the three young men laughed. Gathering up the last of the watering containers, they walked the short trek through the hau bush and lauhala trees to a truck they kept parked in a small gulch, hidden from view of the main road. Don and Leonard would be staying behind to camp near the crop. It was too close to harvest to leave the plants by themselves anymore. So far, it seemed that their new spot was undiscovered, but all three of the young men had felt as if they were being watched lately. They carried rifles now. Luckily, they had never found themselves in a position to use the guns.

The Visitors

Once Don and Leonard had thrown the old milk cartons into the back of the truck, River started it up. He did not wait to watch his friends return to the plants. A storm appeared to be gathering and he was just glad that it was not his turn to sleep outside tonight. As he pulled the truck forward, a movement caught his eye. It looked like a person in the bushes. Straining to see, he thought he caught a glimpse of dark hair and a white arm. Leaving the truck running, River reached for his gun and quietly opened the door, jumping down on the ground littered with the large, brown fronds of the lauhala trees. The dried leaves made a crackling sound under his weight as he made his way around the truck. He scanned the bushes but saw no one. Still feeling uneasy, he went back to the truck and cut the motor. He would need to go and warn Don and Leonard that someone was slinking around.

A thick fog was descending from the east, giving the air a moist feel, promising the threat of rain. In the fast-approaching darkness and mist, it was hard to see and he cursed himself for not grabbing a flashlight. Pulling back the hau bush, the mist cleared momentarily and River felt his heart rise to his throat at the sudden sight of a woman standing silently before him. He had seen her before in the past few days, always from a distance. Once he thought he'd seen this same woman looking in on him through his bedroom window when he had suddenly woken from a fitful sleep. But the image had been fleeting.

Don and Leonard had enjoyed joshing him lately about his lady stalker. Now here she was. Her pale, luminous green eyes stood out milky bright in the swirling fog. As she gazed upon him, her eyes darkened, her pupils widening in her unnaturally white face. Menace seemed to radiate from her being, yet he felt drawn to her. Raising her arm, she beckoned for him to step closer. A compulsion to want to touch her overtook building terror. Reaching out his hand, his fingers lightly grazed her extended arm. Jolted by the fact that he felt nothing, although he could see his hand on her white shoulder, he snatched his hand back. A faint smile played upon her thin lips. Wordlessly, she retreated farther into the bushes, the hau branches folding around her until she disappeared from view.

There was a loud crashing noise like something big coming through the foliage and River fumbled with his rifle.

"Don't move," he heard Don call out. River raised his hands above his head, his body shaking.

"Dude, it's me."

He could only make out the vague silhouette of Don in the last dredges of daylight. An ashy darkness had descended upon them in the bushes, relieved only by the last strands of fading light filtered through the trees where the truck was parked.

"What the hell are you doing, man?" Don asked. "Why are you creeping around in the bushes?"

River lowered his arms and Don lowered his rifle.

"I thought I saw someone walking around here. I was trying to see if I could catch em."

"Oh, sorry, dude. Me and Leonard totally thought you were a scavenger. Did you find anyone?"

River hesitated. He hated to bring up the White Lady again, and somehow he felt that she wasn't there for pot plants.

"No man, whoever it was must have hightailed it when they saw I was onto them."

"OK, dude," Don said. "We'll just be extra vigilant tonight. I guess someone's going to have to stay here twenty-four-seven now until those plants are ready to harvest."

"Yeah man, we're on it," River said, but a cold fear had swept over his body. The idea of seeing that ghostly woman again was disturbing. It was terrifying to even walk back to his truck alone.

"Hey man, you alright?" Don had walked up to River, his rifle hanging at his side. River shook his head.

The Visitors

"I guess it's just the adrenaline."

"Shit, it's getting dark," Don said. "I was in such a rush to catch whoever it was, I forgot to strap my light on my head." The two walked back to the truck, much to River's relief. He handed Don a flashlight from inside the cab.

"OK, man, be safe." River said. Don headed back to the bushes, waved and ducked back into the trees. Starting up his truck, River didn't feel comfortable to drive home. He had seen that woman before, lurking around his place. Always, he had felt her watching him before he would see her. Was she real or some strange Hawaiian entity? River rubbed at his face and pulled at his sparse facial hair. There was that myth about the White Lady. Was that who she was? He shivered, thinking about the ghostly story of the dead hitchhiker.

Following the curve of the road, he found himself out on the highway. He had a desire to be around lights and people, in a town. He desperately wanted to talk to someone about his experience, someone who might understand and not turn it into a joke. Then he knew who might take him seriously and maybe explain things—Pono. He was the *haupa haole* half-bother of his friend Akamu. Both brothers were into the sciences, following in their parent's footsteps. Their mother was a marine biologist from Florida and their father an astronomer. Pono himself was a fascinating bundle of contradictions. While most local boys his age were interested in outdoor sports, Pono spent much of his time studying physics, yet he was also greatly fascinated with subjects on the supernatural. There were many times that River had gone to hang out with Akamu and spent most of the time talking with Pono.

It was a twenty-minute drive to Paia. Just before he entered the town, River made a sharp left into an unmarked driveway. The lights were on in the main house and the *ohana* just next to it. Pulling his truck up behind the blue Subaru station wagon that belonged to his friend's mother, he sat in his truck for a moment contemplating whether or not it was a good idea to talk to Pono and what he might say. Making up his mind, he cut the engine and jumped from the truck, heading for the *ohana* where Akamu stayed, and Pono spent most of his time.

The first drops of rain hit the young man on the nose. Within seconds, great sheets of water began to pour from the sky. By the time River had walked the twenty feet from his truck to the *ohana*, his hair and clothes were soaked. The rain stopped as quickly as it had come. All that remained was the wind screaming and whistling through the yard. River knocked on the door.

"Yeah," Akamu called from within. Opening the door, he found Pono sitting at a small table, studying a chessboard. Akamu came from the kitchen holding a Corona. River held up his hand in greeting as the lights flickered and died out.

"Oh shit. No power," Akamu said.

Chapter Fifteen

Pono tore open a shoyu packet and drenched his spam musubi before taking a large bite.

"That's got to be way salty," Steve commented, shaking his head.

Pono grinned and took another bite, a clump of rice falling to his plate. He had grabbed several of the musubi at the lunch line. It was his favorite school lunch.

"So are we on for D and D at your place?" Eric asked.

Pono shook his head, his mouth too full to speak. Eric rubbed at his nose, his eyes enlarged behind the thick lenses of his glasses.

"This is the second week in a row that we're missing, and you're the DM master."

Pono swallowed and took a quick swig of milk as his friends waited for him to talk. "Something came up. It's kind of important. I need to meet up with River."

"Who, that hippie guy?" Steve asked.

Pono nodded, unwrapping a second musubi and drenching it with more shoyu.

"Ey, Pono!"

The three boys turned to look behind them.

"Oh great, what now?" Eric said under his breath, pushing his glasses up against the bridge of his nose as they watched Sunami sauntering over in their direction.

"Wus up?" Pono said, falling immediately into pidgin.

"Got time?" Sunami asked once she had made it over to their table. Her dark eyes took in Eric and Steve in one quick, shrewd glance. Finding them inconsequential, her focus returned to Pono.

"What up?" Pono asked.

Sunami lifted her chin and inclined her head toward the door, motioning that they should go outside.

Pono frowned, puzzled that Sunami was seeking him out. Shoving the remaining half of his musubi in his mouth, he pulled his long legs over the bench and stood up to follow her outside. She said nothing more as he walked behind her through the courtyard where throngs of kids milled around. There was the occasional, "Ey Sunami, wus up sistah!" but after the brief greetings, they kept moving. They walked down the hallway that was a wing for the various science classrooms and finally out to the football field and behind some bushes. A thin redheaded girl sat on the grass waiting. Pono's eyebrows rose up in surprise as the girl looked up at him.

"Dis is Jenny, and dis is Pono," Sunami introduced them.

"Hey," Jenny said. Pono said nothing but he was intrigued.

"Look, we need your help to solve something, brah, but you got to promise not to tell no one, not even those lame nerds you like go round with."

"OK..." Pono crossed his arms.

"You once wrote one paper on multiple dimensions," Sunami said.

"Well, multiple dimensions were addressed, but it was really on Hugh Everett's many-worlds interpretation."

Pono's pidgin switched back to Standard English and he grinned, watching Sunami's face slip into a fierce scowl. A look, he knew, that either meant she was thinking or wanted to scrap. He had

The Visitors

known Sunami for as far back as he could remember. In elementary school, they had played together. She had always been a tomboy, but in junior high she had become more of a *tita*, a tough girl, and it often appeared that she had a chip on her shoulder. She was smart, a lot smarter than she liked to let on, but her tough girl attitude Pono found wearisome and gradually the two had gone their own way.

"What's up, Sunami? Why the sudden interest?"

"I know you like study freakish things and there be something not right that took place regarding a mirror that don't make sense."

Pono's eyebrows drew together as he stared at Sunami, who stood with her arms crossed. Although her stance was challenging, a look of worry flitted across her narrow face.

Pono looked at the redheaded girl, her knees drawn up to her chest. It was unusual to see Sunami hanging out with a *haole*, and this girl seemed to emanate fear.

"A mirror?" he echoed.

"It really has to do with that girl, Sara Deureaux," Jenny said. "Do you know her?"

The image of a quiet girl, always sitting alone reading came to mind.

"Yeah, I don't really know her. I see her around. She likes to keep to herself."

Sunami nodded. "She get these cousins, come visit her. There's something not right about them, brah. They is white, more white than her."

Sunami pointed at Jenny, and Pono felt the hair rise up on his neck.

"Is one of them a woman with dark hair and green eyes?" he asked.

Both girls' eyes widened.

"You seen em?"

"No, I've heard about, well, just the one, the woman."

"Who went told you?" Sunami asked, dropping her arms in astonishment.

"This is weird," Pono said quietly. "My brother's friend, River, came by my place last night. He told me about this White woman that's been stalking him. He said she was really creepy because she didn't seem natural. He wanted to know if I had ever come across anything like her before when I've read about the supernatural. I mean in a way it was hard to take him serious, but he seemed so spooked. I was going to meet up with him today. But you're saying that this woman is Sara's cousin?" The girls nodded. "But what has this got to do with a mirror and other dimensions?"

"When you look at Sara in the mirror," Jenny said, "it's like she's only partially there. She can't see it, though. It's so strange."

"What?" Pono wrinkled his brow at this new bit of information. "Is this some kind of joke? I mean come on, you expect me to believe this thing about the mirror?"

Sunami's worried expression changed to one of anger.

"Look punk, I get better things to do than make up some stupid fantasy like that dumb ass game dungeons and dragons you and your retard friends get sucked into. We're serious. That spooky White lady that's stalking River, she might be stalking Mele."

Jenny sucked in her breath at this last comment of Sunami's; this information was obviously new to her. "On top of all that, I think that girl, Sara, is in deep shit. I no believe those be her cousins, brah. I don't know what they are, but they is not like regular peoples."

Pono was silent after Sunami's lash of anger. There was no humor on either girl's face; instead, they both stared at him in earnest.

"Well what do you want me to do?" Pono asked.

Sunami took a visible breath and seemed to relax a little. "Can meet us after school?" she asked

"I'm supposed to meet River at my house. But since you both seem to be talking about the same woman, just meet me in the parking lot after school. You can ride in my truck. I think we should all get together."

"K' den." Sunami held her hand up, and Pono placed his palm against hers, briefly clasping their fingers around each other's hand before letting go.

Jenny stood up and waved.

As Pono walked away, he thought of the fact that he had seen Sara earlier during break. She had been sitting by herself on one of the benches in the courtyard. At the time it hadn't meant much to him that she was sitting looking off in the distance at nothing in particular. Usually she was reading.

As Pono walked up the grassy hill from the football field and onto the main campus, he was startled to see Sara walking up ahead. She was clutching some textbooks in her arms, looking straight ahead, although she didn't seem to be focused on anything. Pono noticed that she looked tired and as if she were in some kind of shock. He jogged to catch up to her and then slowed to a walk as they came face to face.

"Hey," he called out, smiling. She looked in his direction but did not acknowledge him. Her eyes were deeply ringed with dark circles. Pono watched as she kept walking.

Sara waited until she and Jenny were out of Mrs. Knowles' classroom before she approached her. Earlier that morning, she had decided that she would confide in Jenny. After jostling for position to get outside the classroom door, Sara remained behind her classmate, keeping sight of her red hair. She was surprised when she saw her turn toward the student parking lot instead of the buses.

"Jenny," she called out.

Jenny turned around, her features brightening with surprise as she stopped to wait for Sara to catch up with her.

"I was hoping to talk with you," Sara said. As the words left her lips, she began to feel unsure of her plan.

"Oh?"

"Aren't you catching the bus?"

Jenny's stared at her feet, and she nudged at the grass with the toe of her sneaker. "Actually, I was going to ride back with Sunami and Pono."

Sara was not sure of what to say. *This is a bad idea*, she told herself.

"What did you want to talk with me about?" Jenny asked.

Sara shook her head, backing away. Jenny took in the dark circles under Sara's eyes and the fact that she looked like she hadn't slept.

"Are you OK? Do you want to come with us?"

"No, it's private. I should really get going."

"You could come over later," Jenny said.

"Maybe."

Sara turned around then and began her walk across the yard to the buses. The thought of going home churned unpleasantly in her mind. She hated the idea of snooping around in her parents' bedroom, but maybe Samuel was right to suggest it. What other choices were there? With no information coming forth from Maman and Papa, she needed to know the truth. Were the people in her neighborhood in danger if she didn't listen to Samuel? But surely her parents wouldn't allow a situation that would put others in danger, would they?

After watching Sara walk away, Jenny ran to the parking lot. It was a fairly large lot, and she realized that she was going to have to walk around until she found Pono and Sunami. Kids were hopping into their vehicles and pulling out everywhere. With the glare of the sun in her eyes, it was hard to see clearly.

"Look, I ain't your babysitter," she could hear Sunami yelling.

The Visitors

Jenny spotted Pono first; he was standing next to a gray truck, his arms folded as he squinted in the direction of Sunami's voice. One of his friends, a boy with glasses, was also standing with arms crossed.

"Why is she going with you?" the boy was asking Pono as Jenny came up to join them.

"Hey," she said quietly. Pono's friend turned to look at her, startled to see her there. Pono gave a brief nod; he was focused on Sunami, who stood a short distance off, scowling.

"You weren't home last night, nor the night before," a young woman was yelling at her. The woman appeared pregnant, and a toddler was crying on her hip. Sunami's scowl deepened.

"I told you, I got tings to do. You freak."

The young woman's eyes grew so wide they looked like they were about to pop out of her head. "Who you callin a freak!"

Other kids were coming to stand and watch the scene that was developing. Sunami, noticing Jenny, motioned to Pono to get in the truck.

"You're not going anywhere," the woman screamed, trying to grab the sleeve of Sunami's t-shirt.

"Get in da kine!" Sunami yelled. "Where da hell you been?" she shouted at Jenny, darting away from the woman's hand.

"It's open," Pono told Jenny, so she scurried in, with Sunami sliding in after her. Pono jumped in the driver's seat and turned the key. The engine roared to life.

"Screw you!" the woman screamed over her baby's cries. Pono's friend stood with his mouth hanging open as they shot out of the parking space and peeled out of the lot, tires squealing on the asphalt.

Clouds hung low, threatening more rain, but the wind had not returned. Sara stepped from the bus at the top of her road and swung her backpack over her shoulder. The thought of going to the house terrified her. She wondered what new development she would find.

The boys from the red house ran ahead, laughing and yelling. Soon they were out of sight. Two women came walking up from the valley, chatting companionably. Their dogs ran ahead of them, their pink tongues lolling, mouths slack, the corners turned up in what Sara thought of as a doggy smile. Seeing the creatures so happy and hearing the comfortable conversation of the women relaxed Sara's mood. However, as the dogs drew closer, they suddenly stopped, their bodies stiffening. One of them let out a low growl and the other began to whine while backing up, both sets of ears flattened.

"Suki!" one of the women called. "Stop that!"

But the dog's growl only grew deeper, rattling threateningly in its throat. It was a large Ridgeback with tufts of fur between its shoulders standing out more prominently in its agitation. Both of the women ran up to the dogs.

"Suki, stop that!" the dog's owner commanded, grabbing the dog.

"I'm so sorry. She never acts like this," the woman said, and then pulled back in surprise as the dog turned on her, its teeth bared, and snapped at her hand.

"Shit, what's wrong with her?" the woman yelled. Her friend stood as if frozen, observing the scene. Sara took a slow step back. The dog lunged forward.

"Suki, no!"

Sara didn't see the truck barreling toward her. Her last visual was of the other woman throwing her hands up to cover her eyes. Dust and metal were suddenly before her. The driver's door flew open and an arm reached down.

"Jump in!" a man yelled. Sara scrambled up into the cab, climbing over the driver in a burst of adrenaline. Once in the passenger's seat she stared in disbelief at the dog throwing itself upon the truck, its teeth bared as it tried to bite at the door. The two women stood

The Visitors

motionless, both pale with shock. Their other dog stretched its neck out, giving a low mournful wail. The man backed the truck up and turned it around. He then pulled up beside the women and rolled his window down.

"Are you crazy?" he yelled. "How can you let a monster like that run around unleashed? Your dog was about to tear this girl apart." Both women were silent. The huge Ridgeback was still lunging at the truck.

"Where do you live? I'll take you home," the man asked. Sara turned around to see the women still standing where they'd left them, Suki growling and barking, her powerful face growing smaller with the distance.

"That was a close one. It's a good thing I was able to get between you and that thing. What are people thinking letting an animal like that run loose?"

Sara stared at the man as they drove down the dirt road. He was young and shirtless and wore his long hair in a ponytail.

"You must be in shock," he said. "I'm River."

Sara swallowed. "Thank you. I'm Sara. I just live up on the ridge."

"No problem, I'll drop you right at your doorstop. Yeah, sure is a good thing I was headed out to town just now." Sara did not reply.

River eased the truck slowly down the steep incline of the road and whistled as they passed over the bridge. "That's a narrow one." She nodded. They continued uphill, following the natural curve of the road and he pulled into her driveway.

"Thank you again," Sara said, opening the door of the cab.

River looked around, his brows pulling together. "This place looks familiar," he commented.

Sara was not sure what to say. She nodded again and stepped out of the truck.

River waited until she had taken a few steps away from the vehicle before backing it up. *It's strange*, he thought to himself, *but there is a sense of déjà vu about this place, like I've been here before.* The White Lady flashed through his mind. It would be good to meet up with Pono and see what information they could find.

"Sara?" Samuel called as she walked through the door.

"*Oui,*" Sara called back. It was quiet and she knew immediately that her parents were not in the house. Feeling jarred from her experience with the dog, she was not sure she could keep it together to appear calm and collected around Samuel and the older girl. She was not sure she could endure any more harrowing experiences. Samuel came into the kitchen, assessing her for a moment.

"Something has happened," he stated, noticing the receding shroud of panic dissipating from her being. "Tell me."

"It is the animals. They are either frightened or they want to attack me. A dog almost got me, if it weren't for a man who happened to come driving up and was able to get his truck between us, I think that dog would have…" her voice caught. She did not want to finish the sentence, or think about what might have happened. Her chest felt heavy and her throat thick with unexpressed emotion.

Samuel pulled out one of the chairs from the kitchen table. "Come and sit down." Sara walked to the chair. Setting her backpack on the floor, she eased her slim body into the seat. "Now close your eyes," he directed. She looked up at him and he took a few steps back in an attempt at reassuring her that she was safe. Sara shut her eyes, feeling her heart speed up.

"Do not go there," he said, as if he could feel and hear her quickening pulse. "Find your breath and focus on it." She took in a breath and exhaled. She had never focused on her breathing before and the added attention gave her the feeling of not breathing correctly.

"Slowly draw in breath."

The Visitors

Samuel's voice had a hypnotic quality and Sara followed his directions. "Slowly breathe out and listen." He stopped talking.

What was she supposed to be listening to? She continued with her breathing, straining her ears. She could hear a faint scratching coming from the living room. Focusing, she realized that it was the sound of Michael's pencil on paper as he drew in that rapid way that was so amazing to see. There was the sound of a page turning in a book: Carmilla reading. Sara felt her breath grow slower as she began to take in other sounds. Scuttling—was that a roach? The sounds expanded, creaking, rustling. Sara opened her eyes and stared at the wall before her, but was taken aback when the room suddenly rounded out and expanded so that she was seeing from every direction. Just as quickly, she was back to looking at the wall before her. The momentary three-dimensional view made her body shudder and she wondered if she were hallucinating again.

"You see what you're capable of," Samuel said. Sara looked up at him and calmness descended upon her. Noticing the change of mood, he came to sit at the table with her.

"Animals are more in tune with other senses than the five senses that men rely upon. They can see beyond what is considered normal, even for them. Just because they have this capability does not mean that they understand. If an animal can't understand, it grows frightened or wants to attack."

"What are they seeing?" Again the fears came fluttering back. He paused, looking into her eyes.

"I can see when you let the darkness ravage your being. You must learn to quiet your mind, Sara. There is no other option for this life that you have. Learn to rise above yourself."

"Samuel, I don't know what I am or even what I am working with."

"No. However, you will learn. For now focus on strengthening your perceptions. Let us move away from this subject. I wanted to tell you that Annette left the house not too long ago. Also," Samuel raised his eyes and lifted his face, motioning to the bedrooms above them, "*She* has fallen ill. *She* did not come down today. I gave her some medicine this morning."

"But I saw her walking around in the early morning hours! It must have been two or three when I heard her come into the house. That is probably why she is still in bed."

"*She* always goes out in the night," Samuel said.

Sara blinked at him.

"That is nothing unusual. You may go up and see for yourself. The fever has already started."

Sara fell silent, thinking. "What does it mean when she gets sick?"

"Her transformation."

Sara did not ask what the transformation would be. Not wanting to hear anymore, she stood up and walked to the living room. There sat Carmilla and Michael, drawing and reading as usual, but they had aged since the morning. The two were visibly taller. Carmilla no longer looked like a girl but a young woman. Michael's jaw had widened and his shoulders were broader.

"Yes, they grew." Samuel said coming up behind her. "While we have this time to ourselves, I need you to look in the room of Annette and Louis. I can keep watch." Sara turned to face Samuel. His face was earnest, as much as it could be.

"What would I look for?"

"Anything. Notebooks, letters."

"I don't understand why you and *She* haven't done this yourselves a long time ago. You are left alone for hours. Why do I need to do it?"

"We physically can't go in."

"What? Why not?"

Samuel motioned her back to the kitchen when Carmilla and Michael glanced curiously at them.

"Come, come," he motioned to the hallway. Sara followed him.

The Visitors

"They are developing a little differently. Their memories are coming back slower. I am not sure which ones they are."

"What does that mean?" Sara could feel a new wave of terror building in her. She tried to steady her breath as Samuel had showed her, but it was difficult.

"Good," he said, taking notice of her effort. She swallowed, hugging herself. "OK, I'll look. Wait by the front door and call my name if you hear anything."

"Right. I will wait by the door like you ask." There was a low moan from up above.

"It is the fever," he whispered.

Sara nodded, walking to her parent's bedroom.

It felt strange to open their door. She couldn't remember ever having been in their room. It was neat and clean as expected but a peculiar musky odor seemed to hang in the air. It was so strong that Sara felt she could almost taste it. There was a four-poster bed that took up most of the space, a colorful handmade quilt covering the top with matching pillows. Nightstands were on either side of the bed and a propane light was centered on the wall directly above. Another larger dresser was pushed up against the opposite wall alongside a small closet.

Sara swallowed, moving toward the closet first. She opened the doors and stared at the neatly hung clothes. Pulling a box down, she found nothing much, just some odd scraps of fabric. She carefully put it back and pulled down another only to find various knickknacks. Not wanting to waste time with more boxes, she closed the closet and moved to Maman's nightstand. There was a bible, which Sara had never seen before. She picked it up and noticed the edge of a photograph sticking out from between the pages. Opening the bible, she stared at a black and white picture that made no sense. There were Papa and Maman, looking very young. Maman was even pretty in a healthy, strong-looking way.

Her dark hair was pulled into one thick braid that hung over her shoulder. She wore a white dress that came in tight about her hips, pearly buttons accentuating the bodice. Papa stood next to her, fresh with youth. Among them were three young girls, the oldest looking very much like Maman. Who were these children? Sara turned the photo over. The neat crisp writing on the back was Maman's, it read: *1948, Louis Deureaux, Annette Deureaux, Olivia, Juliette and Carlotta Deureaux.*

Sara felt stunned as she stared at the photo. Maman and Papa had other children? Where were they? Fumbling with the bible, she slipped the picture back between the pages. Walking over to Papa's side, Sara opened his drawer and saw the journal that he wrote in every night. Feeling guilty, she flipped through the book. Her breath caught when a wispy envelope came flitting out from among the pages. It was the letter. The words were written in feathery lightness with fancy curlicues. The kind of penmanship one might expect from someone that lived in the 1800s.

My Dearest Annette,

There has been a sudden turn of events. I must report to you that the plan has failed. Time runs out as I write this letter. Indeed I do not expect to keep my life once they find that I have been serving the fatalists. I know that I can trust both you and Louis to follow orders.

Four Masters you will receive soon after this letter. Samuel, whom you both know well, he has broken forth already, and is growing steadily each day. Lilith is also still, of course, under our care, and I regret to place her in your home, as this is a crucial time, and we have worked hard to capture her. Also we are sending you Carmilla and Michael. Take care around them. Both shall break open any day now. We will, of course, be sending them by ship. They can survive several days packed in boxes with no nourishment. I trust you have saved plenty of the dried blood pulp, as they will need it to grow. It is

The Visitors

only for a month, at the most. You will receive a second letter when we are ready to send someone from the infantry.

Annette, please remember to hold your temper. Lilith will feed off of any negativity, however small, directed at her, and so will the others. Samuel to a lesser degree. Do not succumb to self-pity over your loss. It is sometimes the fate of the slave. Remember instead, what great favor and regard you have always been held in.

I often wonder how my own daughter, whose care I have entrusted you to, thrives? Have you found a more suitable name other than Lilith for her? Lilith has always been vain in passing on her name to her First Maidens. What must her life be like I often wonder, living as a human. It needs not reminding that you are not to breath a word of this to her.

It is not safe for you to write me, but you may freely write to the enclosed address. I don't believe it has been tainted yet. There is a master there that has been working with Samuel. His servant, Davon, will intercede all posts.

May you find comfort in your God.
Myrina

Sara's hands trembled as she read the letter. So Samuel was right, her parents were slaves of some sort, but from where? And she was obviously this woman's daughter. There was a subtle tone about the letter, an edge to her words that hinted at the fact that she might be a cruel and cold person. The oldest girl's name was Lilith. Sara wondered why her name was such a secret. It was Sara's name as well… Lilith. Sara tried to make sense of the letter. Her heart crashed in her chest as the strange words echoed in her mind. What had this woman meant when she had written, *'What must her life be like I often wonder, living as a human?'* She forced herself to push the turmoil of thoughts from her mind, focusing on the papers in her hand. The third page held the address for the contact. It was in the state of Louisiana, in Appaluses. She would look that up later. Carefully folding the papers back into their familiar creases, she began to replace them in the envelope. The author of the letter had dated it June 30th, 1984, but it was postmarked on August 27th. Sara held the papers in her hand, thinking about what that meant. Were the children meant to arrive earlier? Unsure, she slipped the remaining bit of paper back in the envelope and replaced all before returning to the kitchen where she found Samuel waiting.

"I found the letter that we initially received before your arrival," Sara whispered. Samuel nodded, his face set in that odd, immobile way that made it hard for Sara to know what he might be feeling. "I think we should talk about it later when we go walking and there is more privacy," she continued. "One thing I noticed, though, is that the letter was dated in June but it was sent toward the end of August. I think all of you were supposed to arrive here sooner than you did." Samuel straightened his posture. He did not say anything for a good minute as he thought.

"It is what I suspected. There has been some deception," he finally remarked. "You are right though; let us discuss what you have discovered later. I am not trusting of the others." Without another word, he went upstairs to his bedroom, leaving Sara to contemplate her situation. She felt incredibly tired, and although she knew she ought to start on her schoolwork, she went to her room, falling on her bed. In moments she was asleep.

Chapter Sixteen

As River pulled his truck into Pono's driveway, Pono emerged with two girls. River frowned. He thought he had made it clear last night that he wanted to talk to Pono alone. Climbing from his truck, he walked over to meet the small group, clasping hands with Pono, who gestured with his head toward the girls.

"They know about that woman you were talking about."

River rolled his eyes, exasperated. He had expected more from Pono. "You've been telling people about this?" he asked.

"No dude, they approached me."

River glanced at the girls. One of them was local. Lean and wiry, there was attitude in every bit of her posture: the way she held her chin up in a masculine fashion, the glint of her dark, round eyes, and her stance with her legs spread apart. The other was pale skinned with bright red hair. She stared back at him uncertainly. Her hands were clasped together tightly and held in front of her as if she was waiting to be reprimanded. The two girls couldn't have been more different.

"Pono went told us how that White Lady be stalking you, brah," the local girl spoke up. "We know where she lives." The redhead was looking more uncomfortable.

"I don't think you should tell him where she lives. We don't know for sure it's the same person."

The local girl shot the redhead a look and the redhead was immediately quiet.

"You girls know her?" River asked, feeling aghast. Here was the first proof that he wasn't just imagining things.

"Yeah, we've been talking." Pono said. "My folks won't be home for another three hours if you want to come in. But I'm still not sure what you need me for. I thought the three of you could talk. By the way, this is Sunami and Jenny."

The small group stepped into Pono's home. It was a typical American family room with a plush brown sofa, two easy chairs, a coffee table and an entertainment center; the only thing that was different were the stacks of books everywhere. The bookshelves were overflowing; books crammed on top of books that lined the shelves. Pono led them up a flight of carpeted stairs to his bedroom. A single bed was pushed up against the northern wall of his room and directly across from it sat a desk with a grey computer. There were more books stacked everywhere. A poster of a man in a shiny Stars and Stripes leather outfit astride a dirt bike was tacked over Pono's bed.

"Evil Knievel!" Sunami said, her eyes lighting up. "Brah, that's bad." She turned to study the other poster next to it of Bruce Lee air bound, in mid kick. Sunami smiled in appreciation and then wandered over to Pono's desk.

"Brah, you get one PC?" She looked up at Pono reverently. Pono grinned.

"OK," River said, "it's agreed that Pono's room shreds. But we need to talk." He looked at Jenny. "How do you know this woman?"

Jenny frowned, not sure where to begin. The idea of bringing up Sara, her home and the fact that the woman lived at Sara's seemed unfair to her. She thought of her classmate approaching her earlier and wanting to confide in her. It was unusual.

The Visitors

River stared at Jenny, who didn't appear to want to speak. Feeling exasperated, he tried another tact. "I don't see how we're going to get anywhere if no one wants to talk," he said.

Pono sat at his desk and grabbed a sheet of paper and a pencil from a side drawer. The other three came to stand around him.

"This is what we know so far," Pono said. He wrote on the paper in neat capital letters, underlining the heading for emphasis.

RIVER'S EXPERIENCE

A. For the past week, spotted unnaturally white woman lurking around his place.
B. Twice woke up to woman looking in on him through bedroom window.
C. While out hiking, encountered strange woman. (River grimaced, reading the lie: "while out hiking.")
D. When touching woman there was an odd sensation of touching nothing

"Right?" Pono asked looking up.

"Serious, you went touch her?" Sunami asked.

"That was the same feeling I got when I touched Sara!" Jenny exclaimed. Both girls had spoken at once and Jenny clamped her mouth shut as soon as the words came out.

"Who's Sara?" River asked.

Jenny lips tightened.

"You never told me Sara feel like air," Sunami remarked accusatively. She turned to Pono, "Put this down."

Pono made another heading.

SUNAMI AND JENNY'S EXPERIENCE

"Sara looks like a ghost in the mirror and she feel like one too."

"Who is Sara?" River asked again.

"She's the cousin to the White Lady, but I no think they is blood related. I no think the White Lady is like peoples."

River was quiet, turning over this information in his head.

"Is Sara like a person?"

"Yeah brah, me and Pono been knowing Sara since we was in kindergarten."

"Animals are afraid of her," Jenny added.

Pono wrote it down, waiting.

River felt the hair rise on the back of his neck.

"What does Sara look like?" River asked.

Sunami shrugged, but Jenny spoke up. "She has dark skin, but I don't think she's Hawaiian. I'm not sure what her race is. She's kind of tall and thin with long, sort of wavy, curly hair."

"What happens when she's around animals?"

"They go berserk," Sunami said, eyeing him. It did not slip her notice that his face had gone ashen, a shocked look descending upon his features. "Why? You know her?" Sunami asked, looking at him.

"No, not really, but I think I just met her today on my way over here." He recounted the dog incident. The girls nodded as he spoke. Pono looked stunned.

"For real?" Pono exclaimed after River was done talking. "This kind of thing happens every time she gets around animals?"

Sunami launched into her horse story and told them about Blackie. Pono wrote all this down, furiously scribbling. When Sunami was done, Pono sat back.

"Wicked," he said, exhaling in disbelief. The four of them stared down at the paper.

"Put down that she's stalking Mele too," Sunami added.

"Who's Mele?" River asked.

"Her cousin," Jenny said. "Oh, and there was that bit about your uncle and the book." Pono waited, pencil poised.

Sunami recounted the incident about the book and the picture of the women that looked similar to the White Lady. Again they were silent, each rereading what was written.

"What do you think it means?" River said aloud to no one in particular.

"Well," Pono began, "the White Lady sounds like a classic vampire, except vampires don't exist."

"How you know they no exist?" Sunami asked.

Pono laughed. "They're mythical beings. Of course they don't exist. Besides, if I didn't know Sara my whole life, I would say she sounded like a ghost, but we all know she's not. I'm sure there's some explanation for what you saw in the mirror. Um, the light could have been coming at a funny angle and given the illusion of her being transparent. Besides, you both told me that she couldn't see what you were seeing."

Sunami jabbed her finger at the paper on his desk.

"Pono, you goin try to explain away all these strange things?"

"It is strange." He shrugged. "But there is probably an explanation…"

"Pono!" Sunami snapped. "You believe in Night Marchers!" she yelled. "We saw them together, brah. You remember dat one, eh buggah?"

Pono's face reddened. "That's different," he said.

"How so?" Sunami asked, tilting her head, her hands on her hips as she stared down at him. "Night Marchers is ghostly warriors. If Night Marchers exist, why not vampiahs? And just because we been knowen Sara since kindergarten, don't mean nothin," Sunami jabbed at the paper, reiterating her point.

Pono held up his hands to stop the onslaught of her temper. "Okay, what do you want me to do?"

"We came to you because you is some smart, Pono. I no have good feeling bout this situation. Try help us." Sunami lowered her voice as Pono stared up at her. "Physics, supernatural, what eva. Dis stuffs no make sense right?" she asked, pointing at the paper.

Pono nodded.

"Use what eva you got. The White Lady, she sound like one vampiah, you say, maybe she is. Think about it. She's unnatural white, she's spooky, when River went touch her, he no feel nothin, and she is stalken peoples, she's stalken Mele, my baby cousin."

Pono steepled his fingers together. There was a long silence. Finally he spoke, as if resigned. "I'll see what I can look up."

Sunami slapped him on the back and turned to Jenny. "If we cuts school tomorrow, we can go by my uncle's house and get the book. River, you can pick us up?"

River looked startled at this suggestion. "Hey look, you girls are underage. You're talking about me picking up underage girls in the middle of school and breaking into a house. I could go to jail for that in a heartbeat. Have you noticed? I'm *haole*."

Sunami grinned at his answer.

"Besides, Sunami," Jenny added, "my mom would notice if I cut school. She's my teacher for last period."

"For real?" Sunami said, looking stymied for once.

"I'll go with you," Pono volunteered. "If we get busted, I'll probably just get one lecture."

"Okay, so we get one plan," Sunami said, grinding her fist into the palm of her hand.

River leaned over the paper on Pono's desk, reading it again, his brow furrowed in thought.

"What about that White Lady myth that you guys have here in Hawaii? Something about a woman hitchhiker? If you pick her up, sometimes she disappears?"

The Visitors

Pono shook his head. "No, that story about the disappearing White Lady is pretty tame next to what you guys are talking about. This woman kind of sounds like the White Lady ghost that preys on men and children. It's a common ghost story that has a lot of the same facts and is told not just in this country but other countries. For example, she appears usually out in rural areas and she stalks people to get revenge. The only thing, though, is that she's always seen at night and no one has ever spoken with her or found her living in a house as a person, like how this woman is living at Sara's."

Sunami nodded. "That's why I think she is one vampiah."

"But don't vampires have to stay out of the sunlight?" Jenny asked.

Pono rubbed at his cheek, thinking. "Yeah, you're right. I'll do some reading, see what I can come up with."

"Or maybe she's not supernatural like Pono was suggesting earlier." River glanced at Sunami, but she appeared distracted and didn't respond. The conversation was making him feel increasingly jittery and he wondered if it had been a mistake to make such a big deal out of his experience. It was possible when he touched the strange woman that he had been so jacked up on adrenaline that he thought he couldn't feel her at first. Now as he stood in the room of his friend's kid brother with two young high school girls, talking about ghosts and vampires, he was beginning to feel a little foolish.

"So what kine grinds you get here, Pono?" Sunami asked.

"All kines," Pono replied with a shrug. "We get fried chicken, rice," he stood up, leading the small group out of his room.

"None for me, man," River said as they filed down the stairs. "I'm vegetarian."

"Vegetarian," Sunami said, "So what? You only eats nuts and salad like?"

River laughed. "Something like that," he replied.

Sunami made a face at Jenny and rolled her eyes, but she kept her opinion on the subject to herself.

Chapter Seventeen

It was not quite night when Sara awoke. Shadows lengthened across her room and there was an empty stillness that filled the house like an entity; the absence of Maman's bustling movements was starkly noticeable. Regular routines had ceased to exist the last few days. Her head felt heavy and thick and she noticed that her pillow was wet from drool. A low moan emerged eerily out of the silence, followed by rapid panting. It was Lilith. Sara closed her eyes; she could almost feel her agony.

"Sara," she heard the young woman cry. Sara sat up but immediately lay back when her head began to throb. Was she getting sick as well?

"Sara…"

Again there was the same pitiful voice. Sara forced herself to sit up and then she stood. The room seemed to sway. She steadied herself, placing her hand on her bed. Gradually the dizziness subsided but her head was still heavy and wooden feeling. She found she could keep her footing by moving very slowly. She walked out to the hallway. Samuel, Carmilla and Michael were standing at the edge of the stairs looking up, but turned to stare at Sara when she emerged from her room.

The Visitors

"She is asking for you," Carmilla said. All three were quiet, their pale faces almost glowing in the dark hall. Sara did not want to go up alone, but she did not want either of them to go with her. All of them terrified her to a certain extent.

"She will be okay," Sara said. Again the moans started. Sara could almost feel that awful, excruciating, burning pain, a pain that squeezed and ripped at the insides.

"Sara," Lilith called.

"You must go to her," Michael said, his face expressionless. Sara walked toward the three and they parted to let her go by. Grabbing the banister, Sara walked slowly up the steps; all the while, Lilith's moans grew louder. Once she was at the top of the stairs, she swallowed and made her way to the girl's bedroom. It was dim in the room and Lilith lay beneath the covers, her arms thrown over her head. Sara lit the propane lamp. A golden glow of light illuminated the room. What she saw took her breath away. There the older girl lay with color in her cheeks, lips red and plump; she looked like a young woman, a real woman. Her face moved naturally, although still flushed with fever, and her green eyes were glazed and glassy.

"Sara," she called, holding out her hand. Sara hurried over to her. Lilith's skin was moist with sweat, her dark curls clinging to her forehead.

"Don't let them hurt me," she cried.

"Who?" Sara asked. Lilith did not respond, suddenly taken over with a fit of violent coughing. Her body began to spasm.

"Sh, sh," Sara ran her hand gently over the young woman's hot forehead in an effort to sooth.

"I won't let anyone hurt you," she whispered.

"They will," Lilith rasped. "They will kill me. The gypsies."

"Maman and Papa would never do that," Sara said, taken aback at Lilith's words.

"Please help me, Sara," she whispered, closing her eyes. Sara started when she heard footsteps behind her. Whipping around, she saw Samuel standing in the doorway with a glass of the medicine.

"She needs to have more of this. There are only a handful of days left before she transforms."

Lilith gave a sudden gasp, her body arched and her eyes flew open. It was awful to watch and Sara tried to calm her. Of its own accord her body relaxed and she lay staring up at Sara, her mouth open as she panted, her chest rising and falling rapidly. The fetid odor of her breath filled the room.

"Give her the medicine," Samuel said, "It will help break the fever."

Sara took a spoonful of the medicine and carefully ladled it into Lilith's mouth. It was swallowed and followed by another. Sara kept feeding her until half the contents of the glass was gone. Lilith closed her eyes again. Sara watched her fall into a deep sleep, amazed at how human she looked. Her dark lashes seemed to have thickened and lay against her flushed cheeks. Her lips were slightly parted and a thin whistle of air came through her open mouth. Her face gleamed with moisture and her hair was a dark canopy all around her. She was the most beautiful thing Sara had ever seen. Here she was helpless, begging Sara to protect her, yet only the other day she had been so menacing and alien.

"Come, it's growing dark and there is much to talk about. We must leave before Annette comes up the hill and finds some chore for you to do. She cannot bear to be alone with us anymore," Samuel said. Sara stood up and again had to wait a moment to steady herself as the room began to sway.

This did not escape Samuel's observation. "The headache will clear soon," he said. "It is the result of going into the room of a slave. They, all of them, carry the stones that keep us at bay."

Stones? Suddenly too nauseated to talk, it was all she could do to follow Samuel back down the stairs.

The Visitors

Maman had not returned yet and Sara did not think she would come back for quite a while. The two stepped outside. The air felt refreshing after being in the stagnant environment of the house. It was getting darker earlier, she noticed, as they walked toward the road. Samuel stooped to pick up a rock that he examined for a moment in his long fingers. It was a porous stone and he seemed fascinated by it.

"It is interesting the story nature tells through objects left behind from long ago events." He tossed the stone and turned to look at Sara. "What did you discover?"

Sara thought of the old photo and the letter and took a minute to compose her thoughts.

"I found a picture of Maman and Papa. They were with three girls that looked like their daughters. I am almost sure that they were." Sara looked at Samuel, and while he seemed interested in this bit of information, it did not seem to spark any memory for him. "The letter was written by a woman who seemed to know you. She mentioned something about a plan that went wrong. She is also, I found out, my mother, and is hiding me here."

Samuel nodded. "I thought as much; that someone was hiding you. It is your mother, though?" His brow furrowed. "I did not know that any of the servants had this sort of feeling. Many, many years ago, yes, there were definite attempts to escape and contempt was to be expected. However, I digress. You say she knows me?"

"Yes," Sara swallowed. "She also seemed...she said she regretted having to send the eldest girl, who she calls Lilith." Samuel stopped walking and he turned to stare at Sara, his face awash in disbelief.

"Lilith?" His blue eyes rolled up to the sky, which was nearly dark now. "You must be mistaken," he whispered.

"No. Her name is Lilith and it was my name too, until Maman changed it."

Samuel's hand came slowly to his chest. He stood for a long time like that, not moving. Sara waited. "Who was the author of the letter?" he finally asked.

"Myrina. I think that's how you say her name."

"Myrina," he whispered. "So you are Myrina's daughter, a servant of the first line. *She* was right, *She* knew." He did not say anymore, only continued to walk. Minutes later they reached a muddy, narrow path that led down to several natural pools. The bushes and stones stood out like greyish clumps in the rapidly growing darkness.

"Here, take my hand," Samuel offered. Sara placed her hand in his, used to the momentary absence of feeling. He clasped his fingers around hers firmly, leading her down the path with sure movements, undeterred by the absence of light.

"Watch, there is a large root just there." He guided her off to the side and back onto the path. The sound of rushing water spilling over the cliff filled her ears and the cool air that gathered off the pools swept over her skin, raising goose bumps. Once they emerged from the trees, the pools became visible. Large, flat stones enclosed the inky depths of the water below. Samuel continued to hold her hand until they were standing over the swimming holes. Sitting down on a cold, damp rock, they watched the rippling darkness below them.

"Do you remember your illness much?" Samuel asked. Sara hugged herself. A disturbing thought had been niggling at the back of her mind.

"Please don't tell me," she whispered. "I don't want to know."

Samuel turned to look at her. "It is not necessary that I tell you. I can see you understand."

Sara felt her chest grow heavy as tears filled her eyes and spilled down her cheeks. She wiped at them but they kept coming. "I died last year, didn't I?" She could barely speak the words.

The Visitors

"Yes. A part of you no longer exists." He placed his hand on her shoulder as her body convulsed with grief and terror.

"It is a shock, but you will eventually grow used to the idea."

Sara pulled herself away, hearing the indifference in his voice. He sighed, staring at the pools below them. "There is a perceived separation, Sara. For instance it seems that you and I and the rocks we sit upon are three different entities. Is this not so?"

Sara pulled her knees up to her chest. She didn't want to answer.

He interlaced his fingers. "Dimensions overlap and weave together. A human spirit experiences life on earth and for a time only knows the three dimensional world. The spirit forgets what it is and enters a dreamlike state, which is what life is here. Humans are ghosts embodied. When the body matter dies, than the spirit is free. A spirit that is too attached to this dimensional existence experiences amnesia of the true physical and becomes just a ghost without the flesh suit of the body. Further lessons cease because the essence takes on the shadow self. This type of amnesia can persist indefinitely." Samuel held out his hand. "Take it," he said.

Sara reached for his hand, waiting for the moment to actually feel it.

"Why is there this odd sensation, you've been wondering? For reasons I cannot explain, I reside in overlapping dimensions and so do you, to a lesser degree. There is my human spirit and there is the other." He was quiet for a while letting his words sink in. "You have seen how Lilith has changed. Now human-like, a body suddenly flush with color. It is not Lilith but the human who once was. Soon the old personality will begin to emerge. The spirit is unconscious, in a dormant state, but for a brief while it wakens and overpowers the other. You will see."

Sara stood up, the seat of her dress damp and clinging to her skin. "I don't want to hear anymore. Just please stop talking." She stared down at Samuel, the cold creeping into her flesh. "You wanted to know what I found? That woman who is supposed to be my mother left another address for Papa to write to. I can get the address for you, but I don't want to talk about any of this anymore, do you understand? I wish to God that all of you were gone." As Sara's voice rose, her breath became more labored and her throat constricted, cutting off further speech. Samuel stood up and grabbed her shoulders with a strength that startled her.

"I cannot begin to explain the danger that all of us are in when Lilith goes through her complete transformation. Yet she must be kept safe." His voice was quiet and steely, catching Sara's attention.

"What kind of danger?" she whispered. Samuel's face settled into that odd expressionless mask.

"I hesitate to make clear what is in store to a servant with no training, no experience; a servant that should be hardened by now to certain realities. It is not wise to stand out here in the night, frightening you. If you had been raised properly, you could take what may come in stride, but you have been raised as a human child. Yet you are not, you belong to us." Sara shivered. "This is as much as you should know. Tomorrow, you will go back into Annette and Louis's room and copy down the address for the contact. I will compose a letter and you will go to the post office and have it sent special delivery. We are running out of time."

Sara shook her head, feeling the flow of blood begin to constrict in her arm as he still held her in his iron grip

"Special delivery?" she echoed.

"Yes, it must be sent by the quickest route."

"Sometimes Papa sends things through express mail."

"Is that what it's called today?" Samuel asked. He finally let go of her arm and she rubbed at it, trying to regain feeling. Without further discussion, the two of them made their way back to the house. When they arrived at the entrance of the driveway, Sara spotted her parents walking up the hill from the stable. Papa had his arm around

The Visitors

her mother, whose shoulders were rounded, her head bent down. Neither of them noticed Sara and Samuel as they entered the front door.

Angela frowned at the meatloaf in the oven before reaching in with her hot mitts and pulling the pan out. It was getting late, and although Jenny had called earlier to say she was at a friend's, it would soon be 8:00 and she still wasn't home. Angela had taken down the phone number and knew she could call, but she didn't want to appear over protective.

"Smells delicious," Tim said, walking into the kitchen. The theme song for his favorite show Cheers, rang out from the living room.

Yesterday had been the beginning of first attempts at conciliatory conversation between them. Tim pulled two wine glasses from the cabinet and placed them on the counter before pulling a bottle of Pinot Noir from the small wine rack that they kept on the kitchen counter and filling each glass. He smiled and handed Angela a glass before lifting the lid of the pot on the stove and looking appreciatively at the mashed potatoes: creamy and fluffy just how he liked them. "Looks great."

Angela took a sip of her wine and watched her husband grab two of the folding tables, carrying them to the living room. Coming back, he looked at his wife, who leaned against the sink, cradling her glass, her brow furrowed.

"Something bothering you?"

Angela shrugged. "It's just getting late. I thought Jenny would be home by now."

"Well you have the phone number, just give her a call and tell her to come home, if it's worrying you." Angela took a deeper drink of wine, before setting it on the counter.

"I know I can call her, but I don't want her to think I'm trying to squelch her newfound independence. It's just that when I talked to Jenny, she didn't seem like herself." Angela waved her hand as if to sweep away her words, feeling awkward.

Tim sighed, reaching out to give her shoulder a reassuring squeeze.

"Look, it's great that she's finally making some friends. You were worried about her not having friends and being bullied. Now she's taken the reins of her social life and she's out there."

Just as Tim finished his sentence, they heard the sound of a vehicle pulling into the driveway. Tim lifted his eyebrows and a wave of relief washed over Angela as the sound of her daughter's voice carried through the stillness. Angela brushed past her husband and went to stand on the porch, shielding her eyes from the glare of headlights. A young man stepped out of the driver's side to come around to where Jenny stood.

"Don't worry about it," he said, lifting her door and pushing it closed. "It's kind of tricky."

"Hey mom," Jenny called as she began walking to the porch. The young man turned and, seeing Angela, waved before getting back in his truck and pulling out of the driveway.

"Hi Sweetie. Who was that?"

"Oh, that's River. He gave me a ride home."

"I can see that," Angela said, her stomach knotting up.

"Jenny, I thought you said you were at a girlfriend's?"

"I never said that," Jenny said, looking taken aback. Tim had come to stand in the doorway and Angela could see that their daughter coming home with a young man was not sitting well with him either.

"Why don't you two come on into the house," he said. Jenny shifted her backpack, brushing her bangs from her face, and followed her mother into the living room. She watched as her father went to turn off the TV before focusing on her.

The Visitors

"Jenny," his voice had deepened to a tone he used when Jenny knew he wasn't pleased. "What was that man doing riding you around in his truck? And what do you mean? You weren't at a girlfriend's? Whose house were you at?" Jenny looked at both her parents' worried faces and she finally understood.

"Oh no, I wasn't hanging out with River, well I was… kind of, but we were all at this boy Pono's house. Pono is a friend of Sunami's"

"Sunami?" Angela echoed. "Honey, I'm not so sure how I feel about you hanging around with her. Isn't she one of the main kids that's been giving you a hard time at school?"

"She's not so bad," Jenny said quietly. She looked to her father. His brow was creased, his mouth turned down hard.

"Were Pono's parents home?" he asked.

"It's not like that, dad. We're just friends. River is actually a friend of Pono's older brother. That's why he was there." Jenny felt her face redden at this partial truth. "River lives here in the valley and Sunami stays here a lot at her uncle and aunt's house, so he gave us a ride home. He dropped Sunami off first because her place is before ours, and that was all."

"Look, Jenny, I want you to have friends," Angela began, "but I'm not feeling comfortable about this group that you're getting in with. These kids make a lot of trouble at school. Who knows what goes on in their family life?"

"Mom, you don't even know Pono." Jenny could feel her voice rising.

"Your mother's right," Tim interrupted. "We want you to have friends, but I don't like the idea of you hanging around with some of these rough locals and that hippie who brought you home in his truck. I'm sure there are some very nice kids at school that you can meet."

"Oh you're so full of yourself!" Jenny found herself yelling at her father. "You think you know everything. You never wait to hear what anybody has to say before telling people what they should and shouldn't do."

"You stop right there, young lady," her father said, taking a step toward her, his face flushed with anger.

"No, I won't stop! I don't even know why we are still living in someone else's house. This isn't our place and you know it!"

Tim raised his hand and struck his daughter's red face.

"Tim!" Angela cried, watching in dismay as Jenny's cheek turned white from the imprint of her father's hand and then blotchy as it began to welt. Tears gathered in Jenny's eyes and Tim lowered his hand, looking stunned at what he had just done.

"You are exactly the kind of *haole* that has the locals so angry, and then I have to suffer for it." Jenny could barely speak; her throat felt like it had closed up on her and her words came out in breathy whispers, as tears dampened her face.

"Jenny, please," Angela said, but Jenny ran to her room, slamming the door behind her. Tim stared down at his hands and then looked up at his wife.

"That's it," he said quietly, "She is not allowed to hang out with those kids anymore. They are filling her head with nonsense." Angela shook her head and walked away, leaving Tim standing alone. Shame and despair washed over him and for the first time, doubt crept into his mind.

Jenny threw her backpack down and began to pace. Catching her reflection in the mirror, she stared at her swelling cheek and touched it gingerly. It was awful, this fight she had had with her father. Why couldn't she have controlled her temper? This was not a good time for her parents to forbid her from seeing Sunami. Every fiber in her body told her that Sara was in some kind of danger but she couldn't figure it out. While in the moment, Sunami's argument that the White Lady might be a vampire seemed convincing, now as she thought about it, it seemed ridiculous. Pono was right; there had

The Visitors

to be a logical explanation. Breaking into Sunami's uncle's house to steal a book that had pictures of women that might look like Sara's cousin didn't seem the best plan either. She sat on her bed and then laid back, thinking over the list Pono had made and Sara's eerie reflection in her mirror. Closing her eyes, her mind reeled with the conversations and events of the day. Minutes later, Jenny's breathing became even as she dropped off into sleep.

Something brushed her face and Jenny found herself waking up to a dark room and a light blanket that had been thrown over her. There was a soft glow of light by her door, as if it were glowing from within. Jenny rubbed her eyes and sat up, peering at the light that now appeared to be arranging itself into some kind of form. There were the beginning outlines of a woman and Jenny gazed harder, trying to make out what she was seeing. It was an older woman. She was standing where the door should have been. Her face was sad and she beckoned for Jenny to come to her. Jenny stood up, unafraid, and felt as if she glided to the woman. They were suddenly out of doors and she blinked in astonishment. It was daytime. Local people were about in the yard, laughing and talking, part of a gathering of some sort, and then there was a shriek, so piercing that the sound sliced through the conversations and bantering, rendering a sudden silence. A few men ran off in the direction of the cry, followed by some of the women. Jenny found herself gliding after the others, the older woman just ahead, beckoning.

A woman was kneeling on the ground. She was cradling something, her face contorted in grief as she rocked back and forth.

"She fell from the tree," a boy was saying. Jenny felt herself zoom down as if in one great whoosh. The woman was holding a girl whose neck was at an odd angle, blood gathered at her nose, her eyes open and vacant as her young body spasmed in the woman's arms.

"Mele!" the woman cried. The men stood silently. Some of the women came to kneel by the woman, their crying intermingling with the mother of the girl. Jenny felt herself gliding away. Always ahead, the older woman waved her arms as if continually gathering an invisible substance. There was the red house and the pit bulls tied to their various posts. The dogs stirred as Jenny glided past them. One of them awoke and began to growl. But she floated into the home, into a bedroom where a small girl lay in bed, tucked protectively into the curve of an older girl, the two deep in sleep. Jenny recognized them. It was Sunami and Mele. The dogs began to bark and a man yelled out for them to quiet. Faintly Jenny could still hear the women crying. Again she was gliding away, and now she made her way to Sara's. This time she fought the forward momentum of her astral travel with all of her will. It made no difference. The familiar driveway loomed up before her, and the brown house now looked sinister. Jenny fought harder as she floated into the house and up a set of stairs. There sat Sara next to a young woman, applying something to the woman's head. The woman was asleep. The odd force that pulled Jenny into the bedroom pushed her closer. Sara looked up in surprise.

"Jenny?"

"Jenny, it's time to get up for school." Her mother was shaking her. The girl nodded, turning on her side, pulling her body away, hoping the shaking would stop.

Dogs barked in the distance.

"Ey, quiet!" a man yelled.

Light flooded her room before her mother stepped out. It penetrated through her closed lids and she rubbed at them, grimacing when her hand came into contact with her cheek. The smell of oatmeal and coffee wafted into her room. Jenny heaved herself up and with lumbering steps, walked to her bedroom door, grabbing the knob. It was ice cold. She pulled her hand back in surprise, the shock instantly dissipating the last dredges of sleep.

"Was the air conditioner on last night?" Jenny heard her mother ask.

The Visitors

"No," her father said.

"The knob to Jenny's door was unusually cold." There was no response from her father. "Tim, you should apologize."

"I don't think so."

Jenny listened to the sounds of her parents moving about in the kitchen. She could hear her father's footsteps retreating, the front door opening and closing behind him. Feeling relieved that he was gone she stepped from her room, again surprised that her doorknob felt like it had been in a deep freeze. Curious, Jenny touched the rest of her door; it felt as cold as the knob.

So strange, she thought to herself before stepping out of her room. After a quick shower, she brushed her teeth and returned to her bedroom to put on fresh clothes. When she finally came into the kitchen, Jenny found her mother sitting at the table, drinking a cup of coffee and staring off at nothing. She did not even look in Jenny's direction or say "good morning" with her usual bright, energetic smile. Jenny pulled out a bowl from the cabinet and began to spoon some oatmeal into it.

"The milk is over here on the table," Angela said.

"Oh," Jenny turned to face her mom; their eyes met for just a moment, and then Angela looked away.

"I shouldn't have said those things last night," Jenny said, bringing her bowl to the table. She sat down, searching her mother's face. Fine lines had crept around her mouth and her eyes were ringed and hollowed. Jenny watched her mother's lips tighten before she spoke.

"No, you shouldn't have," Angela agreed. "Today, I'm going to take you home after school and when your father gets home, we are all going to sit down and talk with each other."

"OK," Jenny agreed, pouring milk over her oatmeal and watching the sugar and butter dissolve. It hurt to have her mother this angry with her and to see her so unhappy. Jenny wanted to get up and walk over to her mom and tell her she was sorry and that she loved her, to give her a hug, but she felt rooted to her seat. A lump formed in her throat as she stirred her cereal.

"It's getting late. You'll need to hurry with that if you're going to make the bus. I don't want to have to ride into school early."

Jenny nodded, taking a bite of her cereal, the warm sweetness filling her mouth, gliding easily down her throat when she swallowed. She did not look up when she heard her mother's chair scrape against the floor as she stood up, leaving the room.

Chapter Eighteen

Sara stumbled from her father's truck, rubbing her eyes. She longed to crawl into bed and go back to sleep. Most of the night she'd spent tending to Lilith. Samuel had helped some as well, but whenever Sara left the room, Lilith cried out for her pitifully. Maman would not go near the young woman. In fact, her contact with the children had become almost nonexistent. Household routines seemed to have evaporated overnight. There was no particular time for meals, and lately it was just Sara and Papa in the kitchen preparing food. Papa would bring Maman's food down to the stable where she presided more and more when she wasn't gardening, washing clothes or tending the cows. Samuel prepared the medicine now. Carmilla and Michael still spent all of their time in the living room consumed with their hobbies. Sometimes Sara would hear them talking quietly to each other in another tongue that was foreign to her. When Sara asked Samuel what language they were speaking, he made a circular motion with his hand.

"They are speaking many different languages, mostly they are communicating in Vlaheste, an ancient Vlach language of Eastern Europe."

In the morning, Sara had left two pillowcases stuffed with sheets and night-clothes of Lilith's for Maman to wash and hang out to dry. Twice Sara had needed to change Lilith's bedclothes and once her sheets. The second set she had lined with a few towels to soak up the sour smelling perspiration that came in waves. At least it had cooled her body down and allowed the young woman to sleep for thirty to sixty minutes at a time.

It was in the dark of morning that Sara had seen Jenny. She had sat cooling Lilith's face with a damp cloth, trying to bring down another bout of heat that had seized the woman's body. Stretching her limbs out stiffly, Lilith's mouth had opened as she gasped for air. It had been just a moment that Jenny had stood before them.

"Jenny?" Sara had called, feeling half out of her mind with fatigue and wondering vaguely what Jenny was doing in their room. A shadow had passed, blocking her line of vision and then there had been nothing there. The next thing Sara knew, she had awakened with a start in the chair next to Lilith's bed. It had been quiet except for the clicking of the coconut fronds outside, stirred by a light breeze. Lilith lay sleeping, her breathing even. Stiffly, Sara stood up. Grabbing one of the tapered candles, she lit it and walked to Lilith's gas lamp, turning it off. *Carmilla must have gone to sleep in the boys' room,* Sara thought as she descended the stairs and lit the kitchen light. The small clock on the kitchen counter read 5:30am. Morning had come and Sara doubted whether she slept more than two hours the entire night.

Now here she was at school, expected to stay awake through seven classes. Kids walked up and down the halls, milling about the quad, talking, laughing and yelling. Sara's head throbbed and she made her way to the cafeteria, hoping to get a cup of coffee. There was still fifteen minutes before the first bell. Opening one of the double doors, she was surprised to see Jenny standing there about to walk out. For a moment they both stood staring at each other.

The Visitors

"I—" Jenny began. "You wanted to talk with me yesterday. I can talk now, if you like." Sara nodded.

"Let's sit down," Jenny suggested after Sara had poured herself a cup of coffee. The girls walked to an empty table next to the drama arts stage.

Sara opened her backpack, pulling out the drawing that Michael had made.

"My cousin drew this," she said holding out the drawing.

"Wow, this is amazing." Jenny replied, studying the picture. "Your cousin made this?"

"Yes," Sara took a sip of coffee while watching Jenny's face. She didn't look like she'd slept much either. Her eyes were slightly puckered.

"Which cousin drew it?"

"Michael, he draws all the time."

"The oldest boy?"

"No, the younger one." Jenny looked up then, and Sara could see that her answer was disturbing. She knew that Jenny had noticed when she had stopped by on Saturday that the children were different, bigger.

"Michael says the woman in the drawing is from a band of people called Night Hunters. I was wondering if you had time, could you maybe look up that name in the public library? I'll never get a chance to go there and I was curious. You could hold on to the picture if you like."

"Yes, of course," Jenny readily agreed, carefully slipping the drawing into one of her textbooks.

"I would also like to ask you one more favor. There will be a letter that I will need to express mail. I don't really have money, but later, maybe in a few weeks I could pay you back. It's urgent. Otherwise, I wouldn't ask." Sara could feel her face grow warm at this last request. Jenny was nodding yes, though, and didn't seem at all put off.

"Sure, I can do it."

Sara took another sip of coffee and said nothing more. She desperately wanted to ask Jenny about last night. It had seemed so real when she saw her standing in Lilith's room, yet she didn't want to alienate a burgeoning friend by asking eccentric questions. It was entirely possible that she'd been asleep and dreamt the whole thing.

"Today I have to go home after school, but tomorrow I'll go to the library."

"Thank you." Sara took another gulp of her coffee before the shrill sound of the bell cut through the loud noise of student chatter. Both girls stood up and walked out of the cafeteria together. Sara turned and gave a slight wave before heading off to her classroom. Jenny watched her walk across the field. *She looks more haggard than yesterday and thinner as well,* Jenny thought. Someone pushed up hard up against her, knocking her off balance. Jenny turned around to see Junior glowering down at her.

"Hey shithead, I saw you sneakin round my place this morning,"

She swallowed, stepping away from the boy. "I wasn't in your house."

"You callin me one liar? What you want with my little cousin Mele?"

"What?"

"Goin deaf, bitch? You and that other *haole* chick better stay away. You hear me?" He jabbed a thick finger into her chest and spat at her feet with a curled lip.

Jenny stood breathless as he swaggered to class. But it had just been a dream. How could he have seen her? When she looked up, she saw Sunami standing at a distance, an odd look on her face. Jenny braced herself as the girl walked over to her.

"Junior told me you went snuck in his house this morning."

Jenny shook her head. "No, I never went there."

Sunami studied her as if trying to decide something.

The Visitors

"I think it was that one cousin of Sara's," Sunami finally said. "Me and Pono is going to cut third period and go to Uncle Fess, find that one book."

An idea sprang to Jenny's mind and she pulled her backpack off her shoulder. "I want to show you something."

Sunami moved closer to see what Jenny was holding.

"Sara gave me this drawing this morning. She said her cousin Michael made it."

Sunami sucked in her breath, examining the drawing. "A kid went make this? Sis, that's bad."

Jenny felt her cheeks flush with pleasure at Sunami's referring to her as a sister. "She wanted me to go to the library and look up Night Hunter. This woman in the picture is called a Night Hunter."

Sunami was studying the drawing and she pointed at a second woman barely visible in the mist that shrouded the trees. "She's hunting her. You see that?" Jenny nodded. "Can I take this drawing? It look kinda like *da kine*."

"Like the drawings in the book?" There was the shrill ring of the second bell and both girls looked up, realizing they were standing alone. Jenny shoved the drawing into Sunami's hand.

"We're going to be late. Just give it back to me tomorrow."

"OK Sis." Sunami gave a lift of her chin and Jenny ran off in the direction of her classroom.

Chapter Nineteen

In town it was warm and sunny but as Pono and Sunami traveled farther east, the sky grew overcast. By the time they reached the town of Paia, rain began to hit the windshield. Pono turned on his wipers and turned up the music on his tape deck. "*I Shot the Sheriff*" blasted from the speakers. He hummed along to the Bob Marley tune. Sunami craned her neck to look at the ocean that zigzagged below them.

"Get six footers," she remarked, watching a few surfers paddle away from a mounting body of water. Pono slowed his truck and glanced appreciatively at the waves a few times. The rain came down harder and he increased the speed of his wipers. A moment later the rain stopped and clouds parted, exposing golden rays of light. A rainbow appeared, arching just ahead of them, and the two grinned at the beauty of it.

It was 10:30 am when they left school and they were able to make it to the valley by 11:15.

"We still get plenty time, brah," Sunami said as they turned onto the familiar dirt road. "Boda dem don't get home from the art gallery until 5:00." They followed the road until it came to a dead end.

The Visitors

There stood Uncle Fess and Uncle Manuel's house. It was a massive structure with white cement walls, a red tiled roof and arching doorways. The interior boasted marbled counters and floors, large picture windows and modern space-age looking furniture. *A home you would expect two mahos to live in,* Sunami thought to herself.

Pono parked the truck a little ways away and the two jumped out.

"They always leave the back open," she said.

Pono followed her lead as she opened a small gate and they entered a narrow passageway that wound around to a screened, sliding glass door. Pushing her face up to the glass, Sunami peered through the window. It was empty inside. Opening the sliding door they stepped into a house mildly warm from the muggy weather. Instinctively, they kicked off their slippers and stood barefoot on the cold marble floor.

"His study's dis way." Sunami turned left. Pono gaped at the various statues of Hawaiian warriors and oil paintings of ancient Hawaii. At the end of the hall, a door stood slightly ajar, and Sunami slowly pushed it open, poking her face in. Seeing no one, she opened the door wider, revealing a small study overrun with books and papers. A computer sat on a plain wood desk next to an electric typewriter. Immediately, she began searching around on the desk, her thin face tight with concentration.

"What's the book called?" Pono asked. Sunami looked up and smacked her forehead with the palm of her hand.

"Shit! I no remember." The two looked slowly around the room with dismay. It could take quite a while to look through all the many books. Then there was the fact that most of the books were in the art genre like the one that they were trying to find.

Pono sighed, picking up a small hardbound volume that sat atop a stack of ten other books and flipped through pictures of flowers and text. There were at least twenty piles of books just like this stack.

"OK, I'll look through the shelves since I'm taller," Pono said, "and you look through the piles." Sunami sat down in front of one of the piles and began searching. She remembered that it was a medium sized book with a rough greyish cover. It didn't have a jacket. She flipped quickly through the books, not seeing it, then moving on to the next pile.

"Ey Sis, try look in this one." Pono was staring into a cabinet. Sunami jumped up to see what he was looking at. There was a row of about six books, each bearing odd titles. The first read *Humans, Can We Survive Without Them?* Next to it was a slim volume called *Entering The True Physical.* There was a thicker book with swirly letters called *Daemons, faeries and vampyres.* A few had foreign titles, and then Sunami saw it: a greyish, plain looking volume, something that could have been easily overlooked if one hadn't known what one was looking for. Snatching the book down, her eyes widened when she opened it staring at the cover page: *Wolf Clan, A Brief History of The Night Hunter.*

"Jesus, Pono, try take a look at what dis says."

"I see it," he said under his breath.

Sunami reached into her back pocket and produced the drawing. Unfolding it, she handed it to Pono to hold and then flipped through the pages of the book. The artwork was gruesome and the two stood silently staring at pictures that Sunami had never dreamed a person would paint. The hunters were dark, muscled women with sharp knives, swords and hatchets, all tools they used to kill, destroy and dismember men and women that looked very similar to the cousins at Sara's house.

"Look," Pono said pointing to the signature of the artist on each of the pieces. It was a single M, like the M on the drawing that Pono held in his hand. There was no doubt about the similarities of the artwork. Pono felt his mouth go dry.

"Are you sure a kid drew this? Because this book," not finishing his sentence, he flipped to the opening pages and they both read:

The Visitors

First Printing, 1800. There was no copyright. Sunami could feel her heart knock against her chest. She could see they were onto something but she wasn't sure what exactly. They did not hear the footsteps that moved quietly on the marble floor until they heard the yell of Uncle Manuel. Sunami jumped, dropping the book.

Uncle Manuel stood shirtless, his large belly as hard and round as a *hapai* woman in her seventh month. His eyes bulged with rage and he gasped when he looked down and saw the book that Sunami had dropped.

"What are you doing here?" he yelled. "You come into my study, get into my private things!" In three strides he crossed the room, his olive complexion ruddy with blood that flooded his thick cheeks. Huffing, he bent over his enormous stomach and swooped the book up off the floor.

"You good for nothing thieves!" he screamed, shaking a fat finger in Sunami's face, which remained impassive, her dark eyes narrowing into slits.

"Uncle, we're sorry," Pono began but Sunami laid a slim hand on his arm and gave a gentle, but firm push back.

"Ey Uncle," she called. "Why you have dis book?" She jutted her chin at the book that he gripped tightly in his hand.

"It is none of your business what books I keep. Now get out of this house!"

"No!" Sunami said sharply, unimpressed when Uncle Manuel's eyes bulged even wider and looked like they might fall out of his head.

"Sunami, come on," Pono said quietly. "He's right. This is his home, we're wrong."

"That no matter. We is in some kine trouble and he get the answers."

Uncle Manuel's eyebrows pulled together as he listened. "Why are you here?"

"What kine people are those in that book, Uncle?" Sunami asked.

"Listen, girl," Uncle Manuel almost growled, "I think it is best you tell me why you are interested in snooping around my study. What are you hoping to find?"

Sunami pointed at the book and Uncle Manuel looked down at it, cradled protectively in his arm.

"Pono, give him dat drawing." Unsure, Uncle Manuel took the drawing from the boy's hand and glanced at it. His breath caught in his throat and his red face turned grey.

"Where did you get this?"

"That's the same artist, no?" Sunami asked.

"Yes," he whispered. "Who gave this to you?"

"First tell us what's in dat book."

Uncle Manuel glanced at Sunami's pinched face and shook his head. He looked as if he had seen a ghost. "I can't help you," he said quietly. "I simply can't. You must leave now."

"There are *haoles*, Uncle, not da normal kines but like the ones in the book, and they are living here on the ridge."

Uncle Manuel closed his eyes and beads of sweat began to form on his forehead and nose. "That's impossible," he said softly.

"Possible," Sunami said. "People is hidin tings, but I no get good feelin bout dis, Uncle. You know about these kine *haoles*? What kine people white like dat? What kine keikis grow inches in a week? And animals be spooked by dem." Uncle Manuel's breathing grew heavy as Sunami spoke and Pono, fearing that he might be having heart failure, rushed to his side.

"Uncle, you need water?" When Uncle Manuel didn't answer, Pono turned to Sunami. "He needs aspirin and water. I think he's having a heart attack." The older man waved Pono away and lumbered over to one of the sitting chairs in his study, collapsing into it. The chair creaked in protest under the bulk of his body as he stared up at Sunami in disbelief.

"How many are there?"

The Visitors

"I tink four, meybe."

Uncle Manuel rested his forehead in his hand.

"Dear God in Heaven," he mumbled.

Sunami bent down so that she sat on her knees in front of her uncle. "There is one, some spooky, she be stalking peoples. Dat hippie River, he went tole us bout her watchen him, and Mele. Mele says the White Lady is watchen her when she be in bed."

Uncle Manuel looked up sharply. "She must be removed immediately from that house. She and the man you talk about are in terrible danger. How long have they been here? When did they start to grow? I don't understand how you know them." Uncle Manuel looked from Sunami to Pono, but Pono only looked bewildered. Uncle Manuel looked back to Sunami; her face had hardened with determination.

"I no know, how dey get here but that girl Sara say's they are her cousins."

"Who is Sara?"

"She lives wid peoples dat looks like you, but she look like da kine in the book."

Uncle Manuel shook his head. "What kind?"

"Night Hunters, only she's skinny, not muscled up like those *wahines*."

"I need my cigarettes." He stood up and ran a meaty hand through his thick, wavy black hair and walked to the desk. Hands shaking, Uncle Manuel pulled a cigarette from a shiny box and tried to light a match, but the book fell from his fingers. Pono stepped forward, picking it up, and lit the cigarette for him. He took a long drag before holding the carton out to Sunami and Pono. "Smoke?"

Sunami took the cigarettes, pulled one out and lit hers from her uncle's. Pono shook his head no and Uncle Manuel threw the cigarettes back in the drawer.

"We are in trouble," he said through a haze of smoke, "this whole valley, possibly the island. I can't imagine…I thought I escaped."

"Escaped from what?" Pono asked. Uncle Manuel did not answer him. Instead he walked out of the room. Sunami sucked on her cigarette, watching Pono, who stared back at her, his expression a mixture of bafflement and unease.

"You guys are freaking me out," he finally said.

"And you was tinking there be some logical explanation," Sunami said mockingly, blowing out a great puff of smoke. "Explain dis. Can?" she challenged. Pono shook his head. She took another drag from her cigarette. Uncle Manuel came back into the room with a cordless phone to his ear.

"Just close the gallery and get over here," he was saying. He cradled the phone against his ear, listening. "No, no, Fester, listen to me, just get your ass over here. This is important, damn it!" He clicked off and stared coolly back at Sunami and Pono. "When Fester gets here, we are all going to sit down and talk and I want you both to tell me everything." Sunami shrugged, unfazed by his sudden change of tone.

"I'm not sure I want to be involved in this," Pono said.

"You are already involved," Uncle Manuel replied. "It can't hurt for you to wait a little until Fester gets here to talk with us."

"Fo' real," Sunami snapped at Pono. "So you goin to get all nerjus and pressure out on us, brah."

Pono's face twisted into a grimace and he reddened at her comment. Unsure of what to say, he said nothing.

"Have a seat," Uncle Manuel offered, "I'll get some cokes." He left the room again.

"You heard him say that we could be in danger," Pono said lamely.

"So you goin to chicken shit out on me? What about Mele? I got to move her like Uncle Manuel said."

"What can I do about that?"

Sunami flicked ash into an ashtray that sat on a little table. It consisted of a delicate woman's hand carved out of glass holding a small

The Visitors

cobalt blue dish in the center of the palm. She rolled her eyes, staring at the art piece.

"Look at this *mahu* shit," she said, her voice dripping with disdain. When she looked up, she found Pono was standing near a small easterly window looking out at a manicured side garden. "You tink I'm not afraid Pono?" she asked. His broad shoulders were slouched forward and he didn't respond. Sunami stubbed out her cigarette and let the subject drop. Pono could get stubborn, and one thing she remembered was that the more you pushed him to do something he didn't want to do, the more obstinate he became. *One thing is for sure,* Sunami thought to herself, *she had to convince Auntie Leilani and Uncle Keoni to let her have Mele for at least a few days, possibly longer.*

Chapter Twenty

Sara was relieved to see Papa's truck waiting for her at the top of the road. After explaining to her father about the dog incident yesterday afternoon he reassured her that he would begin picking her up at the top of the road rather than let her walk. Her father's cab smelled of a freshly smoked cigarette. Deep lines etched his forehead and his cheeks were taking on a gaunt look. There was no greeting between them as she climbed into the truck and they ambled down the road, her father carefully negotiating potholes.

"The oldest girl is feeling better," he said, breaking the silence between them. "She has been asking for you." Sara looked at her father but his eyes remained on the road. "She might confide in you Sara, or request favors of you, but it's best that you ignore her words. Come to me first if she asks you to help her in any way." Sara did not reply to her father's comment. For the first time she wondered to herself when it had happened that she had ceased to obey her parents.

"Sara," Papa was looking over at her now. She gritted her teeth and nodded consent. "The children can be very enticing when they like," he continued, "and they may tell you fantastic things." Sara could

The Visitors

not stand to listen to him anymore. She wished she could just place her hands over her ears and block out his lies. Did he think she was a small ignorant child that noticed nothing?

"I have a lot of homework to do today," she interrupted him. "I don't have time to sit and visit with people. I was up all night with the eldest girl."

Papa said nothing more. They rode the rest of the way home silently, the tension between them almost palpable.

Again Maman was nowhere in sight when they arrived home, but Sara was surprised to find Lilith up and sitting in the living room with the others, a shawl wrapped around her thin shoulders and a book in her lap. The fever had taken the little weight she once carried, and she appeared frail now, but there was still color in her skin. Next to the other children she looked like a normal person. When she saw Papa and Sara, she smiled prettily. Her incisors, Sara noticed, were slightly longer and more prominent than her other teeth. Papa did not smile back, but his words were cheerful enough.

"I see you're feeling better," he said.

Lilith held out her hand to Sara. "Come to me," she called, her voice full of affection, her pale green eyes alight with the joy of a young woman greeting a close friend. Sara felt her heart quicken with relief and happiness to see Lilith looking like this.

"Careful now," Papa said in a low voice. The others looked on with flat expressionless faces. Only Samuel frowned. Sara hurried over to Lilith to take her offered hand, the sensation of feeling nothing at first was still there, but a second later she felt the woman's hand warm in hers. Lilith's face glowed with pleasure and she stroked Sara's hair.

"My friend," she said softly and was suddenly taken over by a violent fit of coughing, her thin shoulders shaking. Sara pulled away slightly, the rotten smell of her breath repugnant. Lilith's grip tightened with a strength that Sara never guessed she possessed in her weakened state. "I would have you sit here with me awhile, my dear friend," she said after gaining control of her vocal chords.

"Sara has homework to do," Papa said. "Perhaps when she is finished the two of you can visit." Lilith's eyes grew wide and sad as her grip loosened on Sara's fingers.

"I should like to take a walk this evening and feel the fresh air."

"Are you well enough?" Sara asked.

"Just a short walk to build my strength. Will you accompany me, dear Sara?"

Sara nodded, wondering at Lilith's sudden strong affections, her strange intonations, and her switch to speaking English. She sounded like a character from a turn of the century American novel.

"OK, a short walk." Sara agreed.

Papa remained standing, watching them, and Sara realized that he would continue standing there until she left Lilith. She stood up and saw that in the brief moment of sitting at Lilith's feet, Michael had sketched the two of them. Carmilla stood up as well and walked to Lilith, her dark eyes almost glowing in her white face.

"Lilith," she whispered.

Papa's body grew tense at the mention of the young woman's name and his eyes darted to Sara. Carmilla's white hand caressed Lilith's hair and the young woman closed her eyes. Sara watched in disbelief as Carmilla knelt before Lilith and began to gently kiss her face with small delicate kisses.

"Carmilla!" Papa barked.

Carmilla stopped and smiled at Papa, her features gruesome to look at. A sensuous smile stretched across her white lips, while the rest of her face was paralyzed, her eyes grown quite large with excitement—a sort of bestiality lurking in their depths. Her excitement was catching, for Samuel and Michael now had the same look.

The Visitors

Papa's voice rang out, steady and neutral, but Sara could hear the warning tones.

"Sara, go do your homework. Lilith, you will do best to get more rest, undisturbed in your bed. Sara will take you out for a walk later this evening."

Talk of the mundane seemed to diffuse the tension that had built up in the room. Papa strode over toward Lilith and helped her up, walking her out of the room. Sara followed, again feeling as if she had just escaped danger, the odd scene playing over and over in her mind as she made her way to her room. The doorknob had been replaced on her door. This one had a lock.

"He has also replaced the knob on his own door," Samuel told Sara later after Papa had left the house and Sara was alone with the cousins. How could her parents have noticed that she had been in the room, she wondered. She had been so careful to put everything back the way she'd found it.

"I should have copied the address when I saw it the first time."

"We might have some luck if we pick the lock," Samuel suggested. "Do you have a small clip that women wear in their hair sometimes? It is a brown, wiry thing."

"A bobby pin you mean?" Sara went to her bedroom where she kept hair ties and clips. There were several bobby pins. She grabbed a few and went back to the kitchen. Samuel took one of them and opened it up, handing it back to her.

"If you place the end in the key hole of the knob and wiggle it about, you may release the catch," he explained. After fetching a tablet and pen to copy the address, Sara went to her parents' room but had no luck.

"I can't do it," she called out. "Do you want to give it a try?" Samuel appeared in the hall, hesitant in his stance.

"I am not certain how long I can be here," he replied. She held the bobby pin out to him. He took it, closing his eyes for a moment before working gently at the lock. Again he closed his eyes, this time bringing his hand to his head and standing very still as if trying to gain his equilibrium. He blinked rapidly, tears rolling down his cheeks, his nose dripping. He worked more frantically as his body began to sway. There was a click, and he pulled away, stumbling down the hall. Sara watched him for a moment before entering the room, remembering that he had told her the night before about some stones that may have adversely affected her when she was last in her parents' room. Going straight to Papa's nightstand, she opened the drawer but it was empty. Shocked, she ran to Maman's nightstand and pulled the drawer open, the bible was gone too. Sara stood very still then trying to think. Where would they have hidden these things? She thought of the room in the stable where the two spent so much of their time now. With one last effort, she looked under the bed, pulled back the pillows, opened the closet again and found that it was bare. But where were all their things? Why were all their things gone? Were they leaving and not telling her? An icy feeling of terror prickled her skin.

There was one thing, a necklace with small brown beads hanging from a nail over the bed. Sara went to it, lifting it from the nail. Immediately, a wave of dizziness washed over her so strongly that she felt she might faint. Her body teetered and she caught herself by placing her palm on the bed. She studied the necklace in her hand, marveling at the beads on it, even though her head was growing quite heavy and the room felt like it was beginning to spin. First they were brown, now they were turning an unusual color that she had never seen before, almost glowing. The hand that held the beads felt numb. She set the strange necklace down, and within seconds, her head began to clear, and feeling returned to her hand.

The Visitors

"Louis is coming," Samuel called. Sara hated to touch the beads again but she grabbed them. This time the feeling of dizziness was stronger. With great effort, she hung them back on the nail. "You must hurry," Samuel hissed loudly. Grabbing her tablet, Sara darted from the room, locking the door behind her. She ran to her own room, closing and locking the door. She did not want to see Papa or talk to Samuel. She felt very tired. So tired. She stumbled toward her bed but her knees gave out and she collapsed to the floor, falling into a deep dreamless sleep.

There was a pounding sound that felt like it came from inside her head. Sara moaned, trying to edge away from the sound and creep back into the oblivion of sleep.

"Sara," someone was calling. The pounding continued. "Sara, open the door." It was Samuel's voice and Sara realized that he was knocking, not pounding on her door. Sara pushed herself up, her head felt very light now and her mouth was terribly dry. She felt so weak. "Sara." Now there was the sound of something clicking and the door came open. Samuel stood in the doorway. Finding her on the floor he came to kneel by her side. "You touched them," he said. Sara tried to sit up farther but the effort created more dizziness. Samuel stood up and left the room. When he returned he was carrying a glass of the medicine. "Drink this. It will help." He held to her lips. The bitter, acrid taste woke her up a bit and she began to gag. Moments later her head was feeling clearer. "A few more sips," Samuel coaxed, tipping the glass again to her lips. Quickly she drank down more of the stuff and then stopped as a feeling of intense nausea gripped her insides. She thought she might hurl the liquid back up but the feeling passed and instead she was beginning to feel normal. Samuel sat back, gazing at her. "Did you find some small stones and touch them?" he asked.

"They were beads." Her voice sounded gritty.

"They are stones," he corrected. "Otomic stones, and they are very toxic for us." Sara thought of his reaction when he worked the lock; it began to make sense now. The stones had a stronger effect on him. He could not even get near the room.

"Where do they come from?"

"There are many conflicting stories that explain their existence, of which we don't have time to discuss. Did you find the address?"

Sara shook her head. "They took everything Samuel, their clothes, everything. I don't know why. Do you think they will leave us?"

"It would not matter at this point," he said, disappointment clear in his voice. "No, I don't think they will leave." Sara found that she was growing used to his extreme expressions and the unnatural immobility of his face.

"Lilith waits for you," he finally said. "She is downstairs."

Sara struggled to stand up and Samuel placed his hands under her arms. She saw them hook under her shoulders before she felt them. He pulled her up swiftly and she noticed as she stood that she felt much better.

In the living room Sara found Lilith sitting in the same chair. She was dressed this time in one of the linen dresses that Maman had had her make for herself and her hair was pulled back from a freshly washed face. The young woman smiled and stood when she saw Sara. Again Sara took notice of her incisors, sharp and prominent next to her other teeth.

"I am ready for our walk," she said in a singsong voice. Sara was not feeling the same sort of relief or happiness at seeing Lilith recovered and normal in appearance. Instead she felt a growing trepidation and looked to Samuel. He did not look pleased.

"I am still weak," Lilith said conversationally. "I think a short walk around the property will be sufficient. May I hold your arm for support, my friend?"

The Visitors

Sara held out her arm. Lilith's hands grasped Sara's arm in a vice-like grip: a strength that belied the frailness of her frame or the weakness she spoke about.

"Are you coming?" Sara asked Samuel as she began to walk to the front door with Lilith.

"No." Samuel sat in the chair that Lilith recently occupied and picked up her book, glancing at it without really looking. A moment later he tossed it to the floor and it made a loud slapping noise on the wood. Sara hurried out the door with Lilith, walking a little quicker than she intended down the hill toward the garden.

"Please slow down, Sara. You must remember I cannot keep that pace."

"Yes, I'm sorry." Sara slowed her steps and Lilith tilted her face up to the sky, closing her eyes for a moment. A light breeze played at their dresses, rippling the fabric as they strolled. Lilith paused to examine a cluster of pale, pink ginger, picking one of the bulbs and crushing it between her fingers before bending her slender neck to inhale the pungent, spicy aroma. She was delighted with everything, but by the time they reached the bottom of the hill fatigue had set in again. Sara led Lilith to a soft patch of grass where they both sat.

"You are so different from before you became sick," Sara remarked. Lilith's brow furrowed as if she were remembering something unpleasant.

"Was I different before?" she asked and giggled. With the harshness in her voice gone, her laugh sounded innocent and girlish. Lilith placed a hand over Sara's and cocked her head as if contemplating something. "Why do you go by the name Sara?" There was a faraway look in her eyes.

"Is there another name I should have?"

Lilith scrunched her nose and giggled again. "You silly thing. Why do you vex me with odd questions? We both know your name is Abigail." Lilith smoothed her hair back, smiling all the while. "Oh, it's growing dark and I do feel tired. We should return. Mother has made an iced cake. If you like, you may join us for cake and tea. I must confess that although you are only a mulatta, Abigail, you are my only friend here and you have always been a good and devoted girl like a negress should be with her mistress."

Sara swallowed, her skin feeling icy as she observed Lilith and her strange change of character. "Lilith, I'm not Abigail," Sara said quietly, watching the young woman's face.

Lilith laughed again. "Oh Abby dear, how you do carry a joke too long." Lilith looked down then at her hands and spread her fingers. "My ring," she said softly. "My ring." Sara looked at the young woman's hands, but there was no ring there. When Lilith looked up again, her face was greatly flushed and her eyes looked glazed.

"Sara, take me back to the house." Sara could see that all at once she was back to herself. It was a much more laborious experience going back up the hill than going down. Several times, the girls stopped so Lilith could catch her breath. The air had grown still and quiet, allowing the girl's to hear snatches of conversation as they drew closer to Papa's workshop. Once they were within six feet, Lilith motioned for Sara to stop, the young woman's body growing rigid as she strained to listen.

"We can't keep her," Maman was saying. "You know what will happen after the transformation." There was a long pause. "She can't live, Louis," Maman's voice was sharp.

"If they come, how will we explain?" Papa asked.

"No one is coming! They have abandoned us with those creatures. You must kill her soon." Again there was a long pause and then Papa's voice anguished, "It is not easy to kill someone who looks and acts like a young woman."

"She is not a woman or a girl. We cannot keep that…" Maman's voice broke. "You saw what she did. We both know what she can do, what *they* can do. We can destroy them one at a time. If a high

The Visitors

servant from the infantry comes to take them, then whichever one's have not transformed they may take."

"Of course you understand that our punishment could be death for destroying Lilith," Papa said.

"Do you want to set a monster like Lilith loose in this small valley? And what about Sara? What if something should happen to the girl? Do you think Myrina will be understanding of that Louis? It does not matter if she arranged to send the masters here to be hidden. You know Myrina, she is never reasonable and she is very protective of her children. Our deaths will not be quick with her."

"Of course Myrina may be dead by now," Papa said in a quiet voice. Maman did not seem to hear him because she continued with her own train of thought.

"When *She* is at her weakest you can lead her down by the cliff and kill her. Don't forget to remove the head and organs before you bury her body."

Lilith's hand squeezed Sara's and the girls turned away from the workshop, walking the long way around to the house, neither one saying a word to the other. Once back inside, Sara saw that Lilith was more flushed than before and touching her forehead, she could feel that the fever had returned.

"Let's get you into bed," Sara said gently. Samuel came into the kitchen from the living room. In one glance he took in the fact that Lilith was consumed with the illness again.

"Samuel, come upstairs with us," Sara said. He nodded and the three climbed the steps to Lilith and Carmilla's bedroom. After lighting the lamp, Sara helped Lilith out of her dress and into a thin, short gown. Pulling back the covers, she eased the young woman under the first sheet, folding the top blanket back to the end of the bed.

"Sara." Lilith grabbed her arm. "Don't let them kill me." Tears gathered in her eyes and Sara felt her own eyes water while Samuel watched, his arms folded. "Please don't leave me," Lilith whispered.

"I won't let them do it," Sara promised, anger and sadness building in her chest. Lilith's tears spilled from her eyes. Sara noticed that they were oddly tinged pink.

"So it's come to that," Samuel said. He did not sound surprised.

"We overheard my parents talking in the workshop. They are planning to murder her!" Sara said in a low, fierce voice. How could her parents speak of killing a girl like that, to call her a monster? The more she transformed the more she became human -like, couldn't they see this?

"We are running out of options," he said. "If no one comes for us, how can we live here? We could put our own kind in peril. It would not be wise for humans to know we exist. "

"No!" Lilith cried, she struggled to sit up, her teeth chattering. "You are a fatalist, Samuel, a traitor." Lilith sank back on to her pillow, her body shaking with chills.

"Samuel stop!" Sara hissed. "I will try to find the address and we will write to the contact. I won't let Papa kill her."

"No, you wouldn't," Samuel said, and left the room, gently closing the door behind him.

Chapter 21

Little more than two hours passed before Uncle Fess arrived. He was a large, swarthy man with tattoos on both shoulders. A set of paddles crossed over each other showed his passion for canoeing on one deltoid, and the *pueho*, a small, fluffy owl, advertised his family crest on the other. Laugh lines ringed his jaw and permanent fine lines crinkled around dark eyes that sparkled and lit up at any hint of humor, which he seemed to find in almost every situation. The sticky, slapping sound of his bare feet padding along the marbled hall announced his entrance into the study. He paused in the doorway, observing the scene before throwing his head back with a loud laugh. This elicited a small smile from Sunami. Pono, who had been sitting with his elbows on his knees and his face in his hands, looked up in surprise.

"Whose funeral?" Uncle Fess asked.

"Maybe ours," Uncle Manuel said. This extracted another burst of laughter from Uncle Fess. After he recovered he waved his thick fingers over at Uncle Manuel, motioning at the cigarette in his mouth.

"Gimme one." Uncle Manuel pulled the cigarettes and matches from the drawer and handed them to Uncle Fess along with the slim grey book. "I don't need a book," Uncle Fess said with a friendly guffaw but placed the book under his arm as he lit up and took a long appreciative puff. "Well now, what we got here?" He pulled the book out from under his arm and opened it. The cigarette dangled from his full lips as he read the title page. Slowly his smile faded and he looked up. "Why you give me dis?"

"There are four not yet matured divs on the ridge, Fess, they are here with a young high servant named Sara and slaves posing as her parents," Uncle Manuel replied.

Uncle Fess set the book down on the desk. Sunami could see that his hand shook some. No one spoke as a hush fell over the study, the only sound being the crinkling of burning paper as Uncle Manuel sucked on his cigarette. He had been chain smoking since he put the first cigarette to his lips that afternoon. His skin appeared clammy and sallow. Late afternoon shadows played across his face, emphasizing the bags under his eyes and his sagging jowls.

"Sunami and Pono, why they here?" Uncle Fess finally asked.

"They know about them. I found them here in the study, looking through the book," he pointed at it sitting there on the desk, an innocent looking image of obscurity. Uncle Manuel picked up the drawing and handed it to Uncle Fess whose eyes grew wide as he studied it.

"Where you get dis?"

"Sunami says Sara's cousin drew it." Uncle Manuel's lips jerked on his face in an effort to smile at the ludicrous notion of a div being any ones cousin, and a vein began to throb at his temple. Fess turned to Sunami and Pono.

"How you both be knowing bout dis?"

Pono shook his head and crossed his arms, but Sunami spoke. "Uncle, you remember Sara?"

Uncle Fess nodded. "The girl with the family who like keep to dem selves?" He paused, realizing something. They spoke French.

The Visitors

All the while, he thought they had come from France. They were an odd family that attended church on Sundays. He went to church so seldom that he had not given them much thought over the years, and Manuel had never set foot in the chapel. If Manuel had met them, he would have recognized them for sure…

Sunami launched into her story explaining everything while Uncle Fess listened quietly. When she was finished, he replied, "Dis girl Sara, it sound like she not knowing what she is."

"No, she doesn't." Uncle Manuel agreed. "She has obviously already gone through her illness."

Sunami frowned. "She said she was real sick last year." Both men nodded, affirming her comment.

"It's a common effect, what you saw," Uncle Manuel said. "High servants are transparent in mirrors, but divs do not show up at all, and animals sense what they are."

Pono uncrossed his arms. He looked badly shaken. "How does that work?" he asked. "A person not having a reflection or being transparent in a mirror? Because it doesn't really make sense." His voice trembled as he continued. "Any person or object that is placed in front of a mirror would cast a reflection. Mirrors work because the smooth surface bounces the light back at the same angle that it hit the surface and that's what creates the reflection. Anything that we can see with our eyes should show up in a mirror." Pono wiped at his upper lip, which was beading up with sweat from the humid heat of the room and the disturbing conversation.

"Yes, that's true." Uncle Manuel said. He raised his eyebrows, impressed.

"It is not clear why there is this effect, but some theories have suggested that it has to do with an overlap of dimensions."

"What?" Pono was incredulous but Sunami's eyes lit up.

"Brah," she said turning to Pono. "Didn't I mention dat?"

Pono sighed. "No disrespect Uncle, but what you're saying is not even…" Pono looked flustered as he stumbled over his words. "It just sounds like bad science," he finally mumbled. Uncle Manuel nodded.

"Pono, have you ever heard of demons?"

"Yes, but…"

"They exist, Pono. The white *haoles*, Sunami calls them, those are not people, and Sara is partially on the other side, only she doesn't know it."

"Alright." Pono whistled and rolled his eyes. "I gotta go. I'm outta here." The boy walked to the door but Uncle Fess blocked his way.

"Go sit down," Uncle Fess said, his dark eyes hard and flat.

"I don't want to be a part of this," Pono said, his voice cracking as he tried to walk around Sunami's uncle. The large man grabbed his arm and his voice rose deep and threatening.

"I said go sit down."

Pono backed away to sit in his chair again.

"Let me explain something to you two," Uncle Fess began, remaining by the door. "This is not a game and all a us, we all be in danger. We don't know why they are here, but you need to understand something. The girl Sara, we need to talk to her and see what information we can get. You can't go to the police about dis one. You know what I'm saying to you. The woman that be stalking Mele and da kine," Uncle Fess snapped his fingers, trying to remember the name of the young man.

"River," Sunami said.

"She will kill them," Uncle Fess finished. "River needs to leave dis valley and we need to hide Mele. If she is watching dem, it's not long until her transformation." Sunami's breath caught and her hand came to her mouth.

"I don't think Auntie Leilani will let me take her no wheres," Sunami said. Uncle Manuel was sitting with his legs spread and his

The Visitors

hands firmly placed on his thighs as he looked sadly at Sunami, Pono and Fess.

"The road to hell is paved with good intentions," Manuel said quietly. "I should not have settled here, Fess, it was selfish of me." His shoulders began to shake and he covered his face with his hands, crying out. Sunami turned away, embarrassed. She had never seen a grown man cry and hoped never to see it again. Pono shifted in his seat while Uncle Fess hurried to his partner, placing his arms around him.

"We goin work this out," he said soothingly.

"It is not just the two," Uncle Manuel said between gasps. "They will work their way through this valley. Being a slave, I've seen what they can do. Even if servants come to retrieve their masters, they will destroy all of us anyway just for knowing." Sunami felt the blood leave her face and Pono made a motion as if to stand but then sat back, his face pale with fright.

"Uncle, what can we do?" Sunami asked.

"We should kill them," Fess said.

"No!" Manuel interjected. "Do you know what they would do to your family if we destroyed the masters, assuming they're here for us?" Fess said nothing, despondency descending upon the small group. Getting up, Uncle Fess left the room but was back shortly. In his hand he carried two necklaces made of small brown beads. He handed the necklaces to Sunami. "Place this around the *Keiki's* neck at night and you wear the other one. It will help for a little while."

Sunami took the necklaces, studying them.

Pono, curious, stood up to take a look.

"What kind of beads are those?" he asked

"They are stones," Uncle Fess said. "Sunami, make sure Mele no discard dis one."

The stones had a musky odor and the longer Sunami held them in her hand, the stronger they smelled. Pono put his hand to his nose as he examined the necklaces. His brow creased and he turned to Uncle Manuel.

"So you were a slave?" he asked

"Yes," Uncle Manuel said, his eyes bright with tears and enormously puffy.

"I was born a slave. My tribe has been bound to the div species even before the Night Hunters were taken as servants."

"But what is a div?" Pono asked.

Uncle Manuel sighed. "I could use a beer, Fess," he said.

Within a minute, Fess left and came back with an icy bottle of Budweiser, handing it to Manuel, who took a long drink and belched with his mouth closed before opening a new pack of cigarettes. Once he was lit up and comfortable, he sighed again, his gaze transfixed on the smoke that wafted through the room.

"Divs are a different species from ours, although they have many strengths, they do not flourish like we humans. There is something peculiar about their existence that no one has been able to understand or explain. It appears, although it is not proven, that they are possibly living between two worlds. Another theory is that somehow they are caught between dimensions, and still another theory is that they are viral in nature; they were never alive to begin with. So, like a virus, they cannot function without the life force of a host. Divs have performed experiments on their own kind, and what was discovered is that if a div is deprived of a host, it will go dormant.

"Deprivation sends them into early incubus. When they awaken, they are much weaker than usual. Their life span is generally four hundred years, but they never really die, just cocoon and are born again, growing rapidly to physical maturity. There is a second dying process and then the transformation. It's the initial transformation that's the most dangerous because this is when they begin to feed for the first time. They are ravenous and need to feed often. Human blood restores their system, and a newly transformed div needs

The Visitors

lots of blood at first. After a while the feedings become infrequent. During the course of a lifetime it becomes less and less, until the very end of life when they once again ingest enormous amounts of blood in preparation for incubus. That is the way of a div that was once human, which is why we have wondered about overlapping dimensions and other worlds. Most divs were once in human form, and what is strange is that the person they were comes back. It is like the spirit is trapped and does not know to move on from the body. Or maybe the spirit re-enters the body. I have seen in the infantry full amnesia and a return to the original character of the person that once was. It is as if they are living again as their old human selves."

Uncle Manuel took a sip of his beer and his face crumpled into such a forlorn look that Sunami could not help feeling sorry for him, although she was more afraid than she could ever remember.

"Uncle, you said that those are divs that were human. Is there another kind?" Pono asked.

"There are the pure ones. A pure div was never human. It is a super creature the likes of which I hope never to see or encounter. The half-breeds are bad enough. I have only heard about them but from what I know, they don't have a transformation. After they reach maturity they just begin feeding. Only high servants interact with the pure ones and they are commonly not part of a regular infantry." He swiped at his forehead as he spoke and grabbed his mouth, twisting his lips in agitation. "There are not many pure ones left and I don't know very much about them." His eyes fell to the drawing and he took another drag from his cigarette. "A master drew that. I hope to high heaven that the M on this drawing does not stand for Michael, the same Michael who illustrated and authored the book of the Night Hunters."

"Why?" Sunami asked.

"He is a pure one," her uncle said. He stood up, then and began to pace. "Is there any way to talk to the girl Sara?"

"I can talk to her at school tomorrow," Sunami said.

"She goes to school?" Uncle Manuel looked surprised. "Do you think she would come here?"

Sunami shrugged, "Sara she kine na, you know, private like."

"With good reason," Manuel said under his breath.

"Manuel, you tink it's a good idea to bring a high servant to our house? If she don't know you escaped, why reveal yourself?"

"From what Sunami told me, I don't think Sara knows too much about who she is and, besides, it is too late to be worrying about what they know and don't about us. We are all in trouble. I wish there was some way to at least get your family to leave here with some explanation that would make sense to them." It was quiet again as everyone sat thinking.

"In any case," Manuel said, "I don't think I need to tell you to keep all of this to yourself. Jenny and River must keep quiet too."

Sunami nodded emphatically, but Pono only hung his head.

"May I go now?" he asked.

"I don't think there's anything more we can talk about, so go ahead with you."

Pono stood up and hesitated for a moment. It had grown dark out, and the conversation of the last several hours had him rattled.

"Sunami will go with you," their uncle said, noticing his hesitation. "She needs a ride home anyway."

Pono breathed a sigh of relief when Sunami stood up to follow him out.

"Oh, Uncle, I need that one drawing back to give to Jenny. She has to give it back to Sara." Uncle Manuel picked up the drawing and placed it in the book.

"I would like to hold onto it one more day," he said.

After Manuel heard the door close behind Sunami and Pono, he turned to Fess. "I have failed you, Fess. It was not the right decision to hide here. I cannot promise your family will survive this, and I don't see how *we* will."

The Visitors

Fess was silent.

"I'm sorry, you can't imagine how sorry."

"No, I saw," Fess whispered. "I saw what she did to those *keikis* when we hid in the barn and you went told me put my head down."

Manuel closed his eyes to dispel the image Fess spoke of. Oh, but he had hoped all his life to escape...he had for a while. There were twenty good years behind him. Twenty years as a free man, free from the shadowy existence of fiends that committed unspeakable acts and their high servants, once a noble race, contaminated with the virulent blood of the masters, which rendered them little better than the divs they served. Manuel fingered the small cross that hung around his neck. The warmth of Fess's hand on his shoulder was comforting. He placed his arm around his lover's waist, and the two men stood like this in the study. There was nothing more to say; they could only wait and see.

Chapter 22

"There you is," Aunt Linda called out when Sunami walked through the door. The smell of pork and rice permeated the house and there was the usual mayhem that resulted from five children and four adults all sharing a small space. Pono's truck pulling out of the driveway had alerted the woman to peer out the window.

"Who dat?" she asked over the blare of the TV and the loud, raucous laughter of Kawika and Ikaika playing with two of the dogs on the back porch. Junior stood behind his mother with a beer and cigarette in hand, smirking.

"It's Pono," he said in a high voice, in imitation of a girl in love. Sunami stared at Junior and he quickly jumped away in anticipation of a hard slap, but she had nothing to say.

"What's wrong with you?" Aunt Linda asked.

"Jus tired, Auntie."

Junior's smirk disappeared. He took a drag from his cigarette, watching Sunami thoughtfully.

"Your sister been callin," Aunt Linda said, letting go of the curtain. "She needs your help with dem babies, Sunami. Tomorrow

The Visitors

you should go home and help her." Sunami nodded and Aunt Linda wrinkled her nose. "What's that musty smell? You some stink, girl."

Sunami's hand instinctively went to the pocket where she had stashed the necklaces. Mele came from the kitchen wearing a hula skirt and top that her mother made for her. Every night she put the outfit on and begged her father to play his ukulele so she could dance hula.

"Mama says come get *kau kau*," the little girl said.

Sunami went to the kitchen where Aunt Leilani had dished up a plate piled high with kaluah pork, teriyaki chicken and sticky, white rice. There was a tall glass of 7Up next to the dish. Her aunt stood at the counter, placing swaths of Saran Wrap over the pans of food, her long, thick hair in its perpetual braid down the center of her back. Sunami's throat felt thick. She had no appetite for the dinner on the table but she sat anyway and pushed the food around with her fork, watching Mele spin circles in the kitchen, singing "Pearly Shells".

"Sunami, you coming down with something?" Aunt Leilani asked, placing her hand over her nose. "Girl what have you been into?" She shook her head. "After you eat, you go take one showah."

"Yes, Auntie," Sunami said and took a small bite of rice. She chewed it slowly and swallowed, but it seemed to just sit in her throat. Taking a sip of soda, she placed her elbow on the table, leaning her face into her hand as she watched her baby cousin. Uncle Keoni lumbered into the kitchen and grinned at his little daughter.

"Leilani, grab me one beer," he said.

"Daddy, play 'Pearly Shells'," Mele begged as she pulled at her father's shorts.

"Huh?" Uncle Keoni said. Leilani handed her husband a beer and he took a long deep drink, almost finishing the can. "Get one more for Ben," he said. Leilani grabbed a six-pack from the fridge.

"Just take the pack, you goin finish dem anyway."

"Yeah, but I likes keep em cold," he said with a friendly smile. She sighed as Keoni tore away three from the pack and handed the rest back to her.

"Daddy, 'Pearly Shells!'" Mele cried.

"Play the girl 'Pearly Shells'," Leilani said in exasperation. Keoni left the kitchen with Mele skipping after him. Moments later, he returned with ukulele in hand, smiling at his daughter who ran ahead of him.

"OK, ready?"

Mele nodded. Junior came into the kitchen and sat at the table grinning. Uncle Keoni struck the first chords and Mele placed her hands on her hips swinging them exuberantly. This produced laughs all around and her father's voice rang out deep and resonate over the twang of the small instrument as Mele used the language of her hands to tell the story that he sang.

Pearly Shells, from the ocean.
Shining in the sun, covering up the shore
When I see them my heart tells me
that I love you more than all the little pearly shells.

Sunami couldn't help smiling, watching the two, but her smile dissipated when she caught Junior watching her. He looked away, his face reddening when she glanced in his direction. Sunami felt her stomach flutter and she put her hand to her belly, scowling at the strange sensation. There were a few more songs and then Auntie Leilani was shooing Mele off to bed. Sunami sat upright, the lull from the warmth of her family forgotten at the mention of bedtime.

"Sunami you finished with that?" her aunt asked.

"Yes Auntie." The plate was whisked away as her aunt shook her head. "I hope you're not coming down with that flu that's goin

The Visitors

round. Go showah, and you should go to bed early, sleep is the best remedy for the flu."

Sunami got up from the table but she did not go to the bathroom; she followed Mele into her bedroom. Carefully, the girl removed her hula outfit and folded it neatly before putting on her nightgown. Waiting until Mele got into bed, Sunami pulled one of the necklaces from her pocket, and sat next to her young cousin.

"Mele, remember the White Lady you was tellin me about, the spooky one that was looking in on you?" The girl nodded, her dark eyes growing wide in her round face. Just the mention of the woman had frightened Mele enough for her small arms to reach out to Sunami.

"Don't leave me alone. I afraid."

Sunami gave Mele a quick hug. "Look, I have dis necklace." She held it up for the girl to look at. "Uncle Fess gave me dis to give to you. When you wear it at night, the White Lady can't get at you."

Mele put her hand to her nose. "It no smell good."

"I know," Sunami said softly, "but you'll wear it for me?" She placed it around Mele's neck and her cousin didn't protest as she tucked it under her nightgown. "Mele, don't take dis off OK? In the morning, put it…" Sunami looked around. "Put it under your pillow and at night it goes around your neck." Sunami pulled the second necklace from her pants pocket and placed it around her own neck. "Dis one be protectin me," she explained. Mele reached up her arms again and Sunami held her this time. She could feel warm breath on her neck and the rapid beating of a little heart. Gently Sunami unwound Mele's arms from around her neck.

"I'm just goin take one showah and I'll be right back. The necklace will keep you safe."

Mele remained sitting up, so Sunami fluffed up her pillow and guided her back. When she stood, she was startled to see Junior standing in the doorway. There was an odd look on his face. Sunami walked past him, deciding to ignore his presence, but he grabbed her arm as she left the room.

"I seen her," he whispered. "What Uncle Fess tell you?" Sunami pushed up her chin and remained silent. "You smell strange. Is that the necklace?" Junior asked, glancing at her chest.

"Look Junior, I need take one showah and go to bed." Sunami turned away from him, but he held her arm tighter and pushed her up against the wall, away from the door. He stared down at her with half-lidded eyes and Sunami felt that strange flutter in her stomach again. Then it happened before she realized what was happening, his lips came down on hers like a quick caress, and she was responding. Sunami opened her mouth, feeling Junior's tongue warm against her own, tasting of tobacco. She pushed him away, her scowl fiercer than ever.

"Junior, you need stop. You're my cousin."

"Not by blood," he whispered and pushed his body firmly up against hers, his expression challenging. Sunami closed her eyes and pushed back, moaning a little.

"Ey! What you guys doin?" Ikaika had come down the hall and Junior pulled away quickly. Ikaika stood staring at the two until Junior gave him a rough, friendly shove.

"Did you tie the dogs up?" he asked Ikaika, and Sunami, her body full of sensations that she had never felt before, hurried away to the bathroom.

Chapter 23

It was almost ten pm and Tim still had not come home. Jenny laid in bed thinking of her mom's face, which had grown increasingly tense as the evening had worn on and there was no sign of her dad, not even a phone call. At six o'clock, the two of them sat down to a silent dinner. After dinner, her mom retired to the living room with a glass of wine, correcting papers while Jenny washed the dishes. Her mind had flitted back and forth between her dad's unusual absence and the book that Sunami and Pono hoped to find.

Now it was late but her mind was restless. Disturbing thoughts harassed her; there was no finding sleep this night. The nightmare from the night before replaced earlier broodings. She thought of many things: the girl Mele lying on the ground with a twisted neck, her icy cold bedroom doorknob, Junior accusing her of sneaking into his home, and Sara's cousin with the green eyes and malignant smile. Jenny turned to her side, scrunching up her pillow, trying to get comfortable. She closed her eyes as more thoughts crowded her mind. She heard the front door opening and the sound of her mother's voice, although she couldn't make out the words. Now there was the sound of her father talking. Jenny sat up and walked quietly to her door where she could hear the conversation better.

"I just needed some space."

"You could have called." Her mother's voice rose higher. "Tim, are you drunk? Where have you been?"

"Look, I'm going to bed, we'll talk tomorrow."

"No, we'll talk now! How dare you come home so late, no phone call and intoxicated? You get on your daughter's case about appropriate behavior. Is this the kind of example you want to set, Tim Knowles?"

"Shut up!" Jenny's father's voice rose up deep and loud. "First I have to listen to my daughter tell me what a shitty *haole* I am for providing a home for my family. Now I have to listen to you nag at me. You want to know why I was out? Because there's no respect here, none!" His words were slurred as he yelled and Jenny, not wanting to hear anymore, went back to her bed and put her pillow over her head.

Her chest felt heavy and she squeezed her eyes shut, forcing her thoughts, the yelling and the awful feelings to go away. For a long time she lay curled up, her pillow pushed against her ears, until she was finally asleep.

Chapter 24

The wind had picked up again, pitching its force against the house. The foundation swayed some, the wood creaking and shuddering. Every so often there would be a high shriek, all at once lonesome and eerie. The glow of the gas lamp sputtered from the drafts of air that whistled through crevices in the walls. Sara had once again fallen asleep by Lilith's bedside. It was the loud slamming noise that suddenly broke her dreamless sleep. Lilith slept through this noise, mouth slightly open, full lips pulled back revealing teeth that had lengthened and sharpened even since earlier that evening. Sara sat for a moment, mesmerized by this change. Lilith's face was a contrast in diabolical innocence.

Getting up, her limbs felt stiff and cramped. The banging continued and she went down stairs to see what the noise was. Moonlight illuminated the kitchen. The front door pitched back and forth in the gusts. Papers blew across the table and along the floor. Frowning, Sara shut the door, pulling the handle tight until there was the sound of a click. Gathering up the papers, she jumped when a great bluster of wind shook the house, rattling the windows. The papers were all of Michael's drawings. He usually kept his work in a pad, putting it away every night. An odd feeling came over her as she tidied the stack of papers in her hands and walked to the living room to put them away. It was just a sigh sounding like the wind, but it made the hair rise on Sara's neck.

Shadows played on the white face of someone standing next to the window.

"Who's that?" Sara called out. Panic fluttered through her windpipe like a trapped moth.

"You know who I am." The voice was grating and deep. Something about the movement of the head was familiar and the thin lips that smiled, revealing long, sharp teeth.

"Carmilla?" The shadow of a cloud passed over the moon, throwing the room into darkness and momentarily disorienting Sara. When light returned, the strange figure was now only inches away.

"Are you a good servant?" she hissed. "We don't know."

Her eyes were large and liquid, much too big for her skeletal face. Sara took a step back and the girl appeared to vanish, only to reappear with sickening speed in the kitchen. Cabinet doors were flung open and slammed closed and then only silence, but for Sara's own shallow breathing.

"Come out, come out," Carmilla sang softly. "I have a present." The lithe figure was at the doorway now, Maman's butcher knife in hand. It gleamed even in the dullness of the muted light.

Sara opened her mouth to scream, but Carmilla was already on her, the bony hand covering her lips in a vise-like grip, the point of the knife pressed against her chest. In one swift move, the creature sliced through Sara's skin. Searing hot pain shot across her chest as blood welled up from the gaping flesh. She fell against the armrest of a chair as Carmilla watched in fascination. "Do you heal like us?" she said almost to herself, and raised the knife. Sara covered her face, the papers fluttering from her hands.

"Carmilla. No!" a woman's voice shouted.

The Visitors

There was a clattering sound of the knife dropping. Sara pulled her hands from her face to see Carmilla standing before her, expressionless, watching Lilith. Lilith stood in the doorway hunched over, too weak to stand straight. She was panting slightly but she spoke again.

"Sara, come to me. Come, you would leave me so long."

Although her legs felt like wooden stumps, she hurried to Lilith, her chest on fire, blood soaking through her dress.

Once they reached Lilith's room, Sara pushed her chair up against the door handle before easing her back into bed.

"Lilith, please help me. What do you know?" Sara begged as the young woman closed her eyes in apparent exhaustion.

"Abigail," she called out a moment later. Sara did not answer, recognizing that Lilith had gone into another world again. "Abigail, I don't feel so well. Would you not stay with me a little longer?" Turning her face toward the window she spoke so softly that Sara had to strain to listen. "I fear something haunts me." Sara took the young woman's hand and pressed her other hand to her aching chest, damp and sticky with fresh blood. In this way she watched as Lilith returned to sleep.

For Sara, the remaining hours of the night that gradually gave way to day were painstakingly long. Her chest throbbed and every groan of the house from the wind struck her with terror as she wondered if Carmilla was coming up the stairs. At times she would close her eyes and see the kitchen knife in that white hand coming down at her. Her eyes would fly open again at the horrifying image.

It was Samuel who found her later that morning. Somehow she had managed to doze off and the continuous banging finally got through her foggy mind. Opening her eyes, she watched the chair trembling under the intensity of the noise on the other side of the door.

"Sara?"

Sara jumped from the end of the bed where she had been resting and pulled the chair away from the knob, throwing open the door. He stood staring at her, his face impassive.

"I saw the knife and the blood on the floor this morning."

Sara's hand rose to her chest. The fabric of her dress was stiff from dried blood and it stuck to her skin. Samuel looked over her shoulder at Lilith sleeping.

"It was Carmilla," Sara whispered. "She tried to kill me. Lilith made her stop."

Samuel's eyes wandered back to the girl. There was no surprise or empathy when he spoke. "Today you must find that address and give it to me, Sara. If you care for your life, you will not continue to stay here with us. Already Annette and Louis have abandoned nights in this house. Tonight you will stay with them down the hill."

"What about Lilith?"

Samuel's lips twisted into a wry smile. "My but Lilith has a hold on you." His eyes grew cold and he poked a finger into her chest. "If you knew what kind of master you serve, you would not be so quick to defend."

Sara swallowed, wincing as he pressed on her wound. Her eyes filled with tears and she wondered what had come over him, but Samuel was not moved by her show of emotion. "If you had a proper upbringing, you would not debase yourself with useless self-pity. Tears mean weakness, Sara. Take care that you don't flaunt pain and injury. Those who are wounded are easy prey." There was a low moan from Lilith. The soft light of morning cast a gentle glow on her face, flushed and beautiful in her illness.

"Is Carmilla downstairs?" Sara asked. She could not stand to be with Samuel in the room but to face Carmilla terrified her.

"Carmilla went out last night and she has not returned. She is not one of us. I know that now, and neither is Michael."

When Sara went downstairs, she found the knife still on the living room floor with blood congealed on the blade. There were splatters of more blood browned and hardened on the plywood. The papers were gone and Sara felt a fresh jolt of fear when she took notice for the first time of Michael sitting with his note pad. He'd grown tremendously in height, his shoulders wide as a grown man's. He wore surf trunks and a t-shirt; clothes Papa picked up for him in town. Several weeks ago he had been a small boy and now he looked to be a man of twenty.

"I saw," he said without looking up, his dark hair falling in thick waves over his white face, his hand moving rapidly over the paper in front of him. "What lies ahead for a servant such as you?" he asked his apparently rhetorical question because he continued without waiting for an answer. "Dull in wit, a stranger to our customs, lousy with human virtues. You cleave to Lilith and the human she once was." Michael looked up and Sara grew rigid, but his gaze fell back to his drawing pad.

"You needn't jump away. Unlike Carmilla, I know what you are. I do not need to slice your flesh open to understand." He tore the drawing from his book and let it fall by his feet. "At one time, we did not have a chance against your tribe." He sighed and Sara stared at the gruesome story that he had drawn. Several women were strung with rope by their feet from the low branches of a tree. Their heads were removed. Two other darker women, strong, and muscular, worked diligently gutting their insides. Blood pooled on the earth beneath their gaping necks. A third woman squatted separately from the macabre scene, tying the hair of the severed-heads together. Two wolves of great size sat lazily near the industrious women, their tongues lolling from their mouths.

Sara left the living room then cleaned the knife to take it with her to her room for protection. Grabbing her backpack, she emptied it and stuffed it instead with several dresses, underclothes and a sweater, which she shoved without folding into the bag. Pausing, she thought of the necklace in her parents' bedroom. Samuel suffered when he went near the room just from the necklace being in it. Sara thought about taking it and changed her mind when she weighed the consequences of the effect it had on her. She could not afford to fall asleep suddenly with Carmilla around. Once she was packed, Sara went to the bathroom and removed her dress, peeling the fabric from her chest. Already the wound had closed up but it still ached. She washed away the dried blood with soap and water, cleaning the rest of her body, all the while trying to listen for the sounds of anyone coming into the house. As she dried herself, she noticed her toothbrush and the toothpaste and dumped these items into her bag, not bothering to clean her teeth. Knife gripped tightly in her hand, she edged slowly down the hall toward the back door.

"Sara," Lilith's voice called piteously from upstairs. "Sara, where are you?"

Sara stood rigid for a moment, Lilith's cries tearing at her but she heard then the mummer of Samuel's voice. He would take care of her, she told herself. Even if he was upset with her, it seemed the four of them needed each other, needed to stick together. Sara opened the door, stepping out to an early silent morning devoid of the usual birdcalls. She would find a way to check on Lilith later. With this resolution in mind she headed down the hill to the stable where her parents were.

The grass was damp with moisture under Sara's bare feet and she realized she had forgotten shoes. Still she continued on. As she got closer to the pasture, she noticed the two milking cows standing near the stable. Their heads shot up as she approached. One gave a low moo as both blew air from their large, wet nostrils. The mooing grew louder. They were obviously in distress. The stable door opened and Papa came out shirtless, his curly hair askew, face gaunt and tired with stress lines etched deeply into his features. Around his neck was the Otomic stone necklace, with its obscure, brown beads. As Papa's eyes focused on her, the cows took off charging to the other side of the pasture.

"It is time for school?" he asked. Sara had forgotten about school and the prospect of leaving the property felt like a relief. His eyes wandered down to her hand that held the kitchen knife at her side.

"What happened?" he asked.

"Carmilla, she's changed," Sara said. Papa stood silently for a moment as if trying to think.

"Come in here, Sara," he said after a bit. She walked to her father and the two went into the room connected to the stable. The tools and lumber had been cleared from the front section and there was a domestic feel about the space that hadn't been there when Sara explored the stable room earlier. Maman sat on her knees holding the rosary, an Otomic necklace also around her neck. She looked up when Sara entered. Her eyes were sunken and ringed with dark circles. Much of her weight had disappeared and her hair, having turned almost completely gray in a few days, fell down her back instead of being wound tightly in its usual bun.

"I don't want her here," Maman said and looked away. She bent her head to her rosary, fingering a bead and praying, her lips moving wordlessly. Papa took Sara back outside and sat her down on a narrow bench in the stable.

"How has Carmilla changed?" he asked.

"She tried to kill me last night with this knife. Lilith stopped her."

Papa stood and he seemed to weigh this information before he asked the next question. "Has Carmilla been ill at all?"

"No," Sara said, watching her father's face. He could not hide his expression, although she saw him wrestle with himself. Sara could see that her answer was deeply distressing.

"Where is Carmilla now?"

"I don't know."

Papa's weathered hand stroked a chin thick with stubble. Sara waited, her attention drifting to a colony of ants that formed two rows, marching up and down the trunk of a banana tree, carrying bits of leaf and gummy residue from the tree itself.

"I think I will take you to school and then we will try to figure out something later. Is it possible that you may have a friend whose house you could spend the night at?" Her father's question jolted her with surprise. But before she could answer, Maman came running out from the stable room, her eyes wild. She ran at Sara, who stood up. Papa grabbed her mother, wrestling with her arms that reached to Sara, the fingers curled like claws.

"Away with you!" she screamed. "You devil! You devil!"

Sara stumbled over the bench, knocking it over in her haste to escape Maman's wrath. Papa held her securely and spoke quietly into her ear. Slowly the wild look receded along with the fury and she slumped into herself. Papa took her back to the room.

"Stay here. Lock the door behind you. I will be back Annette." Papa came out and Sara could hear the sobbing: loud, wretched sobs that made Sara ache inside.

"God be with us," her father said as he motioned Sara to follow him. "We cannot keep you here. Maman is obviously not herself and your cousins are no longer safe."

"Those are not my cousins," Sara hissed. "I do not know why you insist on keeping up this false pretence of family, Papa. You know that I know."

"And what is it that you know?" he asked. They trudged up the hill but were distracted by the sight of Lilith standing in her thin gown at the top of the hill.

"Papa, look!" The two hurried toward the young woman who stood with teeth chattering.

"Abigail, there you are," she called. "Where is mother? Where has everyone gone? I don't understand where I am. What is this place?"

"Lilith, you need to come back in the house," Sara said, catching her by the arm. Her eyes were glazed but they seemed to clear when she looked at Papa.

"Louis," she said quietly, her eyes tearing up. She began to swoon. Realizing his necklace was overpowering her he took several steps back from Lilith, who seemed to recover a bit. Taking in Sara's backpack, she began to plead with the girl. "Do not go to school. I beg of you."

"Lilith, you are not well. Let's get you back to bed," Papa replied firmly. The three walked back to the house. Once inside, Sara noticed for the first time that their home was beginning to take on a desolate look. A vase on the kitchen table held flowers that had died days ago, the water giving off a sour smell. Dust and bits of food covered the floor that had not been swept in several days. Some of the counter had splotches of coffee and dried residue of the medicine so often dispensed. There was no one in the living room now and it had an equally abandoned feeling. Sara took Lilith back to her bed while Papa went to look in the other bedroom.

"Are you sick, Samuel?" she heard Papa ask, but she could not hear the answer. Lilith grabbed her arm again.

"Please Sara, don't leave me," she whispered.

"I will be back," Sara said, gently pulling her arm from the firm grasp. Walking to Samuel's room, she noticed that Papa had removed his necklace and hung it on the doorknob of the small bathroom that stood between the two bedrooms. Samuel was lying in one of the twin beds, his white face clammy with sweat, eyes closed.

"Where are the others?" her father asked. Samuel opened his eyes.

"They have left. I'm not sure where," he said weakly.

"What about the sun?" Samuel closed his eyes again and flung his long, white arm over his face. Papa swallowed and Sara watched him cross himself while a look of absolute terror overtook his features.

"Have they changed?" he whispered.

"No, not quite," Samuel muttered. "It is Lilith who will have her transformation soon." Papa left the room, leaving Sara standing awkwardly in the doorway. Samuel didn't seem to notice. He lay quietly, his breathing even. Sara could hear the clinking sound of Papa stirring medicine in a glass, then his footsteps coming back up the stairs. He held out two glasses, giving Sara one.

"Give Lilith her medicine and then I will take you to school. If you have a friend who could put you up, I would prefer that you spend the night out."

Returning to Lilith's room, she found her sitting up, although Sara could see it was a great effort for her. How she was able to muster the strength to walk down the stairs in her condition or to go outside was a wonder. Sara could remember being very sick like this and the agony of it. Every bone had ached constantly and there were times that she could barely breathe from the crushing, squeezing feeling inside. Then there were the fevers so hot it felt like being roasted from the inside out.

"If you leave, Sara, I won't be here when you return," Lilith said. "He means to destroy me." Sara could not think of a single thing to say. She knew Lilith spoke the truth. "Sara, you must hide from him. When evening draws near, come back and help me to escape. He will come for me in the night hours. We need to leave while there is still some light in the sky."

"But where could you go?" Sara asked, alarmed. "And the sun. You and Samuel are so sensitive. It burns your skin."

"In the evening hours, take me down to the shore. There is a place there where I can rest in the day away from the sun." It suddenly made sense, Lilith's late night excursions before she became ill. She must have seen this coming and scouted a safe place for herself. Lilith sat back, sighing from her effort.

"Drink some of your medicine." Sara brought the glass to the young woman's lips and she sipped a bit at it then turned her head.

"It is enough. Set it on the night stand." Sara did as she was directed.

"I will come back then," Sara said just as Papa called her name. Lilith closed her eyes and Sara left, closing the door behind her. Papa stood waiting at the bottom of the stairs.

"I'll meet you in the truck," Sara told him. "I just need to grab a few more things if I'm going to sleep away from home." Papa nodded. He was wearing the necklace again.

The Visitors

"I'll wait on the porch," he said. Sara knew that he did not want to risk her being alone in the house if Carmilla or Michael were to return. She waited until he was outside before she came down the stairs. In one of the kitchen drawers, Sara grabbed a flashlight. Then opening and closing her door to mimic the sound of going into her bedroom, she quietly crept to the back door and let herself out. Once outside, she ran down the hill through the banana orchard and to a narrow footpath that led to a wire fence, which she scaled. On the other side she landed in dense vegetation. A great twisted, jumble of hau bush ran as far as the eyes could see. She stepped through an opening between gnarled branches. Taking out the knife, she began a trek that would lead to the next valley, an undeveloped, lush piece of land where she could wait undetected. Stray dogs were the only foreseeable danger until nightfall.

Chapter 25

"Pono, hey! Where are you going?" Pono turned around to see Eric and Steve approaching him. Sunami and Jenny stopped as well, waiting with Pono as the two boys approached.

"I thought we were going to meet for lunch," Eric said, his blue eyes enlarged behind thick glasses. Steve hung back a little looking at the girls curiously. Tall and skinny he still wore braces with the small rubber bands connecting the top and bottom rows. He reminded Jenny of Ichabod Crane from *The Legend of Sleepy Hollow*.

"Yeah, I can't." Pono said. "We've got a project we need to work on." He motioned at the library that all of them stood in front of.

"What are you working on?" Eric asked.

"It's, huh," Pono looked uncomfortable as he stumbled for words.

"Dimensions and stuff," Jenny said quickly.

Eric pushed his glasses up against his nose, staring at her.

"Dimensions and stuff?" he echoed.

Sunami rolled her eyes and stepped up to Eric, pushing her chin out. "Hey retard, he said we're busy, so make like da wind and blow."

The Visitors

Eric's mouth, twisted as if he had tasted something sour and his eyes narrowed before he turned to Pono, gesturing at Sunami.

"Really Pono? You couldn't come to us for help with your project on dimensions and stuff," he emphasized dimensions with a lift of one eyebrow.

"Look, you stupid *haole*, we don't get time..."

But Pono interjected, holding up his hand to Sunami. "You goin raise yo hand at me punk?"

She sauntered over to Pono, her dark face red with anger.

"Sunami quit it!" he yelled. "Let me talk to them alone. I'll meet you and Jenny in there."

Sunami was silent, her face one giant scowl before she spun on her heel with Jenny following her.

"What are you doing hanging around with that *tita*?" Eric asked as soon as the two girls were out of earshot. "I mean, the redhead's not too bad, but Sunami? Man, get real. What the hell are you doing with her?"

"It's complicated," Pono said looking over his shoulder. "Look, sorry guys, but I gotta get in there."

"What about D and D?" Steve asked.

"Yeah," Pono ran a hand through his hair and looked over his shoulder again. "Maybe I'll call you later after school." He took off before either one of them could ask any more questions but groaned silently when he almost walked into Junior, who stood blocking the library door.

"Hey brah," Junior snarled.

Pono groaned inwardly, but he gave a flick of his head in greeting and was careful not to meet Junior's eyes as he said, "Hey."

"So you been spending a lot a time with my cousin." He stayed firmly planted at the door.

Pono lapsed into pidgin. "We get one project assigned us in science, brah."

Junior lifted his chin. "What you be workin on, cuz?"

"Physics, I get assigned mentor." The door suddenly opened with a great whoosh and Junior stumbled back as Sunami came out of the building, glaring at him.

"We get work to do Junior."

Junior stepped away, tucking his head down. He glanced up quickly at Sunami, who continued to stand with her arms crossed and her perpetual scowl. Hanging his head again, he walked on, passing some of his friends who tried to high-five him, but he just pushed past them and kept walking.

"Get in here, Pono," Sunami demanded, opening the library door wide for him.

The library was a small, boxy room. Several oak wood filing cabinets filled with card catalogues took up the center of the space. Behind the low-lying cabinets was the librarian's desk. Rows of books were on either side of the room. Jenny was already looking through a catalogue arranged by subject matter. She looked up when Sunami and Pono approached.

"I've already looked up Night Hunters but there was nothing under that subject," she said in a hushed voice.

"I no think they have anyhow."

"What are you looking up now?" Pono asked.

"Vampires."

"Didn't your uncle call them divs?" Pono asked Sunami.

"Oh yeah, you is right, brah," Sunami said excitedly. "Look up dat word." Jenny moved over to the D section.

"May I help you find something?" The three looked up to see a young, pretty woman standing before them. Her nametag read Mrs. Halls.

"You is the librarian?" Sunami asked, frowning. "What happened to Mrs. Nakashima?"

The woman smiled. "Mrs. Nakashima is taking a leave of absence. I am actually her niece."

"Oh, I thought only librarians could work as da kine," Sunami's brow wrinkled; disappointment was evident on her features. Mrs. Halls laughed a little.

"I am a librarian. That is why I was able to fill in for my aunt."

"Mrs. Nakashima, she some smart. She traveled all over the world."

Mrs. Halls nodded agreeably as Sunami spoke and then she tilted her head. "Are you Sunami?"

"Yes, Miss."

"My aunt spoke a lot about you."

Sunami's face reddened and she looked down.

Mrs. Halls noticed her discomfort and discreetly changed the subject. "What may I help you find?"

"We are trying to find anything you have on divs," Pono spoke up.

Mrs. Halls' forehead wrinkled. "I've never heard of that before, how is it spelled?"

"Um, I'm not sure," Pono said feeling silly for not knowing.

"What does a div pertain to?"

"I think it's a kind of vampire," Jenny interjected. Mrs. Hall's features cleared and she smiled again.

"Probably it is best to start with the subject of vampires," she said helpfully, moving to the V section. "They're a fascinating myth, aren't they?"

The three were silent. Mrs. Halls observed their serious expressions and said nothing more. Her slim fingers with nails painted a light shade of pink rapidly flicked through the cards until she came to the subject they were looking for. Grabbing a blank index card she wrote down where they could find the books. "It looks like there are only three," she said as she handed the card to Sunami.

"Thank you," Sunami mumbled. Jenny and Pono crowded in to see what Mrs. Halls had written down. In neat, small writing she had listed:

1. D368 Vampires, Myths, and Legends
2. D362 A History of the Undead
3. D369 Vampires From Around The World

"Section D is on the left, it's one of the middle aisles," Mrs. Halls said before returning to her desk. Pono looked at his watch.

"We only have fifteen minutes. We need to hurry."

The three walked in the direction Mrs. Halls had indicated. Within seconds of their search Jenny called out, "Here they all are." She pulled one off the metal shelves. Sunami grabbed the other two books and they went to sit at one of the long tables situated in the back, settling in to the plastic chairs as they each opened a book.

"We'll check the index for divs," Pono said.

"Duh, really," Sunami hissed, her dark eyes snapping at Pono, her mouth tight with irritation as she opened her book to the last pages. Pono bent his head over his own book, saying nothing.

"Hey, I think I found it," Jenny said, flipping through her book. Both Sunami and Pono looked up.

"In Persian literature," Jenny read, "div (demon, monster, or at times Satan) carries many different forms. Divs are completely independent of, and different from, people. In relation to the vampire, one branch of the div is the daeva clan: sensual predators that seduce unwitting victims. The daeva are thought to be one of the oldest, if not the oldest, clan of the damned. Often daeva are compared to the demon of lust and anger, Aesma Daeva. This demon personifies violence and works hand in hand with Asto Vidatu, who preys on the souls of the dead."

Jenny stopped reading and looked up at Sunami and Pono; both were frowning down at the text.

"Are you sure your uncle said that Sara's cousins are divs?" Jenny asked. "Because this is really..." her words trailed off and she looked to Pono. He met her eyes, making no effort to conceal the naked fear in them.

"That's what they is," Sunami said quietly and she knew deep down that it was the truth.

"I better go find River today and let him know," Pono said.

"What you goin tell him?" Sunami asked.

"Well, I don't know, I guess I'll tell him that it's not safe for him to stay around where he is."

Sunami rubbed at her temples. "I gotta get Mele outta there, my whole family. It's not safe for no one."

Jenny shivered as a ball of nerves began to form in her belly. If it was not safe for Sunami's family, it wasn't safe for her or her family.

"What about Sara?" Jenny asked. "What will happen to her—living with these," she waved her hand over the book, "demons?"

"We goin have to warn Sara too," Sunami said. "Oh shit, I forget. I have to go home today and babysit, my aunt told me I had to go home." Sunami blew air out of her nostrils angrily as she sat and thought. "Pono, you can take me when you go talk to River. Then I can remember Mele to wear the necklace before she go to sleep. Then you can take me home." Pono nodded. "I only goin sleep one night away. I no like Mele be by herself in dat room at night."

"What about your uncle wanting to talk to Sara? Have either of you seen her today?" Pono asked.

"I don't think she came to school," Jenny said. The three fell silent, thinking about what could be the possible reasons for Sara missing yet another day of school, and if she wasn't at school, what might have developed at home.

"See dis be why my sistah need to get her own life. Here we goin through some life threatenen shit, and I have to go babysit so she can clown around wid peoples goin no wheres fast." There was the shrill sound of the bell warning them that there were three minutes to get to class.

"I'll check out these books," Jenny said as she scraped her chair back.

"OK, so I'll meet you in the parking lot after school," Pono said to Sunami. "Do you want a ride too?" he asked Jenny.

"Of course she wants a ride," Sunami said. "What? She's goin to catch the bus when you is goin out dat way?" Sunami shook her head in disgust.

Pono ignored her but shot Jenny a side-glance, his expression questioning. Jenny shrugged, watching Sunami leave, striding off in her boyish, loping walk.

"What's with her?" Pono asked under his breath.

"I don't know," Jenny said. She had noticed that Sunami's temper was worse than usual. Something else was bothering her.

Chapter 26

Gray storm clouds rolled out from the ocean, covering the sky in billowy ashy clusters. A fine drizzle blew at a slant, misting the valley. River grabbed his raincoat from the back porch and folded it before stuffing it in his backpack.

"Want me to roll you up a doobie?" Don asked as he finished rolling his own joint. There was still a bit of the dried, crumpled plant, which Don pushed into a small pile with his matchbook.

"Yeah, sure," River said. It was his turn to go and sit with the plants. Later in the evening Leonard would come join him. Leonard stood smoking his own joint.

"Are the boards on the car, man?" Don asked. Leonard nodded.

"How were the waves yesterday?" River asked as Don handed him the joint from the final bits of bud.

"The waves were shredding yesterday dude. It was total awesomeness except for all the grommets that were out." Leonard said

"Yeah, but I think you got a piece of ass with that chick," Don said with a grin.

"Hey man, mind your own business," Leonard said, but he was smiling.

"What chick?" River asked. Leonard took a long toke on his joint but he wasn't talking. Don's grin broadened.

"You boned her, dude."

"Yeah so... she wanted it," Leonard said through the smoke he held in his lungs, and then exhaled. "OK, you ready man?"

Don nodded.

"Catch a few for me," River said as his friends left, the screen door banging after them. He looked around him. The place definitely needed some serious cleaning. There were empty beer bottles everywhere and various dishes and cups with bits of old food or partially consumed liquids, doubling up as ashtrays. The smell of mold permeated the four-room shack that the three of them dwelled in for only $60.00 a month. With this final crop, River looked forward to having his own place. At twenty-three, the bachelor scene was beginning to wear a little thin for him.

The sound of a vehicle pulling in the driveway broke through River's thoughts. He peered out the window to see a familiar grey Toyota truck. Pono emerged from the drivers' side followed by the two girls he had met the other day. All three appeared somber and washed out like they hadn't slept since he'd seen them last. Panic fluttered in his chest as he opened the door and stepped out.

"Hey, what's up?" he called out in greeting. None of them smiled.

"Hey," Pono said with slumping shoulders. Jenny's eyes met his briefly, and then she looked away too, swiping at her bangs with jerky, unsure movements.

"What up?" Sunami said with a brief lift of her chin.

"Uh, yeah, come on in," River said holding the screen door open for them. The three filed in and Jenny walked toward the couch to sit down but changed her mind when she glimpsed a pile of smelly clothes on one end and a huge stain on the other.

The Visitors

Sunami threw her shoulders back and looked hard at River. She did not mince words. "We came catch you up bout that *haole* you say was stalking you. She means to kill you. You're not safe here."

"What?" River exclaimed. "What do you mean? And how did you find this out? I mean who is she?"

"She's not like a person," Jenny interjected.

River glanced at Pono, who stood with his head hanging down. "Um, who is she?" River asked again.

"We think she might be a demon," Pono mumbled.

"And you think this because?" River stared at the three of them, but none of them were forthcoming with any more information. "Shit you guys, are you shitten me?" River asked. But the expression on Jenny's face was his answer. She was pale and her fear-filled eyes seemed to be silently begging him to believe them.

"Look—" River began, "I appreciate you guys coming out here, but I'm going to need a little more information. I can't just pick up and go."

"River, it's not just you," Sunami said. "We all gotta leave here, none a us is safe. That's all we can tell you, brah. If I was you, I wouldn't stay here no more and who eva else be living here."

River frowned. "But, well this is just hard to swallow. A demon?"

"We talked to some other people that know about her," Pono said.

"Who? Your uncles?" River asked.

Sunami lifted her chin slightly. "Brah, we gotta go. It's up to you. We just came to warn you."

Pono turned to head for the door and River watched incredulously as the girls followed him.

"Is this some kind of Joke? Man you guys, this is wacky," he laughed, but Pono only opened the door, holding it for Sunami and Jenny, who stepped out onto the porch. He glanced briefly back at River.

"Look man, if you have no place to go, you can crash at my place for a while until whatever this is blows over. I'll talk to Akamu tonight."

River shook his head. "I don't know. This is crazy. Its possible people are just being overly superstitious, you know?"

Sunami rolled her eyes. "What eva, come on let's go."

The three walked back to the truck. River watched as Pono and Sunami got in, then Jenny raised one of her long, lanky legs to hoist herself up, but paused and brought her leg back down. She ran back to where he stood, grabbing his hand, her eyes filled with tears.

"Please don't stay here, River. I know we sound crazy. If we're wrong, then we're wrong and all that happened is that you spent a few nights at Pono's. But what if we're right? I've seen her too, and the other ones. In just weeks two of them grew from small children to teenagers. People don't do that. Just come stay at Pono's for a little while." Jenny blinked and her gathering tears spilled down her cheeks. River's throat tightened and he felt he could cry watching her.

"I'll think about it," he said thickly. Jenny nodded, brushing the tears off her face with the back of her hand.

"OK," she breathed and walked back to the truck. Pono's truck roared to life as she climbed into it. He watched as she closed the door and Pono backed out of the driveway and onto the main dirt road, where they disappeared around a hedge of bushes. River went back inside, badly shaken. A moment later he remembered the pot plants. "Shit!" he cussed under his breath. He couldn't go anywhere. The plants were almost ready to harvest and he needed to be out there right now. Picking up the joint that Don had rolled him, he squeezed it hard between his fingers. Those kids had him scared out of his mind. He lit the joint, inhaling long and deep. Get a grip on yourself, he thought as the smoke filled his lungs. Demons! Demons don't exist.

The Visitors

"Just drop me off here," Jenny said as she saw her driveway loom up ahead of them. The last thing she wanted was another encounter with her parents over what kind of friends she was hanging around with, although she doubted either of them was home.

"Yeah, sure." Pono pulled over to the side of the road, Jenny grabbed her backpack, hopping out of the cab.

"Hey, Jen, wait up," Sunami suddenly said. "Let me give you my two numbers for at my auntie, uncle's and my house. Pono, write your number down here too, brah." Sunami reached into her backpack and pulled out one of her notebooks. As she opened it, some papers fluttered out and fell to the ground near Jenny's feet. Jenny picked them up, glancing down at what appeared to be two tests from Mr. Ikeda's biology class. Sunami had received a perfect score on both of them.

"Wow, I didn't know that you did so well in biology," Jenny remarked. "Those tests were really hard, I barely made a B-."

"Sunami doesn't like people to know she's wicked in science," Pono said with a grin.

Sunami frowned, snatching the papers from Jenny.

"Ey Pono, shut up! Is your name Sunami? Was she talking to you, cuz?" The playful smile evaporated from Pono's face as Sunami, producing a pen from her bag, rapidly wrote down her phone numbers and handed the notebook to Pono to do the same. When he was finished, she grabbed the book and gave it to Jenny. "Put your number down there." She pointed to the bottom half of the page. When Jenny was finished, she ripped the paper out of the book, tearing it in half, handing Jenny her portion. "Get trouble, call us." Sunami reached over and closed the cab door. Pono slowly pulled the truck away. Jenny stood watching.

The sound of someone walking up behind her made her whip around in alarm.

"Hey."

It was Charlie. Jenny breathed a sigh of relief as she watched him approach. The black dog that had been slinking around his place walked several paces behind him.

"Sorry, didn't mean to startle you."

Jenny bit at her lip as she took in his bronzed skin and muscular body. He was wearing surf trunks and slippers, but no shirt. A cigarette dangled from his full lips. He assessed her for a moment, glancing briefly off in the distance at Pono's truck ambling down the road. He grinned.

"Didn't know you were cruizen around with Sunami, especially since she's got a major chip on her shoulder when it comes to *haoles*, more like a giant *pohaku*." He laughed and Jenny could feel herself relaxing as she smiled at his joke. Charlie stared at her thoughtfully. "Smoke?" He reached for his pack in his pocket. Jenny shook her head. "Thought not."

"Why?" Jenny asked.

Charlie shrugged. "You just don't seem the type."

"And what type is that?" she asked, crossing her arms, surprising herself with her own boldness.

Charlie lifted an eyebrow. "So where are you headed? Back home?"

Jenny let her arms drop, her attitude deflated from the change of topic.

"Yeah." She glanced down at the dog again. "So I guess you've made him your pet."

"It's more like he adopted me." The dog sat patiently while they talked, tongue lolling lazily. Jenny bent down to stroke his head, smoothing the dark fur. Something jogged her memory as she scratched under the animal's neck.

"He likes that," Charlie said as the dog stretched its neck out farther toward Jenny's fingers. She smiled and looked up at Charlie. He was staring down at her with an intensity that made her stomach tighten and her face grow red. A moment later his own face seemed to darken and he looked away. Jenny looked quickly back at the dog.

When I try walk Blackie to her, he quick bit my arm and run away. She could hear Sunami's voice in her head. He was Sara's dog, she suddenly remembered. Jenny stepped back, staring at the animal. It blinked back at her, rising to its own feet as if understanding her thoughts.

"Blackie?" she said hesitantly. The animal cocked its head. "Come Blackie," she called louder. The dog immediately walked over to her and sat at her feet.

"You know its name?"

"I think this is Sara's dog."

"The girl that lives on the ridge?"

Jenny nodded.

"Oh. I wonder why he's hanging around here lately? I guess I'll walk him up. She's probably missing him."

"No! Charlie, don't do that." The words flew from her mouth before she had time to think what she was saying. Charlie's eyebrows drew in tight as he took in Jenny's rapidly reddening face and the stark naked fear in her amber eyes. Her expression displayed more alarm than his casual remark warranted.

"What's going on? Why shouldn't I bring him home?"

Jenny swiped at her bangs and looked away.

"It's just that her family's really private."

"Well yeah, but I'm sure they would want their dog back if he was missing."

Jenny couldn't think of a single reply that would make any sense and she was feeling increasingly uncomfortable under Charlie's scrutiny.

"Maybe you could let her know that I have her dog then," he suggested, breaking the tense silence that had built up between them. Jenny nodded, shifting her backpack strap so that it was higher up on her shoulder as she stared across the road at a some chickens and a few ducks pecking at the grass in someone's yard. The birds sat comfortably in the late afternoon sun, fluffing their feathers contentedly. All around there was a sense of calm and normalcy, yet the mention of Sara brought all of the worries and fears back to the forefront of Jenny's thoughts. "So, did you find anymore ti leaves hanging around your house?" Charlie asked with a grin, changing the subject.

"No." Jenny shuddered at the mention of the ti leaves. She did not like the idea of being alone in her house. Having been so focused on Sara she had forgotten about her experience that morning when she thought she heard someone moving about the living room and found no one there. The memory made her think of her nightmares.

"Hey," Charlie said softly. "You look really freaked out."

Jenny swallowed, meeting his gaze. She wanted to confide in him. For some reason, she felt comfortable in his presence.

"Do you want me to walk you the rest of the way home?" he offered. She nodded and they walked the short distance to her house in silence. Neither of her parent's cars was in the driveway she noticed, feeling a sharp stab of fear.

"How about a coke?" she blurted out.

Charlie grinned. "Yeah, why not?"

His acceptance of her offer flooded her with immediate relief. They walked up the front steps together, leaving Blackie to sit waiting on the porch. The door was unlocked like all of the houses in the area. With Charlie by her side there was a sense of the ordinary as they deposited their shoes near the door and walked through the living room to the kitchen. Charlie glanced out the windows that enclosed the space around the dining room table while Jenny searched through her fridge for the soda.

"How is your dad keeping up with the maintenance around this place? I remember Uncle Keoni was always out in the yard mowing the lawn, cutting back bushes, whacking away at something with his machete."

"My dad hires a couple of landscapers to come out. They've been out twice so far. He doesn't have time to work in the yard because he works full time as a manager at the Hyatt on the west side." Jenny located a large bottle of Coca Cola and pulled it out along with a lemon-iced cake that her mom had made.

"Thanks," Charlie said appreciatively, as she cut a large slice, placing it on a salad plate and poured him a tall glass of soda. The two sat at the table and quietly took bites of their cake, sipping their drinks.

"I think this house is haunted," Jenny said and winced as soon as the words left her lips. Now he *was* going to think she was a freak.

Charlie's eyebrows rose up, he set his glass down. "Why do you say that?"

Jenny traced the rim of the plate with her index finger as she told Charlie about the morning she had come out of the shower and the odd experience of hearing someone in the house, but finding no one there. She also told him of her nightmares, except she left out the part about traveling to Sara's house. When she began to talk about seeing a girl named Mele, who had fallen from a tree and broken her neck, he leaned forward, his eyes widening.

"What?" Jenny asked, observing his expression.

Charlie seemed like he was about to say something, appeared to change his mind, and sat back. "No, nothing. I just thought it was interesting."

Jenny frowned. "You know something. What is it?"

Charlie's eyes dropped to the table. "Look, I can see you're really scared." Jenny felt the warmth of embarrassment creep up her neck at his words. "And I don't want to add to that."

"But what?" she whispered.

Charlie's lips twisted in an effort to smile and reassure her, but instead it was more of a grimace. "You never knew about the other Mele that lived here? My great Aunt Margaret's daughter?"

Jenny shook her head, feeling her skin grow cold from his words. "Shit," he said under his breath. "No one told you about Mele?"

"What about her?"

Charlie pushed his chair back and stood up. Jenny pushed her own chair back. "Where are you going?" He inclined his head toward the living room.

"Come here, I want to show you something."

Jenny followed him through the room and out the front door. Blackie lay on the front porch waiting. His tail began to wag, thumping the wooden slats as they came out. Charlie jogged down the steps and Blackie picked himself up, running after him. He was headed toward the back yard area.

Jenny slowed her gait as they began to walk over the knoll that led to the small cemetery. The cluster of headstones rose up, lonely and foreboding. She had not been back to look at the cemetery since they had moved in. The overwhelming guilt she felt for displacing the Kahiamoi's dampened any enthusiasm she might have had to explore the area.

Charlie paused before the headstone that read *Beloved Tutu Margaret Kahiamoi 1879 to 1979 May She Rest in Peace*. He stepped up to the brown headstone and then walked around it to another that sat behind it and a little off to the right. Jenny closed her eyes for a moment, feeling sick. She did not have to look at it. She already knew what it read.

"This is Auntie Margaret's daughter, Mele. She's buried here." Charlie turned around as he spoke but stopped when he found Jenny standing off at a short distance, her eyes screwed tightly shut, her face white. "Jenny?" She shook her head jerkily, stepping away.

"I don't want to see," she said in a hushed voice. "I can't look at it."

The Visitors

"Hey," Charlie walked back toward her rigid frame, placing his hands on her shoulders. "Sorry, I guess I shouldn't have brought you here. I just thought it was so strange how you dreamt of Mele not knowing that she existed."

She was shaking and her breathing was getting quicker.

"Oh God, something's not right. I feel so strange." Pulling herself from his grip, she turned around and began to run back toward the house.

Frowning, Charlie ran after her, followed by Blackie, who began to bark, thinking it was a game. When he caught up to her, he found her leaning against the porch banister.

"Are you OK?"

She stared at him, perturbed. "What's happening?"

"You got upset."

She nodded, the frenzied look receding from her expression, replaced by one of thoughtfulness. Charlie glanced up at the house.

"What do you know?" she finally asked.

Their eyes met for a moment and he reached out, brushing her bare arm with his fingers. She took a step toward him. He felt his pulse speed up.

"What time do your folks get back?" he asked. Jenny glanced at her watch; it read four-thirty.

"My mom should probably be back in the next half hour or so."

"That's good," Charlie said under his breath, not able to pull his gaze from hers. "I should probably get going. Are you going to be OK?" She stared at the ground, but when she looked up his breath caught and he didn't dare touch her again for fear of kissing her this time.

She nodded.

"I'll see you around then."

"Yeah." She swatted at something imperceptible and began walking back up the porch steps. He stayed to watch her go inside before heading out to the road.

Uncomfortable thoughts swirled around in his mind. He remembered hearing an argument between his mom and dad. His mom had insisted on knowing why they weren't helping the Kahiamoi's when the house went up for sale.

"He's had all of the responsibility of taking care of tutu, Jack. We can't let them be turned out of their home." His father had not answered right away. "Jack!" his mother had snapped. "It is the *pono* thing to do."

"He doesn't want to keep it," his father had finally responded.

"What? What do you mean?"

"I offered. He said no. Keoni says it's under the wishes of tutu."

"That makes no sense."

"There is a presence. I'm not sure. Apparently there was some history there on that land before the house was built. A girl was murdered. I've been trying to find what I can about it because ghost stories are not a reason to let your house go. I couldn't get past a certain point with him, Kanani. He said tutu told him the spirit has been plaguing the house for years. She believed that it's why Mele fell from that tree." There was a long silence that stretched between them.

"No one has ever spoken about that," Kanani had said. "I've never heard of this before."

"It's something he's been keeping to himself. He says there's been strange incidents that have made him uneasy. Before Margaret passed, she made him promise that if he had a girl he would keep her in the easterly room."

"What?" his mom had exclaimed in disbelief.

"There was no talking him into keeping the place. He's never even spoken to Leilani about this. You know how much she loves the home. He's made a deal with the realtor to stay on as a caretaker for Leilani's sake but if it were up to him he would vacate now."

Without warning, Charlie's mother had suddenly stepped out of his father's office, where he had been standing before the closed door listening. She stood stunned for a moment, staring down at him. But it was his father who called him into the room and sat him down, wanting to know what he'd heard. He had been twelve then, and he had promised his father he wouldn't talk about it. He'd kept that promise, even when his father came out looking bad, the secret dampening his integrity with the rest of the family.

Charlie's brows drew together as he thought over his short visit with Jenny. When he was younger, he had fully accepted the idea of the Kahiamoi house being haunted without giving it much thought. It wasn't until maybe a few years ago that he'd come to the realization that his blind acceptance of such an implausible story was childish. Respectfully chalking it up to more islander superstition, he hadn't given it much more thought until now.

Jenny had said she hadn't known about the tragic accident of the first Mele, yet she had described it word for word as he had heard the story. Pausing at the mouth of the driveway, he looked up at the white clapboard cottage. Light glanced off of the low-pitched roof, the windows dark as if holding secrets.

Chapter 27

"So you finally decide to come home."

Sunami pushed past her sister who stood blocking the entrance of the front door, a cigarette in one hand and a can of beer in the other. Her nephew Mitchell sat watching a cartoon on TV, the sound blasting through the house. Joseph sat in his playpen amid plastic toys and stuffed animals, his nose encrusted with dried snot. The rank odor of feces in old diapers permeated the house and everywhere Sunami looked she saw a mess. Kayle slammed the front door and strutted over to the TV. A sarong was tied low under her protruding belly, raked with stretched marks. She wore a thin tank top, her large breasts barely contained in a shirt that she had outgrown years ago. She turned the channel and Mitchell began crying.

"Shit, Kayle. Can't you see he's into that?"

Kayle rolled her eyes and flopped down on the sofa next to her son.

"We been watchin this crap all afternoon. It's my turn to look at my show." She took a deep drag from her cigarette and set her beer down, scratching her belly with her long fingernails, leaving red marks.

The Visitors

"You're not supposed to be smoking and drinking neither. The doctor told you with the last one. That's why he get breathing problems."

Kayle held up her middle finger and stared silently at the TV. Mitchell had stopped crying and scooted off the sofa, toddling over to Sunami, pulling on her hand.

"Auntie get one?" She stared down at the small boy, wondering what he was talking about. "Get one, Auntie."

"Get what?" Sunami asked.

"He wants a popsicle," Kayle said, glancing over in their direction. "And can you make Joseph's bottle while you is in there?"

Sunami took Mitchell's little hand and walked with him to the kitchen. It seemed every dish, pot and pan that they owned was either used or already had something in it. There wasn't a single clear surface and the rubbish next to the back door was overflowing with two full bags next to it. *The lazy bitch*, Sunami thought angrily as she reached into the freezer for a Popsicle. She unwrapped the treat and handed it to her nephew. *Couldn't even be bothered to put the rubbish in the bin outside.* Sunami looked for the paper towels to wet one down and wipe Joseph's nose but there were none to be found. She went into the bathroom to look for a washcloth but found more of the same kind of filth. Dirty towels were draped everywhere. In exasperation she grabbed Joseph from his playpen and washed his face over the kitchen sink, which immediately elicited shrieks of protest.

"Ey! What the fuck you doin to da baby? He was good and quiet."

Sunami ignored her sister, cleaning the last bit of mucus off of his face, while Mitchell stood watching, contented with his treat. Having nothing to dry the baby's face, Sunami used the bottom of her t-shirt then brought him back sniffling to his playpen. Putting him back in only brought on more crying. "What da hell are you doing?" Kayle yelled. "You went make him all *huhu*." Sunami gritted her teeth, reminding herself not to hit a pregnant woman.

"Kayle, it no bodda you dis house be m'lepo to da max. You get rubbish piled in the kitchen, every ting *pilau*."

Kayle pushed herself up from the sofa and walked over to the playpen, roughly pulling up her small son into her arms, taking him back to the sofa with her. "Save the leccha and make him one bottle."

Sunami swore under her breath and went back to the kitchen where she picked up the first two rotting bags of rubbish, tossing them out to the yard. Fortunately after she brought out the third bag, she found a full box of clean bags and relined the rubbish container. Next she set about washing all the dishes, Mitchell following by her side. When he was finished with his popsicle she washed the sticky sugar from his face and hands and set about mixing formula.

Hours of cleaning stretched out before her. Dinner needed to be made and there was overdue homework. Mele's face flashed through her mind and a flutter of fear took up residence in her belly. She needed to call Junior and remind him later about the necklace. The thought of Junior sent a small frisson of pleasure through her body, which she mentally stamped out, scowling at her own weakness. That was just what she needed, to fall prey to Kayle's situation. If it took every last bit of her strength, this would never happen to her.

She was going to go to college. She had told no one of her plans to become a doctor. She knew that getting good grades was her first step in being accepted into a university, preferably one far away from her life on the islands. Having babies at fourteen and fifteen like many of her peers was not in her future, and neither was Junior.

Linda brought in the last of the box of groceries, laying it down in the bed of the truck next to the others. Leilani had already slid into the cab. She was resting her elbow on the armrest of the passenger door, looking out the window. Ever since that new *haole* family had

The Visitors

moved into her home, she had been depressed, not her old self at all. It didn't matter that Linda kept a small garden at the back of her place, which she offered Leilani full use of, but she stayed uninvolved, pining over her loss.

She was young, only twenty-five. Pregnant at seventeen, she had moved into the house with Keoni at the end of her senior year of high school. Linda had watched her put her heart and soul into the place and Keoni was proud to have such a beautiful home for his family. Why he was too proud to let the rest of the family know about the mounting medical bills, Linda would never know.

It was true that they could afford to get their own place. With Leilani's salary as a nurse's aide and the odd jobs Keoni picked up in construction, there was enough to get by, but whatever they found would never compare to what they had had in the Kahiamoi home. Still, Leilani needed to get out of her funk. It didn't help that her older sister had been incarcerated recently for burglary, a crime she had committed to support a long time cocaine addiction and a growing bevy of grandchildren. And Sunami looked so much like the sister that Leilani had once looked up to.

Sunami had come by that afternoon with some nonsense about all of them needing to move because they were in danger. When Linda had pressed her for more information Sunami had said she couldn't tell her. Linda shook her head as she started up the truck. That girl was too much and probably up to no good. She wondered if Sunami had begun dabbling in drugs. The house was getting full and she had no room or patience for family members that were choosing to go down the wrong road. It would not surprise her for one minute if Sunami wound up pregnant like Kayle, who not long ago had looked forward to a future as a talented hula dancer but was now burdened with babies, two deadbeat dads and a self-defeating attitude. *When will people learn?* Linda asked herself, as she pulled onto the two-lane highway that wound its way back to the valley.

It was a short drive home from the little market and as they pulled into their driveway, Leilani perked up a bit when she saw her small daughter waving exuberantly from the front porch. The two women climbed out of the truck as Linda's boys began unloading the boxes of groceries.

"Mommy come, me and Ikaika went pick flowers for you." Mele was hopping up and down on the porch, a large smile on her round face. Leilani's eyes lit up and she climbed the stairs, picking her daughter up to give her a hug. The girl squirmed in her arms and when she put her down, ran into the house. Leilani and Linda both followed to her bedroom. But what both women noticed immediately was an over powering, musky odor. Leilani wrinkled her nose and Linda covered her face with her hand.

"Look! Look!" Mele cried out, she ran to grab a loose bouquet comprised of the various flowers that grew in their yard. Ikaika and Junior stood in the doorway grinning. Leilani took the flowers from her daughter's hand, looking around the room.

"Mele, what is that smell in here?" The girl frowned.

Linda had already begun looking around, picking up toys, squatting to look under the dresser. "Mele, did you bring something in here that smell *pilau*?" Leilani asked. Mele was quiet, looking up at her mom, and Linda came to stand over the girl as well.

"You hiding something, Mele?" Linda asked as the small girl walked backward to her bed.

"No, Auntie." She sat on her bed, her dark eyes solemn and Linda stepped toward her, watching her grow rigid.

"Alright, what kine nasty thing you hidin in here, Mele?" Linda demanded.

"It's mines. I need it," the girl responded pleadingly.

"What is yours?" Leilani asked gently, coming to sit next to her daughter. But Mele was quiet again.

The Visitors

"Mele, get up," Linda said. When the girl didn't budge, she pushed her aside, lifting her pillow. Mele grabbed her aunt's arm as the two women and the boys stared down at two coiled, beaded necklaces.

"No, no, those are mines!" Mele screamed, hanging on to her aunt as the woman swooped up the necklaces. Leilani pinched her nose to block out the smell and tried to hold her daughter back with her other hand. "I need em. Sunami gave em to me to keep away the White Lady!" Linda handed the necklaces to Junior.

"Take these things and throw em far away from heres," Linda commanded.

"Yes, Mom," Junior said, and left the room with Ikaika following him. Mele let out a blood-curdling shriek and tried to run after Junior, but Linda held her back.

"Mele, sit down!" she commanded.

The little girl sat, her chest heaving as she stared at the now empty doorway.

"Tell Auntie what Sunami was telling you."

"Sunami give me doz necklaces to keep away the White Lady."

"What white lady?" Leilani asked. She glanced at her sister-in-law but could see that Linda had no idea what Mele was talking about.

"The White Lady that be watchen me in the window at night."

"Sunami outta know better scaring a small child like that," Linda remarked angrily but Leilani put her hand up, signaling Linda to stop talking.

"Mele, tell Mommy about the lady that stay spying at you in the night."

Mele looked up at her mother and Leilani could see a fear so clear in her daughter's eyes that it tugged at her heart and knotted her stomach. "Mele?" Leilani prodded gently. But Mele wouldn't reply, instead her arms snaked around her mother's waist and she buried her face in Leilani's belly.

"I'm going to have a talk with Sunami. What has got into her? Making a small child all scary like that and then tellin us we're all in danger and need to move."

"What? When she tell you dis?" Leilani asked.

"A few hours ago."

"What kine danger she talken about?"

"She didn't say. When I see her, she's goin get it though."

"I will talk wid her," Leilani interjected before Linda went off on another tirade. She felt tired of Linda and her superior attitude. She knew that her sister-in-law looked down on the family and that for some reason she felt extra spiteful toward Sunami. The girl was rough, Leilani knew that, but she had been through a lot. There was another side of her niece that was good and loyal. She also knew that Sunami cared too much about Mele to frighten her like that. If Mele said there was a white woman, then there was somebody. The idea settled uncomfortably in her mind. She needed to talk with Sunami. It was not like the girl to go around warning people for a joke. Linda stood up sighing and left the room. Leilani felt relief to see her leave. She longed to be in a home of her own again. Staying in the valley was too painful and staying under Linda's roof was smothering. Looking down at her daughter, she pulled the girl away from her mid-section and lifted her small face.

"Mele, please tell Mommy what you been seeing." Mele shook her head.

"OK," Leilani said. She would just have to talk with Sunami and find out what this was all about.

Junior slipped out the back door with the necklaces, Ikaika following him with a wrinkled nose.

"Those tings some stink," Ikaika said, watching Junior curiously.

"Yeah, I goin throw em far from heah," Junior replied. "I tink I heah your mom callin you."

The Visitors

"I don't heah nothin," Ikaika said after standing still for a moment, straining to hear.

"Just go see anyway," Junior urged. Ikaika shrugged, leaving Junior alone. When his cousin was out of sight, Junior went to the back bushes of the yard, finding a large stone to place the necklaces under. Somehow in the night he needed to get that necklace around Mele's neck like he had promised Sunami. He had seen the woman that Mele was frightened of, and Junior felt equally terrified of her. She was definitely one of those *haoles* up on the ridge that Sara claimed were her cousins, although Junior wasn't buying it. He knew Sunami wasn't either. There was something not right about them. For one, their skin was too white, whiter than any *haole* he had ever seen.

He remembered that night when the dogs had been whining. They had sounded scared. Sitting up, he had listened to their low wails and then pulled back his blinds to look out into the night but had seen nothing unusual. Yet the dogs had not let up. Quietly, he had risen from bed and walked through the still house and out the back door. There stood one of his dogs, Pele, her body trembling, tail between her legs. Junior had never seen her like that before. When he walked around the house, he had found the other two dogs, Jack and Kila Boy exhibiting the same behavior as Pele.

Only when he walked over to the side of the house where Mele's window was had he seen her...a young woman standing silently in the night. Her white skin had gleamed in the darkness. Her large, liquid green eyes held him enraptured for a moment. Then something odd happened. After that night, he played the incident over and over in his mind to make sense of what he had seen but was not able to reckon the images. It seemed the woman disappeared yet at the same time he was sure he saw her back away toward the road. The two images seemed to superimpose upon themselves. At the time it appeared ordinary but later when he thought of it, he realized it had been anything but.

Watching Sunami place the necklace around Mele's neck last night, Junior heard her say that Uncle Fess had given it to her to protect Mele. *What did Uncle Fess know?* he wondered. The boy stood up and walked to the edge of the property that bordered the steep, sloping road that lead down to the bridge and up again to Sara's house. Sunami had said they were in danger. He thought about grabbing Jack and Kila Boy and walking over to Sara's to investigate what was happening over there but realized as soon as he had the idea that the dogs probably wouldn't come with him. They were frightened as hell, like Sara's own dog. Realizing that there was nothing he could do at the moment made him clench his fists in frustration. He wished Sunami would come clean with him about what she knew instead of holing up with Pono and that skinny redhead who jumped at anything that came her way. Pono? Why him? The thought angered Junior, but he shook his head at his rising temper. The main thing was that he needed to get that necklace around Mele's neck and back out of the house by morning without his mom catching on.

Chapter 28

It was growing cool as the sun dipped into the west. Sara swallowed, trying not to focus on how thirsty she was. When she packed her bag, she hadn't thought to bring water and now her throat felt parched. She had been following a sluggish stream through dense vegetation, but was not sure if it was safe to drink. Papa had lectured her in the past about drinking stream water and the possible harm of picking up bacteria that could make her very sick. The rocks were slick and slimy with algae along the water's edge. Sara stayed farther back, swatting from time to time at mosquitoes as her skin grew incessantly itchy from the many bites she received over the course of the day.

Earlier in the morning, she hiked across a hill that started from her property, following the narrow footpath for a few miles. It had led her to a vast gulch that stretched every which way she looked, the stream running through the center of it. At one point she stumbled upon a steep, narrow opening between two cliffs. Farther back where the stream divided, the water plunged down the chasm to a large pool below.

It was at that spot that she had spent the majority of the day sitting on the cliff, trying to think clearly about her situation. Many times she thought of running away, but continuously rejected the idea. Where would she go? And how long could she hide on an island? She had no friends, no money and no survival skills. Confiding in someone outside of her family seemed a bad idea. It might put that person in danger if they tried to help. As the day wore on, she realized that her only option was to go home and help Lilith. Her stomach cramped with fear as she stood up, her legs stiff from sitting too long. How was she going to get Lilith out of the house without her parents noticing? And what if she came across Carmilla? Sara hopped across some rocks, trying not to think of it. Lilith was so weak Sara wondered how she would get along without the comfort of a roof over head, a bed or medicine to help her recover. Sara began to make a mental list as she retraced the route back to her house. If there was time, she would need to pack extra medicine for Lilith, warm clothes, maybe some of Maman's special cream. She bit at her lip. It all seemed so implausible. She wished she could talk it over with Samuel and get him to help. But he was different now, and sick as well. Was he in danger of her parents killing him? Sara picked up her gait, but was mindful to pay attention to what was under her feet. The last thing she needed was to fall and sprain her ankle far from anyone knowing where she was.

It took longer to walk back than she realized. The sky was already darkening and clouds were gathering as a cool breeze passed through the thin fabric of her dress. She shivered, her skin instantly rising in bumps from the cold air. Pausing a moment, she stopped to rummage around in her bag for the sweater she had thrown in there. Once she pulled the thick material over her head, she scouted the shadowed terrain before her and made a guess that she was closer to her property than she'd previously realized.

Minutes later, a thicket of hau bush, scrubby mountain apple trees and some young pine came into view. Sara's heart beat quicker as she made her way through the bushes where it was harder to see the last bits of daylight almost blocked out by the canopy of dense branches. Gingerly, she pushed at the scratchy foliage until she finally came to an opening and a wire fence several feet in front of her. Trying not to focus on her rising fear, she climbed the fence, landing quietly on moist ground and dampened leaves. She could see the stable now.

Taking a side path, with the kitchen knife firmly in one hand, Sara stayed along the outer edge of the property, following the fence until she had climbed the hill and was level with the main house. The small library building was blocking her view. *Please let no one be there*, she repeated over and over in her mind as she ran up to the library, peeking around the structure. It was clear and desolate looking. The grass had grown long and there was an unkempt look about the front yard. Sara dashed around to the backside of the house, looking jerkily over her shoulder down the hill to where the stable building was.

Only the long grass rippled from the increasing wind and a fine mist of rain began to fall from the sky. Easing the back door open, she slipped silently into the house, keeping a firm hold on the door and not letting it close too quickly lest it make noise. The door clicked shut. She stood for a moment in the dark hall, listening. It was completely silent. Not waiting a moment more, she hurried to the stairs, climbing them as fast as she could. She froze when she heard the sound of her parents' bedroom door opening and Papa's voice.

"Who's there?" he called. The sound of his footsteps coming toward her prompted her to keep moving.

"Sara?" Sara turned to see her father standing at the bottom of the stairs. He was terribly haggard looking, still shirtless, wearing the necklace, but at his side he carried a small pistol. They stared at one another before he made a lunge toward the stairs. Running up the remaining steps and down the short hall to Lilith's room, she threw open the door, whirled around and shoved the chair under the handle.

"Sara! Open this door!"

Backing away from the pounding, she went to sit on Lilith's bed.

"You came back," Lilith whispered, struggling to sit up.

"I told you I would." It was almost dark, but Sara could see that Lilith was greatly flushed. The sheets and mattress were damp from her sweat and the medicine that Sara had given her earlier in the morning was not finished, the glass still half full on the dresser top.

"Sara, you are not safe with her!" Papa yelled. Lilith's hand, hot and clammy from the fever, covered Sara's, her green eyes beseeching. There was more pounding and then it was quiet.

"He will get in," Lilith said after a bit, "and then he will kill me."

Sara's heart hammered in her chest. She stood up, listening to the rain begin to drum hard against the tin roof. Lilith was right, she knew. There was no way she was going to be able to get her out of the house. Once Papa was successful in removing the door handle, it would be all over with, unless...

Sara walked to the window, looking down. They were too high up to jump. But if she had something to tie to the thick piping just outside the window, they could climb down part of the way. If she had some rope they could maybe escape. Sara scanned the room, her eyes falling on the bed where Lilith sat helplessly.

"Lilith, get up," she whispered. The young woman sat up a bit more. Sara reached under her arms and hauled her up. She felt very light. Lilith stood trembling and Sara grabbed the top blanket, throwing it over her shoulders. Next she stripped the sheets off of the bed and began twisting the fitted sheet. Giving up on the twisting, she made rips at the top of the sheets with the knife, creating strips, which she tied together, making a knot of the fitted and flat sheets. Again there was more banging on the door. Sara jumped.

"Sara, I am not the enemy."

Her father was using his calm tone, trying to reason. "I don't want to force anything. But at some point I will be coming in. I will give you a few minutes to cooperate and then I will remove this door handle. It is important that you do not fight me, Sara. This is beyond your understanding."

The knot was tight; Sara yanked at it, testing its strength. She went to the window. It was small but they were both slim enough to slip through. Sliding the window open with as little noise as possible, she stared at the screen. Pushing the screen up, she tried to pop it out of the grooves but it wouldn't budge. Impatient with the process, she grabbed the knife and stabbed through the wire mesh. Lilith stood behind her, watching as Sara reached her hands through the opening she had made and tried to rip it apart. It was harder than she had anticipated and her hands were slippery and wet with the rain drumming against her. Lilith pushed past her, reaching her hands through, and in one fluid movement, she ripped the screen completely apart. Sara was astonished for a moment at the power she still held, even in her weakened state.

Rushing to grab the tied sheets, Sara leaned out of the window, throwing the material over the thick rectangular pipe. She had to straddle the sill, resting one foot on the gutter, hoping it wouldn't collapse under her weight as she leaned out farther to tie the sheet. It took several minutes in the darkness and the rain. Her fingers grew numb from the cold and trying to secure thick material tight enough that it would not give way under their weight. When she thought she had it, she gave a tug at the piping; it seemed stable enough.

Bringing her wet body back into the room, she stared despairingly at how frail Lilith was. How was she going to survive in the rain? Sara opened the young woman's dresser to scan what clothes she had. There were a few sweaters, but no pants; Maman thought pants were crude on women. Removing her own damp sweater, Sara pulled two dry sweaters from the dresser and put one on, giving the other to Lilith. Grabbing the sheet rope, Sara threw it out of the window and leaned over to see how far down it dangled. There would still be quite a jump but from where she stood, she wasn't sure how many feet.

"I will go first," she whispered, "and then you follow me."

Lilith nodded.

Sara straddled the sill again, trying not to look down as she reached for the sheet dangling from the pipe. Once she grabbed hold of it, she would have to pull the rest of her body out of the window and let go. The danger of what she was about to do engulfed her body in an icy fear. Before she could give it much thought, she eased the rest of her body out of the window, still holding the sheet tightly. The gutter under her feet began to crack as she tried to get closer to the piping. She slid her body down to get past the gutter, the hard lip scraping her back. She was now dangling. The rain was hitting her hard while the wind pushed her back so that the tip of her ear hit hard against the thick, solid plastic. Holding tight, she inched her way down, pitching crazily in different directions from the force of the growing storm.

When Sara neared the bottom of the sheet rope she looked down. It was not such a far jump, only eight feet maybe. Letting go, she landed on the mushy, wet ground, her bare feet stinging a little from the force of her fall. She looked up and saw that Lilith was already straddling the sill.

Sara stood on tiptoe, reaching the very tip of the sheet and guiding it over so that Lilith could grab it directly. Half way down, Lilith stopped and suddenly hunched over, her body shaking violently as she was pitched to and fro in the wind. There was the sound of creaking metal and Sara noticed that the piping was beginning to bend. Afraid to yell out, she clinched her fists, taut with frustration, hoping Lilith would continue to climb down.

It seemed minutes went by, although it was only seconds, as Lilith hung onto the sheet, not moving. There was a louder creaking and Sara watched as the piping began to bend farther. Lilith noticed it too and, slowly, she resumed the descent. Once at the bottom, she let go and landed in a perfect crouch, although she began to tremble uncontrollably again. Sara grabbed the young woman's arm and they hurried as best they could in the direction of the library. Looking behind her she thought she saw a figure standing in the driveway. Sara's heart rose to her throat as she realized that she had left the knife in her hurry to escape from the room with Lilith.

Lilith's hand tightened on hers, and through chattering teeth she whispered, "Carmilla can't hurt you."

The two continued down the slope of the property, pausing at the bright flash of lightening that lit up their surroundings. "We need to cross to the other side," Lilith panted. "There is a path that leads to the ocean. I know of a place where I will be safe." Sara knew what path she was talking about. Continuing to lead Lilith down to the bottom of their land and the fencing that held in the two dairy cows, they crossed back to the other side of the vast yard.

Sara searched the bushes, looking for the path, it was not easy to find in the storm, but Lilith pushed forward, parting some branches, her own night vision keen. The skinny footpath had grown slick and muddy from the recent rains and now the hammering of sheets of water made it treacherous. Once hidden by the bushes, Lilith stopped again, her body overcome with trembling. She began to cough. A deep rattling sound rose from her throat. Sara put her arms around her, feeling Lilith's body grow rigid as her mouth opened wide, her teeth long, sharp and curved like that of a feline animal. The sight made Sara shrink back. Lilith bent her head down and opened her mouth wider, gagging, her body hunched. She gave one great push as clumps of something fleshy and rotting came up from her insides. Once she spewed the strange, clotted contents, she began to sag into herself. The smell was vile and Sara was afraid to glance at whatever it was that Lilith had thrown up. They waited as she clutched herself, fighting with every fiber to keep standing.

The distant bobbing of Papa's flashlight finally prompted Lilith to keep moving. It was not easy on the slippery mud. Some parts of the path had eroded into small holes of cold water, giving Sara a jolt whenever she plunged a foot into one. Shivering now herself, mild relief came when the rain turned back to a fine mist. However, the wind grew stronger, lowering the temperature. It was almost unbearable. At one point they both slipped, sliding a good way down the path. It was almost half an hour when they finally reached the bottom.

Huge waves pounded the shore only six feet away. The noise was thunderous and created vibrations in the earth that could be felt from where the girls rested. Lilith leaned against a sapling as Sara waited for her to reveal where the shelter was. There was a great, explosive sound in the sky that made Sara jump: thunder followed by lightening. It lit up the beach before them, the ocean ghostly silver blue in the white light. Lilith sagged to her knees and collapsed completely, panting harder than before. Sara knelt down and lifted the woman's head up off the muddy ground to rest on her own wet lap.

"I can't go on," she said between breaths.

"We can rest. Please, don't give up." Sara felt her throat tighten as Lilith's body began to tremble violently again.

"I…" her panting became more rapid, her body suddenly growing lax.

"Lilith?"

The woman's head moved slightly, followed by a low moan. "Mother?"

"It's me, Sara." Lilith turned her face up, her eyes resting on Sara.

"Mother, I'm frightened," she whispered. "I'm so frightened. The White Lady. Please don't leave me alone." Sara stroked Lilith's head, unsure of what to think. A moment later, her body was limp.

"Lilith?" There was no answer. Sara shook her gently, but her head only moved back and forth like a rag doll.

The Visitors

"Oh God! Please." Sara shook her again. Streaks of lightening intersected across the sky and Sara saw the vacant green eyes that were almost purple staring up at her. In that one second, Sara could see that her eyes had sunk deep into their sockets as if she had already been dead for longer than just the few moments that had passed. A deep wrenching cry rose up in the girl's chest as she struggled to stand and move away from the dead body. Grief and terror engulfed her. She stumbled back up the mess of mud that was the path. Climbing up was much harder than coming down. Sara slid back countless times, clawing frantically at the wet earth for roots or low-lying branches to hang on to. Her body felt weak and she was terribly tired. She realized for the first time that she had not eaten the whole day. With a supreme force of will, she continued climbing the path until she was finally back on the ridge! A patch of circular light cut through the darkness and Sara froze.

"Don't move!" It was Papa's voice. Sara remained where she was, listening to the soft swish of his feet in the grass. His hand grabbed her shoulder, squeezing tightly. Sara gave out a sharp cry. "Where is she?" her father growled. "How dare you disobey me? You have no idea what you're protecting Sara. Where is she?"

"She's dead! She's dead. I tried to save her." Warm tears flooded her eyes but Papa's hand tightened even more on her shoulder, creating pain.

"Where?"

Sara looked past him at the path she had just come from. "Where did you leave her?" he yelled.

"Down by the ocean."

Her father released her shoulder. "Dear God in heaven, but you have no idea what you have just done. Show me." He bent down to pick up something. It was a machete. The handle of a pistol stuck out of his pants pocket. "Hold this light," he commanded. "Take me to exactly where you left her."

"She's dead, Papa," Sara cried, taking the flashlight from his hand.

"No Sara, she's not."

He marched forward, machete in one hand and pistol in the other. It was exhausting to think of making the trip down the trail for the second time, and horrifying to imagine having to view Lilith's body again. Her father's footing was sure. They reached the bottom in half the time it had taken her with Lilith.

She had left the body several feet away from the path. Shining the light near some spindly, young trees she scanned the bare ground.

"I left her here."

Papa grabbed the light from her, waving it all around.

"She's gone," he said bleakly.

"But she was dead."

Her father took a step toward her and for the first time in her life, his hand fell hard against her cheek. She bit against the side of her mouth, the tangy taste of blood flooding her tongue.

"You have unleashed a monster." His words were quiet. Sara felt numb. He pushed the flashlight back into her hand. "Get up the hill now. I must take you from here." Sara stumbled forward, making her second round trip. Her legs ached and her mind swirled with the fact that Lilith, obviously dead before, was now gone.

They did not stop by the house. Instead Papa had her rinse off the dirt with the hose from the water catchment tank. He rinsed as well.

"Do you think Mrs. Knowles will let you stay the night?"

"Yes. I think so," Sara replied through chattering teeth. Not bothering with drying off, Papa went briefly to the workshop where he retrieved his keys. His jaw was set hard and firm as they got into the truck.

Sara rolled down her window, her head spinning from such close proximity to the stones her father wore. She felt she might pass out, but forced herself to stay cognizant.

"Where does she live?"

The Visitors

"Make a right."

They passed the red house, which set off an alarm of growling and barking from the three dogs that lived there. The front door opened and Sara saw Junior step out onto the porch.

"Slow down. The driveway is just around this curve," she said. Sara's heart sped up as they pulled in. He kept the engine running and seconds later someone came out the front door.

"Hello?" a man said.

"Aloha. Louis Deureaux here. We're having a bit of an emergency. My wife's not well. I wonder if Sara might stay here for the night?" The man was silent but he walked down the steps and into the driveway. Light flooded the porch, revealing, Jenny and Mrs. Knowles.

"Sara?" Jenny called out.

"Jenny." Sara took a step forward, trying to control her shivering. "May I stay here tonight? I'm sorry…"

"Yes, of course," Jenny replied, echoed by her mother.

"Thank you." Papa had backed out of their driveway in seconds, leaving the four standing quietly.

"Well, come on in, Sara," Mrs. Knowles finally spoke, crossing her arms against the cold breeze and misting rain.

"Thank you," Sara said quietly, ducking her head as she walked past Tim into the shelter of the house.

Chapter 29

Junior stepped down from his front porch after Sara went by. The dogs were still going crazy. He walked farther out into the yard to look around. To his relief, he found no one lurking around. Moments later, the barking and whining died out and the dogs began to wag their tails, vying for his attention. He knelt down and petted Jack brusquely on the top of the head, wondering why Sara was out with her father at night. As long as Junior could remember, he had only seen her in the truck going to the bus stop, school, or on Saturday mornings on their way to the swap meet. They had always been headed to the highway, not farther into the valley.

The truck came by again and Jack stiffened, letting out a low growl, but the other two dogs were quiet. The truck passed their house and continued back down the steep road that would eventually lead up to the ridge where Sara's family lived.

What the hell was that all about, he asked himself. He wanted to call Sunami and talk with her but there was no privacy. The phone was mounted to the wall in the kitchen and there was always someone there. Junior sat on the ground next to Jack, whose wide face

The Visitors

rested on his paws. Loud conversation, boys laughing, the TV blaring and Uncle Keoni playing his ukulele rang out from the house. Junior knew Mele was wearing her hula outfit, dancing to her dad's music; this brought a fleeting smile to the boy's lips. Sunami came to mind again, but this time he saw her pinned under his body, pressed against the wall, her eyes closed as he kissed her. She had pushed herself against him. The memory made him squirm with arousal. He stood up, flooded with frustration. Jack lifted his head, keeping his eyes on Junior. The dog's eyes were red with fatigue. He was a good guard dog. Bending down, Junior gave Jack one last pat before he went back into the house.

"Alright it's time fo bed now. Keahe, you need take one showah," Linda called out to her son. Ikaika emerged from the bathroom in his pajamas, black hair slick and wet. Kawika sucker-punched his brother as the younger boy slunk past. Keahe howled with laughter, watching this interchange between his cousins while Kawika's face darkened with anger. He took a swing at Kawika, who jumped away just in time.

"Stupid!" Keahe yelled.

"Ey!" Linda stepped in grabbing the top of Kawika's ear, pulling him toward her. Keahe smirked, satisfied with the justice. "Go to your room!"

"Yes Mom," Kawika meekly ducked his head, pushing past his baby cousin, who stood watching her aunt with wide, dark eyes.

"What you need, Mele?" Linda asked.

"My necklace," Mele said quietly.

"Mele, you can't have that necklace in heah, now go to bed." The girl stood, her eyes filling with tears.

"Sunami said I need wear it at night."

"What did I tell you?"

Junior watched this exchange and his stomach clenched as tears began to spill down Mele's cheeks.

"Mom, I'll walk her to her room. She's just scared." Linda's eyes flicked over her son.

"I want my necklace!"

Junior pulled Mele down the hall and into her room where he knelt down in front of her.

"Mele," he grabbed her shoulders as she shook with sobs.

"I want Sunami," she cried.

"Mele, listen to me," Junior whispered, looking over his shoulder to make sure they were alone. "I never went throw your necklace away." Mele's cries quieted. He had her attention. "I hid em." He looked over his shoulder again. "I gone sneak it to you latah. Now go to bed." Mele was completely quiet now but she turned to look at the window by her bed and her body shuddered.

Junior sat on his bed looking at *MAD* Magazine, straining his ears to hear what was happening in the house. The TV was finally shut off. His dad and uncle had gone to bed, followed by his mom. His cousin Ikaika curled up against the wall in the bed they were forced to share, jerked in his sleep, mumbling something. Junior glanced at the digital clock on his nightstand. It read 10 pm. He hadn't heard his aunt leave Mele's room. She was probably still reading to her. Getting up, he walked quietly to the kitchen so he could pass the girl's room. The door was shut and light shone from the gap underneath. He continued on to the kitchen and poured himself a glass of water. A moment later, the door to Mele's room opened and his aunt padded down the hall and into the kitchen.

"Goodnight," she said, pausing as if wanting to say something more and then changing her mind. Junior watched her leave, heard the front door open and close as she made her way to the one room *ohana* that she and his uncle were staying in while they lived with

The Visitors

them. He slipped out into the yard. The fact that the dogs were quiet was reassuring. Pushing aside the branches of hau, he felt around for the large stone where he had hidden the beads. Grabbing the musky scented jewelry, he made his way back to the house, negotiating his way through the unlit hallway to Mele's room. Carefully, he opened his young cousin's door, peering into the darkness. She lay fast asleep sprawled on her back, her mouth open. If he could just slip the necklace around her neck without disturbing her, that would be easiest. He didn't want her to wake up and start crying for him to stay. Junior put one of the necklaces in his pocket, and held the other one open. As he crept toward her bed, something grabbed roughly at his arm, squeezing hard. Junior's throat constricted and he spun around to a see a woman standing before him. It took a second for him to realize that it was Auntie Leilani glaring at him.

"Junior," she hissed. "Why you be sneakin in heah?" The terror he had suddenly felt left him speechless for a moment. Leilani's hand squeezed his arm harder, her face a mask of rage so intense it looked like she could easily kill him. When he didn't answer, she yanked him toward her and out of the room. When they were in the hall, she gave him a rough shove so that he stumbled back.

"You bettah tell me why you is sneakin in Mele's room right now." As she spoke, her eyes fell to the necklace in his hand and she snatched it out of his fingers.

"What the fuck is you up to, Junior?" she growled.

"Auntie, I'm sorry. Sunami told me that Mele needs to wear that at night."

"Why!"

The door to Kawika and Keahe's room opened as Kawika came out, rubbing his eyes.

"Go to bed," Leilani said and pushed the boy back into the room. His eyes widened, but he silently complied. Once she had closed the door herself she examined the necklace in her hand, wrinkling her nose. "You need to come out wid it Junior, and I don't wanna heah no bulai."

He ran his hand over his hair, his heart pounding. Sunami would never forgive him, but there was nothing he could do.

"There's been a woman; I saw her auntie. She's been sneakin round Mele's window. She's not like regular peoples." He was going to tell her about Sara and her strange cousins, but thought better of it. There was a reason Sunami wasn't bringing it up and until he had a chance to talk with her, it was probably best to keep that part a secret.

"What you mean she not like peoples?"

Junior's confession was disturbing and there was something about his stance and expression that did not give Leilani the impression that he was lying.

"Sunami has seen her and I saw her." He explained the strange incident of seeing her in the yard, watching her disappear and walk away at the same time. "Uncle Fess gave Sunami these necklaces. He said it would keep the lady away."

Leilani's brow furrowed deeply as she listened.

"Why you both nevah come talk to me? You go to Uncle Fess, who tink every ting be one big joke. He give you dese pilau beads and is probably laughin himself sick." Junior was silent, not sure what else to say. "Tomorrow we goin get to the bottom of dis one. Go to bed now. I goin stay wid Mele."

Junior watched his aunt scrunch up the necklace in her hand as she turned on her heel for her daughter's room. Leilani stopped and opened her hand, staring at the beads nestled in her palm. They were somewhat rough feeling and as she held them she was fascinated as they began to turn from plain brown to an odd color that she had never seen before. She stepped into her daughter's room, thinking. Tomorrow she would talk to Sunami and Junior both. For now she would leave Linda, Ben and Keoni out of it. Whatever her niece and nephew were up to, instinctively she felt that the fewer adults involved, the more information they might volunteer. Sitting on Mele's bed, watching her daughter sleep, worry gnawed at her. *Why did they go to Uncle Fess?* She wondered. Mele's arms rose to rest above her head, as she gave a deep sigh. Leilani stroked her forehead, glancing out the window into the darkness. Maybe it would be a good idea to stay at her sister's for a while, but the thought of Kayle and the dysfunction she created around her immediately caused her to reject the thought. There had to be somewhere else for their family to stay. It was time to start looking.

Chapter 30

Angela sat opposite Sara watching the girl eat. It felt almost surreal to see her student sitting at her kitchen table in her daughter's bathrobe eating leftover pot roast. She ate quickly, shoulders rounded in, and asked for water. The first glass she downed without coming up for breath. She drank half of the second glass before taking a few bites of food and finishing the water. Sara ate as if she hadn't been given food in days.

It had been a shock to see her standing in their driveway earlier, just left there. Under the porch light they had seen that she was a mess. Her arms and legs were streaked with dirt, her hair hanging in wet clumps. Parts of her dress were ripped; the fabric caked with drying mud. "We should call the police," Tim said after they stepped into the living room.

"No!" Sara grabbed his arm, startling him. He stared down at her grimly, his jaw tight.

"Tim, let me handle this." Angela stepped forward, gently taking Sara's hand. She could see that the girl had experienced something terribly traumatic. "Jenny, why don't you take Sara to the bathroom, show her the shower and give her a pair of your pajamas and a bathrobe."

The Visitors

"We need to call the police," Tim whispered, as soon as the girls were out of earshot.

"I agree that things don't look right," Angela told him, "but let's give her a chance to get comfortable. She has obviously been through something terrible. She is not in any position to be dealing with the police at this moment. You saw her, Tim. She's wet and dirty. Right now she needs a hot shower, dry clothes and possibly some food. Once she is feeling a little better, we can sit down and talk to her to get to the bottom of this."

"Yes, you're right," he had said quietly.

Sara swabbed the last bite of bread over the smear of gravy on her plate before putting it in her mouth and chewing more slowly.

"I know this is hard for you," Angela began, "but could you try to explain to me what happened?"

Sara looked up, her large dark eyes swimming with tears that collected on her lashes and finally spilled down her cheeks. "Please don't call the police. I just needed a place to stay for the night."

Angela reached out to take her hand, but she withdrew it, placing it on her lap.

"But why? What happened exactly?"

Sara searched for something to tell Mrs. Knowles. What would happen to her parents and cousins if the police came? Whoever they were, instinctively she knew that they needed to return to wherever they had come from without others knowing about them. She looked at Jenny, whose face was tight and pinched with worry and Jenny's father, who sat frowning at her.

"My mother had an accident and she had to go to the hospital." Sara said quietly. "Papa needed to hurry. He told me to tell you thank you."

"What happened?" Tim asked. His frown deepened. Sara could see that he didn't believe her.

"She got hurt on the path down to the ocean. We didn't know where she was. She fell and couldn't move. I heard her yelling. It was muddy." The image of Lilith's sunken, purple eyes flashed through her mind. Involuntarily, her hand went to her mouth.

Angela flinched, watching the girl. Whatever accident her mother had must have been awful to see. She looked at Tim, whose features softened while watching the girl.

Angela glanced at Jenny. The stark terror on her daughter's face was unsettling. Did she know something? "I think you could use some rest, Sara. We can check in on your parents in the morning. Jenny, why don't you show her where the guest bedroom is?" The girls rose up from the table and walked silently out of the kitchen. Tim stood up as well and opened the cabinet, pulling out a bottle of Grand Marnier. Angela watched as he poured some into a goblet.

"She's hiding something," he said

"Tomorrow, I'll look into it," Angela replied, "I think I may need to report this incident to Child Protective Services and let them investigate to see if there is any abuse. Did you see how frightened Jenny looked?"

Tim shook his head, taking another sip from his drink.

"I feel like Jenny knows more than she's letting on," Angela said.

"I put in a request for a transfer," was Tim's reply.

"What?" Angela glanced sharply at her husband.

"We need to leave here. This place is tearing our family apart." He stood up, glass in hand, and left the kitchen. A moment later, canned laughter filled the living room from the television. Angela followed her husband. Something was not right. She could feel it down to her bones.

Jenny pulled back the blanket on the twin bed and watched as Sara sat down. Drawing her knees to her chest, she looked up.

"I'm sorry," she said quietly.

The Visitors

"It's OK. Whatever it is that happened, I'm glad you chose to come here." Jenny sat on the edge of the bed and fidgeted a moment with the fabric of her nightgown. "Sara, I know more than you think."

Sara blinked. Her face seemed to close up.

"Sunami and I know that those…" Jenny paused, searching for words. "They're not your cousins, are they?" Sara did not respond. Jenny waited and tried a different tact. "I want to help."

"I don't think you can help me," Sara said quietly. "And I don't want you to get hurt."

"Do you remember that drawing you gave me?"

Sara nodded, bringing her legs back up and burying her chin on her knees. "Sunami's uncles have a book with drawings that are like the one your cousin made. She told me that the book is a history of the Night Hunter clan." Jenny could see that she had Sara's attention.

"Where did they find this book?"

"That's the thing. Her uncles said they know about, um, your cousins that are staying with you. Who they really are."

"How do they know about them? Do you think Sunami's uncles would maybe talk with me?"

"Yes. They told Sunami they want to meet you." Both girls fell into a thoughtful silence.

"What happened tonight?" Jenny asked in a low voice. "Why did your dad just leave you here like that?" Sara's expression grew tense as she stared at Jenny. A raw, naked fear emanated from her eyes. Her lips moved as if to speak, but no words came out.

"It's OK," Jenny said softly and reached to hug her. She felt nothing. Disconcerted, she pulled away.

Sara began to tremble. "You can't feel me, can you?"

Jenny frowned deeply, edging away, and then stood up, backing toward the door.

"Why do you feel like air?" Jenny whispered. "Are you a ghost?"

Sara shook harder. "I don't know. I don't know what I am. Please Jenny, don't be afraid of me."

Jenny grabbed the door handle as she felt the blood drain from her face. Sara stared back at her wordlessly, her body shaking violently. Jenny opened the door, slipping out of the room. She needed to call Sunami and see what to do.

The sounds of someone up and about moving around in the living room had her groaning inwardly. The last thing she needed was for her parents to ask her why she was using the phone at this hour. It sounded like someone was dragging the furniture around. Expecting to see her mom or dad when she entered the living room, she was surprised at finding no one there, the room dark. Not sure what to think she slowly headed for the kitchen, where the cordless phone was mounted to the wall. She stopped, hearing what sounded like the feet of a child pattering across the linoleum.

"Hello?" The house creaked slightly from the wind. Jenny turned on one of the lamps in the living room. Everything was in its place. Nothing had been moved. She took a few more steps into the living room. "Hello?" There was only silence. Running the rest of the way across the living room, she threw on the light. Looking quickly about, she saw that there was no one there. Without wasting any more time, she grabbed the phone. But it was when she turned around to flip the light off that she saw something...it was so brief that she wasn't sure. A white, hot terror flooded her insides. There was a girl. Or at least she thought she saw a girl. The image vanished before Jenny had time to really register what she was looking at. Suppressing the urge to scream, she flew back through the living room, not bothering with the lights, and into her room her heart crashing in her chest. Her legs felt like Jell-O and her fingers seemed uncoordinated as she dialed the number for Sunami, all the while continuing to listen for movement outside her door.

The Visitors

Someone picked up the phone on the second ring.

"Hello?" There was a lot of noise in the background, reggae music playing, people laughing and talking. "Who is dis?"

Jenny cleared her throat, not sure if she had dialed the number correctly. She wasn't expecting a teenage boy to answer.

"Is Sunami there?"

"Sunami?" the boy said, puzzled.

"I think I might have the wrong number," but just as she said this the boy called out.

"Ey! Is there a Sunami here?"

"Gimme dat phone," a girl said. "So stupid. Dis be Sunami's place. She's Kayle's sistah."

"Oh," the boy sputtered laughing. "Shit, I'm stoned."

"Hello? Who is dis?" the girl spoke into the phone.

"This is Jenny. Is Sunami there?"

"What you want with that mean ass *tita*?"

Jenny gripped the phone, not sure what to say. But the girl burst out laughing. Jenny could hear Sunami in the background asking who was on the phone.

"I'm just playin wid you," the girl said. A second later Sunami's voice was growling into the phone.

"Who is dis?"

"Sunami? It's Jenny." There was a short silence.

"What up?" she asked in a quieter voice.

"Sara's here. Some strange things have been happening. Is there any way we could take her to your uncle's tonight? I don't know if there will be a chance tomorrow. I think my parents might call child protective services."

"Shit. Fo real? OK. I gone call Pono. We'll be there soon." Sunami hung up. Jenny took a deep breath. Hearing Sunami's voice had settled her nerves somewhat. Afraid to venture back out to the kitchen and place the phone on its mount, she went to sit on her bed and wait. The letter her friend Becky sent her sat on her nightstand. Jenny picked it up, pulling out the contents for the fourth time. She stared at the Polaroid pictures of her two best friends. Tara had cut her hair short. It was red like Jenny's, and for years people had asked them if they were sisters. In another picture, Becky was sitting in a booth at a diner with a boy. She had written that he was a college sophomore and he thought she was a senior in high school. Jenny looked over the letter again, tears filling her eyes. They thought she was having such a great time. That her days must be filled with tanning at the beach, hula lessons and meeting hot guys. They were the lucky ones, Jenny thought. She longed to be home again, with her friends, having a normal life.

Sunami took the phone to a quiet corner of the living room to talk. The house had begun to fill up with Kayle's crowd a few hours ago. The babies had been placed in the playpen to keep them from underfoot and now and then someone would lean over to talk or play with them. Sunami had watched with dismay when the dinner she prepared of ham, cabbage and rice, the way Auntie Leilani had shown her, was mostly gobbled up by three younger men. They showed up soon after dinner was cooked. Kayle had all but taken one bite of the meal, eating a snickers bar and Fritos instead, guzzling down Coca Cola as she laughed, telling her friends that Sunami was keeping an eye on the beer.

The phone rang several times before someone picked up.
"Yeah?"
"Ey, Pono."
"Nah, it's Akamu. I'll get im. Sunami, yeah?"
"Yeah." A moment later Pono picked up, he sounded tired.
"Pono, come get me. We need go by Jenny's. Sara's there." There was a long pause.
"Sunami, I have a lot of homework. I'm kind of behind."

The Visitors

"What? And I no have da kine? You da only one behind? Jenny says it's important." Pono sighed.

"Shit Sunami. I'm seriously behind right now."

"And I'm telling you, you need to get your damn ass ovah heah, and come pick me up." There was a click. Sunami realized he had hung up. Stunned, she stared at the phone before slowly placing it back on the receiver. Shit! That chicken shit!

"What up, Sunami?" Sunami looked up to see Paul watching her. Out of Kayle's crew, he was probably one of the better ones. At least he worked a regular job in construction and would once in a while give Kayle money for food or stop by with groceries. Why he hung around with all the rest of the bozos, Sunami wasn't sure. She pressed her right knuckles into the palm of her left hand, cracking them all at once.

"Hey, what's up?" he asked again.

"I need one ride. A friend of mine get trouble."

"Oh, yeah. I can ride you." Sunami raised an eyebrow and Paul grinned, realizing his word choice.

"You know what I mean, Sis. You wanna ride?"

"Yeah? *Mahalos,* brah. Let me go get my tings." Sunami went to her bedroom and grabbed her backpack, ignoring the three girls that were lounging on her bed smoking doobies. Dashing back out to where Paul stood waiting, she could hear her sister laughing in the kitchen. Relieved that Kayle wouldn't notice her leaving, she slipped out the front door with Paul behind her.

"Thanks, brah," she said again.

"No problem." As they drove down the highway, rock music blared from the speakers. Sunami scrunched up her nose, glancing at him.

"What? No reggae?" He shrugged, turning the dial until there was the sound of familiar Jawaiian music. Sunami sat back, gazing at the empty highway that stretched out before them. She wondered what had caused Sara to show up at Jenny's. The glare of oncoming headlights made Sunami squint, and she sat up straighter as the vehicle became visible. Recognizing the familiar gray truck, Sunami leaned over Paul, pressing on his horn. The other truck slowed, and Paul braked, rolling down the window. The gray truck rolled back. A moment later Pono stuck his head out the window.

"I was just coming to get you," he said.

"Can drop me here," Sunami said to Paul. They clasped hands quickly before she grabbed her bag and flung open the door of the cab, hopping down to the street. Paul gave a quick *shaka*, before pulling over to the shoulder to turn around. Pono leaned over, unlocking the passenger door. He said nothing as Sunami climbed in. Her dark eyes snapped with anger but she was quiet. They drove out to the valley in silence.

As they approached Jenny's driveway, Sunami waved her hand for him to keep going.

"Park up ahead. We goin walk ovah. She's in Mele's old room. We can get in through the window there."

"So her parents don't know what's going on?"

"If they knew, would we be sneakin around?" Sunami pointed a finger at her temple, a sign for him to think. Pono rolled his eyes. If she didn't have such a crappy attitude, she would be a cool kid, he thought to himself. The sound of their footsteps were masked by the cacophony of crickets and the high whistle of the coqui frogs. Pono followed Sunami around the eastern side of the house, where a light shown from a large window. Inside he could see Jenny standing in a nightgown at her closet. Sunami knocked on her window. Jenny jumped, whipping around to stare at the glass. Sunami knocked again and this time Jenny walked over, peering out for a moment before bending down to unlatch the window. Pono watched as she pulled the glass up, her features relaxed into a look of pure relief. Sunami hoisted herself up and climbed in, followed by Pono.

"Why you still in your PJs?" Sunami asked.

The Visitors

"I was just thinking that I need to change before you arrived."

"It's a good ting we nevah catch you naked."

Jenny smiled wanly. She was feeling strange with Pono in her bedroom when she was just in a nightgown.

"Where is Sara?" Sunami asked, looking around.

"She's in the guest bedroom. I'll go get her." Jenny walked to her door, paused and turned to look at Sunami. "Do you mind coming with me?" Sunami shrugged but Pono noticed that she didn't look as assured as she was pretending to be for Jenny. The girls left the room. Not sure what to do, he leaned up against the wall, his hands in his pockets. There was a lack of something about the place, he noticed. The homey feel that he usually had when he went to friends' houses was absent at Jenny's. Instead it felt bleak in the girl's room, almost menacing. Pono pulled his shoulders up, frowning. He would be glad when they were done with all this business.

It wasn't long before they returned with Sara, frail and thinner than Pono remembered. She looked like she'd been sleeping. Her hair was a wild tangle of thick, half damp curls falling dramatically to her waist and her eyes were deeply ringed with dark circles.

"We need to change," Jenny whispered.

"Pono, go wait by the truck," Sunami said. Pono hesitated. The idea of going out alone was extremely unappealing. Jenny picked up on his uncertainty.

"Maybe it's best if we all stick together," she said. "Pono just turn and face the wall." Sara remained quiet. She appeared almost catatonic. Jenny handed jeans to Sara, careful not to touch her. Next she searched her dresser for long sleeved shirts. With Pono's back to the girls they quickly pulled on their pedestrian clothes.

"OK," Jenny called out. Sunami lifted the latch on the window as Sara went to crawl out first. It was then that Pono saw the odd reflection in Jenny's mirror. There stood Sunami solidly reflected holding the window, but Sara was just a wisp of herself. The strange sight made Pono's insides cramp and his mouth go dry.

"Shit," he whispered under his breath. Jenny caught his expression and looked in the direction of the mirror, shuddering at the image. She quickly looked away and waited for Pono to go out next, not wanting to be anywhere near Sara.

Chapter 31

This time they approached the front entrance. Sunami pressed the doorbell as the other three waited behind her. The house was dark, but moments later a light flooded the upstairs window, and there was the sound of movements, along with more lights coming on. Two fake tiki torches, mounted on either side of the bottom porch step illuminated the darkness, and then the door opened. Uncle Fess stood before them, heavy-eyed in a thin, silk robe. All vestiges of sleep vanished when he saw the four of them standing there. Sunami could see Uncle Manuel coming down the winding staircase, hair on end as he pulled his robe tighter over his bulging belly.

"Can we come in?" Sunami asked.

"Yeah, yeah, come in." Fess stepped aside, watching curiously as the four stepped through his doorway. Manuel stopped midway on the staircase, staring down at them. A moment later, he crossed himself and then hurried the rest of the way down.

"What's happened?"

"Uncle, we get Sara," Sunami said. Both men turned to focus on the thin, dark girl, who stood hugging herself. She was tall like her people, with the same high forehead, prominent cheekbones, narrow nose and wide jaw, yet she lacked the aquiline nature of a high servant. The sharp, steely hardness was absent in her deep-set, almond eyes and she was terribly thin. While they stared wordlessly at the girl, she began to sway and seemed as if she might fall over. Uncle Manuel suddenly stood up straighter, fumbling with something on his neck.

"Fess, the necklaces, they're overpowering her," he hissed. Stepping back from Sara, he pulled a string of beads over his head. Fess did the same, handing his necklace to Manuel, who strung them around the doorknob. With this done, Uncle Manuel turned his gaze back to the small group. This time his eyes fell on Jenny and he grimaced deeply, his gaze flicking back to Sara. He spoke something in French and Sara responded by nodding.

"Let's sit down," Fess suggested. The children all left their shoes on a polished koa wood foot rack.

Leading the small party into a mammoth sitting room, Fess quickly moved about turning on lamps. Jenny's mouth hung open as she took in the marbled floors, Persian carpet, crystal chandelier, Victorian furnishings and paintings that all seemed to bear a melancholy, haunting quality. A large wet bar with a wraparound counter and high backed stools with plush, fabric seats filled one corner of the room. Sunami carefully sat in a wide, flaming red, oblong chair, the back curving off to one side.

"Is this one chair or a bed?" she asked, scowling at Uncle Manuel. This brought a faint smile to Sara's lips and Fess threw his head back and laughed at her comment. She looked completely incongruous within the chair in her blue jeans and t-shirt, one leg resting over her knee, exposing a dirty, roughened foot. Pono and Jenny laughed nervously while Manuel stared at all of them in disbelief.

"This is not a time for jokes," he admonished. The laughter dissipated as quickly as it had come.

The Visitors

"I'll go put on some coffee," Fess said, breaking the tense silence. Sara and Pono took seats on a stiff, claw-foot couch a lighter shade of red than the chair and Jenny chose one of the delicate, neutral-colored chairs next to the fireplace. Uncle Manuel stared at all of them for a moment before walking to the bar, where he retrieved a pack of cigarettes from the counter and lit up. He pulled a second cigarette from the carton, lighting it with the first and handed it to Sunami, who took it coolly.

"And who are you?" he asked Jenny.

"I'm Jenny. I just moved here. We all go to school together."

Something cleared in his expression as she spoke.

"Do you live in the Kahiamoi home?" She nodded slightly, looking away. He sucked on his cigarette, inhaling the smoke deeply. It was Sara who spoke up.

"I was told that you might know something of my situation. Maybe you could help." Manuel's brows drew together sharply.

"Help with what exactly?" Sara wanted to talk with Sunami's uncle, but not with an audience.

"*Mes cousins.*" She continued in French, "I was told that you understand who they are and where they come from." Uncle Manuel nodded, smoke curling out of his nostrils. He sat in the matching chair that Jenny was in.

"What were you told?"

"My mother and father told me that they are cousins, but I noticed strange things as soon as they arrived. They were so white and thin; they didn't speak. At first I thought that they were recovering from an illness. There were other things too. Maman said they weren't allowed to eat but could only take the medicine that she kept."

"It is a grey powder that you mix in water," Manuel said.

"*Oui,*" Sara agreed. "When I first touched one of the boys, I noticed that I couldn't feel him." Her eyes flitted to Jenny, whose face was an open book of intense curiosity, for she didn't understand a word. "It took a second before I could actually feel his body. It was like that with all of them." Sara shook her head, recounting her mounting frustration. Everything about her expression and body language was a plea for help, Manuel noticed. As she went on with her story, he was struck by her innocence and benign nature. In all his years he had never meant a servant of her age that did not mirror back the darkness of the masters that they served with the utmost loyalty. Servants were loathed and greatly feared by slaves. A young servant could be particularly cruel as they were usually drunk with power in the beginning.

"How many are there?"

"Four." The sound and smell of coffee percolating had Jenny standing up.

"I'll go see if he needs some help," she said. Uncle Manuel glanced at her blankly before the English words registered.

"Yes, yes, that is a good idea," he said. Sunami for once was sitting patiently. She inhaled on her cigarette, a thoughtful expression on her sharp face, and Pono, bless the boy, Manuel thought, looked tired and lost. Sara continued coming to the last part of her tale.

"I knew all of their names except the eldest girl's. For some reason my parents did not want to say her name out loud and did not want me to know it."

"What are their names?" Manuel interjected.

"Samuel is the oldest boy. Then the younger ones are Michael and Carmilla. The oldest girl, it turns out, is Lilith, although when I mentioned her name to Samuel, he seemed shocked." Sara watched as Sunami's uncle gripped the armrest of his chair at the mention of the names.

"You are certain that these are their names?" His features were slack with disbelief. Sara nodded, feeling herself begin to tremble again with fear that came in surges, wracking through her body. She suddenly felt very sick as she watched a look of pure terror

The Visitors

take over his expression. This had not escaped Sunami and Pono's notice having read their expressions easily. Pono leaned forward and Sunami sat up straighter.

"What?" Sunami finally asked, but Uncle Manuel stood up and walked with quick strides out of the sitting room and down a hallway. A moment later Jenny emerged with Fess, each carrying a silver tray with delicate gold-rimmed cups and a matching teapot. Fess looked around.

"Where is Manuel?"

Sunami shrugged, getting up to take one of the cups and pour herself some coffee.

"He just went took off," she said, avoiding the cream and spooning sugar into her cup. Fess picked up a cup and poured the steaming black liquid, handing it to Sara, who sat with her legs curled under her, shivering.

"I can make one fiah," he said, taking pity on how frail and miserable she looked. Sara held the cup in her hands and tried to respond but she began to shake so violently that some of the coffee began to splash up out of the cup. Pono quickly took it from her as Fess opened a mother of pearl armoire, producing a thick woven blanket, which he threw over her shoulders, pulling it snug around the girl. Her teeth were chattering. His large hands began to briskly rub her arms, but stopped as his eyebrows rose in surprise. He felt nothing, though he saw his hands resting on her arms. Seconds later he felt her, and began again the brisk rubbing. It was that effect, he remembered. They all possessed it. He tried to keep his expression neutral. She was obviously suffering from severe shock. Jenny held her own coffee, her throat tight, understanding why he had paused that way. As Fess continued to rub her arms, her trembling subsided and by the time Uncle Manuel returned loaded down with books, she was able to relax enough to speak.

"I apologize," she said softly. "May I have my coffee?"

Pono, who had sat frozen holding her cup, suddenly came to life, handing it back to her. Uncle Manuel set the stack of books down on the glass table. Squeezing his bulk past Sunami's legs, he clumsily came to sit between Pono and Sara. Opening a book, he thumbed through the glossy pages. It was a fat volume filled with painted portraits of people who looked like the strange children posing as her cousins. Each picture was accompanied by a short biography written in several different languages. He flipped through the pages and came to a section simply called Portraits of Lilith. Jenny and Sunami came to stand behind the couch so they could look down at the book.

"Tell me when I come to her picture," Uncle Manuel instructed. Although these women looked like the visitors who had come to stay with Sara, they also looked different. Their skin was even paler, something that Sara did not think could be possible, and their features more chiseled. The mouths were cruel and hard, the eyes reflecting an evil that even from the page made one's hair stand on end. They carried a human form, but they were so obviously not human.

"That's her!" Sunami called out. There was Lilith, staring back at them, thin lips pulled back in a small, tight smile. She seemed to be looking up coquettishly. Penetrating green eyes, set in a white, skeletal face gazed back at them. Her dark hair hung in carefully made ringlets down her shoulders, her hands rested in her lap, the nails curved and sharp. On her right ring finger was a delicate, silver band that housed a small ruby.

"Her ring," Sara whispered.

"Patience D'wolff 1st, November 1751/52," Sunami read aloud, "What does that mean? Was she born in 1751 or 1752?"

"It is the change of calendar," Sara said quietly. "The old calendar was the Julian calendar. Patience was born in November of 1751, but when we changed to the Gregorian calendar, she was technically born in 1752."

The Visitors

"Fo real? No one never told me that we changed dates like dat. How you know about dis?"

"I read a lot," Sara replied under her breath. She glanced quickly at Manuel, who sat watching her thoughtfully before dropping her eyes back to the book. Sunami continued to read out loud.

"Born in Bristol, Rhode Island, to Joseph D'wolff and Caroline Collins. Married to Master Michel Moreau 25th, August 1771, via his impersonator, Slave Louis Deureaux. Death and rebirth into Lilith line, 1st November 1771."

"Louis Deureaux, that's Papa's name," Sara said.

"Then this man is his ancestor," Manuel replied. "It was common in that time for educated slaves to pose as a master in conducting business, as you can see." Manuel waved his hands over the pages. "These creatures don't look very human, although high servants were actually the real masterminds in conducting and organizing business for divs. In delicate situations such as this, the slave would step in to fill the role of societal expectations. A male high servant would have been too dark to have married Patience." His finger ran down the page. "She was a D'wolff. Her family made their wealth in slave trade. They called it the triangle trade. Ships would leave Europe with rum, trinkets, beads, guns, ammunition and the like, sailing to the west coast of Africa, where they were traded for slaves, gold and ivory. The ships then traveled through the middle passage to America and the Caribbean where the human cargo was sold."

"What's the middle passage?" Sunami asked. Manuel opened another book, pulling out a map draping it across Pono's lap. He traced his finger from the coastal countries of Africa to the Caribbean islands, Cuba and the New England states.

"This stretch of the Atlantic is the middle passage. If you follow from these European countries here—France, Spain, Portugal—and slide down to these west African countries, cross the Atlantic over here," the children followed his finger to America and the Caribbean and back to Europe, "it becomes a giant triangle. You see?" He looked up, staring at their studious faces. "This particular branch of the D'wolff family held three slaving ships, plantations in Cuba and some rum distilleries. They were quite wealthy and their trade in humans would have made them interesting to div society. It was and still is common practice to take over the branch of a wealthy family such as this one, marrying in through the one that is in a position to hold the most power. Most often, the newlywed is killed after legal arrangements have been made of transference of documents, assets and the like. There must have been something about Patience for a Lilith to take an interest in pulling her into that line."

"But women didn't have any power back then," Sara said, frowning at the map in Manuel's lap. "And if she were to marry, her family's money would have stayed with them."

"Yes, you're right, but there were ways around these problems. Louis posing as a master would most likely have ingratiated himself with the family, bringing his own portfolio of wealth and pomp to entice the D'wolff family into combining assets. In the end, signatures are forged, then unneeded parties are done away with."

Jenny shivered, wandering over to the now roaring fire that Fess was attending. Manuel picked up the larger portrait book again. He nodded to himself. "It took ten years to secure the family business. Patience must have been sent away long before. And here it says that Joseph and Caroline both died around that time as well." Manuel scrunched up his forehead in thought, looking off into the distance. "If my memory serves me correctly, in Rhode Island during the late 1700s and a long time after there was thought to be vampirism amongst the young women and girl children, although later it was chalked up to tuberculosis. Lilith must have been there all along. I wonder how they kept her."

Manuel fell silent. The only sound was that of the crackling fire. Sara sipped at her coffee. Her heart had sped up and now crashed against her chest. Lilith's sunken, purple eyes flashed through her mind. *This is what she is,* she told herself and shivered. She had seemed so human the last few days.

"Still cold?" Fess asked. Sara shook her head.

"Uncle Manuel," she inquired. "What about Samuel? I heard Lilith call him a fatalist, and there was a letter I found in my parents' bedroom, it was sent by a woman named Myrina, who is my real mother. She mentioned something about fatalists, being an accomplice and tampering." Sara shook her head in confusion as she spoke, but Manuel's eyes lit up at her words.

"*Mon dieux!*" He smacked his head at her words. "You are a daughter of Myrina? A servant of the first line. And Samuel is a fatalist?" He threw the larger book aside and picked up another. Again he flipped through the pages. "I do not see him in here. These are the fatalists. Many of them have been destroyed already." Pono picked up the larger book that Manuel had cast aside in his excitement, opening it to the index.

"Samuel, page one thirty nine," he read aloud and turned to the page. Sara's breath caught as she stared at his portrait.

White bulging eyes with the just the palest rim of blue; the pupils dark, malevolent pinpricks glared back at them. Power and evil poured from his imposing figure, clothed in a scarlet mantle, dark medieval breeches, stockings and pointed shoes.

"What's that?" Jenny called out, grabbing her arms and looking about her. Manuel looked up sharply, as did the others. The sound of someone whispering faintly snaked through the quiet room like a wisp of smoke and evaporated as suddenly as it had come. "Did you hear that?" Jenny's amber eyes were wide as she looked about her.

"Yeah, I heard it," Pono said in a low voice. Fess stood up and Manuel rubbed at the stubble on his face.

It was felt rather than seen; an icy wave of air and the barely audible hiss of a voice that seemed to come from the northern wall of the house.

"Shit! What the hell is that?" Sunami cried.

"Close the book!" Manuel demanded. Pono slammed the pages shut and tossed the large volume off of his lap. The spine of the book hit the rim of the heavy glass table, falling with a loud smack to the marbled floor. The chill that had descended upon them began to recede. Manuel turned to Sara.

"What do you know of yourself?" he asked. Sara wrinkled her brow, setting her coffee cup down, the liquid now cold.

"What do you mean?"

"Why are you being raised away from the community that you belong to? Can you guess at any reason why you and four divs are being hidden here by people of my clan?" Sara shook her head. Manuel stood up, pulling at his lips, his posture emanating frustration. Sunami came from around the sofa and pushed gently at Pono.

"Ey, scoot ovah," she said softly, before sitting down and drawing her thin legs up to her chest.

"I'm scared," Jenny whispered. "I just want to go home. I want to go back to California and my life there..." her words were cut off by a sudden force that pushed at them, a louder hiss, voices, barely audible were suddenly all around them, accompanied by a whirring sound. Jenny ran into Fess' arms. Sunami and Pono held hands tightly and Manuel's eyes bulged as he stared at Sara. Understanding lit up his features.

"You are a channel," he said, his voice rising over the strange sounds that wound through the room. Sara closed her eyes, her father's words coming to mind.

Mary watches over us, child. You must pray for yourself, Sara. Wash away the darkness that clouds your mind.

"In the name of Jesus," Sara whispered, "I rebuke you, spirits of fear. I command you to go directly to Jesus!" her voice rose as she spoke. "Without manifestation and without harm to me or anyone, so that he can dispose of you according to his Holy Will."

The Visitors

"Sara!" a woman shrieked. "Help me." The voice seemed to suck back into the walls. Sara threw back the blanket from around her shoulders and jumped up from the sofa.

"Lilith!" It was quiet. "Lilith, where are you?" She made to run toward the hallway. Manuel grabbed her arm, wincing when he felt nothing at first, but he tightened his grip and yanked her toward him. Sara tried to pull her arm from his large hand, but he only held her tighter. "It is Lilith," she cried out frantically, "she is stuck somewhere."

"I see," he said quietly. "Hold still, please," he said in the same even voice. Sara tried to steady her breath and push away the anxiety that rose in her chest. Manuel slowly lifted her mane of thick curls, pushing her hair over her shoulder to expose the back of her neck. Along the hairline, just barely visible in the same color as her skin was the coiled image of what he knew would be there, a sleeping serpent. "You are her handmaiden," was all that he could say. "Has Lilith been ill?" Sara covered her mouth with her hand as a tremendous sadness came crushing down on her.

"She died tonight, or that is what I thought. I tried to save her. Papa was going to kill her." Her chest heaved as she remembered the horrid experience. "She told me to take her down to the ocean. That is where she died. She was so sick." Jenny pulled her face away from Fess's chest, her cheeks wet with tears as she listened to Sara's story. "When Papa found me, he made me take him to her, but she was gone." Manuel loosened his grip on Sara's arm, his shoulders slumping forward in what looked like defeat.

"Tomorrow we must all leave here before the sun sets again."

"But I tried talk to Auntie Linda, she won't listen," Sunami cried out.

"I will talk with them," Fess interjected.

"What were those voices?" Pono sat up a little straighter as he released Sunami's hand.

"They are spirits," Manuel said plainly. "There is always some paranormal activity in connection with divs, usually spirits with unfinished business that want to communicate or warn us about something. They become stirred up with the proximity of the masters and high servants. My people, we have many different rituals and prayers to keep spirits at bay. But you," Manuel looked down at Sara. "You are a channel of some sort." He rubbed at his chin, thinking. "I have heard of this, but I have never seen it. You are a source of power. Lilith is weak right now. It is her way to stir up malevolent entities and to psychically travel through the wind. If she can borrow energy from Sara, it will revive her to full strength. Right now she can only gather her strength slowly through feeding. Sit down, Sara."

Sara sat back on the sofa hesitantly as Manuel reached for more cigarettes. After lighting up, he inhaled deeply.

"Fess," he turned to his partner.

"Yes?"

"We must cover all the mirrors in this house. Lilith has tapped into Sara's energy. If Sara were to step before a looking glass while Lilith is actively searching for her, it could become a gateway for Lilith to access her. We must slow the process down for as long as possible.

"I am going to need you to tell me everything, Sara. Everything that you know about your life from the beginning, and I need you children to also tell me of anything unusual that you may have experienced lately," he said looking around the room at five pairs of eyes riveted on him.

"But before we begin I must explain something to all of you which may be hard to understand. First, you cannot talk of this to your family. Second, and this is the hardest to understand, I know." He swallowed, and took another drag from his cigarette. "It is not certain that we will live through this. The more others get involved, the more lives will be at stake." Jenny gasped and Fess pulled her tight against him.

The Visitors

"Oh God!" she cried. "I need to tell my mom and dad. We have to leave." Uncle Manuel pushed Pono's legs aside, squeezing past him and Sunami as he rushed over to Jenny and roughly pulled her from Fess's arms. She gave a shriek, but he did not care as he grabbed her face, his thumb and index finger pinching her cheeks. He pulled her head up so that they were eye to eye.

"When I was a child," he whispered, "I saw other children dismembered. I have seen the unborn ripped out of their mother's wombs and powerful men torn to pieces. If you want your parents to have a chance of living, you will not confide in them. People, innocent people that go investigating, that get involved, disappear. The same with those close to them." Manuel let go of Jenny's face, the imprint of two prominent white marks left on her reddened face. "The slave has always been a private person, as I am sure Sara can attest to, having been raised by two of my race. We are private for good reason, to protect others. Yes we may seem harsh, or unfriendly, but you see it is the only way." Manuel shook his head, and went to the front door where he and Fess had left their necklaces hanging on the knob.

"Sunami," he called. "Come here." Sunami stood upon wiry legs in bulky jeans, seeming to shake a little as she walked to Manuel. He placed one of the necklaces around her neck. "Go with Fess and cover all of the mirrors. Some may be turned around to face the wall. I will stay here with the others. Fess, how many more of these Otomic necklaces did we have?" Fess frowned, thinking, as he went to gather his necklace.

"Dunno, five meybe."

"Bring what's left. I need to make sure that these children leave here with some kind of protection."

"How many mirrors are there?" Sunami asked with a slight lift of her chin. Sara could see that this subtle gesture was her attempt at being brave and for the first time she felt a deep sorrow for the girl. What would happen to her? What would happen to all of them?

"There are only a few," Fess said. "Manuel has never cared for them."

"If you knew what could happen with mirrors you would not care for them either."

"That's enough," Fess replied angrily. "You went scared these *keikies* enough Manuel."

"Have I, Fess?"

Fess dropped his gaze and motioned for Sunami to follow him. The two disappeared down the hall. Manuel sat in the red oblong chair, briefly regarding Jenny. In a matter of minutes, she had become pale and washed out looking, her eyes swollen and her nose red from crying. Pono leaned forward and buried his face in his hands, rubbing at his eyes.

"A few days ago you told me that River and Mele were being stalked by Lilith, correct?" Manuel asked, his question directed at Pono. Sara sat up straighter. She had not heard this before. Pono nodded. "And what has been done about it so far?" Pono lifted his face from his hands. His eyes were rimmed red from exhaustion and shock at the desperate circumstances of their situation. He shrugged.

"We tried to tell River what we knew. We even told him that probably his friends weren't safe, neither. But I don't think he believed us."

"And Mele?"

"Sunami brought those necklaces over there to give to Mele."

"I'll talk with her when she gets back," Manuel said. The four fell into uneasy silence, each in their own thoughts. The hiss of a voice, soft and pleading, had all sitting up rigidly. A girl crying seemed to come from one direction, and then another

"That is Lilith," Sara called out

"Stay where you are," Manuel commanded. He was amazed at the hold Lilith's voice had over Sara. Earlier the girl had seemed to grasp the direness of their situation, but hearing Lilith, it was like she had no previous knowledge of what they were up against.

The Visitors

Having been away from high servants for so long and meeting one as benign as Sara made him forget just how strong the Master's blood was that ran through the veins of a servant. The crying grew louder.

"Sara, help me. Sara." It was not certain where she was; from one moment to the next her voice came from different parts of the room.

"We cover dim all," Sunami said as she and Fess came back into the living room. Something hard hit the wall behind the fireplace and a burning log came flying out onto the marble floor, landing at Jenny's bare feet. She flew from her seat to Pono, jumping into his lap as a loud scream of fury whipped through the room, blasting their ears. The lights flickered out.

"Shit! What the fuck was that?" Sunami said in the darkness. Manuel wiped his face. He had not realized how much he was sweating until droplets landed on his eyelashes.

"She is connected to Sara," Manuel said quietly as Fess went to attend to the blazing log on the floor. "She fortunately doesn't know where she is yet, otherwise she would be here now. If she can get Sara to look through a mirror, she will be able to see with the girl's eyes. Tonight she will search out her marks for sustenance."

"What about Mele?" Sunami asked quietly.

"Did you explain to her about the importance of wearing the necklace at night?"

"Yes. I even went tole Junior before I go by my house to make sure she wears it."

"Than if she is certainly wearing the necklace, Lilith cannot go near her. She is too weak yet to deal with Otomic stones. But in a few days she will be stronger and that is why we need to hide Mele." Manuel lapsed into silence, seeming suddenly lost in reverie. "Mele," he said. "Her name means song." He turned to Fess than in the semi-darkness. "There is no use explaining anything. Tomorrow we will just have to take the girl and keep her safe somewhere else."

"What about Lanai?" Fess asked. "I get one elderly aunt over der. We can send Sunami go stay too. She don't have a phone and so it could bide us some time."

"Yes it may be a good plan," Manuel said. He stood up then to go to the bar where a few candles and matches were kept in a drawer behind the counter. After lighting the tapered candles, Manuel focused his attention on Sara. He needed to find out all he could from the girl. She had no idea what sort of power she held and the danger that she posed to her friends and herself. It was doubtful, he realized, that he would live; but possibly he could save these children and maybe Fess.

Chapter 32

It was 5:30 in the morning by the time Sara was finished telling her story. Manuel wanted to know every detail of her life from her earliest memories up until the present moment.

Pono's head lolled onto Sara's shoulder. Sunami and Jenny remained awake, although their faces were puckered with fatigue. After Sara finished they sat sipping their coffee while Manuel thought to himself.

"I think the best plan for now would be for all of you children to go to school today. When school lets out, come back here. I would like to speak with Sara's parents, if that's possible. From there, maybe we might have a better idea of what to do next. Fess, let's call Clive and see if he can open the gallery today." Manuel looked over at Pono, whose head was back, mouth open, as he slept deeply, emitting a quiet snore. "Wake him up," he motioned to Sara. Gingerly Sara poked her finger at the boy, gently nudging him.

"You goin put him in one coma, rockin him like that," Sunami said and roughly shook him. Pono's head snapped forward, his eyes flying open as he looked around, bewildered.

"You awake?" Fess asked. Pono wiped at his mouth, his eyes bloodshot.

"Yeah."

"After school all you all is going to come back here," he reiterated. Pono nodded, rubbing at his eyes and yawning. Fess got up, pouring a cup of coffee and handed it to Pono.

"Sara and I need to get back home, before my mom and dad notice that we're not there," Jenny said, noticing the gray light of morning outside the windows. To her relief, Manuel agreed. As they filed to the front door, they were each given a necklace to place around their neck, all except Sara, who put her hand to her head, stumbling back slightly.

"Try not to walk too close to her," Manuel said, as the four stepped out the door. The air was cool and fresh outside. Sara took deep breaths, her head pounding from exhaustion and the heavy feeling of the stones that were sapping her last bit of energy. They walked to Jenny's house, parting ways before her driveway. They did not bother saying goodbye to each other. Pono and Sunami climbed into his truck. Sara kept her hand on her forehead. It hurt to look up. Following Jenny's footsteps, they quietly crept around to her bedroom window, pushing the glass up and climbing through the opening. It was still inside, but moments later gun shots exploded through the quiet, followed by a cacophony of birds jabbering away, as dogs began to howl and bark. Rustling movements of Jenny's parents suddenly up and about and then a sharp knock on her door made both girls freeze with alarm.

"Jenny?" it was her mother. Jenny quickly locked her window before moving to her closet as if she were examining the contents. Mrs. Knowles opened the bedroom door and stood staring for a moment at Sara, who stared back at her. Jenny cursed under her breath, realizing that she had forgotten to turn on the light. Her mother would wonder why they were standing around in a dark room.

"Did you hear gun shots?" Jenny could hear the tension in her mother's voice as she nodded yes. Mrs. Knowles stepped into the room, assessing her daughter. "And you're both already dressed." Sara remained silent, unsure what to say. "Why are you girls standing here in the dark?"

"It's the light—my lamp," Jenny said. "It went out, and then it was on, but now it went out again."

"It probably just needs a new bulb." Mrs. Knowles smiled tightly at Sara before walking over to Jenny's lamp and twisting the small metal switch. Light flooded the room. "It seems to be working," she said and turned to look at the girls. In the full light they both looked haggard, as if they hadn't slept at all, and Jenny's face was puffy, like she had been crying. Angela paused, staring at them, an instinctive feeling of uncertainty flooding her body. She wanted to ask her daughter what was wrong, but thought better of it. Whatever the girls had been up to, she realized that they probably wouldn't be forthcoming with the truth at that moment. "I'm going to get breakfast started. And I'll take you girls to school after we eat," she said instead.

Half an hour later, Angela slid behind the steering wheel of her Volvo and closed her eyes for a moment. Last night she and Tim talked about his decision for a transfer request. She had wholeheartedly agreed that it would be good to leave the island and to put the house up for sale. Even if the house didn't sell right away, as long as she and Tim could transfer their employment, they could always rent an apartment. Starting up the car she pulled out of the driveway, ambling slowly up the dirt road. By the time she reached the main highway, both girls had fallen into a deep sleep. For the second time an instinctive feeling that something was terribly wrong gripped at her insides. The girls hadn't slept last night. It hadn't been much past six in the morning when she had knocked on Jenny's door and found them already dressed. Where had they been?

The gunshots jolted Leilani from her sleep, the explosive sounds rousing the dogs as well. They began to bark all at once. She had slept the rest of the night with her daughter cradled in her arms. The sudden noise and commotion of the animals had Mele yawning and stretching. When she opened her eyes and saw her mother beside her, she smiled and nuzzled her face under Leilani's neck. Holding Mele tighter, Leilani kissed the top of the girl's dark head before sitting up.

"Why you stay here, Mommy?" Mele glowed with delight at this unusual occurrence.

"I know you miss Sunami, so I came to stay wid you." Mele smiled wider at these words. "OK little one, it's time to get up now," Leilani said gently to her daughter. "And I need to get ready for work." Mele followed her mother into Kawika and Keahe's room, but the boys were already awake.

"Kawika, go and wake Ikaika and Junior," Leilani said softly. "I goin take Mele to the bathroom." Kawika rubbed at his eyes.

"I think they is already awake, Auntie. That gun was so loud." Kawika's comment sent a small chill down Leilani's back. She left the room only to come face to face with Junior. For a moment they just looked at each other and then Leilani took Mele to the bathroom.

Linda had already started making breakfast by the time Leilani came into the kitchen. She watched her sister-in-law's broad back bent over the mixing bowl as she whipped up more than a dozen eggs. Link sausages were sizzling in a skillet and a full pot of coffee was already made. Leilani pored herself a cup, as Linda glanced in her direction.

"You hear those gunshots?" Linda asked. She frowned as she poured the eggs into a pan. "Someone's up to no good."

"Yes, I heard them." Linda moved the goopy mass of egg around with a spatula.

"I also saw Sunami go riding by with Pono in his truck."

The Visitors

"Sunami?" Leilani asked, startled.

"There's no room for that girl in this house if she gets pregnant," Linda said, and with that, she gave a snort of contempt before stirring the eggs.

Tonight when she returned from work, she would talk with both Sunami and Junior, Leilani thought. Something was definitely not right but she would get it out of them.

Chapter 33

River pounded on the door, glancing over his shoulder at the empty road.

"Is anyone home? Jesus someone be home!" his voice caught as he looked over his shoulder again, rapidly scanning the gardenia hedges and pine trees that enclosed the yard. The dirt road, which dipped and curved behind him was unnervingly devoid of traffic.

"Who is it?" a male voice called from within.

"My name is River. Please help!" He could hear the locks unclasping, and then the door was opening. A hand reached out and grabbed his arm, pulling him into the house. The door was shut and locked again. Two men stood gazing at him and then everything went dark.

Manuel lunged for the gun that slipped from River's fingers, as Fess caught him before he collapsed. Rushing from the room, Manuel returned with a jar of smelling salts, waving the potent contents under the young man's nose and grunting with approval when he took a ragged gasp, turning his head away. River's eyes fluttered open. He looked up at them, disoriented.

"We have heard about you," Manuel said. He placed the lid back on the smelling salts, and set it aside, staring down at the longhaired youth.

The Visitors

"Who are you?"

"We are Sunami's uncles."

Fess helped him up, and he stood looking from one to the other, a wild, unhinged look in his eyes.

"My friends..." he whispered.

"What happened to your friends?" Fess asked.

"There was this woman...she killed...." he paused, licking his lips. "I shot at her when she took off after Don. Those kids tried to warn me yesterday. I didn't believe them." A wave of nausea, fear and grief overtook him, as the image of Leonard being eaten alive paraded through his mind. His legs felt weak and un-sturdy as he took a step and found the contents of his stomach rising to his throat.

"We need to call the police," he whispered. Manuel glanced at Fess, giving a slight shake of his head no.

"Yes, of course," he soothed. "Come into my study. There is something that I would like to show you there. Fess, make him some tea, it will help to settle his nerves." River followed the stout man down the hall. "Have a seat," Manuel offered.

Sitting in the chair next to the window, he was somewhat bewildered and still in shock when a package of cigarettes was produced from a desk drawer and he was offered one.

"Smoke?"

"No." Something shiny disappeared in the older man's meaty palm and he closed his fingers around it, smiling stiffly.

"If you don't mind waiting a moment, there is something I need to get. I will be right back." River frowned at the sharp feeling of uncertainty that stabbed at his intuition. It was only when the door closed that he realized what was about to happen. Springing from his chair he heard the click of a lock.

"Hey man, what are you doing?" He slammed his fist against the door. "Hey!"

Manuel wiped his forehead, hurrying back to the living room. Fess stood waiting for him, his face grim.

"We cannot have that boy calling the police. Not just yet anyway. I must go to Sara's and talk with those slaves. It is all I can think to do at this point."

"What about the other children?" Fess asked.

"Whomever you can successfully take with you to Lanai before the sun goes down would probably be the best plan."

"And you?"

"I cannot go with you, Fess." Manuel turned away from his partner, willing his emotions to stay in check. His duty now was to make sure that Sara made it back to society. He would not live, but possibly his death and the deaths of the slaves pretending to be her parents would be the end of it. The less that was known of his connections with Fess or the other children, the better their chance of escaping the fate that had befallen River's friends. There was not much time left.

"OK, everyone that was bringing one food item, you can put em on da table over here." Mrs. Sakamoto pointed to a wooden fold-out table that she had set up at the side of the classroom. She watched, smiling, as kids filed into the room carrying the homemade goods that they were assigned to make last week. As her students got situated and the bell rang for the second time, she quickly started with taking roll. Looking over her list of eight students that were to bring either a main dish or a dessert, she called their names, putting a check mark next to each one that was present and had fulfilled their homework assignment. She finally came to the last name on the list, Sara Deureaux. Next to her name was written *bran muffins*.

"Sara," Mrs. Sakamoto called out, scanning the classroom.

The Visitors

"Yes," Sara said quietly.

Mrs. Sakamoto finally saw the girl sitting toward the back in jeans and a long sleeved knitted top. Surprised to not see her in her usual homemade dress, she stared for a moment, not missing the fact that Sara looked as if she hadn't slept in days. Dark circles ringed her eyes, her whole face seeming to droop with exhaustion. "Did you bring the bran muffins?" Mrs. Sakamoto asked gently. Sara shook her head, staring at her desk, and folded her slim fingers together, letting them rest contritely on her lap. Mrs. Sakamoto moved on, outlining the lesson for nutrition and announcing that they would be sampling the various food items in the last twenty minutes of class.

"Open your nutrition books to page 75. We will be learning about the different food groups and what constitutes a healthy diet." It did not escape the teacher's notice that Sara Deureaux didn't have anything with her. As she moved toward Sara, a wave of pity flooded her when she saw the girl's expression change to tense worry.

"Sara, I want you to stay behind after class." She patted the girl's back in what she hoped was a reassuring touch and gave her a quick wink. Returning to the front of the class, she continued with the lesson. Three minutes into her lecture, Sara had slipped off to sleep. She did not wake up amidst the commotion of kids rising from their desks, chattering amongst each other as they went to sample the various dishes that were brought in. Some of them glanced curiously at her, but all left her alone.

She could see them from the window: slave children. They stood alone in the empty courtyard below holding hands. Waiting. It was cold and their breath clouded into white plumes, obscuring their pale, young faces with every exhalation.

Pressing her face against the glass, she gave a sharp knock, catching the attention of the eldest girl. Their eyes met briefly.

"Come away from there, Lilith," a woman said, her voice curt and brusque. The sound of heavy boots hitting the concrete echoed amongst the cloistered buildings, and the girls drew closer together. A bearded man ran toward the children, followed by a woman who appeared to be desperately begging to someone, a dark figure hovering over her.

"Please, Miss, please."

"Papa," the eldest girl screamed, grabbing hold of the man's leg. He peeled her fingers away.

"Run!" he shouted. The thick, brown curtain was whisked over the window, obscuring the desperate scene.

"Don't look!" The woman said, inhaling sharply at the gruesome sounds that carried up to the room.

She did not struggle this time when frantic hands pulled her away and led her to the closet.

"Hide in here!" Light illuminated the hiding space, revealing another child crouched amongst the clothes. The door closed, blocking out the shrieking of the children, the sound of flesh tearing and the anguished cry of their mother.

Sara gasped, her head shooting up from her desk where she had fallen asleep. She looked around, bewildered for a moment by the empty classroom. As her eyes adjusted, she saw Mrs. Sakamoto talking on a phone mounted to the wall. Her teacher hung up and walked over to her.

"I am going to give you a pass," Mrs. Sakamoto said, handing Sara a slip of paper. "I want you to go to the counselor's office. You're not in trouble. Understand? But I would like you to talk with the counselor. I can see that something is bothering you and you look like you haven't had enough rest."

Sara took the paper, glancing down at it. Her mouth felt dry and her heart still pounded rapidly from the nightmare. Students for the next class began to file into the room. She stood up stiffly, and without a word, headed out the door.

The Visitors

Mrs. Sakamoto, deep in thought, watched as Sara made her way down the hall amid the clanging of lockers, conversation, laughter and shouting.

The counselor's office was in a side building that was adjacent to the main office of the school. Sara's head pounded as she walked to a yellow door that already stood ajar. Poking her head into the room she was greeted by an older Japanese man. He was writing something down in a folder, but motioned for her to sit down. A moment later he looked up, giving Sara his full attention.

"Sara Deureaux?"

She nodded. He pushed a jar of hard candies in her direction, his smile widening magnanimously. "Help yourself."

"No thank you." Her voice was barely audible. The man cleared his throat.

"I'm Mr. Nakashima." He held out his hand, but Sara's gaze remained on her lap. "Yes, well, it's come to my attention that you have been missing quite a bit of school, but previous to that we have you on record as having excellent attendance and top grades." Sara did not respond. Her head was killing her. She rubbed at her temples and looked up at Mr. Nakashima trying to focus on what he was saying. Something about attendance and grades, it was so simple, why couldn't she follow him?

"Are you not well?' he asked, a note of concern in his voice.

"*Come to me*," a voice whispered.

"Did you say something?"

"Yes, I asked if you were not well?"

"I have a headache."

"Have you been getting headaches often, or is it just today?"

Sara rubbed at her eyes. She wished he would stop talking, asking questions. She needed to sleep.

"Sara?" Mr. Nakashima waited for her to answer, but she did not reply. She was very thin, her face gaunt and her eyes shadowed and puffy. He had seen students like this before when they were involved in drugs, especially crack cocaine, which was becoming a problem these days. Mrs. Knowles had told him that Sara spent the night at her house last night due to some problems at home. He was made to understand that this was unusual, as she had never spent the night away from home before.

"How are things at home?"

Her facial muscles twitched at this question. He had struck a nerve. But she seemed to compose herself. "I'm sorry Mr. Nakashima, but may I speak with you another time. I did not get much sleep last night, and my head...May I go to the nurse's office?" He was struck by her polite, mature conduct.

"Yes, of course. I want you to know that I am available to talk anytime. I would like to help you keep on track. Maybe tomorrow when you're feeling a little better we might talk some more."

She stood up, her dark eyes assessing him sadly. "Possibly."

As she turned to leave, an icy cold descended upon the room, surprising the counselor. It was a warm day but suddenly it seemed the temperature had plunged to almost freezing. There was a strange hissing sound, like someone whispering. Mr. Nakashima stared down at the phone, wondering if he'd left the speaker on. When he glanced up at Sara, a look of intense fear had replaced her previously composed features.

"Sara, is something bothering you?" Mr. Nakashima waited for an answer. The whispering grew louder. He frowned, his attention drawn back to the phone. Picking up the receiver, he was startled when the louvered windows began to rattle, followed by a shriek of fury. The malevolent sound sliced through the office, piercing his eardrums. It's decimal of intensity left his ears ringing and every hair on his body standing on end. When Mr. Nakashima looked in Sara's direction, he found the room empty. She had slipped out the door. The counselor stood up, his body shaky. He noticed that the icy cold dissipated as quickly as it had arrived. Picking up the phone to call the main office, he realized that he was damp with sweat. He set the phone back down, letting his pulse return to normal. What had just happened?

"Hey Jenny," Charlie Baldwin called. It was lunchtime and she stood in a tight huddle with Sunami and Pono near the student parking lot. They were all hoping to avoid Pono's friends and Junior, who just minutes before had tried to start a fight with Pono, demanding to know what was going on.

Sunami had intervened, pushing him into the onlookers—several of her girlfriends. One of them had called out to her, "Hey Sunami, why you went dissing us for one *haole*?" referring to Jenny. Sunami's face became a mask of rage at this question and the girl who spoke fell silent. Pushing Jenny and Pono ahead of her, Sunami shepherded them toward the parking lot for privacy.

Charlie's smile slowly evaporated as he drew closer to their small group and saw how serious each one looked.

"Hey," he said again. "What up?"

Sunami lifted her chin in greeting, but she looked on edge and wiped out. All of them looked beyond tired. He stood for a moment, unsure of what to do or say as the three of them stared back wordlessly. There was no friendly outward gesture of even a hello, other than Sunami's signature chin lift of acknowledgement.

"See you guys around then," Charlie said after a few moments, feeling uncomfortable with the unnatural reticence.

"All right cuz, catch you later," Sunami replied. Charlie nodded and continued on his way to his truck. He was done with school for the day. Looking back at their group as he put his key into the lock, he caught Jenny gazing at him, a look of hope in her amber eyes. Biting his lip, he focused on unlocking his door.

"He's got a girlfriend," Sunami said. Jenny snapped back to attention, tearing her eyes away from Charlie and focusing back on Sunami and Pono.

"Yes, I know."

Sunami's gaze remained fixed on Jenny, her eyes hard. "If you know, then you shouldn't be lookin at him like dat."

Jenny swallowed, her face growing warm.

Pono felt sorry for her. "Let's talk," he interrupted.

"So are you in for Lanai?" Sunami asked.

"It makes sense to hide out there," Pono said, "but my parents and brother would be worried."

"You still don't believe, after everything we just saw," Sunami cried out.

"That's not what I said. Why you gotta jump down everyone's throat? Just because your uncle says we need to go to Lanai, doesn't mean that's what we should do."

Jenny was silent, thinking of her own parents. She had to find a way to get them to leave the area. After Manuel had grabbed her like that, she had lost all trust in him. Sunami turned to her.

"You with me?"

"It's harder for me and Pono," Jenny said. "If you went to Lanai, no one would care." As soon as the words left her mouth she wished she could take them back. Sunami's face darkened.

"You know what bitch, go figga it out fo yourself." She turned to Pono. "Can pick me up heah after school?" Pono nodded.

"Sunami, I'm sorry. It's not what I meant." Jenny took a step toward her, but Sunami whipped around, jabbing a finger into her chest.

"Don't come near me," she hissed. Hunching her narrow shoulders, she shoved her hands in the pockets of her sweatshirt and walked away in her familiar loping style. Jenny turned to look at Pono, speechless.

He shook his head. "Why would you say that?"

The Visitors

"I just meant because her mom…"

He held up his hand, grimacing with disgust and walked away. Jenny's hands fluttered to her face. The heat of embarrassment and shame flooded her body. There was only one way out of this situation and that was to leave the island. Tonight she would tell her mother everything. If she could convince her mom to believe her, then maybe her dad would listen. Jenny hugged herself, biting her lip. What if they didn't believe her? She shook her head. It was a risk she would have to take.

Chapter 34

Angela carefully arranged the stack of quizzes she had administered into a brown folder.

"Mom, it's getting late." Jenny was looking out of the louvered windows for the third time in the past ten minutes as Angela tidied up her classroom. She had told the girls to wait in the room. She wanted to take Sara home and then have a talk with Jenny.

During lunch hour she approached Glen Nakashima in the teacher's lounge to ask him about his take on Sara. Usually easy to talk to, the counselor was distant and appeared mildly disturbed about something. His only answer being that due to what he could observe; it might be in Sara's best interest to have someone from CPS pay a visit to her home.

Sara was sitting quietly at one of the desks. On closer observation Angela realized the girl had fallen asleep sitting up.

"Mom," Jenny called out again. "We need to leave." Angela frowned as she watched her daughter. She was terribly agitated, her face tense with worry. Jenny's repeated requests that they head home soon were odd and disturbing. Why the hurry? Angela was keenly aware that she wouldn't get a straight answer if she asked.

The Visitors

Glancing over her desk once more to make sure she hadn't left anything, Angela grabbed her bag and then went to wake up Sara. The girl woke easily, and saying nothing, stood up to follow them out of the classroom. Upon opening the door, Angela struggled with the wind that had almost snatched the doorknob from her hands, as the three stepped outside into the tumultuous weather. It was hard to see straight or walk, as they seemed to be assaulted from every which way. Already branches and sticks had broken off from nearby trees. Jenny ran ahead through the empty campus to wait huddled up against the car until her mother and Sara came to join her.

It was a slow drive home. The car swayed several times from the high winds and odd bits of debris flew up against the windshield. No one spoke and it was only minutes into the drive before Sara was asleep again. Jenny remained awake this time, her window rolled down a crack to stave off her carsickness. As they drew closer to home, Angela took notice that her daughter seemed to grow more rather than less agitated. She sat up straighter as they left the highway, turning onto the road with the mailboxes, but when Angela made the right turn that would take them to Sara's house, Jenny gasped.

"Mom, where are you going?"

"I'm taking Sara home." She glanced at her daughter in the rearview mirror and saw that her face had grown pale. Jenny said nothing else, collapsing back against her seat to look out the window. It was not that late, but the growing storm made for a dusky sky and as they descended down the driveway lined with Norfolk pines, it was almost dark in the shade of the trees. A minute later, they were pulling into the wide driveway of Sara's place. The familiar gray Ford truck was parked off to the side alongside a blue Toyota Camry and a red Corvette. The Corvette looked familiar to Jenny; she felt as if she had just recently seen it somewhere. Angela gently nudged Sara awake.

"I've brought you home," she told the girl softly. Sara sat up, wiping at her mouth as she looked about, her face registering immediate concern. The girl's expression made Angela hesitate. She knew that Tim wouldn't be pleased to see her back at their house again this evening, but it was obvious that she was panicked at just being in her own driveway. Angela turned to look at Jenny for some kind of confirmation. Her daughter's expression held such terror that it made her heart skip a beat.

"Sara, are you afraid to be here?" Angela asked. The girl only stared back at her. She appeared almost catatonic. That's it. She would just have to deal with Tim's irritation. The girls were afraid of something. For whatever reason, it was obviously unsafe to drop her student off here.

She put the car in reverse, but was distracted by a woman walking through the yard and into the driveway. Tall with dark skin like Sara, the wind whipped at her carefully coiffed hair that was elegantly wrapped into a high bun, creating a halo of curly tendrils that accentuated her high forehead and cheekbones. She was dressed warmly in a pale, creamy turtleneck sweater and blue jeans that hugged strong, lean legs. She smiled, waving her hand, and Angela put the car in park, turning the engine off.

Stepping out into the howling wind, the girls followed her a bit more slowly. The woman who had come out to greet them was saying something, but her words were lost in the rush of air. Finally she beckoned good-naturedly for them to follow her to the house. Well this is an unusual turn of events, Angela thought to herself. They hurried through the yard, stepping into the warmth and sanctuary of the house.

Once inside, the strange woman turned to them laughing, her eyes dancing with mirth as she smoothed back the wisps of curls clinging to her face. Her friendly demeanor brightened the bleak, dour atmosphere of the home. There was an unkempt look about the place since the last time Angela had been there.

The Visitors

"My, but that is a strong storm." Her voice was pleasant and friendly and she smiled so charmingly that Angela felt completely disarmed. "Forgive me. You must all be wondering who I am. My name is Analise." There was a subtle accent to her speech, so mild that only Sara detected it. "You must be Sara," she said with another laugh. "*Je suis une cousine. Oui une autre,*" she added, rolling her eyes and raising a slim, friendly eyebrow at Angela. Angela laughed, relieved to see someone so normal and vivacious at Sara's, but when she glanced at the girls, she noticed they appeared guarded. Jenny had barely cracked a smile. Angela held out her hand.

"I'm Mrs. Knowles, Sara's history teacher, and this is my daughter Jenny." Analise took her hand briefly. She had a fresh, floral scent about her, the odor pleasing.

"Stay a bit and have some tea," she offered. "We are a popular place this afternoon." She led them into the living room. "Have you met Manuel? He is a neighbor from down in the valley." Jenny's heart skipped a beat when she saw Sunami's uncle sitting stiffly in a wicker chair. Next to him sat Sara's father, unshaven and distressingly thin in rumpled clothes. His eyes were hollowed and deeply sad. Jenny watched her mother pause with uncertainty when she saw the two men and the look of tension on each of their faces. With an imperceptible shake of his head, Manuel's eyes shot Jenny a warning look.

"Is something wrong?" Analise said from behind them, a touch of hardness in her previously friendly manner.

Manuel stood up, a wide smile spreading across his full face. "I'm not sure I've had the pleasure," he said taking Angela's hand. "Here, have my seat." Angela sat down slowly, glancing at Mr. Deureaux, who nodded her way.

"Mrs. Knowles," he said politely. The girls took the other two chairs as Manuel leaned against the bookshelf. "I just came to see how Annette was doing. I heard she wasn't very well."

Analise laughed, but there was an edge to it. Angela's stomach tightened. Something wasn't right.

"Annette can be over dramatic," the young woman said. "I'll put some water on." With Analise out of the room, there was only the sound of the rushing wind and the tremor of the house swaying on its foundation. The tension on Mr. Deureaux's face was almost palpable and Sara looked apprehensive, as did Jenny. Angela made to stand up, certain now that something was very wrong. Her first impulse was to flee with her daughter but Manuel's voice cut through her thoughts.

"Storms are always unsettling, isn't that right, Analise?" he called out in a jovial voice.

"Quite," Analise called back from the kitchen, sounding once again bright and cheerful. "Oh dear. Sara, would you help me find the tea? I'm not sure where Annette keeps it."

Her father sprang from his seat. "Let me help," he said going into the kitchen. It was then that Jenny thought she heard something like a child crying.

"Did you hear that?" she asked quietly to no one in particular.

"Hear what?" Analise asked coming back into the living room.

"I thought I heard someone crying," Jenny whispered. Analise threw back her head and laughed. The sound was like bells. It reminded Jenny of Lilith's laugh, without the harsh, sharp quality. But there it was again, a child crying; Angela was sure she heard it too.

"I think I did hear a child's voice," Angela said.

Analise stopped laughing, her smile gone. She fixed Jenny's mom with hard, cold eyes. "It is the wind," she said simply. "There is no child here."

"Yes, the wind is like a song," Uncle Manuel said, his eyes locking with Jenny's. There was something he was trying to relay. Analise laughed again.

"*Oui, oui, le vent chante,*" she agreed, her French so pretty and airy that she almost sounded as if she were singing herself. "There seems to be quite an assortment of teas that Annette keeps. Do you prefer herbal or black?"

Jenny stood up then, taking Manuel's cue and trying to appear as normal as possible. "Actually Analise, I'm sorry, but I can't stay. I have a ton of homework and I thought we were just going to bring Sara by to ask if she could stay over another night. We're working on a project at school." Sara sat up straighter in response to Jenny's words, but her father came back into the living room.

"I'd like Sara to stay here," he said. "We have company. Another time."

"Oh, but I am sorry that you have to leave so soon," Analise said with disappointment. Angela was up and ready to go, impressed with her daughter's quick thinking.

"What are you working on?" the woman asked.

"A history project," Jenny said quickly.

"History." Analise smiled widely. "It is my best subject. You shall get plenty of help from me, Sara." Sara's eyes were cast to the floor. She did not look up. Jenny made a beeline for the door, followed by her mother.

As they walked to the car, pushing against the storm, Manuel's words played over again in Jenny's mind.

Yes, the wind is like a song.

"Song," Jenny said to herself. She ducked into the car, breathing a sigh of relief. And then it struck her. That was Mele she heard crying. Manuel had said her name meant song. Somehow they had gotten a hold of the girl. That was what Manuel was trying to tell her.

Chapter 35

Linda put the last of her cigarette out and set her book down, pouring herself a cup of coffee from a freshly brewed batch. She did not add anything to it, blowing on the hot liquid before taking a small sip. The sudden storm prevented her from getting any gardening done, and since she'd thoroughly cleaned the house yesterday, there were only a few things to put away. She had spent the majority of her day reading a romance novel, transfixed by the unrequited love of the heroine in the story, while Mele played quietly by herself. As the afternoon wore on, Linda turned on the TV for her niece, flipping to the cartoons that the little girl looked forward to. Now the sound of the dogs suddenly barking and growling prompted her to poke her head out of the front door to see what they were fussing about. There was nothing but the empty road that wound its way through the valley.

"Hush up," she called to Jack, who strained rigidly against his leash, growling low under his throat. "For the love of God," she complained bitterly to herself. Over the last few weeks, the dogs had been acting up to the point that she was thinking of maybe giving one or all of them up. They barked at every stray cow they heard in

The Visitors

the distance, waking people up at night. Why they had begun this strange behavior, she couldn't understand. It was chilly out, and in the few moments that she stuck her head out the door, the wind had turned her hair into a matted mess on her head. As she pulled herself back in, the door flew from her fingers, slamming shut in the storm. A moment later, she realized why the door had blown closed with such force. There was a cross draft coming from the living room.

"Mele, did you open the glass door?" Linda called, trying to make her voice heard over the cheerful sounds of banging and clanging that came from a *Tom and Jerry* cartoon. When her niece didn't answer, she rolled her eyes, stepping into the living room. The sofa was empty and the glass door wide open. Linda closed the door and turned the television down.

"Mele?" Now where had she gone? She couldn't have gone out into that weather, although why she opened the glass door to begin with was a mystery.

"Mele?" Linda put her hands on her hips, frowning. She could still hear Jack barking. A feeling of uncertainty took hold of her. Hurrying to the girl's bedroom, she found it empty. Panicking, she ran through the house, searching all of the rooms, and then she ran outside, shouting into the wind. There was not a soul in sight

"So you are Myrina's other daughter," Analise said.

After Jenny and Mrs. Knowles left to go home, all pretences of tea and good humor were dropped. Analise stood over Sara, her eyes narrow, hard and suspicious. Sara did not reply. She did not dare to look in Manuel's direction either. Unsure of what role he played in the events that seemed to be spiraling out of control, Sara realized that he could possibly be in danger as well.

"Louis tells me that you have no knowledge of our legion or your lineage, yet you went above and beyond to aide your master." Analise raised her eyebrows, smirking, but she also seemed mildly impressed. "It is interesting to witness the effects of a high servant such as yourself, steeped in human values, rally to the defence and protection of a holy one in her most vulnerable state." Analise looked about the small room, her expression thoughtful. Louis and Manuel remained silent.

The sounds of footsteps on the stairs and voices caught Sara's attention. A moment later, an old woman emerged. She was dressed similar to Maman but there were small differences. She wore a scarf of brilliant blue on her head. Under it she appeared to be bald. A pale, yellow apron was tied around her middle, the border made of light brown gingham. It accentuated the light blue of her long cotton dress and the darker, piercing blue of her scarf. Her round, brown eyes were as sharp and observant as a bird. She smiled when she saw Sara, her face dimpling and folding into many crinkles.

"Ah, my lady." She curtsied, bowing her head respectfully and stepping aside to let someone else through. Sara gasped as she glimpsed the girl who stood behind her and heard Manuel whisper.

"*Mon dieux!*"

It was like looking into a mirror. Sara felt faint as she stared at the girl who held all of her physical attributes. But that was where the similarity ended. This girl stood with quiet arrogance, her expression discomforting. She wore stylish, modern clothes and around her neck was a simple delicate, silver choker. The centerpiece was a ruby that rested attractively against her dark throat. Crossing her arms, she gazed down on Sara, unsmiling

"Your sister, Selene," Analise said.

When she looked in Manuel and Papa's direction, they lowered their eyes immediately, giving a slight bow. Apparently, Manuel's reaction was not fast enough because the girl strode across the room, grabbing a fist full of his hair. She yanked his head up, slapping him hard with the backside of her hand.

"Impudent slave," she hissed. Manuel said nothing, only lowered his eyes again. Releasing his hair, Selene moved over to Papa, her eyes boring into him.

"We are disappointed in you, Louis. Annette tells me from the window of the little room that she hides in, about the plan between you two to destroy our master. If it were not for my sister, Lilith would be wandering aimlessly through the corridors of time. And Samuel?" She paused. "Is it true he is a fatalist?" There was a hint of incredulity in her voice, her tone similar to Manuel's when Sara had told him this bit of information. Although where she heard this, Sara wasn't sure.

"We have always just followed orders," Papa said quietly.

"I did not ask you about orders." She flicked her finger at his forehead. "Do you take me for a fool?" He did not answer. "Tell me this, Louis. Were you ordered to destroy Lilith?"

"No."

"With all due respect, my lady," the old woman interrupted, "Master Samuel is consumed with the sickness. He is caught in the full grip of amnesia. Thinks he's a lad again in the 1300s." She clucked to herself at this information.

"Just the same," the girl responded, "I would not dare to decide Samuel's fate outside the court of his peers. He will return with us."

She looked at Analise, who said, "Darious has spotted Carmilla. That means Michael can't be too far from us."

"Shall I coax her with the child?" the old woman asked eagerly. Sara winced at her words, her stomach turning at the thought of it.

"No," the girl said. "Now that my sister is here, I do not have to struggle so hard to communicate with Lilith. We will save the child for her." Her dark, cruel eyes fell to Sara. "Her handmaiden is a direct vessel. We just need a mirror."

317

"There are no mirrors here," Papa said, pausing and adding, "my lady." The girl smiled smugly.

"I thought it would be the case. I have brought my own glass." Again the faint sound of crying made Sara strain her ears to listen. But Samuel's sudden moans and coughing drowned out the dim sounds of distress.

"Why is the child crying?" the girl snapped. "When I brought her here, she was happy."

"My lady," the old woman shrank back at the servant's sudden fury, "all children cry when they feel the end is near."

"Where is she now?"

"I have put her in the closet in the room down the hall, locked her in tight."

Sara jumped to her feet. "Please let her go! I know her. Please!"

"Sara," Papa said in a warning voice, but instead Selene turned on him, her face contorted with rage.

"You dare to reprimand her!" Sara ran to her father, throwing her arms over him, he felt like a bundle of bones.

"He is my father. I only know him as that." She could hardly breathe as she stared in horror at Selene. She was nothing more than a monster with her face. Sara's action seemed to calm her sister, for she composed her irate features.

"Very well. You heard Lilith. Bring her the child, Brenda."

"Yes, my lady," the old woman said. She quickly curtsied before rushing from the room.

"Analise, come and help me tend to Samuel. I wish to see if we might catch him in a lucid state." The girl paused, looking over her shoulder.

"Do not bother running away, my sister. We will find you. Those that harbor you do so at their own risk." The two left the room and Sara buried her face in her father's chest, all of her anguish bursting forth in a flood of grief. His arms slowly wrapped around her trembling body.

The Visitors

"Sara," he said softly. "Listen to me, child."

She raised her head to gaze into his kind, sad eyes. His face was worn and creased with the misery of the last several weeks. "You are better than this," he whispered. "Maman and I cannot protect you anymore, but we will always be in your heart. Try and remember our Father in heaven and what we have taught you. Pray always."

Sara shook her head as if to dispel all that was around her, but Papa reached out and held her face in his rough hands. "The fiend's blood runs through your veins, but it is not you." He leaned forward and spoke into her ear. "Do not give Samuel away. He is your only ally." Straightening up, he stroked her hair. "One day you will step into the true physical, and your spirit will be free."

Manuel was silent, watching this interchange. The sounds of crying grew louder and then the old woman, Brenda, was back, holding the small hand of Mele, whose chest heaved, her body trembling between terrified gasps. She hung back, distrusting of Sara and the two men, and Sara suddenly realized why. Her sister had mentioned getting Mele herself. Mele must have been tricked into thinking that Selene was Sara.

Sara walked over to the girl who watched her with wide eyes, confusion and fear on her small face.

"It's OK, Mele," she spoke soothingly, reaching out gently to take the girl's hand. Mele stepped into her arms and Sara picked her up, walking back with her to one of the chairs, where she sat holding the girl protectively on her lap.

"Sara, can take me home?" she asked between gasps.

"Yes, soon." Sara stared at Brenda, feeling disgust for the old woman whose round eyes never left Mele. She did not dare to look directly at Sara, but smiled submissively.

"There, there little one," she soothed. "Don't you see our lady has taken a liking to you?" Her overly subservient nature and pandering ways made Sara feel repulsed.

"She is a kid snatcher," Manuel said. He spoke in French to keep from frightening Mele. Sara turned to look at him and his own face mirrored her disgust. "She would woo even our own children to give up to a master, although it doesn't take slave children long to avoid the clutches of these women. A slave child of six knows that to listen to the coercion and promises of a kid snatcher means to disappear."

Sara held Mele tighter in her arms, noticing that it was growing darker out. Maybe she could convince her sister to let Mele go. Brenda left the room and Sara could hear her bustling about in the kitchen. But what if they kept Mele? She swallowed, thinking of what the girl's fate might be. Sara stood up, continuing to hold Mele tight in her arms.

"Papa, I have to take her home," she whispered.

"It is too late," he said quietly, also keeping to French so as not to worry the little girl any further. He pointed out the window at the storm. "There are spirits unleashed. She is hunting for you, child. You cannot possibly make it safely on foot." His voice grew more hushed. "There is the little place I showed you. You could hide the child in there, if you get the chance. But she would have to have the sense to keep quiet, no matter what sounds she hears." He hesitated, and then continued. "Sara, you will be returning home, to a place you do not remember. Manuel, Maman and myself, we will not be joining you."

"Will you stay here?"

Papa's gaze returned to the window. He said nothing.

Chapter 36

Junior stood waiting by Pono's truck. He leaned against the front end, scowling as Sunami and Pono approached him.

"What? Make mo trouble, Junior?" Sunami called out. She felt exhausted and her nerves were on edge. It did not help that just to look at him excited and irritated her at the same time.

"No," Junior replied. "Can get one ride?"

"Do we get a choice?" Sunami asked, opening the passenger side of the cab and throwing her backpack inside. "You missed the bus anyway," she added.

"Look, you need tell me what's going on," Junior said. But this time his expression held no malice, just genuine concern.

"We can't," Sunami said with a sigh.

Pono inclined his head toward the truck and Junior climbed in, followed by Sunami who slammed the door after herself and then situated her body so that she and Junior were not touching in any way. Pono slid into the driver's seat.

"Brah, I'm sorry," Junior began, but Pono held up his hand, saving the other boy from having to continue.

"It's all forgotten." They drove the rest of the way in silence, Pono negotiating the truck around various objects that the wind had tossed into the road. It was an uncomfortable drive, each of them lost in their own thoughts. When they finally arrived in the valley, Sunami sat up straighter, noticing her Auntie Linda standing in the road, her hands over her mouth, shouting something.

"Hey isn't that your mom?" Pono asked. Junior looked up, frowning.

Seeing them pull up alongside the house, Linda ran toward the truck. Sunami's heart skipped a beat and she rolled down the window.

"It's Mele," Linda cried. "She's gone!"

"What?" Sunami whispered. She could feel the blood drain from her face as a cold knot of terror formed in her belly. Opening the door, she swung her legs out of the cab, jumping to the ground, followed by Junior. Pono parked the truck in the carport before coming to join them. It was hard to talk in the storm. The four ran into the house.

"What happened?" Sunami demanded. Linda was taken aback by her niece's tone. Her son and Pono stood with arms folded, both their faces tight with tension.

"She was watching cartoons. I found the sliding glass door open. She must have gone out. I just don't know why she decide to go out in dis storm."

"How long has she been missing?" Sunami asked.

"I don't know. I've only been looking for meybe five minutes." She decided to leave out the fact that she had been lost in reading her novel in the kitchen for nearly an hour.

"She went took her, didn't she?" Junior said to Sunami.

"Who took her?" Linda demanded. Her question went unanswered. Sunami ran from the room.

"Junior, you need tell me what's goin on." Feeling mounting frustration at the lack of respect, Linda followed her son, watching him

The Visitors

open his closet. Her eyes widened when she saw him pull out his hunting rifle and the buck knife that his father had given him last Christmas. "Junior, why you need those things?" Linda yelled, her heart in her throat now as she watched him load bullets into the gun.

"Junior!"

Her son's jaw was hard. He glanced up at her, determination emanating from his dark eyes. "Mom, I can't talk wid you right now. But we goin find Mele."

"Why do you need a gun, Junior?" He squeezed past her.

"Sunami!" he called. Pono came out into the hallway.

"Sunami wants to know what you did with those necklaces," Pono said.

"Auntie Leilani took em from me last night. She caught me trying to put the necklace around Mele's neck."

"Yeah, but it smells strong in her room." Pono said. "She must have stashed them somewhere."

"Those *pilau* necklaces?" Linda echoed.

"Why we need those?" Junior asked.

Sunami joined them in the hallway, the necklaces dangling from her fingers. Her features and thin, wiry body radiated a fierceness that Linda had never seen before in the girl.

"Put this on, Junior," she said, throwing him one of the necklaces. He caught it and slipped the brown beads over his head. "Me and Pono get our own in our bags. You too, Auntie," she commanded, holding the other necklace out to Linda. Having had enough, Linda stepped in front of her son, pulling back her thick shoulders and straightening herself to her full height as she glared at her niece. She was not tall but her figure was like that of a female linebacker.

"I'm not taking that nasty ting and wearing it, and what's more, I'm goin to call Ben and tell him come straight home, because all you all has lost your minds. Mele's probably hiding, gettin a good laugh at all a us." As she heard her own words, she knew deep down it wasn't true.

"No she's not!" Sunami exploded. "You weren't watching her and she was taken. Taken! You get that, Auntie?"

"Ey!" Junior yelled. "Don't talk to my mom like that." Sunami wiped at her nose that was beginning to run. Junior's face softened.

"We goin find her," he said. Sunami nodded, not daring to speak. Pono cleared his throat.

"I think we should let Uncle Manuel know that Mele's missing."

"Uncle Manuel? What has he got to do with it?" Linda asked. She was feeling increasingly sour and frustrated with every second. No one answered her. *I may as well be a ghost*, she thought to herself.

"We don't get time," Sunami said. "Maybe we can call him and let him know what."

"I'll get the dogs," Junior said.

"Aren't animals afraid of them?" Pono asked.

"I'm goin bring dem anyway," Junior said over his shoulder, as he headed for the front door. Pono followed him, bracing himself against the wind. Jack pulled at his chain as the boys approached, his wide head and powerful jaw straining as he stretched his thick neck against his collar, whining and barking. *It is too bad he can't speak*, Pono thought. Junior handed him his gun.

"Here, hold dis." Pono took the gun as Junior unhooked a metal clasp. The sound of a car rolling past them caused both boys to look up. It was Jenny and her mom. The car slowed, coming to a stop. Flinging open the door she jumped out, holding her red hair down with her hands to keep it from being whipped around by the strong gusts. Jack made a lunge in her direction, the dog's mouth peeling back to reveal his sharp teeth. Junior grabbed hold of his collar as Jenny froze. Her eyes then swept over to Pono holding the rifle.

"Mele's gone," Pono yelled above the wind. Jenny did not look surprised, but her fear was visible.

"They have her?" she called back. Pono nodded, his eyes tearing

The Visitors

up from the cold air that blew against his face. As Jenny held tighter to her hair, the wind grew stronger. All at once it stopped, like a switch being turned off.

Junior looked up, frowning at the sky. It was oddly still like the depths of the ocean when diving a hundred feet below. The air felt thin and oppressive.

"Mom, call the police," Jenny said, her voice sounding small in the unnatural quiet that surrounded them. Jack and the other dogs began to bark, growling and snapping at nothing.

"Someone's missing?" Angela asked. There was a tremor in her voice.

"Junior's baby cousin, Mele. The little girl that used to live in the house we live in now," Jenny said. Angela's hand fluttered to her mouth in alarm.

"I'm going to stay here," Jenny said, stepping away from the car.

"No, Jenny I'm not comfortable with that. I would like you to come home with me. There is a lot we need to talk about."

"Mom, I can't go with you right now. I promise that I will explain everything later, but right now I need to be here."

Angela's throat tightened as she took in her daughter's determined face and the tense looks of the young men.

"Just call the police and tell them that there is a child missing. Her name is Mele Kahiamoi. I promise I'll be home soon."

"I'd like you back home in the next twenty minutes," Mrs. Knowles said, before climbing back in the car. She sat for a moment, watching her daughter walk up to the red house that belonged to the local family whose residence filled her with overwhelming guilt every time she drove by it. The boys followed Jenny, all three walking into the house. Angela headed for home. She would call Tim as well as the police.

Sunami pulled back the kitchen curtain, peering out of the window while she cradled the phone up against her ear, counting the rings. *Pick up Uncle,* she repeated over and over in her head. She frowned when she saw Jenny pull up with Mrs. Knowles in front of the house. The sting of Jenny's words still echoed in her mind, and she felt her body grow warm with anger. Auntie Linda stood next to her, arms crossed.

"Why you callin Uncle Manuel?" she demanded. Sunami watched Jenny get out of the car, her hands on her head, holding her hair down. She was shouting something over the wind at Pono and Junior. Mrs. Knowles got out of the car. She looked strained and frightened.

"Hello?" a male voice said into the receiver.

"Uncle," Sunami breathed.

"Sunami?"

"Mele went turned up missing." There was a brief lapse, the sound of static crackling.

"Uncle Fess?"

"Yes. I'm still here." His voice was tired and strained.

"Where's Uncle Manuel?"

"He left hours ago to go to Sara's house. He never come back." Sunami's heart quickened as she stared out the window at Jenny lowering her arms from her head, and crossing them instead. Junior was staring up at the sky.

"Sunami, you kids best come here and I'll take you to Lanai."

"We can't leave Mele."

"River…"

Auntie Linda grabbed the phone from Sunami putting it to her ear. Her expression grew slack as she listened to whatever it was that Uncle Fess was saying.

"Hello?" she said into the phone. She pulled it away from her ear and put it back again. "Hello?" Linda looked at Sunami, real worry clouding her features for the first time. "The phone went dead. Who's River? Who's Lilith? Uncle Fess says someone named Lilith went killed River's friend."

Sunami did not bother to answer her aunt. She darted out the front door, her aunt on her heels.

The three looked up as Sunami stood on the porch staring down at them. Jenny's wan face was a mix of emotions; sadness, chagrin and fear all displayed at once.

"They took her," she said. "I just came from there."

"You get one more gun, Junior?" Sunami asked. Junior nodded. Their voices had taken on a peculiar quality, as if they were all talking on a phone that did not have very good reception. Linda watched helplessly as her son ran back up the front porch. She did not bother to say anything, realizing now that her words, reprimands and demands meant very little to any of them. He was back within the minute with his father's hunting rifle, tossing it to Sunami.

"Bullets?"

"It's loaded," Junior said. Sunami held the rifle with confident ease. She went to release Killa Boy. Junior unhooked Jack again, hanging onto his collar.

"You bettah go inside with my mom," he said to Jenny. Jenny slipped into the gate, as Jack and Killa Boy growled, sensing her fear. She climbed the steps, glancing one more time at Sunami. Sunami did not look up but her jaw, held tightly shut, flexed as if she knew that Jenny was watching her.

Once Jenny was inside, the dogs were let loose. Pono went around back to untie Pele, but what he found made his stomach turn. Junior's mother had never noticed that Pele's leash was stretched all the way toward the back bushes. He found the dog sprawled in the grass, her throat gouged ear to ear from what looked like a blade. How someone had managed to even get hold of a powerful animal like this and kill it with one swift stroke was unimaginable. Letting the dog's head fall back against the grass, Pono was about to stand up but Jack and Killa Boy came racing over to him, sniffing and whining at Pele. *They know she's dead,* Pono thought. When he looked up, he grimaced, watching Junior and Sunami come around back. Junior looked perplexed for a moment, but Sunami's face seemed to close up as her eyes swept over the whining dogs and Pele's immobile body.

"Pele!" Junior called, his voice catching. He quickly knelt down to examine his pet. When he looked up, his dark eyes were moist and his lips and cheeks twitched uncontrollably. "Who would do dis?"

Sunami and Pono were silent. Anger contorted his features as he stood up, clenching his gun.

"Do you think guns would work?" Pono asked.

"What do you think?" Sunami snapped.

"It's just, the reading I've done on demons. I don't think you can kill them with guns."

"Demons?" Junior echoed, incredulously, but even as he spoke the word inside it felt like the truth.

"Pono, we don't get time for you to act like one sissy. You wanna chicken out, brah, go wait inside with the rest of the girls." Pono gritted his teeth, but he said nothing more.

As the three made their way out of the yard, they were startled to see Kawika, Ikaika and Keahe walking home, having forgotten about the younger children and the school bus. There was a solemnness about the boys as they made their way to the house.

"Ey!" Kawika called out. "Where you guys going?" But he didn't wait for a reply. Instead he turned to Keahe and Ikaika. "It's like someone is snatchen the words outta my mouth. You hear how sissy I sound?" The other two boys nodded. There was a glum look to all their faces. They took in Junior and Sunami holding hunting rifles and Pono hanging back behind them with the dogs. Kawika wanted to ask them why they had the guns, but it was too unsettling to speak. He said nothing.

"Go on into the house," Junior commanded, his speech halting at the strange effect of his words. It was as distracting as listening

The Visitors

to an echo of one's voice when speaking. The boys obeyed, walking slowly up the steps, looking over their shoulders at the older kids departing down the road. Kawika opened the door and drew back in surprise when he saw Jenny standing with his mom in the hallway.

"What's she doing here?" he asked, before he had time to register the worry and concern on both their faces. "My voice. It's normal again," he commented. His brother and cousin came in behind him, gaping at Jenny.

"Go wash your hands," was all his mother said. The boys took off their shoes, standing for a moment and staring at Jenny, who stared uncomfortably back at them.

"Ey! What did I say?" Linda yelled. They immediately began making their way to the bathroom. The woman sighed out her mounting frustration. *At least some people are listening*, she told herself. She sized Jenny up. The girl was all arms and legs, with skin that looked like it burned after ten minutes of sunlight. Her hair was a striking red.

"You going to tell me what's going on?" she asked.

Jenny's hand fluttered to her bangs, she brushed them off her forehead. As she glanced toward the front door, she noticed Sunami's backpack lying open, partially glimpsing dull brown stones. *She forgot her necklace!* Jenny thought, walking to the bag and kneeling down to pull the stones out.

"What are those for?" Linda asked. Jenny looked up at the woman and back at the stones that she held draped over her fingers. The brown began to disappear and the color started to change to something Jenny had never seen before, casting an ephemeral glow.

Linda gasped. "Why they do that?"

Jenny closed her fingers over the stones in her hand and stood up. "I'm sorry, but I need to get this necklace to Sunami. She'll need it where she's going."

"Where's she going?"

Jenny did not bother answering her, but ran out the door and out toward the road.

"Auntie!" Ikaika yelled. Linda jumped as her nephew ran up to her.

"Someone went killed Pele!" The other two boys darted out of the sliding glass door. Ikaika stood, his chest heaving, waiting for a reply from her. Slowly his expression changed to one of dread as she stood mute and sweating.

"Where's Mele?"

Linda wanted to say something but she felt she might just cry. "Auntie, where's my sister?"

Chapter 37

They were already out of sight, having rounded the bend to the road that would lead them to Sara's. Jenny's legs pumped under her and she tried to push the frightening images out of her mind: Sara's transparent reflection, the voices calling the girl at Fess' house and Mele crying, hidden away somewhere by the strange woman who called herself another cousin. Once she reached the top of the road, she paused. It was empty, the bridge below desolate looking. They had crossed already. Hesitating, she thought of turning back and asking her mom to drive her, but she knew her mom would do no such thing. She took a few steps forward and slipped the necklace around her own neck for comfort. If she ran, she could probably catch up in a minute.

It was very cold as Jenny jogged down the hill. The sky had grown greyer, threatening rain, and the trees and hedges that formed the shady grove created shadows along the way, their effect startling at times, the dark shapes long, ominous and almost human like.

The quiet was like the storm inverted. It was all around, invisible, oppressive and dangerous. A flicker of something, Jenny wasn't quite sure what, caused her to stop suddenly. She waited, scanning the environment. The road was empty, as was the sky—trees, bushes, grass—all were absent of movement. Certain now that it was just her imagination, she began to run again, her breath hard and laborious, the air seeming to suck the oxygen from her lungs.

There it was again, a fleeting wisp of a white arm and fabric. It was gone before she could decide what it was. Her slippers scraped the dirt, sounding loud in the absence of any other life save for herself. But soon her footsteps were matched by a second pair, crunching dirt and gravel behind her. Glancing quickly over her shoulder, she saw no one, only the empty road she had just traversed.

As Jenny ran, she tried not to think about the fact that she was being followed by someone or something she couldn't even see. It didn't seem a good idea to go into the bushes and hide, for even the foliage appeared menacing. Her legs and arms ached as she continued her brisk run, the tension mounting when she found she was getting closer to Sara's. There was still no sight of Sunami, the boys or the dogs. Had they taken a different route? She was too afraid to go back the way she came. Stopping to catch her breath, there was a lightening of the uneasy stillness.

The sheet of grey clouds overhead parted and rays of late afternoon sun filtered through the trees, creating swirling tunnels of dusty light that dappled the ground in golden splotches. She began to walk, feeling a sense of relief, but it was short-lived. Something was following her again at a rapid pace. Tired, she began to run, her ribs hurting from a level of physical exertion that she wasn't used to. Squinting from the sunlight that danced along the leaves, the reflection winked back at her, now bright, now dark. She saw an arm, hair, then nothing; the image dissolved as fast as she could make it out. It was hard to breathe. She pushed faster, keeping her head down, moving forward.

The Visitors

She almost stumbled on her, a woman crouched by the side of the road, head tucked down into long white legs, bedraggled hair hiding her face. Jenny took a step back. Jolts of shock stabbed at her skin. Her mouth went dry.

"Don't leave," the woman said. Her words seemed to hang in the still air. She lifted her head and Jenny placed her hand over her mouth, suppressing the urge to scream. Green eyes too large for the skeletal, demonic face held Jenny's gaze. They were glistening and entreating. Rising slowly to her full height, she was much taller than before, wearing a thin linen dress that was torn and stiff from dirt and blood. A shadow of a smile played on the white lips as her gaze fell on the necklace Jenny wore.

"Otomic stones," she whispered.

It was not clear what happened next, for in one instant, she stood at a short distance, and the next, she hovered over the girl, one bony finger gently caressing the stones.

"How quaint," she rasped. Each word was drawn out like the slow scrape of metal. Her breath was putrid, falling in warm wisps of air over Jenny's face as her fingers wandered over the girl's face and hair with sharp nails. "Things are a little different this time," she said as if speaking to herself. "I don't know quite where I am or why I am here."

When Jenny didn't answer, the thing wrenched her arm without warning. She yelped, feeling something tear in her shoulder.

Lilith laughed softly, her eyes darkening into mesmerizing pits of blackness.

Jenny swallowed, her throat tight and her shoulder on fire. The white hand pulled harder and this time Jenny heard a pop. She began to scream, pleading with the demon that held her in its grip. Warmth spread across her jeans and she realized that she'd lost control of her bladder. Spots floated before the girl's eyes as Lilith brought her face closer. Cold lips grazed her ear, sending a shiver of revulsion through her body.

"Shh," Lilith whispered, "maybe you can help me. Do you know where my handmaiden is? She goes by the name of Sara." She gave another twist to Jenny's arm.

"Please, please,"

"She left me on the shore last night, all alone."

The sounds of dogs barking caused Lilith's head to whip around at an impossible angle. Fast approaching were Jack and Killa Boy with Junior behind them. Lilith pushed Jenny away, knocking the girl hard to the ground. The first dog was on her, tearing into her leg, followed by the second, which was on her backside. Lilith's head righted itself on her shoulders. She gave a great, piercing shriek that shot through Jenny's eardrums. Too weak to move, she watched with horror as the demon's mouth receded far back from her teeth, her fangs dripping with saliva. Lilith pulled away from the dog's grip, her leg deeply gouged down to the bone. In an instant, she snapped the animal in half, as if it were nothing but a twig, throwing its convulsing body against Junior. Sunami and Pono were not too far behind him, but they halted their forward momentum when they saw him knocked flat on his back from the impact of Killa Boy's body, the gun flying from his hands. Jack got a hold of the back of her neck, the animal's eyes bulging, as it tried to shake her but she was unstoppable. Her arms contorted backward, grabbing the canine and tossing it against the embankment. The dog yelped pitifully from the impact. She suddenly sprang on Junior, grabbing his upper lip. Skin, flesh and muscle came away. She ripped open his face as if tearing a page from a book.

A shot rang out, and blood exploded from her chest. There was an odd sound of growling and whining that arose from Lilith, and she stumbled back from Junior's body. Sunami shot again, this time catching one of her arms. She screamed, freezing in action. The black eyes focused on Sunami, everything grown still.

In the next moment, she was gone, springing in one single bound into the dense foliage along the roadside.

The Visitors

Sunami ran to Junior as Pono began dry heaving. Blood pooled around the boy's head, his face a lacerated mess of fleshy pulp. Sunami's chest rose rapidly and she squatted over her cousin, Killa Boy lying prone across his legs. Jack whined, struggling to stand up, but his back was broken.

"Junior." Sunami's voice rose raspy with shock and grief. "Oh God! Oh God," she cried. "He's still alive."

Jenny wanted to stand up but she was faint and weak.

It was the truck moving slowly down the road crunching dirt and gravel that caught Jenny's attention. There was something familiar about it. That was her last thought before the spots returned and everything went black.

Chapter 38

"And now for our breaking news. A young man's body was found this morning at nine am along Hana Highway, about ten miles east of Paia. It appears that he may have been the victim of a dog attack." Tim glanced up at the TV, his turkey sandwich forgotten.

"Don't you live out that way?" Chris the concierge asked as he lit up a cigarette and took a long drag, walking closer to the television. They were the only two in the break room. Tim frowned, listening to the anchorwoman,

"The body was found by a couple visiting the islands from Charlotte, North Carolina." The camera cut to the woman, whose round face was still full of shock.

"We were, you know, sight-seein." There was a mild twang to her voice as she spoke. "And it was right after the road started to get curvy. I remember that we passed this row of mailboxes." Tim's hand tightened on his coffee cup. "And that's when we saw him on the side of the road. At first we weren't sure what we were looking at."

"Something had got to him," the man cut in. "I can't say it was a dog. Looked more like what you would expect from a large cat. The panthers out in the mountains of Washington will take a person's throat out like that."

"Jesus," Chris said under his breath. He turned to Tim. "There's no large cats out here, but a Pit Bull or a Rottweiler can do that kind of damage too. People just let their dogs run around wild. Innocent young kids have been killed by dogs on these islands." Chris's words made Tim's stomach turn as he thought of the fact that his daughter often walked home after school.

"….tell you what, it's not the sort of thing you expect to see when you come to a place like Maui."

"No," the anchorwoman agreed.

"We're staying in Kaanapali." He pronounced it *'can a polly,'* "and I think we'll just be staying put there."

The wall phone rang. Chris picked it up.

"Yeah," he mumbled, the cigarette dangling from his lips. "Yeah, he's here." He handed the phone to Tim.

"I think your wife is trying to get ahold of you."

"Hello."

"Mr. Knowles?" a woman asked in a pleasant voice.

"Yes."

"I have your wife on the other line."

"Yes, put her through."

"Tim?" Angela sounded rattled and he immediately straightened up.

"What is it?"

"I need you to come home. It's Jenny." Tim's throat tightened.

"Dear God. I heard about the hitchhiker. Did the dog try to get Jenny?"

"What dog?" The relief from her question was instant.

"I just heard on the news that there was a hitchhiker killed by a dog out there." Angela did not respond. "Hello?"

"Tim, there is something bad happening out here. I'm not sure what it is, but it involves Jenny and the little girl in the red house,

Mele. She's missing." Tim gripped the receiver so hard his knuckles turned white.

"I'm on my way." He hung up, his head buzzing. Chris looked at him with concern.

"Let the main office know I had to go," Tim said. "There's been an emergency."

Angela hung up the phone, her hand shaking. She would call the police now that she knew her husband was on his way. The awful quiet had followed her home. It was like an entity giving everyday things about the house a menacing quality. Picking up the phone again, she glanced at the refrigerator and the number for the local police posted with other emergency numbers by a magnet. There was no dial tone. Angela pressed down on the receiver and listened…still dead. Hanging up the phone, she willed herself to keep it together as hot fear raced through her system, causing her to sweat. I'll go to Ann's, she told herself. Her neighbor would call the police. She slipped through the front door, jogging down the porch steps. The quiet felt worse outside, the silence almost deafening. She could hear the blood pounding in her eardrums as she crossed her arms, quickly walking the short distance to the house next door. Unlatching the lock of the white picket gate, she was relieved to see lights on through the windows. Closing the gate behind her, she ran up Ann's porch steps and knocked on the door.

It felt as if someone was watching her. Angela took a breath and slowly peered over her shoulder. A man with long, dark hair in surf trunks and a t-shirt was standing in the road. He wore a red baseball cap. Angela wanted to look away, but she couldn't seem to. He was staring at her, his face and skin gruesomely white. His eyes were dark orbs of liquid black. He smiled, flashing unnaturally sharp-looking teeth.

The Visitors

"Who is it?" she could hear Ann's voice.

"Careful, Mrs. Knowles," the man said.

The door opened and Ann smiled. "Angela, how nice to see you." But her smile quickly faded when she noticed the fear on her neighbor's face. Angela looked over her shoulder again before stepping into the house. The man was nowhere in sight.

"What is it?" Ann asked.

"I need to call the police, and my phone's dead."

"Yes, of course. Use ours. Bill, Angela's here," Ann called out to her husband. "There's been some kind of emergency," she added. Bill emerged from the den with a perplexed look on his face. "The phone is just here, dear," Ann pointed to a cream-colored phone sitting on an end table next to the sofa. Angela, grabbing the cradle, put it to her ear and prepared to dial, but found there was no dial tone.

"It's dead," she said looking up. Ann's brow furrowed. She took the phone from Angela's shaking hand and pressed repeatedly on the clear plastic switch…still no dial tone.

"The TV has lost reception too," Bill said, taking the phone from his wife's hand and putting it to his ear. A moment later, the lights flickered out and the stifling stillness that had begun when Angela had dropped her daughter off, felt as if it were seeping into Ann and Bill's house.

"Do you feel something?" Ann asked, pulling her sweater tighter around her body.

"What is the emergency?" Bill asked.

"It's Mele Kahiamoi. She's missing."

"Oh my God!" Ann exclaimed. "For how long?"

"I'm not sure."

"Let me go over there, and see if I can lend a hand in looking for her," Bill said. "It's so gray out, it'll probably be dark before we know it. I'll grab a flashlight."

"There was that hitchhiker on the news. They found him near here this morning," Ann said.

"Ann, don't mention that to them," her husband replied. "It's scary enough that the girl is missing."

"Yes, of course," Ann agreed quickly, "I was just telling Angela." Bill rolled his eyes, leaving the room in search of a flashlight. Moments later, he was headed for the front door.

"I'll go with you," Angela volunteered. She was too afraid to walk the short distance to the red house alone—the strange man standing out on the road ever present in her mind. She would get Jenny and they would wait at home for Tim. This time she would make her daughter tell her what was going on. A picture was beginning to form that she was finding hard to accept or believe.

"It's so strange about the phones," Ann mumbled to herself, rubbing her arms, "and it's suddenly so cold." Ann peered out the window. "It's only four in the afternoon, but it feels like five." As Bill and Angela readied themselves to leave, Ann added, "I'm sure they'll find her. Kids do that, wander off sometimes."

It is unusually cold, Angela thought to herself, as she followed Ann's reticent husband down the road. The lack of traffic and the fact that the air was so still and strange lent an eerie feeling to their surroundings. Bill remarked, "I noticed that the birds disappeared today."

"What do you mean?"

"Just how it sounds," he said, his tone matter of fact.

"Isn't that normal for them to disappear sometimes?"

"Not that I can ever recall."

Shortly the red house loomed up in front of them.

"Hum, dogs are gone." Bill said.

The door opened before they even had a chance to knock. A buxom woman stood in the entrance, worry emanating from her round eyes, as three younger boys came running up to see who was there.

The Visitors

"Hi, Linda, I heard Mele's missing," Bill said. The woman nodded, tears gathering in her eyes.

"She's been missing for a little while now. I think someone went took her."

"I'd like to offer my assistance in looking for."

She nodded. "My son, Junior, he took off wid Sunami and that boy, Pono. They didn't say where they was going, but they took the guns. They seemed to know where to look." Bill frowned deeply.

"Someone killed our dog," one of the boys called out.

"Where's Jenny?" Angelea asked. Her stomach grew cold with this new bit of information.

"Sunami tole her stay heah, but she went took off after dem, something about Sunami left a necklace that she would need where she was going."

"Do you know where they went?" Angela demanded. But somehow she knew. Sara's home came to mind and that odd woman, Analise. Sara's *whole* family was odd. There had been the strange, muffled sound like a child crying. Analise had said it was the wind.

Linda was shaking her head. Tears slipped down her round cheeks.

"Ok," Bill was saying. "Is your phone working? Did you call the police and report this yet?"

"It's dead," Linda replied.

"May we come in?" Bill asked. Linda stepped aside for the two to enter. They followed her to the living room.

"Where have you looked so far?"

"Just around here a bit. Mele was complaining the last few days about a woman. It's no offense," she said, her eyes sweeping over Angela and Bill. "But she's been complaining about some white woman watching her at night." Angela's throat felt dry as the image of the strange man standing on the road flashed through her mind. She wondered if he could have been watching Mele, and the little girl had mistaken him for a woman with his long hair. His words played again in her mind, *Careful, Mrs. Knowles.* How had he known her name?

"Then earlier when the phone was working, Sunami called Fess. I took the phone from her, because ever since these kids get home this afternoon, they is just talking amongst each other, won't tell me what they know. But I heard Fess telling my niece that there is a woman named Lilith and that she already kill someone named Leonard. Before that, I heard Junior say to Sunami, she took her.'"

Bill's mouth opened his features growing slack with shock. "Leonard was killed?" he asked.

Linda nodded again, the three boys standing silent beside her, consternation creating a rigid tension on their young faces. The youngest boy's eyes began to moisten and it seemed he was fighting hard to hold his emotions in check as he gave Linda's hand a tug.

"Auntie, did someone take Mele?"

Angela felt her head spin as she watched Bill place a hand on the boy's shoulder.

"We're going to look for her," he said quietly.

"I heard Jenny say the same thing to Sunami, something like, they took her." Angela said. "When I was at the Deureaux's..." but her words faded when she realized that what she was about to say would not be fair if it wasn't true. Linda fixed her with a hard gaze, sizing her up shrewdly.

"Do the Dereaux's know something?" she asked.

"I think they might." She did not want to go into detail about her visit and hearing a child crying. It was not right to jump to conclusions, incriminating people that might be perfectly innocent, no matter how strange they might seem. After all, it could have been the wind, she told herself. A feeling of dread was nagging at her and she realized that she was still selfishly fixated on the whereabouts of her own daughter. *She is probably fine,* she tried to reassure herself. It was Mele who was missing.

The Visitors

"Why don't you and the boys keep checking around here," Bill suggested, "Angela and I can take a ride up to the ridge and talk with Louis and Annette." Even as he said this, Bill felt doubtful that either one of them would be very helpful, or that Mele would have wandered that far. They were not a particularly friendly family and Mele wouldn't walk all that way by herself in the windy storm. Reason told him that Mele was in serious danger. The Kahiamois family dog was dead and Mele was suddenly missing. It sounded to Bill like she may have been abducted. If it hadn't been for the expression on Angela's face, like she knew something, he would not have bothered to volunteer going out that way.

The sound of a girl screaming sliced through the conversation. It was followed by a gunshot and another scream, a piercing shriek of fury that was not quite human, resulting in more gunshots.

"Oh God! What was that?" Angela cried out. Linda grabbed hold of the cross around her neck, the three boys huddling closer together.

Chapter 39

Sara closed the door gently behind her. It was dark, the last dredges of daylight obscured by the curtain drawn over the window. Samuel lay quietly in his bed. The sour, musky smell of sickness hung in the air. He turned his head in Sara's direction when he heard her come in with Mele. Sara placed the girl in the chair next to his bedside before lighting the gas lamp. She then went to stand next to the child, looking down at Samuel. Again she was struck at how he had changed. A young human man stared back at her, his blue eyes bright with fever, his lips and cheeks red as mountain apples. His gaze slowly shifted to Mele.

He spoke slowly in French. "She will not live," he said simply.

Sara remained silent. She knew it was the truth.

"Sit down."

Sara sat at the edge of his bed.

"There are some things that I must tell you now that my memories are securely in place. Hopefully I shall not disappear for a while into the young man I once was." He began to cough violently, the foul smell of his breath filling the air around them. Mele shrank back, covering her face with her arm, her eyes widening when she saw the length of his teeth. When he had recovered, he wiped the spittle from around his mouth.

"It amazes me what you have done. You have obscured the truth so thoroughly that you have even managed to deceive yourself."

Sara shook her head. Samuel always seemed to speak in riddles, and this time was no exception. "When your memories come, I cannot say." His eyes locked with hers. "This is your doing, Sara. You asked for my help long ago, but it is you that have arranged all of this."

Sara could not digest what he was relaying to her. Numbness crept through her being, as a strange familiar feeling began to take shape in her thoughts, a film of memory that she couldn't quite grasp. He beckoned her to come closer. Sara hesitated but his hand grabbed hold of her arm, pulling her closer to him.

"I wish to tell you things," he whispered, "that I can only speak into your ear." Sara tried to steady herself; his breath was overpowering.

"Soon it will be completely dark," he continued, "and you will look into a mirror and be reunited with Lilith, but you are not exactly her handmaiden. It appears so, but in reality she comes *from* you." Samuel's eyes blazed and his grip grew stronger. "You have successfully died and been reborn. You are not a handmaiden or a servant. Do you understand? You are a Master, and you are Lilith, the first Lilith." Sara's head was spinning with his words. She wanted to pull away, but he sensed this. "You need to know," his voice was urgent. "Tonight, Lilith will feed on that girl that you protect, and other children, presumably, that I am sure the kid snatcher has found and hidden away somewhere." Sara shook her head, not wanting to hear anymore.

"You knew you were not coming back. It was Myrina from the original band of Night Hunters that we captured who was your influence, and mine as well. Together we began the fatalist movement. We are fatalists, because we believe in freeing ourselves. Many others innocently joined, involuntarily indoctrinated in the infantry during vulnerable growing periods as we initially were. When we were finally discovered, a great majority of us were destroyed." He paused, catching his breath.

"Some escaped detection, driving the movement farther underground. In your last years, you knew that you would not be coming back in your old form. You are the first to shift. Imagine the surprise when you did not emerge from your cocoon, your body shriveled and finished. No one guessed that you were safe in Myrina's womb, waiting to be born as was planned. It was not to be expected, but the egg split in two, creating twins, you and Selene. Except Selene is you, as well. Your spirit is divided." He smiled, his lips pulling back from his rancid mouth with a look of triumph on his face that Sara did not share.

"It was an interesting experiment, Sara. You arranged for one part of yourself to be sent far away with trusted slaves who knew nothing of your true nature.

"Would you become a human? That was the question. The other part of you, the part that is Selene, stayed behind." Samuel tensed, his grip loosening on her as his body stiffened from the sickness. When he had regained himself again, he continued speaking. "You even arranged for our capture and disappearance, the four of us, during an impressionable time; the other two, the most virulent of the purists, had no knowledge of this.

"We were to be sent here, a place no one would know to look, while all the other obvious locations would be ransacked in search of us. From here we were to be sent to an undisclosed location that only you knew about, a place where we were to receive the last of our education. Michael and Carmilla are original in nature, like you. It was your wish to see how deeply they could be affected by the experience. However, there is an unfortunate weak link somewhere, Sara. That is what you must learn when you return home. Someone

The Visitors

has deceived you, us. Already there are rumors spreading that I am a fatalist. We were to arrive here months ago. I know not how long I was packed away. Someone purposely sent us here late, just before our transformations."

Samuel let go of her arm, his blue eyes boring into her. She watched his lids grow heavy, exhausted from his speech. Within minutes, he was sleeping deeply.

Sara sat up, shaking, fragments of memories flitting through her mind. She saw a young woman sleeping, a vision of beauty. Her dark hair and green eyes so entrancing, she longed have her, keep her always. It was Patience. Other memories tore at her mind until she thought she might go mad. The sudden scream that ripped through the room, followed by another malevolent, less human sound, drove the dark thoughts back.

The gunshots that came after had Mele crying out, "I want to go home. I want to go home."

Below she could hear the others scurrying about, the front door opening and slamming shut a few times. The burst of noise woke Samuel. He grimaced, his lips pulling back from his long teeth as his body arched and stayed that way, before finally relaxing. Sara grabbed his medicine that sat on the end table near his bed, urging him to sip a little. He did as instructed before turning his head away and closing his eyes again. Mele's face was damp with tears as she stared entreatingly at Sara.

"Please, can go home now?" the girl begged. "Please."

"Soon," Sara said quietly. Mele nodded, drawing her small legs up to her chest, her eyes darting quickly over in Samuel's direction.

Pono flagged down the truck. A girl climbed out. It was Sara. She was dressed in stylish clothes, holding a revolver. Sunami looked up, her face streaked with tears. Surprised, she watched Sara approaching her, pointing the gun in her direction. Having set aside her rifle to attend to her cousin, she now turned to reach for it.

"Don't move," Sara said. Her words were quiet and even. There was a hard edge to her features that Sunami had never seen before. "Stand up slowly, and move over to this other boy."

Sunami did as instructed, glancing at Pono, his face a mask of terror and confusion. Uncle Manuel sat in the back of the truck and Sara's father emerged from the driver's side. He was incredibly thin, his eyes deeply hollowed, lines of age etched like old scars along his forehead and cheeks. Sara walked over to where Junior's body was and picked up both rifles.

"He's still alive," Sunami called out. The girl pointed the gun at Junior's head and pulled the trigger. Pono looked away, but not before he saw bits of skull and flesh explode off the shoulders of the prone boy.

Sunami stiffened, a cry of anguish tearing from her chest and she grabbed Pono, burying her face in his shoulder.

Walking over to Jenny, Sara stared for a moment at the girl, whose right arm stretched over her shoulder at an odd angle. She nudged her with the pointy toe of her high heel. Jenny moaned.

"Manuel," she said, "you and Louis dispose of these bodies." There was a final shot as she put Jack out of his misery. Manuel climbed out of the truck.

"What do you want done with them?" he asked.

"Throw them in the ravine. It does not matter if they are discovered. We are leaving tonight anyway. When you are finished, put this girl in the truck. Lilith will be delighted with her." She pointed her gun again at Pono and Sunami. Pono braced himself, but instead Sara inclined her head toward the bed of the truck. "Get in," she commanded. She joined them, gun still pointed in their direction. Pono pulled Sunami closer to him, bringing her face back to his

The Visitors

chest as he averted his own eyes from the grisly scene of blood, flesh and brain splattered on the road. The two men picked up Junior's body, tossing it through an open space in the bushes, followed by the dogs. The bodies crashed through the vegetation rolling down the embankment to the stream below.

"Lovers?" Sara asked.

What is she talking about? How is it that she changed so drastically and acts like she doesn't know us at all? Pono wondered. He did not answer. She was smiling pleasantly as if nothing had happened and they were all going for a beach outing.

"Ran into some trouble, I see," she said conversationally. She laughed good-naturedly, her even teeth flashing brightly in her dark face, but the humor never reached her flat, cold eyes.

Chapter 40

Jenny's face had lost all color. Excruciating pain shot through her shoulder, leaving the rest of her arm and hand numb. Manuel held on to her good arm, walking her slowly to the plain brown house. The feeling of eyes watching her made her look up. She stopped, her breath catching at the white face in the upstairs window. Dark, malevolent eyes held hers for a moment, before the image vanished.

"Mom," Jenny whispered, her voice faint.

Manuel said nothing. Just a few more hours, he thought, before this miserable suspense would end. The poor, foolish boy slain in the road was the lucky one. He died quickly.

Brenda was there to greet them as they entered the house, bowing for Selene. Her eyes flitted over the children as she smiled, her lips curving nervously.

"My lady," she began submissively, "the Master Carmilla has returned just since you were away. Analise is upstairs tending to her." Selene seemed pleased with this news.

"Michael should not be too far behind then," she said.

"Quite right, quite right," the old woman replied, bobbing over and over, happy that her bit of news had gone over so well. Selene's

The Visitors

eyes hardened, her momentary cheerfulness vanishing as quickly as it had come.

"That is enough, old woman."

"Yes, my lady."

Selene led the small party into the living room, revolver in one hand and rifles under the other arm. She looked them over.

"Have a seat," she said. Pono sat hesitantly, pulling Sunami down next to him in the wide wicker chair. Since they had climbed into the truck, Sunami had become mute with shock. Jenny took the opposite seat. She did not look well and it seemed that at any moment she might pass out again.

"Louis, do get Lilith and the little girl." Upon hearing the name, Jenny shrank back, the last bit of energy that she had encapsulated in the fear that bubbled from her eyes. Selene did not miss this reaction.

"There are many Lilith's, girl," she said.

Louis left the room and they sat waiting in silence for several minutes. They were not prepared for the two figures that finally emerged. Sunami shot up erect, as did Pono, and Jenny, too weak to move much, only looked on. There stood a second Sara, holding Mele's hand, and then Jenny finally understood through the haze of pain. The cruel girl with the gun was not Sara at all.

Mele let go of Sara's hand, running to Sunami, who stood up, catching her cousin in her arms. Her relief at seeing Mele alive and unhurt brought fresh tears to her eyes. She hugged her tightly.

"Can go home, Sunami?" Mele asked. Sunami shook with grief, unable to reply as she held her tightly.

"There, there," Brenda said in a soothing voice. "Such a lucky one. The lady has taken a liking to the girl." Sunami's eyes shot up, and she glared at Brenda as she held Mele protectively. The old woman's words died away.

"A relative," Selene said. "How interesting." Her was tone was heavy with indifference that belied her words. "So much to talk about.

Isn't that right, my dear sister?" She turned to Sara, who remained silent. Although the two girls were similar in looks, their differences were clear now that they stood side by side. Selene was lean, but she looked fairly robust next to Sara, who had grown dangerously thin over the past weeks. Their faces, although identical in structure, were completely different in regard to expression. Sara radiated sadness and compassion, while Selene was as cool and fathomless as a dark, still pool.

"Do you know these people, Lilith?" Selene asked.

"I go by Sara." There was a resolve and strength to her voice that had not been there before. Selene paused, taken aback slightly at this show of defiance.

"Very well, I shall humor you. We will call you Sara." Selene's lips twisted into a smile. "Now, Sara, sister of mine. Are these friends of yours?"

"Yes," Sara said under her breath. She was staring at Jenny. "Her arm. Jenny, what happened?" Too afraid to answer, Jenny said nothing. Sara spun around, glaring at Selene. The girl made her sick. Never in her life had she wanted to hurt someone as much as she wanted to hurt her. Samuel's strange confession swirled around in her head. Sara struggled with the idea that they could possibly be one and the same.

"What happened?" Sara demanded. "Why are they like this, Selene? And Jenny's arm, what did you do to her?"

Selene's eyes widened. "And why is it that you think I have anything to do with her injury?"

Sara looked at Papa, feeling at a loss, but he and Manuel only stood with their heads down.

"What happened, Papa?" Sara asked.

"It is like I told you," he said, his voice low. "She is not dead." Sara felt the blood drain from her face.

"Lilith?" He nodded slightly. "I thought the sunlight…"

The Visitors

"Oh, the sun?" Selene interjected. "This is just one reason among many that our Masters should never have been brought here at such a sensitive time to be looked after by slaves who are not trained for the infantry. You see the sun, *Sara,* is only harmful on fresh, newly developed skin, like an infant's skin." She laughed. "We would not expose a newborn to the full sun with no protection, now would we?" Her lilting voice dropped an octave at the end of her question and her eyes rested squarely on Sara, waiting for her answer.

"Jenny needs a doctor," Sara replied. Selene laughed, her hard eyes flitting over Jenny's still form.

"A doctor, indeed. Tell me, Sara, when a lamb breaks its leg in the slaughter house, does the butcher call in the vet to fix it?"

"They are going home, Selene. I understand that I need to stay here, and maybe Manuel, but not the rest of them. They have nothing to do with this. We should take them home."

Selene raised an eyebrow. "And how do you propose we will go about doing that?"

Sara opened her mouth to speak, but was cut off by the sound of something large hitting the backside of house. The force of it made the house vibrate, causing all of them to jump. It was followed by a hissing, writhing sound of voices that began to wind through the room, bursting like wisps of steam from a whistling kettle. The wind began to pick up but it was the car pulling into the driveway that caused Selene to begin snapping orders.

"Take the children into the back bedroom and lock the door," she said to Manuel.

"They are innocent!" Sara screamed.

"No, my sister," Selene said quietly and evenly. "The people that are about to walk through this front door are innocent." She pointed her gun at Sara as she spoke.

"You would harm yourself?" Sara asked.

Selene's brows came together at Sara's question, and Sara realized that she had no idea what she was talking about.

Jenny sat up when she heard her mother's voice and the sound of footsteps approaching the house.

"My mom!" she cried. Manuel seemed to come to life as he bustled Jenny out of the chair.

"Come with me. Come," he ordered.

"No, we need to leave." Sunami spoke for the first time since she had come to the house.

"If you stay, and Jenny's mother sees all of you here, and whoever else is with her, Selene will kill them on the spot. Do you understand? This is no time for your bull-headed ways, Sunami."

Sunami frowned, her forehead puckered. Mele still clung to her. There was a knock on the door. Pono stood up.

"Let's do what he says. We saw what happened with Junior." He held his hand out to Sunami, who took it. Manuel gently took Jenny's good hand, leading her out of the living room with the rest of them following, Selene bringing up the rear. There was another knock at the door.

"Sara, put some tea water on," Papa said. He turned to Brenda. "Go upstairs with you," he demanded of her. She gave a quick nod. Papa went to the door, opening it slowly.

The ride to Sara's had been grim. Angela insisted on accompanying Bill after the terrible screams and gunshots had ripped through the valley and he suggested she stay behind. When it was clear that she was going with him in his vehicle or alone in her own, he had finally relented. They left Linda's house with a plan that Linda and the boys would keep looking around the property for Mele, while she and Bill went to the Deureauxs.

It was a matter of minutes before they reached Sara's. Angela held her breath, expecting to see something terrible beyond every curve.

The Visitors

The strange stillness that had settled over the valley began to dissipate into a light breeze that did not have the normal pattern of trade winds that blew from the northeast. Instead, the air seemed to have a life of its own, coming from one direction and then another, winding its way along their bodies like a snake when they walked through Sara's yard.

Bill stopped at one point, looking around, confusion furrowing his features. "Something's not right. I have never seen the weather behave like this. And the birds, they've completely vanished."

"Do you think it could be a tsunami?" Angela suggested.

He turned to look at her, his expression thoughtful. "Possibly. You might be right." Leaves and sticks lay scattered in the yard. The grass was ankle high. It looked like it had not been mowed for weeks. "Unusual for Louis to let things go like this," Bill muttered to himself as they stepped onto the porch. He knocked on the door. There was no answer, but Angela heard movement from inside. While they waited, the wind seemed to slip into their clothes, winding more forcefully around their bodies. Bill batted at his ear. There was a kind of hissing and voices, like people whispering.

"Did you say something?" he asked.

Angela shook her head, and knocked a second time. The door opened. Sara's father stood in the entryway. Again Angela was struck by how worn down he looked. She detected an expression of surprise on Bill's face as well. The three stood awkwardly staring at one another.

"Hi, Bill," Louis said and nodded at Angela. "What I can do for you?" He addressed both of them.

Bill cleared his throat. "Keoni and Leilani's daughter Mele is missing. We're just out helping to look for the girl. Is there a chance you may have seen her? It's a long shot, but we thought she possibly may have wondered out this way."

Louis shook his head. "No, I'm sorry. We haven't seen her." He did not offer to have them come in, just stood waiting in the doorway.

"Did you hear someone scream and gunshots?" Angela asked.

He nodded. "Yes, we heard that." There was no elaboration to his answer. He just stood quietly waiting.

"Mr. Deureaux," Angela said, "when I was here earlier, I thought I heard a child crying from inside your house."

Bill turned to look at her, startled at her frank statement.

Louis stepped aside and Angela glimpsed Sara behind him in the kitchen holding a plastic bag of loose tea.

"Why don't you come in," he offered. "I can see you have something set in your mind about us, and you won't feel better until you see for yourself."

"No, that won't be necessary," Bill interrupted. "I'm sure the girl will show up."

Angela felt her face redden, but she wasn't giving up. She turned to Bill with eyes flashing.

"Jenny and I were here earlier. We heard a little girl crying. When we mentioned it, Analise said it was only the wind. I am certain…" She did not finish, as she could tell she was not getting through to Bill, whose mouth had turned down angrily; his eyes, filled with chagrin, darted toward Louis.

"I heard Jenny say to Sunami, 'they have her'," Angela continued. "She was implying that she knew Mele was here, and now my daughter, Sunami and two boys are off looking for the girl with guns. We heard gunshots and a girl scream. It sounded like it came from this direction." Angela was feeling more and more frantic as she spoke. She could see the look of utter disbelief and embarrassment on Bill's face as she tried to convince him. It did not help that Louis appeared indifferent. Only Sara's expression held any level of concern.

"Sara, please, you know something," Angela pleaded with the girl.

Sara looked at the floor.

The Visitors

"Mrs. Knowles, our family has been having a difficult time as of late. I would ask you not to badger Sara. I am sorry about Mele, but we do not know where she is."

Angela gave a sharp squeal when Bill suddenly grabbed her arm, squeezing hard. "I'm sorry to disturb you," he said. "Let us know if you see the girl, or bring her by. Linda's worried."

Louis nodded. "I will."

Bill gave her a powerful yank, pulling Angela off of the porch toward the driveway. She struggled to wrench her arm from his grasp, her anger coming to a boiling point.

"How dare you manhandle me!" she cried out, her face hot with rage. The wind was growing stronger. His arms fell to his side and he glared back at her.

"That was—" he rolled his eyes, shaking his head. "I didn't think anyone could top Ann when it comes to indiscretion, but I think she has just met her match. What are you thinking accusing this family of kidnapping Mele? They might be strange, but you were completely out of bounds here, Mrs. Knowles."

"There is something going on in this household. I don't know what it is, but…"

"Exactly. You don't know," Bill interrupted. He had to raise his voice over the wind that was becoming a force to reckon with. It tore at their clothes and hair, pushing forcefully against their eyelids until Angela's eyes began to tear up and her nose dripped. Unworldly shrieks arose out of the thin air, startling Bill into silence. He suddenly stopped walking, squinting off in the distance.

Angela followed his line of vision. Coming up from the banana orchards was a woman running. It looked like Mrs. Deureaux. Angela and Bill waited, watching her figure draw closer. She appeared to be yelling something. Her mouth was moving, but the words were lost in the rush of powerful air that circulated around them.

Angela's breath caught once the older woman was close enough for them to get a good look at her. She had lost a considerable amount of weight like her husband, and her hair was hacked away, her scalp splotchy with bald spots, tufts of gray hair sticking up here and there.

"Monsters!" Angela thought she heard the woman scream. She and Bill took a step back as Mrs. Deureaux flew at them, trying to grab hold of Angela. Her eyes were wide, burning with an inner light of fanatical fury, neck muscles rigid and strained. "Monsters! They killed my babies. They killed my babies!"

Bill's face seemed to drain of color all at once as he took action to restrain the woman. It was Louis, though, who came as if from nowhere, grabbing his wife and holding her in a bear hug. She continued to scream, her eyes rolling maniacally in her head, her mouth stretching rhythmically into an odd grin.

"She is not well!" Louis yelled above her screams and the wind.

Angela covered her mouth, trying not to cry herself. Her stomach grew ever tighter with a fear and certainty that her daughter was in danger, along with the others. Where were they? Where were the children?

"She needs a doctor," Bill exclaimed.

"Listen to me!" Mr. Deureaux yelled. "You must leave. You are not safe here!"

"What's going on here, Louis?" Bill asked, now uncertain.

"I cannot speak more plainly, Bill. Soon it will be dark. You do not want to be here then. Do what you need to do. Go to the police if you like, but I implore you, for your own sake, do not stay here."

Bill opened his mouth to say something, but no words came. He stood speechless at Mr. Deureaux's odd confession.

Angela wiped at her nose and all three froze when the shrieking wind grew louder, although it didn't sound like wind anymore. It was an unearthly voice that raged with a wrath that intertwined with

The Visitors

Mrs. Deureaux's own cries of madness. Mr. Deureaux began to drag his wife to the house, her face almost purple from her crazed state.

"They said we had to take them!" she was yelled.

"Take who, Mrs. Deureaux?" Angela asked, the hairs rising on her body.

"The children. I didn't want them."

Bill stepped forward, reaching out his hand to try and stop them, but Mr. Deureaux flashed him a warning look of such intensity that his hand dropped.

"Where are our children?" Angela yelled.

"You have a finite amount of time, Mrs. Knowles," was Louis's response, "and then I cannot help you." He struggled with his wife, turning away.

"Come on," Bill said to Angela. "Let's go. We'll go to the police. You were right."

Angela hesitated, staring back at the house. "Oh God," she whispered. Was her daughter in there?

Bill tapped her, and she reluctantly followed his lumbering form.

Chapter 41

Louis struggled with his wife while she tried repeatedly to get free of his arms. Streaks of white, jagged light began to slice through the air. In all his years he had never experienced, only heard of, demonic storms. This was a storm that only a div like Lilith could produce. As a child he had heard stories, while huddling with others around a hearth fire, of a Lilith's fury, the things she could do when she was in possession of her full strength.

His daughters' faces flashed through his mind, the memory of their screams echoing in his thoughts. Forced to watch the brutal killings, Annette's cries had been shrill and raw until she could cry no more. Then they were left alone with the lifeless mutilated bodies. He'd assisted his wife to their cabin, the other slave cabins shuttered and closed, the occupants hiding. When he returned for the bodies, they were gone, no doubt taken by the kid snatchers to be rendered useful in the gray, powdery medicine fed to the masters and servants during the sickness.

Once upon a time, Annette had been young and pretty in a strong sort of way. They had been in love, both favorites with the high servants.

The Visitors

He pulled her toward the front door, away from the blinding streaks of light. Her mouth was stretched into a smile that marked her advanced insanity. Once solid of mind, industrious, proud and pleased with her brood of well-behaved girls, Annette used to laugh and sing, to talk animatedly with friends. Louis opened the door, pushing her in ahead of him. He let go and did not look up when Selene grabbed his wife's hand, leading her away.

"You are a devil!" she cried, spitting in the girl's face. Selene did not even flinch, only dragged the older woman along with unusual strength. Annette's head bobbed back, her cackling echoing through the back hall. She was pulled into the empty bedroom that she and Louis vacated weeks before, the door closing firmly behind them. Sara stood, holding the bag of tea to her chest, the pot whistling. Louis turned off the water, closing his eyes. The sound of a single shot reverberated through the house.

It is over, my love, he whispered in his mind.

Just as Analise appeared at the top of the stairs, Selene emerged from the bedroom. Saliva dripped from her cheek, along with splatters of blood; she staggered for a moment, blinking rapidly. Upon seeing this, Analise came down the stairs, taking them two at a time. Within seconds, she was at Selene's side.

"The old woman was stacked with Otomic stones," Selene muttered. "She pulled a necklace from herself and rubbed it in my face."

"Come Selene, let's wash you up," Analise said. Selene took another step forward before falling to her knees. Gently pulling the gun from her grasp, Analise turned on Sara and Louis, waving the revolver at them.

"Go wait in the other room," she commanded. Sara set the bag of tea on the counter and moved off. She could hear the sink water running and Analise cursing the thin stream of water as she cleaned Selene's face.

"Selene don't go to sleep, try to fight it," Analise said.

"Take all of them and put them in the building with the piano," Selene said. Her words were ponderous. "There is a piano there. Lilith…likes…"

"Selene! Selene!" There was the sound of Analise slapping the girl's face, trying to wake her. The front door opened and Sara glimpsed a tall, powerful-looking, dark-skinned man, already understanding that he was a servant. He took one look at the scene before him before rushing into the kitchen.

"What has happened to her?"

"Otomic stones. The crazy one, Annette, rubbed them on her face." He did not reply.

"Did you find Michael?" Analise asked.

"Yes, he was glutted from a feeding. He was not easy to negotiate with. It seems there is still some confusion on his part. All of the Masters are somewhat disoriented in this strange environment, away from servants that would have guided them through this sensitive time."

"Where is he now?" Analise asked.

"I could not persuade him to come with me," the man said. "However, I told him that we are all leaving here tonight. If he remains behind, he does so at his own risk." There was a lapse in the conversation and Sara listened to the man fussing over Selene.

"She could be out for hours," he finally said. "We'll let her sleep it off for a bit, and then we'll attempt to wake her again. I'll put her in her sister's bedroom."

"No, we have others hiding in there," Analise said.

"Others?"

"While you were away, a group of children showed up. Apparently there was a run-in with Lilith."

"So she is here?"

"No. One of the girls shot her. She is, no doubt, recovering somewhere from her wounds.

"Shot her?" He sounded incredulous. "A girl shot her?" There was a brief pause then Analise spoke again.

"I will move everyone to the other building, as Selene instructed. Then Selene can sleep this off."

"Where is Lilith's handmaiden?" the man asked.

"In the living room." A moment later, the man rounded the corner of the kitchen and stood in the doorway that separated the two rooms. He stared at Sara and Louis, a thoughtful, mildly surprised expression illuminating his features. Striding across the room, he held out his hand to Sara, the fingers long and slim, his skin smooth. When Sara did not take his hand, he let it drop.

"I am Darius," he finally said. Sara did not reply and Darius's eyes moved to Louis, studying him. "There is much to discuss," he said. Louis nodded his head. In the last five minutes, his eyes had sunken farther into his face, his grief stark and prominent.

"You told me earlier that she does not know who she is really, or where she came from. That she has been raised a human girl," Darius said.

"*C'est exact*," Louis replied. His words broke as he spoke.

"It was Myrina who sent you away with Lilith?"

"*Oui.*"

"When it was discovered that Master Romulus was part of the fatalist movement, we searched his belongings and we found your letters in his possession."

Louis said nothing, and Darius became distracted with the commotion of Analise filing everyone out of Sara's bedroom. "Excuse me," he said, and left the room. Sara followed him and found Selene lying on the kitchen floor. Unconscious, she looked perfectly innocent, a girl asleep, not a cold-blooded killer.

Jenny came first with Uncle Manuel assisting her. She was very pale. Her skin had taken on a clammy look, her eyes glossy with pain. Pono came up behind her, followed by Sunami, who still clutched Mele. The small girl had once again buried her face away against Sunami's thin chest.

"Keep moving," Analise said to the small group. "We are going to the other building." Sara joined her friends but Darius laid a hand on her shoulder.

"I wish to speak with you, Lilith." Sara's nostrils flared, and she pulled her body away from his touch.

"I don't want to talk with you."

Darius said nothing more and stepped away from her. Analise paused at this exchange, but the man tilted his head toward the door.

"Let her do as she likes for now," he said. He turned his back, squatting down to pick up Selene. He held her easily, walking with her limp body to Sara's bedroom.

Sara exhaled, feeling slightly relieved that she had won that small victory. Analise marched the children across the small courtyard. They walked in single file into the building.

It was dark and cold in the small room. Once they were all inside, Sara set about lighting the two gas lamps that were mounted to the wall. Bookshelves lined the walls; a piano sat in one corner. Analise pointed to the fireplace at the back of the room and the wood piled domestically in an iron bin.

"Is it in working order?" she asked. Sara nodded. "Well then make a fire," she commanded of Manuel, rubbing at her arms. The small group stood huddled together in the middle of the room, but Analise's demand dispersed them. Pono went to sit on the piano bench and Sunami took one of the overstuffed chairs as Manuel gently led Jenny to the second chair. Analise grabbed the girl from his hand, pulling forcefully at her dangling arm so that Jenny gave a loud, wrenching scream.

"Do not cater to her," she snapped at Manuel, whose face paled visibly, although he said nothing.

The Visitors

No one saw it coming, least of all Analise whose back was turned. Sunami flew from the chair. Grabbing hold of the woman's bun, she yanked her head back, bending her neck at an unnatural angle. Her eyes were full of shock and, for the first time, fear. Analise released Jenny's arm as she tried to right herself. The revolver went off, the bullet exploding into the shelf of books ahead of her. The shot made all of them jump, but Sunami seemed unaffected as her knee rose up, catching Analise sharply in the small of the back. The woman collapsed, sprawling forward, trying to turn around, but Sunami's bare foot came crashing down on the hand that held the gun. Grabbing Analise's head, Sunami smashed her face again and again against the floor. Sara heard something crack, and then footsteps coming up the porch steps. Running to the door, she threw her body against it. Manuel, coming out of his stunned pose, ran to help her. The bulk of his large frame wedged the door shut as they heard Darius yelling from the other side. A moment later, they heard him retreating.

"Stay here," Sara whispered to Manuel. Coming away from the door, she observed the scene before her. Jenny had sunk to her knees, greatly weakened from her injury. Sunami stood panting over Analise. Sara bent down, turning over the prone form. The woman's eyes stared vacantly back at her, the skull cracked. Mele gave a small whimper.

"There is a hiding place that Papa showed me," Sara said. She motioned with her hand for Sunami, Pono and Mele to come to her. Sunami stood up slowly from her hunched position as Sara walked over to one of the shelves of books. She pulled back several of the books, peering behind them. Not finding what she was looking for, she pulled back more books, sweeping her hand behind the spines. She paused when her fingers hit upon the lever that Papa had showed her.

Days before the arrival of the children, he'd taken her into the room and removed the books, showing her the latch.

"You must push in, and then up," he had instructed, demonstrating for her. He had made her practice over and over. "This is for your own safety, Sara. You must not tell your cousins of this. It is not a place to play in. There may be a time when you will need to hide in here. The doors bolt from the inside." She had not asked her father at the time why she would need to hide, knowing he would not explain further.

Sara pushed at the latch. There was no give. It appeared to be stuck, and now Darius was back at the door. Manuel redoubled his efforts, leaning heavily against it.

"Let me see," Pono whispered. She stepped aside as he pulled the books off the shelf to see what she was working at. It was a small, white lever that blended incongruously with the wall.

"Push down," Sara instructed. She watched him push on the thing and grimace as nothing happened. Making his hand into a fist, he gave one swift blow, and the latch gave way; there was the sound of something clicking. "Now pull up." Sara said. He did as she ordered and the shelf suddenly swung open to a dark, musky, smelling space. "It bolts from the inside," she explained quickly. Pono stepped aside to let Sunami in first. She had retrieved Mele and she ducked into the space with the girl clinging to her. As Pono made a move to walk toward Jenny, he froze as he and Sara watched the doorknob being wrenched out of place, the wood splintering.

"There is no time," Manuel hissed.

"Go inside," Sara said to Pono.

"But Jenny."

Jenny struggled to rise up but Sara saw she could not wait another second. Pushing Pono, she shoved him into the musky closet. "Lock it!" she whispered loudly, closing the shelf up and replacing the books. The door came open; Manuel stumbled back. Sara gasped. There stood Carmilla with Darius behind her. She was very tall, her form now lean, sinewy and hulking. Her white skin glowed in the golden hue of the room. Slowly, her demonic eyes took in the scene before her, her long neck bending and turning. Her movements were minute and alien. She held in her hand a mirror; her long bony fingers and sharp nails wrapped tightly around the handle. Sara did not see her move forward. In one instant she was standing by the door and the next she was only inches away. Darius rushed to bend over Analise.

"Where are the others?" he asked.

"Where indeed?" Carmilla said and her eyes scanned the shelves, the shadow of a smile playing on her lips. Sara's heart skipped a beat, but Carmilla's gaze left the shelves and rested on Analise's body and Jenny cowering on the floor. With lightning speed, the creature was suddenly hovering over Jenny. Picking up the girl by her hair, she flung her into a chair like a rag doll. Jenny's eyes flew open and she stared at Carmilla, her mouth opening as if to scream, but the wind was clearly knocked out of her. Sara watched the girl's body tense several times from the physical and mental shock of what was happening to her. Carmilla spoke to Sara, although her eyes remained on Jenny.

"Did you think I would not find out?" she asked. "You have been very foolish, Lilith. Although your experiment is interesting: hiding from yourself."

"What are you saying?" Darius asked. Carmilla's question diverted his attention away from his dead comrade. Carmilla did not answer him. Sara heard Manuel draw in his breath, as if he understood something. This time, Carmilla took her time walking over to Sara. She stood staring down at the girl, her mouth slightly parted, the gleaming dark eyes locking with Sara's. She slowly reached out her hand to caress her hair.

"We have always been together, you and I. You were my beauty. Do you remember that we made Patience into what she is?" Sara shook her head, swallowing as she leaned back from Carmilla's bony hand that now petted her face.

"I hate this image," Carmilla whispered. "I have always hated the Night Hunters. Why did you do it?" As she spoke she raised the mirror.

"Sara, close your eyes!" Manuel yelled. "Don't look in there!" Sara shut her eyes, squeezing them closed but not before she caught a brief glimpse of the reflection; the smirking lips and fathomless eyes, mocking her. Her features animated through no will of her own in the round glass.

A hand was grabbing her and suddenly she was falling, space expanding all around. The hand holding her slipped away. There was a furious shrieking, like something slithering back into itself. Sara kept her eyes closed. She could hear Darius gasping.

"Upon the Devil!" he yelled. "It is Lilith!"

Rounding out of her body, she was traveling at an unbelievable speed, off the property down the road and through a ravine; the bushes and trees were a blur. She could feel herself dispersing until she was the very air itself, and then there was the twisting and stretching. Her spirit fought, but she couldn't pull free.

Her breath...she couldn't breathe. Throwing back her head, she took a long ragged gasp and opened her eyes. All around her it was quiet, dark. Something rough rubbed against her leg. She reached to push it away, realizing it was a branch. Her body ached. It hurt to bend her neck. Where was she? In moments, her eyes adjusted to the night and she could see clearly, as if someone had turned on an iridescent light. Gingerly, she pushed against the ground to pull herself up. It was her hands and arms that caught her attention. She collapsed back to the ground, stretching her arms out before her. What was happening? Her skin, her arms and dress; none of it belonged to her. Someone was breathing heavily close by. Sara turned her head. Her neck hurt terribly, but she could see no one. Pushing herself up again, she pulled herself to a standing position; her chest and shoulder were on fire. She felt dizzy and had to stand for a moment to gain her equilibrium.

The Visitors

"Lilith?" she called. A raspy voice, not her own, sprang from her vocal chords.

"Sara."

The sound of her name sliced through her brain, echoing off of itself. Sara realized that the labored breathing was coming from herself. She looked up. There was only the night sky and the tops of trees that surrounded her. The land sloped upward, the sound of the stream close by. Taking a step forward, she gritted her teeth from the pain that wracked her body as she assessed her surroundings.

She was at the bottom of the ravine. The road to her house was up top. Taking another step, she cried out; the pain was excruciating. She wanted to sink to her knees but something else took hold of her body, forcing her to remain upright and to keep moving up the steep embankment. Never had she felt such pain, not even the illness could compare to the fire that was in her chest, shoulder and her neck. She wanted to stop, but couldn't. In horrified amazement, she watched the white, skeletal hands that belonged to her grab hold of the odd branch, pulling her body up with an enduring strength that obeyed the life force that inhabited her being. She did not stop until she found herself standing on the road.

"Sara," the voice called again, loud and sharp, stabbing at her temples.

Sara looked in the direction of her house. Again her body began to move through no will of her own and then she realized what was happening. She was inside Lilith, leading her back to the house, the others, and herself. Struggling to halt the movements, the energy overpowered her efforts, the legs marching stiffly. There was a great heaving cry, like someone lifting something weighty. "Go!" the voice yelled. In a great whoosh she found herself dispersing as if she suddenly exploded, while at the same time her matter gathered itself up and like an object being cast violently down, she re-entered her own body.

When Sara opened her eyes she found Carmilla watching her shrewdly.

"Lilith?" she whispered. Sara found her mouth opening and foreign words flowing forth that were not her own. She was locked away somehow in her mind.

"I am here," the voice spoke. Struggling to regain herself, Sara found she was being pushed farther into the depths of darkness. A wild panic took flight in her chest and she opened her mouth to scream but instead Lilith spoke through her.

"Carmilla," the voice hissed sensually, "soon I shall be in your arms." A slow smile spread across Carmilla's thin lips. Sharp teeth and bestial eyes blazed with pleasure and lust. She turned away from Sara, fully pleased.

"Go and wake this one's better half. We shall leave here soon," Carmilla ordered Darius.

"And what of Michael?"

She did not reply to his question and a moment later Darius left the room, taking Manuel with him.

Chapter 42

It had not been easy to leave the ridge. The windstorm dangerously rocked the truck. Bill edged forward at five miles per hour, sometimes stopping altogether when blinding streaks of light shot out as if from thin air, assaulting them from every direction. Angela cowered in her seat, her chest heavy with fear for her daughter. There was no explaining the strange events. She and Bill did not even attempt to talk to one another until they found they were back on the main road. Scissors of light sliced through the air, crossing over each other, coming more and more rapidly until it was almost impossible to see a foot ahead of them. Bill peered grimly out of the windshield, bending closer as he continued to move his vehicle forward.

"How will we see to get to the police?" Once the words left her mouth, Angela knew they were trapped. Although she couldn't voice how it was possible, she knew that all of it was connected: the freakish storm, the children disappearing and Sara's odd family.

Bill shook his head. "This is all very bizarre," he said. He could only guess at where his driveway was. Pulling along a stretch of the road where he thought his house might be, Bill cut the engine and struggled to push his door open. The door flew from his fingers, slamming shut. Angela fought against her own door, stepping out into the blizzard of flashing, streaking lights. Keeping her head down, she kept her hand in contact with the truck as she crept around the other side of it.

"Bill!" she yelled. She didn't see him but felt his hand grab hold of hers.

"Move to the right," he instructed, pulling her toward him. She did as she was told, blindly following him until she walked into something hard. They stopped as he began to feel around for the latch to the gate that was blocking them. Again he pulled at her. She tripped over the first step. He paused, helping her to steady herself. Angela raised her leg up high, not sure how to gage the distance of the steps. In this way they made it to the front door where Bill fumbled with the doorknob. To his surprise, it was locked.

"Ann," he yelled, banging on the door. There was no answer. "Ann," he called again, a flurry of dread descending upon him. Angela held tightly to his hand. A moment later, there was the sound of Ann's voice, heard faintly over the shrieking wind.

"Is that you Bill?"

"Of course it's me," Bill yelled, exasperation replacing the momentary panic. Ann opened the door and Bill stepped into his house, closing the door after Angela. The flickering light of candles lit up the living room. His wife stood bundled warmly in a thick sweater and hat, her face pinched with worry.

"After you left, I saw a strange man outside the window," Ann said. She shuddered. Angela's heart skipped a beat.

"A strange man?" Bill echoed.

"He wasn't normal looking. I saw him walking on the road, heading in the direction of the highway. His skin was unnaturally white. He must have felt me watching him because he looked in my direction and saw me at the window. His face was—" Ann's breathing grew heavy. "His face was almost skeletal and his mouth and shirt were bloody. When he looked at me, his eyes were so evil! Oh Bill."

Angela watched the older woman's face crumple. "He stopped walking and was just staring at me. I closed the curtains and locked all the doors. Shortly after, this storm started up. I didn't know what to do. The phone lines are down, you were gone and now there are these strange lights coming out of the air." As Ann spoke, Bill stood, his arms dangling at his sides, worry and bafflement clouding his features. Ann swiped at her eyes, focusing on Angela for the first time.

"Did you find Mele?" Angela shook her head, not trusting herself to speak. Ann looked at Bill. "What are they going to do?"

"We'll have to wait until this storm is over," Bill said, "but then, the police will be our best bet. We went to the Deureaux's. Something very odd is going on there, but I'm not sure what it is. Annette has gone insane. She came running at us, had cut off all her hair and was screaming that someone killed her babies and made her take the children."

Ann's hand flew to her mouth. "What?" she whispered. "What babies? What children?"

Bill shook his head. "Like I said, I think she has gone insane. What really worried me though, was when Louis told me and Angela to leave before it got dark, something about being in danger once the night came."

"Oh God," Ann exclaimed. "I wonder what he's talking about." She turned to Angela. "Where is Jenny?" Angela could hold it in no longer. Her grief burst from her chest and out of her mouth in successive gasps.

"I don't know," she cried. "I think... I think—" Angela shook her head, trying to compose herself, her lips tightening as the tears began to spill, slipping rapidly down her reddened cheeks. Ann hurried to her, gathering her in her arms.

"She'll show up," she soothed. "We'll find them." Angela pushed her face into the woman's shoulder, her body convulsing as Ann patted and stroked her back. Looking over Angela's shoulder, Ann met her husband's eyes. Uncertainty flickered in his expression.

Chapter 43

She walked stiffly up the stairs, her footsteps slow and heavy. Already the flesh had closed on her wounds but they were not yet completely healed. Only the vibrant life of another would restore her to full health.

Inside Sara waited with the others, listening as each foot struck the wooden steps. Her breath was labored but she did not stop until she had finally reached the entrance. The door was split and hanging at an odd angle from Carmilla's entry. Lilith's hulking figure stood slightly bent from the pain that Sara had felt herself just moments earlier. Her green eyes slowly swept the room and came to rest on Sara, who suddenly felt lighter as the last part of Lilith that had invaded her body departed. Lilith gave a sharp gasp as she regained the remnant of her essence.

"You abandoned me," she finally said.

Sara did not reply and Lilith's eyes swept over Analise. "What has happened to my servant?"

Sara pressed her back up against the piano as both demonic women focused on her. There was nothing left that was human anymore. The strange separation of mobility in their features had extended to the rest of their bodies. A bend of their necks remained absolutely separate from all other body parts, which did not move at all. Their pupils dilated rapidly, encompassing the whole eye, yet sometimes movement was so fast that it was missed altogether. Impossibly white skin was stretched tautly over wiry musculature. Their nails were almost claw-like. Thick hair framed their skeletal faces, and the girlish linen dresses that they wore were frighteningly incongruous with their arthropod-like figures.

When Sara remained silent, Lilith turned to look at Jenny, who shrank back under her gaze.

"Your friend hurt me," she said softly, hissing the words out. Jenny swallowed, unable to speak. "Where are the children, Sara?" Lilith spat the words out. Gritting her teeth, Sara turned her face away so as not to look upon the monsters, but Lilith was suddenly before her, grabbing her face and wrenching her neck so that they were eye to eye. "You would deny me? Look carefully at what you have made. I am part of you. Where are they?" Lilith demanded.

"Hiding," Carmilla said with a slight smile as her eyes roamed the walls of the room. Lilith released Sara's face and she too looked about.

"Oh, hiding," she said as if to herself. She walked over toward Jenny, who gave a sharp squeal as Lilith approached her. Grabbing the hand of Jenny's intact arm, she carefully inserted one of her sharp, pointy claws under a nail, slowly peeling it back, exposing the pink soft flesh underneath, watching the blood well up. Jenny's scream reverberated off the walls. "So you want to play," Lilith said quietly, her tone indifferent. An intense heat swept through Sara's body, as she watched Lilith casually take another finger, lift up the nail and slowly peel it back.

"Please! Please!" Jenny screamed.

"Please!" Lilith screamed, her voice a perfect imitation of Jenny's. Carmilla's smile widened, her sunken eyes blazing. Her teeth were bared and saliva dripped from her mouth. Her bony chest rose with fiendish laughter. The whimper of a small child coming from inside the walls caused both demonic women to turn in the direction of the sound, only their heads moving, their bodies remaining poised as they were. Other than Jenny's soft crying, nothing more was heard.

Sunami clasped her hand tightly over Mele's mouth to block out any more noise from the girl. It was a narrow, dark space that they were hiding in and they sat on a cold stone slab, Sunami's back pressed up against Pono's chest. She could feel his heart thumping rapidly against her. When Mele cried out, it became suddenly quiet. Other than Jenny's sobbing there were no other sounds or movements. Sunami bit down on her lip until she tasted blood, the palm of her hand like an iron vise over Mele's face. Sweat beaded up in her hair and forehead, dripping down the sides of her face. She dared not move or breathe.

Jenny's gut-wrenching screams ripped through the room and Sunami fought against Mele's tensing body, bringing her lips to the girl's ear.

"Shh," she breathed shakily, and then closed her eyes, wishing she could close her ears to the sounds of torture on the other side of the wall. The sickening sounds of flesh ripping and the gurgling, bubbling death rattle stabbed at Sunami's insides.

It was after Lilith had removed her arm, ripping the limb completely from its socket that Jenny saw the golden light; it gleamed through the bodies of the creatures, slowly overtaking their forms. An older woman was emerging, smiling, and as Jenny gazed upon her, the woman grew younger. Love emanated from her body, and she seemed to be made of the light that brought her. With a joy she had never known before, she was gathered into the woman's arms, the woman who had been waiting for her, waiting for her to return all these years since she had left the world as Mele Kahiamoi. It was her mother, Margaret.

Jenny had already left her body when Lilith and Carmilla descended upon her, crushing her windpipe as they devoured the flesh and bones of her throat, feeding hungrily on her blood. Lilith pulled back first, blood and tissue smeared across her face. She began to tense and heave repeatedly, her mouth drawing back farther and farther, until her features were nothing but fangs and crowded teeth, the eyes black and bulging, hair hanging over the feral face. A low wail rose from her throat that grew louder and higher pitched until she was screaming, her screams joined by Carmilla's. The screams raked through the room, stabbing Sara's eardrums until she was clasping her hands over her ears. Over and over, the awful sounds rose out of the demons as they hovered over Jenny's lifeless form, her legs sprawled like a rag doll, lifeless eyes staring straight ahead.

All at once the shrieks ceased and both women were straightening back up to their full height. Slowly they were growing, their flesh rounding out, the gaunt faces filling in. Within minutes, they were several inches taller, the skeletal look had vanished and two very human looking women stood before Sara. The features were still sharply defined and the skin too white, but other than that, both possessed astonishing beauty.

No one heard Brenda approach. Sara had no idea how long she had been standing in the doorway. She suddenly spoke, grabbing the attention of the demon women.

"There, there now, my beauties," the kid snatcher spoke, her speech cautious, cajoling and slightly hypnotic. "Brenda has something for my precious duckies." The old woman's round, beady eyes glinted from her wrinkled, dimpled face. In her arms, she carried something bundled up that appeared to be moving. Lilith cocked her head, and although she didn't smile, pleasure lit up her green eyes.

"Ah, it is you, Brenda." Her voice was low and husky.

"Yes, my dearie," the woman crooned. "There are more children. Come, my lovies, come with Brenda." Lilith and Carmilla seemed to

The Visitors

fall under a spell as the kid snatcher spoke to them. In this way, she led them from the building.

Sara remained pressed up against the piano, listening to the old woman lead Carmilla and Lilith through the courtyard, speaking of home, Michael, who had returned after all, and the children waiting for them on the boat that they would all set sail in that night. Sara strained her ears until she heard nothing more, and for the first time she felt how hard and uncomfortable the edge of the piano was against the small of her back. Stepping away from it, she ran to Jenny and stood for a moment gasping at what was left of the girl. Then, remembering Sunami, Pono and Mele, she went to the portion of the bookshelf that hid them. Pulling back one of the books, she knocked on the wall.

"It's Sara," she whispered loudly. There was a sharp tap in return. "Jenny is dead," she spoke through the wall. It took her a moment before she could speak again as her throat tightened with grief. "Whatever you do, don't come out. I think at some point tonight, we are all leaving. There is an old grandfather clock here in the room. When you hear it strike seven times for the second time, it will be seven in the morning. I think it may be safe to come out then." She waited and then heard Sunami's voice, small and faltering. "OK."

Sara replaced the book and went to sit on the piano bench, too afraid to go to the main house. She turned away from the dead bodies, willing herself not to cry.

This was her life now. At one time she had been a creature like Lilith and Carmilla. Something had shifted in her, prompting her to come back as a human girl, to send herself away and to abduct the others. She had to understand what was in her own mind. If she were so evil at one time, what inspired her to turn away from it? Sara brought her elbows to rest on the lid of the piano, burying her face in her hands.

Chapter 44

"Maddie." It was a feeble voice that called the elderly slave woman.

"Yes, Misses, I is here," the old woman rose from her chair where she had been praying for her mistress, Patience D'wolff.

It was late afternoon, but Maddie had drawn the dark, gold and brown damask curtains over the window to block out the sun. In the past fortnight, she had watched her mistress grow weaker and weaker in body and spirit. The strange illness that had descended upon the town of Bristol, resulting in deaths of mostly girl children, had Patience in its grip. What was more, several of the town's people had been found with their throats gouged, their bodies mutilated, the work of presumably a large cat that had acquired a taste for humans and was now stalking people, although there were never any tracks found. The deaths sparked feverish speculation that ranged from a killer on the loose to witchcraft, to talk of the supernatural and curses. Of late, vampirism was widely blamed for the deaths.

Old Master Walker, who owned the neighboring plantation, had lost three young daughters to the strange curse, and a fourth, Sally, was now consumed with the illness. Hannah, one of his house

The Visitors

servants, said the children's nanny, Nellie, told her Master Walker ordered Joe, his field hand, to exhume Beth, the last daughter to die from the terrible sickness, remove her heart, and burn it. Master Walker, afraid that she had become a vampire, was convinced that Beth was responsible for Sally's ailing health.

Maddie bent over her mistress, placing her dark, arthritic hand over the young woman's forehead. It was cool and clammy. "Praise be to Jesus," the old woman muttered to herself. The high fever had come down. Patience opened eyes, which were dull and flat, ringed with greenish brown shadows.

"Maddie," she whispered.

"Yes, Miss Patience, ole Maddie is right heah, chile." Maddie watched her mistress' eyes wander up and focus on her own dark, wrinkled face.

"I fear I am sinking into darkness," Patience said. Her voice was faint and Maddie sat on the edge of the bed, bringing her ear closer so she could hear her mistress.

In the last several days, Doctor Smith, a squat older man with thick gray hair and a black suit had been hired to administer his medicinals upon Patience. He had removed large quantities of her blood with slimy leeches, much to Maddie's silent disapproval. It was clear to Maddie before he came that the blood of the young woman was somehow weakened and that removing it was only hastening her demise. Every time the doctor came, Maddie had rectified his ignorant treatments with a tea of burdock root. Eventually it had been one of the strange servants that had come with Master Moreau, Patience's new husband, who had sent the doctor away.

Maddie had never seen servants like these. All of them were mulattas, or half-breeds, as Patience's father called them. They were tall, imposing, sharp-featured women. These servants wore fine clothing, used proper speech, spoke several languages and appeared well educated.

"Doctor Smith, we will no longer be needing your services," one of the mulattas, Analise, had said just two hours earlier. She swept through the foyer in a rustle of blue silk, the panniers so wide under her dress that the fabric grazed either end of the doorway. Her hair hung in a mass of rich curls and waves over her wide shoulders. She was striking to behold.

"I do not take orders from a negress," the doctor said. Analise paused and changed course, walking up to the doctor. She held his gaze.

"What you do and do not do, Doctor Smith, is of no consequence or concern to me outside of this house. However, under this roof, you will do as I tell you." Dr. Smith's face reddened and looked as if it might explode.

"Now you look here, you nigger wench…"

"Doctor Smith."

The doctor looked past Analise to Master Moreau, who had appeared from his study, standing several feet behind her.

"As you have heard, we are no longer in need of your services. Patience is not improving under your care. Maddie, get the door for the doctor." Maddie, feeling uneasy about the whole exchange, walked as quickly as her elderly body would allow her and opened the door. A shaft of golden sunlight shot through the large, murky hall and the doctor looked with disbelief from one to the other of them. However, he was not finished having his say when he reached the door.

"I don't know what they do in France, but we don't let our niggers behave like this in Bristol, Mr. Moreau." Maddie watched the master bend his head slightly as if to show that he had heard, all the while dismissing the doctor. But it was Analise who spoke up.

"It is ten miles you must travel to your home, is it not doctor?" She had a lilting singsong tone when she spoke, which thinly veiled the sharp edge underneath. Doctor Smith's bushy eyebrows drew together. A small smile played on her lips. "Take care, doctor, that you make it home safe and sound. We would not wish you to fall under

The Visitors

any misfortune. A lonely road in the dusk of day is when the devil likes to play." She did not wait for him to respond but continued on with her business. The doctor's face grew ashen. Collecting himself, he stepped outside and Maddie shut the door behind him.

"Maddie, do make Patience that tea," Master Moreau spoke. "I think it does her well."

"Sho nuff," Maddie responded. It was not Patience's new husband that Maddie found intimidating, but the servants he had brought with him.

Patience shifted her frail body.

"What time is it? Is it almost night?"

"No, chile, it be afternoon. Da sun be burstin forth today." Patience stared wordlessly at her old nanny and reached for the knurled hand. Maddie let the young woman grasp her knotted fingers.

"I'm not sure if I am dreaming. Sometimes the visits seem so real." Maddie felt a chill come over her body.

"What visits you is talkin bout, Miss Patience?"

Patience's green eyes wandered the room, and then settled on her old nursemaid. "There are two women who steal so quietly through the door." Her voice became fainter as she spoke, and Maddie had to strain her old ears to hear what her mistress spoke of. "The white slaves that my husband brought. It is always one of them who brings the women." Patience's fingers tightened around Maddie's and Maddie stared down at the pale hand and dark ruby that adorned the young woman's slender finger. There was something about that ring that had never sat well with Maddie. Its blood-red depths shone brilliantly when the light hit it just so, bringing to mind a feeling of lurking evil.

"They hover over me in my sleep," Patience continued, "and when morning arises, I am so weak." Patience closed her eyes, turning her face away, although her hand still remained in Maddie's. What was she speaking of, the old woman wondered. Could it be another of the girl's spells? As quickly as Maddie thought it, she decided against it. Patience's spells were different, something that took over her body and voice.

Maddie had helped bring Patience into the world, nursing her with rags soaked in goat's milk when Mistress D'wolff's milk had dried up and no wet nurse could be found. The old slave woman had stood by her as best she could, even when Patience had been marked by the curse.

It had begun in the spring of her young mistress' eighth year. Maddie remembered that day well. She had found the girl standing in the middle of the kitchen, blank-eyed in her linen shift, legs bare and spread apart. Her hair, usually clipped up, hung lank and greasy down her back, as it had not been washed yet that spring.

"Patience, chile, watcha be doin half nuded?" Maddie cried in alarm. Instead of answering her, the girl had begun to speak in an odd voice. A rush of words flowed from her mouth. She spoke of soldiers, war, devastation and poverty. Maddie had been stricken silent. It was Mistress D'wolff who found them like that. She gave a shriek, turning on Maddie.

"What is wrong with her? What have you done to my child?"

Maddie had shrunk back from the wrath of her mistress, as the girl continued to spout forth a great mishmash of information. Mistress D'wolff had grabbed her daughter, shaking the girl until she finally seemed to come to her senses. After that day the odd spells continued. There was no telling when they would come on, although as time went by they became more frequent. Soon the strange proclamations were followed by objects that moved on their own and doors that shut by themselves. Once a favorite with her father, Patience became a source of embarrassment, shame and fear.

As Patience grew older, her mother fretted over her marriageability. Most of the people in the town were aware of the girl's odd proclamations that came suddenly in a strange voice that was not her own. Over the years, she became something of a joke among her peers. Slaves told frightening stories to each other of how she was a witch.

The Visitors

There was not a family in Bristol or any neighboring towns that would so much as entertain the idea of their son courting the girl.

Salvation came in the form of a letter sent via the solicitor of a certain Monsieur Moreau interested in investing in the shipping business of Master Joseph D'wolff. Over a period of months a relationship was formed, business contracts drawn up and finally a small farm of fifty acres purchased with a modest manor consisting of twelve bedrooms and a smattering of shacks, along with a dozen slaves already inhabiting the farm.

Monsignor Moreau arrived almost a year to the day of his first letter of interest, with an entourage of white slaves and several mulatta women servants who enjoyed something close to the privilege of free status. This was such a strange occurrence that it caused quite a stir. The mulattas, dressed in the height of French fashion, kept to themselves and had tight reign over the slaves. To Master D'wolff's displeasure, he found the Frenchman demurred and sought out council with these women in all of his business dealings. It was during one visit, when Monsignor brought his servant Analise with him to talk over the matter of rum, that Patience had one of her spells. She screamed of men in red and gray suits rotting in the fields. The great mirror in the sitting room cracked. The wooden shutters on the windows folded closed and the house grew still. Patience stood, eyes blazing, chest heaving. It was Maddie who came to her aide, carefully guiding the girl back to the here and now. Monsignor Moreau looked stunned, but it was Analise, who muttered in amazement, "The gift of Sybil."

"What did you say?" Master D'wolff asked.

Analise turned to him, her dark face lit with excitement. "How long has she been prophesying?"

Master D'wolff's craggy face seemed to close up on itself at this question, and he spoke to Monsignor Moreau instead. Mulattas being treated and acting like white women didn't sit well with him and it was further distasteful to see these women commanding white slaves.

"You must excuse Patience," he said to Monsignor Moreau, "her spells are uncontrollable."

Analise said nothing more, but a few days later Monsignor called on Patience and an awkward courtship began, begrudgingly allowed by the D'wolffs, there being no other suitors. A month later an engagement was proposed and accepted, along with the oddity of the ruby ring. As part of Patience's dowry, Maddie, along with half a dozen field hands and a young girl, Abigail, were sent to join Patience at her new home. From the start, Maddie could see that things were not right. The mulatta servants were each given their own rooms in the big house.

One of the slave women that came with the property, Susan, told Maddie one Sunday afternoon of the events that had followed after Master Moreau had showed up with his household of white slaves and mulatta servants. "First de Master comes wid all dem white slaves. You'd never spect dey is haven even one drop of negro blood, de is no different looken from all de utter whites." Susan's rough fingers flew over the quilting material, the needle dipping expertly in and out of the cloth, creating nice neat stitching as Maddie struggled with her own section. "All dem white slaves, and not one is speakin a lick of English. Dey is speaken only French. Den he put dem tall, high and mighty mullatas in dah house. What you be makin of dat?" Susan's eyes flashed. "Der was some heavy crates came wid em. Cotton Joe and Nettie's son carried dem wooden boxes, and was tole to put one in each room. You know how Master keeps the door locked to dos tree rooms, and a keys wid him." Maddie nodded. She also knew that the white slave women with colorful scarves covering their baldheads and shunned by the other slaves, also held keys to those rooms. They held keys, but Patience, mistress of the house, did not. Maddie witnessed on two separate occasions one of those women going to the southern corridor of the house and unlocking the door to one of the forbidden rooms in order to go inside.

The Visitors

Many of the white slaves split their time between manual labor and study. All made use of bound blank books, which they usually carried with them, writing in the journals with graphite sticks wrapped in string. There was a particular young woman who accompanied Patience everywhere, scribbling furiously in her book whenever Patience had a spell.

"Some say the whole lot a dem, dey is from the devil," Susan said, her voice hushed. She paused and crossed herself. "All dis sickness and den dem murdered peoples found, half eaten. What you be makin of dat?"

"Hush now," was Maddie's reply, but a knot of uncertainty settled in her belly at Susan's words.

Patience grew so lonely before her illness that Abigail became more of a confidante than a servant. There was a polite but general mistrust of the Moreau's within the community.

As Maddie sat on Patience's bed her mind wandered to two startling events that she'd witnessed the day before. The first had been the visit of Mistress D'wolff to see her daughter. The mulatta, Genevieve, had guided Patience's mother up the winding staircase to the suite of rooms on the southern wing. Patience's room was the last after the three forbidden rooms. Mistress D'wolff had paused before the second to the last room, trying the knob, as she had thought it was her daughter's room. A moment later, her hand had been sharply slapped by Genevieve, the mulatta's dark eyes flashing a warning look. Mistress D'wolff had been stunned speechless. After a moment of stilted silence, Genevieve turned away from the shocked woman and stiffly but graciously, opened the last door. Mistress D'wolff had hurried into the room, sending Maddie away shortly after, saying she wished to be alone with Patience.

When Maddie walked the carpeted hall back to the stairway, the sound of a woman's voice rose in anger from the foyer below. Not wishing to draw attention to herself, the old woman hung back in the shadows as she watched with disbelief Genevieve yelling at Master

Moreau in French. He had stood, head bowed, contrite. Her yelling attracted the attention of Analise, a woman whom Maddie and all the slaves had come to greatly fear. Analise had stood listening, arms crossed. When Genevieve was finished with her tirade, Analise walked up to the Master and lifted his chin with her finger, looking down at him. She was several inches taller than the man.

"Louis," she'd said, and continued in French. Maddie's head had spun. Louis, she had called him. But his name was Master Michael Moreau, wasn't it? Afraid to make her presence known, Maddie had slowly crept back toward Patience's room until she was out of view of the people below. There she had waited in the shadows, listening to a strange lilting voice that rose up high and pretty. Someone was singing from one of the locked rooms.

No one kept track of Maddie's comings and goings. It was understood that she put Patience at ease, along with the slave girl Abigail, and so they were tolerated, but they were in no sense needed; all domestic chores were handled by Master Moreau's own slaves and the mulatta servants. Maddie was given a small mammy cottage in the back of the big house, which she shared with young Abigail. She knew that no one would notice if she went up to Patience's room in the evening and never left. It would be assumed she had gone to her own cottage if someone were to look in on Patience and not see her there. It was easy to hide in the large armoire with a keyhole for spying and that was what Maddie did later that night, waiting while Patience slept.

The sound of the great clock below chiming twelve times woke Maddie from her doze. It was dark and stuffy in the armoire, and the old woman's eyes grew heavy after a few minutes but the sound of Patience's door slowly opening caused her to become alert and awake. Fixing her eye to the small hole, at first she saw nothing but darkness, but as her vision adjusted to the thin stream of light that filtered into the room from the hall, she saw two shadowy figures pass by. From where she stood, she could see nothing more, but she heard her young mistress gasp and strange sucking, slurping sounds, almost like kissing. This seemed to go on for quite a while, and then the shadow of one figure passed before her. It looked like a woman. Maddie's throat tightened when she realized how impossibly white the skin of the person was that passed before the closet. These events continued until Patience began to mumble something, and then she was talking in that voice she used when the spells took over her being.

"There shall be an end to your race. Back into the light you shall return, for you belong to him," the girl yelled. There was a brilliant glow and Maddie closed her eyes, her heart beating so rapidly, she was afraid it might burst with the fear that overtook her. The doors to the closet were opening and Maddie stared at the face of something that was utterly unknown to her. An impossibly white woman stood before her, her teeth long and sharp and her eyes devil-like. She was covered in blood. A hand grabbed her, yet she never saw it move. Her last glimpse was of Patience sitting fully upright in bed, her eyes fiery with images marching before her that only she could see. Another creature with glorious, bright red hair stood over her mistress, as a pale, unearthly light passed between them.

Sara's head shot up from her arms as the memories came flooding back, threatening to overwhelm her mind. She was not Lilith! She was Patience. That night, Lilith had entered her body, hoping to usurp that odd power she possessed. The energy that had plagued her all her life as Patience, Lilith wanted and somehow needed.

That night she and Lilith switched bodies, but their souls remained intertwined, impossible to separate, like conjoined twins, except the gift remained with Patience. Sara's head sank back down this time to her hands, clasped and folded under her chin. She began to pray.

Her body shook with grief, but her eyes were dry. She prayed for Jenny, Jenny's family and the others hidden in the wall. Last of all she prayed for Maman and Papa.

It was Brenda who came to collect her. The bodies of Analise and Jenny were left as they were. Sara joined Samuel, who was waiting outside by the banana orchards. Bundled in a thick coat, he shivered from the cold night air.

The others moved forward under the bright stars that lit up the night sky.

"Take my hand," Samuel whispered. He held his hand out, palm up with long slim fingers spread apart. Sara placed her hand in his. The skin was warm and fleshy. Below, the small party came to a halt. Samuel's hand tightened around hers as she watched Papa and Manuel fall to their knees, Darius behind them.

"Look at me," Samuel said. His pale blue eyes held hers as two shots rang out in the distance. Sara's body tensed and a slow numbness crept through her muscles. Samuel pulled her closer. "It is over," he said quietly. "You begin a new life now." The party continued forward to the path that led down to the ocean.

An immense fiery, gold and orange moon sat just above the dark sea, the night stars illuminating the two figures sprawled forward as if praying toward the east.

"May God stay with you, Papa," Sara whispered. Samuel gave her a slight tug and she followed him. Brenda, who moved a few feet ahead of them, turned and smiled, her wrinkled face seeming to fold into itself.

"Soon we will be home, my lady," she called out, her teeth gnashing together. "Such a good lady. Such a fine one."

Chapter 45

Charlie waited by the canoe, holding the conch shell while the waves lapped at his bare feet and the boat. Aunt Clair stood with her arms raised to the heavens. She chanted a *kanikau* before the large group assembled on the shore. Leis of white tuberose, pink plumeria and the green ti leaf lay stacked on the sand, next to them were the urns carrying the ashes of the many that had been found murdered the next day after the strange storm had scourged the valley.

"*I ke ala i ho'i 'ole mai*, on the pathway of no return we bid you aloha cherished daughters, sons, brothers sisters, husbands and wives. You are loved, and never forgotten: Fester Kahiamoi, Manuel La Croix, Junior Ben Kahiamoi, Annette and Louis Deureaux, Jenny Knowles, Don Crowley, Leonard Kahn and an unknown sister who came to our island in an earthly body, but now leaves in a spirit one." Aunt Clair's deep voice rose clear and melodic as she lapsed into Hawaiian again, singing the chant of lament.

Angela stood half supported by her husband, eyes red rimmed. She pressed her hand hard against her lips to stem the flood of grief that threatened to erupt from her. It was all she could do to make it to the memorial service. The past week had been a nightmarish blur. Every morning was a fresh shock that Jenny was no longer with them.

The sight of her daughter's disfigured mangled body at the morgue, when she had gone with Tim to identify her, had caused her to collapse. There were the other bodies as well, and Linda's wail at seeing her son, his face unrecognizable, still rang through Angela's mind. Try as she might, she could not hold back the hot tears that filled her eyes as Clair continued with her chant. By the canoe were the ashes of all the victims except Jenny, Don and Leonard, who were shipped to the mainland to be buried in their own family cemeteries. Angela reached for a tissue in her pocket. As she looked down, she noticed Mele looking up at her. The little girl stood in a white aloha dress, her round eyes large as she held tight to her mother's hand. Since the morning that Sunami, Pono and Mele had come straggling back from Sara's, Mele no longer spoke.

Clair's chant stopped abruptly and the lonesome sound of the conch shell rang out as Charlie blew into it, raising it skyward. Ben was the first to board the canoe then Keoni, Pono, and River. Charlie's father handed the men the urns of ashes and the leis. He was joined by other men that helped push the boat into the small waves before the occupants took over with their paddles. The strum of a ukulele signaled the women to begin their hula and Angela took Mele's hand as her mother went to join the dancers.

An hour later, the party of mourners assembled at Angela's. The kitchen brimmed with food that various neighbors had prepared and brought over. It was a bright and sunny day and most people stood about in the large yard talking quietly amongst each other while Bill and Eric, the realtor, ran the barbeque.

Angela looked about, her eyes heavy with fatigue. She just wanted to sleep, sleep forever, but it was River standing alone with a beer in his hand that caught her attention. Shading her eyes from

The Visitors

the glare of the sun, she made her way over to the young man. He watched her approach and they stared silently for a moment at each other.

"I hear you're leaving," he finally said. He took a sip of beer. "It's probably for the best," he mumbled.

"What happened that night, River?" Angela asked. His jaw tightened and a raw fear lit up his eyes. He swallowed.

"It's like we said, Mrs. Knowles. They were demons. I know you don't really believe us." Angela's attention wandered as he spoke and she noticed Sunami standing in a long yellow mumu, her thin lanky body swallowed up in the dress. Mele stood next to her. A young pregnant woman, Sunami's sister, was talking to a small group of teenagers that clustered around them, but Sunami wasn't paying attention. She only stared at the ground.

The story that the children told was unbelievable, and all were still under investigation and psychiatric evaluation. Angela's eyes wandered back to River, who stood watching her. He was clean and fresh in aloha attire, his long hair neatly tied back in a ponytail. It was said that he had been found locked in a room at Fester Kahiamoi's house, Fester's body partially eaten and abandoned in his own front room.

"If you could just tell me," Angela whispered, and she closed her eyes as the grief burst forth again. Her scream shattered the quiet conversations, resulting in immediate silence. It was Tim who ran to grab his wife, her body trembling, her eyes squeezed shut. She screamed over and over in his embrace. River, pale with uncertainty, stood awkwardly by.

"I just want to know! I just want to know!" Tim gently pulled his wife to the house, joined by Clair and Ann, who assisted him, their guidance quieting the woman.

"There are some sedatives by our bed," he explained. "She needs to sleep." Mele took a step away from Sunami, distracted by a girl following the group of adults who slowly made their way to the house. Shading her eyes with her hand to obscure the sunbeams that washed out her line of vision, she squinted at the vanishing figure of Jenny. Opening her mouth to speak, the words remained stuck in her throat as she watched the last of the red hair dissipate into the rays of light.

About the author

C.A. Wittman spent sixteen years on Maui where she raised six children. She now resides in Los Angeles and continues to write.